More Than Shipmates

PHILIPPA YOUNG

For content warnings, please visit my website:

www.philippayoungauthor.com

MORE THAN SHIPMATES

Edited by Bryony Leah

Character Illustrations by Ivanna Nashkolna

PLAYLIST

In case you'd like to listen to the songs mentioned in the book.
(It's a lot of musical theatre).

If you knew me before I could walk, respectfully, either shut this book or shut your mouth.

All right, fine. Read it. But you might want to skip chapters seven, eight, thirteen and fifteen...
And you should DEFINITELY skip ten, twenty, twenty-one, twenty-two, twenty-four and thirty-two.

The rest of you, I want to see your colourful sticky tabs
ALL. OVER. THEM.

ONE

I'm not sure if it was the jet lag or my subconscious counting down my last few hours of freedom, but I didn't sleep a wink last night. My eyes sting as I frantically tap away at my phone for the last time, engorging myself on the luxury of reliable free Wi-Fi while I wait for the shuttle bus. I say my final goodbyes to an embarrassingly small number of people ahead of my six-month hiatus from the outside world, and in between replies I check who, out of the people I used to talk to every day but would now actively avoid if I saw them in person, has seen my Instagram story. Anxiety surges through my veins. Correction: *excitement*. I must turn my anxiety into excitement if I want to make it through today without having a nervous breakdown.

A surprisingly warm breeze rushes over me, which I take as my cue to look up from my phone and embrace dry land while I still can. To any ordinary person, this hotel car park wouldn't seem like anything special, but to me, the abundance of palm trees surrounding the lot and the small fountains on either side of the entrance make it seem far more exotic than any hotel back in England.

On the flight over to Miami I wrote a list of all the reasons why this job would be good for me – something I'm grateful for now, but which at the time had felt futile. Self-doubt had crept in exponentially; I was finally facing the reality of the impulsive decision I'd made a few months ago. I hate to admit it, but I allowed myself to dance with the idea of not even boarding the plane. As tempting as the thought was, it simply wasn't an option. The consequences of abandoning that flight would've been far worse than the contract I signed up for.

In an attempt to comfort my nerves, I slide my hand into my back pocket to retrieve the list and allow my eyes to scan the first line:

There's nothing left for me at home.

Well, that certainly feels more depressing than comforting. A real reflection of my state of mind when I started scrawling things down. Maybe I was more hopeful towards the end of the list…

This is my dream job. Please don't fuck this up.

No pressure then.

And let's make one thing clear: this is my dream *place of work*, but this isn't my dream job. According to my brother, I'm incapable of doing anything right, so I must have wished upon the wrong star. Or I got it *so* wrong I actually missed the stars altogether and wished upon Pluto, because just like that dwarf planet, I also wasn't good enough to make the cut.

Thankfully, my personal broadcast of Self-Loathing FM is interrupted by a waft of freezing-cold air-con that escapes through the sliding doors behind me, and the sound of suitcase wheels rumbling over the fitted doormat. I look back to see a young guy chasing his luggage as it races down the slope beside the concrete steps. I can't help the small grin that breaks out on my face as he ultimately loses control, sending the suitcase into free fall. He curses under his breath before catching my eye and flashing me a warm smile. His apparent confidence while enduring something so humiliating is almost impressive.

Everyone's so much friendlier here. You smile at a stranger in London and you'll either get the police called on you for suspicious behaviour or be in for a good stabbing. That's something I won't miss, the constant fear of being subjected to mild peril at any given moment.

As he leans over to return his suitcase to an upright position, a few belongings fall out of his carelessly unzipped backpack. A plastic folder glides its way along the pavement, stopping just in front of me. I shove the list I was clutching back in my pocket and crouch to pick it up for him while he takes off his backpack and desperately tries to cram the runaway items back into it. I wait patiently to hand him the file, though he only notices it's missing when he sees me.

"Shoot, thanks. I'd be screwed without that." An American accent tumbles out of his mouth. I should be accustomed to them by now, but each new encounter still pleases me.

He takes the folder from me and shoves it into his bag, then runs his fingers through his now tousled brown hair, pushing the subtle waves back into a small quiff. Despite his scattered energy he's well-groomed. Sunglasses rest on the collar of the plain white T-shirt that doesn't quite cling to his slim body. I think he's one of those guys who's just effortlessly attractive, and suddenly I find myself hoping he thinks the same about me. Though that's tremendously unlikely given this humidity has been about as kind to my hair as I was to it a few months ago when I decided to get this horrendous fuck-it fringe. It's flapping about in the wind and it's driving me up the wall. It's not short enough to technically be a fringe anymore, but it's also not long enough to stay tucked behind my ear for more than a few milliseconds. As for my outfit, there were no strict instructions on what to wear to embark since I'll be given my uniform on board, so after much deliberation, I went for a short-sleeved pink leotard with high-waisted skinny jeans and white trainers. I imagine this will be the last time I wear jeans for a long time considering the heat. This is unlike any September weather I've ever known.

"No problem," I reply.

An inquisitive smirk brushes one corner of his lips, making a perfect dimple on his cheek. "You're not from around here, are you?"

I shake my head. "London," I say with a smile.

If we were on the other side of the Atlantic, I'd have at least told him to piss off by now with my "don't mess with me" eyes, though I've never been afraid to use my words. However, it appears my pupils, usually filled with daggers of contempt for unknown men trying to converse with me, have softened. There's just a certain allure to him that makes me want to engage, so I allow myself one last flirtatious encounter before the streak of celibacy I've resigned myself to. Or to put it bluntly, he's simply too gorgeous to ignore.

But then again, apparently so was Ted Bundy.

"But are you actually from London or just saying that

because you think most of us Americans don't know the difference?" The cheeky flicker in his big brown eyes invites me to play along.

"Are you saying you *do* know the difference?"

"I know you're not from Newcastle…or Essex."

"Oh yeah? What makes you so sure?"

"For starters, your voice is nice and you're not orange. Wait, I didn't mean… I—"

"Is this your first time speaking to someone from the UK?"

"You'd think, huh? I'll go stand over there. Sorry I bothered you. Have a nice day." He moves to walk away.

"No, you're really good at this. Keep going."

He sighs with a smile, taking a second to think before he speaks, which I get the impression he doesn't do a lot. "Are you from Chelsea by any chance?"

"Is reality TV the only reference you have for us?"

"What makes you think that?" His sarcasm elicits a laugh out of me. He has an infectious runaway giggle I'd give my left leg to hear again.

"Want to give it another guess? I'm sure there's some part of the British population you haven't generalised yet."

"Sorry. You're really pretty – my brain's short-circuiting." He scans my face for a reaction, but I'm stunned into silence by his candour. I've never been hit on so forwardly before, and I can't say I hate it. "It's a real impairment for guys. Look it up."

"I think this interaction is all the evidence I need."

"I'm super nervous today too, so that isn't helping. I give up. Put me outta my misery."

"So I'm not a Chelsea girl, but I do genuinely live in London. Or I did." Saying that out loud for the first time knocks me a little off-centre. Just a casual reminder – in case

I wasn't already painfully aware – that I've uprooted my entire life on a whim for a job at sea. "I grew up out of the city though. How about you? I'm guessing you're not local." I point to his now scuffed suitcase.

"No. Well, I guess to you I probably am. I just flew over from Chicago last night. Ever been?"

I shake my head. "I've always wanted to go though."

"You should." Our eyes linger for a little too long. "I'd be happy to show you around." He extends his hand as heat rushes to my cheeks. "Tom."

"Eliza." I bring my hand up to shake his, and a fire blazes through my body the second we touch. Sorrow weighs on me knowing this chance encounter with a handsome stranger will be short-lived. "So, why are you nerv—?"

A chorus of rattling suitcase wheels startles me. I turn to see a handful of people leaving the hotel and heading towards us. We step out of their way, and my gaze follows them to a coach that seems to have miraculously appeared out of thin air despite my fixation on every vehicle that pulled into the hotel in the past twenty minutes. While the driver opens the luggage compartments, a friendly-faced woman steps off the bus brandishing a clipboard stamped with the ship's logo.

I go to break our silence, but Tom beats me to it. "I think this is me."

Wait. "Are you…?" My mind races with questions. I point to the bus, not sure what to ask first.

"Yup. Are *you*?" The shock in his voice matches mine.

"Yup."

"Which department?" he asks.

"Entertainment," I say proudly. I would return the question, but I'm pretty sure I already know his answer now he's smiling from ear to ear.

Over the past few weeks, and especially in the past

twenty-four hours, I've worked myself up immensely about making a good impression on the hundreds of people I'll meet during the next week or so. It's not that I have an aching need to be liked or accepted, that's never fazed me before, but if I'm going to be stuck on this ship for half a year, I want to get on with at least one person. Yet having found that person before my day's even technically begun hasn't relaxed me at all. Instead, my relief is clouded by indignation at how attracted I am to him, and now that we're coworkers – close ones at that – he's instantly off-limits.

We join the back of the small queue, both of us suppressing smiles. Once we're at the front and the woman has ticked off our names, the driver helps us load our suit-cases, and we climb on board. We plonk ourselves down in a pair of seats, and I struggle to ignore the tingles I get when Tom's arm brushes against mine.

"Elizabeth, huh?" he teases, gesturing to the woman I gave my name to, and I shudder. He clearly overheard me. I've never much liked my full name. I don't think it suits me, and neither does anyone else. "So your parents named you after the queen. I love British people." He giggles to himself, and I half-expect to see my dismembered left leg flailing about on the pavement as we drive off.

I looked up pictures of the ship online, but *nothing* could have prepared me for just how monstrous it is up close. With fifteen passenger decks and I don't even know how many more below decks, it has the capacity for almost 5,000 passengers and 1,500 crew. And somehow this thing still floats.

After a lengthy sign-on process, complete with security

checks, uniform fittings, and taking ID photos – which I am *dreading* the results of – we're finally ready to head to our cabins. We stumble upon Tom's first. He presses his key card against the sensor on the door and his shoulders lift with an excited breath. He enters to a friendly reception from his very Scottish roommate, Daniel, whose big smile pushes against his full cheeks as he extends his greeting to me. I can tell Tom is struggling to understand him because he pauses for far too long before answering Daniel's "How are you, pal?" with a simple "Yes."

Daniel and I share an amused glance, and I leave them to get acquainted, setting off in search of my new home.

Alone for the first time since I arrived, I'm alert with unease. From our room numbers, I thought we'd only be a few doors down from each other, but I've been walking in circles for what feels like forever. This place is like a labyrinth. In fact, I'm disappointed when David Bowie and his bulge don't turn up to taunt me with singing puppets.

When I finally arrive outside the door, I compose myself, ready to embrace whatever and whoever lives in there – because good or bad, I'm stuck with them. The green light flashes, accompanied by a faint beep, and I step cautiously inside.

It's empty. The cabin is lived in, but not messy. From the clothes draped over the ladder, it looks like the top bunk is already taken. *Bummer.* On the upside, the bottom bunk appears to have been made up for me. Guess I didn't need to bring my own bedding after all. I'll just add that to the growing list of things in my suitcase I already regret packing.

With the room to myself, I take the opportunity to snoop on my roommate. She's stuck a few pictures to the wall by her bed with magnets. The first photo I examine is of her family all bunched up on a sofa wearing matching novelty

Christmas jumpers. Holy shit, her brother is *hot*. At least, I think that's her brother. I can certainly see a family resemblance.

I scan along to the next photo and see him again. In this one, the two of them are straddling surfboards in the sea. *What I'd give to be that surfboard...* Christ, he looks like a Hollister model, blond and tanned with a rigid six-pack and broad shoulders to die for. I get the impression they might be Australian. I could be wrong, but I'm pretty sure you don't get glowing skin like that from surfing in Cornwall.

The last photo is a selfie of Hollister Boy with a Golden Retriever, and there's no mistaking the dog's smiling at the camera. I would be too if someone who looked like that paid me even the slightest bit of attention.

I force myself to snap out of horny Sherlock mode. There isn't much time before orientation, and I still need to get changed. I place the uniform – which I've been clutching to my chest all this time like a security blanket – down on the desk ready to change into. It's my only set for now. The spares and evening formalwear, along with my suitcase, should be dropped off at some point today.

I'm instantly relieved to be rid of my impractical leotard. They always seem like a good idea until you're hunched over sticking the impossibly stubborn poppers back together or sitting on the loo stark naked like a potty-training toddler. Standing in my underwear, I assess my new clothes. A baby-blue polo shirt with the cruise logo embroidered on the front and white shorts that fit loosely enough to be comfortable, but which aren't so loose that it looks like I'm about to play basketball. "Practical" is the word that springs to mind. If I'd told my twelve-year-old self that one day I'd have to wear what is essentially a sports kit every day, I think she'd have tried harder in school.

To my surprise, the bathroom door opens. I don't scare easily, but apparently, when on the cusp of utter mortification, I'm as skittish as a dormouse. A squeak escapes my throat and I flinch away, my arms instinctively rushing to cover my body with little success. I'm frozen in place as I lock eyes with my new roommate, making a mental note to call the BBC momentarily to cancel that detective series they weren't ever going to commission, because I'm clearly no sleuth. It isn't the girl in the pictures standing in front of me.

It's Hollister Boy.

TWO

"I'm so sorry."

Any question I might've had about his country of origin is instantly solved. Apologising for something that isn't his fault? Classic Brit.

Averting his eyes, he immediately retreats into the bathroom, the quick swing of the door filling the room with his scent. Christ, he even *smells* like a Hollister model, all coconuts and wood and... *Is that pineapple?*

I shove my uniform on urgently. Why is there a man in my bedroom? I glance back at the photos on the wall. Perhaps he's my roommate's boyfriend, not her brother.

"Sorry, I didn't know anyone was in here," I pant, hopping about trying to find the other leg hole to step into.

"You good?"

"Yeah."

He returns, still only wearing a towel around his waist, and we stand in uncomfortable silence waiting for someone to explain themselves, except no one does. In my defence, I'm too distracted wondering what it might be like to be one of the droplets of water clinging stubbornly to his torso.

"So sorry,"—*Yup, definitely British*—"but why are you in my room?"

"Your room?"

"Yes."

"I didn't think they had co-ed cabins." Though I have no complaints if this is who I'm sharing with.

"They don't," he corrects me, looking just as confused as I feel. His kind blue eyes search mine for any obvious signs of distress, of which I'm sure there are plenty.

"I'm new," I explain as if it isn't blindingly apparent.

"I gathered." He smiles.

"This is my cabin."

"That can't be right. I've already got a roommate."

"But this is 276, right?"

His confidence falters, which gives me hope I'm not being a complete dullard.

I hand him the document given to me by the sign-on team. "It must be – my key worked."

"That *is* odd. There must've been a mix-up."

"Great. I'll go speak to them…" I look at my new watch, get distracted by how cute it looks on my wrist – I know it was meant to be a plain and neutral colour, but I couldn't resist getting the one with an iridescent sheen – and then panic strikes. There are only six minutes left until I have to be at the training centre for orientation, and I'd planned on spending at least five of those getting lost trying to find it. "Later…"

"Don't worry – I'll have a word," he offers. It's a considerate gesture from someone who probably can't wait to see the back of me. Although I guess he already has.

By the time lunch rolls around, my inner child is crying out for a power nap. And without stealing a knife and sticking it in one of the weird-looking plug sockets I keep seeing everywhere, I'm not sure how I'll summon the energy I need for what's scheduled to be an intense afternoon.

Along with our official job roles, all crew must be intricately trained on how to deal with a wide range of emergencies. Then tonight, once we've completed various crash courses, we'll be assigned a buddy in our specific departments to shadow. They'll be our mentors for the next few weeks until we're deemed fit enough to run every activity the ship has to offer. That's what I'm looking forward to the most: being allowed to do my job without someone looming over me, waiting for me to slip up so they can berate me for it.

One less thing I need to exhaust myself over is the matter of my room assignment. It turns out someone in the office misread a handwritten two for a seven when making up the key cards, so instead of assigning me to cabin 226 as they should have, they put me in 276. Apparently, the correct room I'm now in I have all to myself – for this week at least – so that's something.

The crew mess is way down in the belly of the ship, but somehow, we still have a perfect view of the waves passing by outside the windows. Tom comes up to my side with a gleaming smile as if he's a puppy bringing me a sock I never asked for.

"I made some friends," he announces.

I load up my plate with what the name card promises is a vegetable lasagne, and he escorts me over to a table where two girls are seated. That's when I see through the illusion: a glitching monitor where there should be a perfect view. *How clever.*

The girl with short auburn hair, a cheery Emma Stone lookalike, eagerly greets us, while the other couldn't seem less interested.

"This is my buddy, Maddison," Tom tells me. "And this is…" He trails off, hoping the other will introduce herself.

"Oh, I'm not your buddy," the girl with wavy black hair rebuffs as I take a seat opposite her.

"Please excuse her. She woke up on the wrong side of the bed this mornin'." Maddison tries to melt away the frosty rejection with her warmth, the Southern twang to her words making me smile.

Her friend takes a deep breath and rolls her dark eyes. "Your buddy's Obi. He won't be hard to find – he's the one who looks like he eats rainbows for breakfast."

That doesn't narrow it down. Everyone probably looks like that compared to her.

"No, she's with Harvey," Maddison corrects her.

"Good luck," teases the ice queen after taking a sharp breath in through her teeth.

Great. I'm going to be lumped with a social pariah – or worse, the ship's sex pest.

"Valentina! Don't wind her up. He's fine. He's a really good guy."

"Too good," Valentina sulks.

At least I can rule out the latter then.

"He's…" Maddison pauses to think of a way to voice whatever thought she's wrestling with diplomatically.

"Uptight," Valentina interjects. I quickly realise she isn't the type of person to beat around the bush. Given half the chance, she'd most likely batter the bush so violently it could no longer be categorised as a shrub.

"I wouldn't say uptight." Maddison shoots Valentina a stern glance. "More…he's all work and not much play."

I guess I can cope with that.

"Don't worry, we'll show you what the nightlife here is really like," Valentina promises in a way that feels like a threat.

I turn to Tom, who forces an "it'll be all right" expression. I thank him profusely for seating us at this table with our new *friends* with a heavy blink and a pained smile.

We congregate in front of a stern-faced, potbellied safety officer in a crew hallway, and even though I'm taking him seriously, Tom has other plans. The man insisted upon dead silence while we walked single file to this location, and the whole time, Tom kept stoking the coals of my amusement. This is one of those times when I know I can't laugh, but knowing that makes me want to laugh even more.

"Fire is the biggest threat to a cruise ship."

"And here I was thinking it was icebergs," Tom whispers in my ear.

I hold my breath to stop a laugh from slipping out.

While the officer explains the key fundamentals of fire safety, smoke starts to fill the hallway from under a door behind him. "Locate the emergency exits!" he bellows over the panicked chatter of the new recruits and a siren that decides to get involved, singing its infamous "Ode to the Flame" in G-sharp. *Seems simple enough.* But before too long I can no longer see anything or anyone around me.

"To those of you coughing, I'm keeping note. It's dry ice. Doesn't make you cough," he warns.

Where did they find this guy?

"Get below the smoke line!"

We're left with no choice but to get on the floor and drag

ourselves along on our elbows, following the fluorescent strips running along the edges of the corridor. The man continues to shout instructions with unnecessary aggression until we're all out of the fog and in the designated safe spot. It takes me a while to dispel the fear that I've inadvertently signed up for an SAS boot camp and not in fact a cruise.

Not only are we role-playing escaping a blazing inferno this afternoon, but we're also getting trained in how to actually *fight* one. We go out to the back of the ship and take turns brandishing a hose so powerful it requires two people to hold down the wielder so they won't each take off like flatulent deflating balloons. Much like a balloon, I breathe a sigh of relief when we're dismissed for the day after attending a muster drill with the passengers, putting an end to this fever dream I hope I never have to repeat. Though after that ordeal, I'm full of apprehension about what's in store for the rest of the week's training. A masterclass in drowning perhaps? Or maybe even a Concordia reenactment ceremony. Judging by the safety officer's flair for the dramatic, I wouldn't be at all surprised if he faked a brain haemorrhage during our first aid training tomorrow just to test our emergency preparedness.

When it's finally time to get our first glimpse of the Entertainment Team in action, Tom and I find a prime spot on an upper balcony overhanging part of the front deck and await the Captain's Welcome and Sail Away Party. I'm not too sure what to expect, but I'm excited to find out.

I'm amazed by the vast number of children on board. I thought cruises were supposed to be floating retirement villages, but there seems no shortage of entertainment here to occupy a younger demographic. With a dedicated kids' team and teen social scene, parents can sink themselves into their all-inclusive drinks packages without fear of dreaded cries of boredom just as they begin to unwind. Meanwhile, voyagers holidaying without kids can continue to do what they've always done: satiate their lust for Bingo, boast about how successful their grandchildren are to people who never asked, and experiment with swinging.

The only thing comparable to the passengers' reaction when the captain takes centre stage is a Miley Cyrus meet-and-greet at the height of her Hannah Montana years. Unfazed by the passionate outcry, she commands everyone's attention effortlessly. Without the uniform, she wouldn't look out of place as a geography teacher or librarian. Understated. But here she's a celebrity, and without a doubt a hard-working one, presumably having to work twice as hard just to override people's stereotypes of what a captain should look like. Passengers cling to her every word, laughing at each over-rehearsed joke and clapping mindlessly as she introduces the key senior members of staff. She eventually excuses herself and hands over to the cruise director, Henry, so she can prepare the ship to set sail.

Clearly no stranger to the spotlight, the tall Black man leaps at the chance to hold the microphone, giving a rundown of the activities available tonight and highlighting a few taking place later in the week. Theatre shows, game shows, quizzes, discos, competitions, and themed dress-up nights. He makes me wish I were one of the holiday-goers. Instead I'll be directly involved in running almost all these activities soon.

Henry wastes no more time and instructs the DJ to get the party started. A swarm of blue polo-wearing hosts jump into action, hyping up the guests to the old-school crowd-pleaser "Hey Baby" by DJ Ötzi. Scanning the team, I don't see anyone even remotely boring enough to be my buddy. Surely they'd stick out like a sore thumb in this line of work, what with everyone bobbing around and waving like those inflatable tube men you find outside car dealerships. Guess I just need to be patient.

A look of utter horror washes over Tom's face. "Everything okay?" I ask.

"I didn't know there'd be dancing." He's unable to tear his eyes away from the action below. I'd hardly call it dancing. Then again, I've been taking classes since I was in nappies.

"It's just two-stepping with a few claps, points, and waves. You've got this," I assure him, and he settles back down – that is until the chorus of "Mambo No. 5" kicks in. He audibly gulps when spins are added to the repertoire.

While the party ramps up, the rumble of the ship steadily increases as it prepares to leave the dock. There's an abrupt and definite shunt forwards, followed by the ship's bellowing horn, which catches a few people off-guard.

"Probably just my legs." Tom raises his voice to be heard over the hubbub.

"What about your legs?" I shout back.

"I was just working out what I'd break if I jumped ship right now."

"You seem pretty confident you'd land on your feet. And on the dock for that matter."

"What would be better?"

"Well, if you land in the water, you'll be chewed up by the motors quicker than you can cry for help. But if you land on the jetty…you might be alive, but it's going to be messy."

"Got it. Aim for the side. Bend the knees."

"Or better yet, save yourself the medical bills and land headfirst."

He considers his options.

"I reckon you've got about eight more seconds to decide."

"Hold my cell." He slaps his phone down in my palm. "I don't want it to get wet." He walks away from me.

"I think that's the least of your problems." I grab his hand with both of mine, sandwiching his phone between our fingers, and use all my weight to drag him back.

"Come on, it's not that bad," I implore him to watch the hosts again.

"It's not that I don't want to – I'm just a lousy dancer."

"I'll help you."

"Fine. Wait, no, I'm not ready."

"Delaying it won't make it any better. Come on, bite the bullet. Let's dance!" I wiggle my shoulders.

"Okay, okay. Next song, I swear."

I wait impatiently for the next track, and our faces drop in disbelief when "Fireball" by Pitbull blares through the speakers.

Well, that's mildly triggering after the afternoon we've had.

"I'm gonna take that as a sign." Tom tries to backtrack.

"Nope. You're not getting out of it that easily."

We copy someone in blue before I twig it's Valentina. I almost didn't recognise her with a smile on her face; she's like an entirely different person out here. I quickly pick up the routine, which doesn't exactly feel like a huge accomplishment – it's just a few box steps, a spin or two, and obviously fiery jazz hands. I look over at Tom beside me to see how he's getting on. Transfixed by my footwork, he's hobbling around like a wounded animal. Maybe he'd be better off with two broken legs after all.

"Ignore the music." I slow the steps right down until he makes some progress. We gradually speed up to match the beat, and I watch him go. I think I finally know how every parent feels when they teach their kid to ride a bike.

We must have attracted an audience as there's a round of applause and cheering coming from behind us. Encouraged by the attention, Tom continues with an accomplished grin and adds some flare to his movements. Unfortunately, his newfound affinity for dance is short-lived as he spins right instead of left, bumping into me and causing half the passengers on our balcony to also collide with one another. Luckily, they see the funny side and burst out laughing too. Tom playfully ridicules them, claiming it's their own fault for watching him, and urges them to copy me instead. He certainly knows how to work a crowd.

It dawns on me that no one's asked us to do this, and I'm almost scared we're going to be told off for joining in. Using my initiative under my brother's thumb always landed me in trouble. Desperate to shake my paranoia, I glance around and notice a sea of cheerful faces. This job is about making people happy, entertaining them, and that's all we're doing up here. I can't get punished for that, right?

Before I get the chance to overthink it any further, I catch Maddison's eye from the deck below. She beams up at us, sticking two proud thumbs in the air, and my heart smiles.

Once the Sail Away Party dies down, Tom and I reconvene with Maddison and the other members of the team, who are standing around chatting.

"You guys looked like you were having fun up there."

"That's one word for it," Tom jokes.

Something steals Maddison's attention in the distance. "Here he is."

I follow her gaze to the jaw-droppingly handsome guy from this morning heading in our direction, clinging desperately to the hope he's not in the same department as me. But with his uniform matching the rest of ours, my faith is futile. All eyes are on him. It's as if he's walking in slow motion.

Ladies of all ages and a few flamboyantly dressed gentlemen abandon any sense of subtlety to gawk at him. But before he can reach us, the jolly cruise director bounds over. I'm genuinely shocked this guy's name isn't Zebedee because he bounces around as if his bottom half is one big spring.

"My new recruits, hello!" Henry greets us. He's the head of all entertainment on the ship so this is one impression I really can't afford to mess up. "Tom!" His voice booms as he shakes Tom's hand with a great deal of enthusiasm, cupping his free hand over where they're joined. "The funny guy! Great to have you on board, my friend. I hope you'll treat us to one of your comedy sets in the crew bar sometime."

"Absolutely!"

So Tom does stand up? That tracks – he can't go five minutes without making a joke out of something. Henry must have been given some highlights from our applications. Apprehension weighs me down as I consider what his immediate assessment of me will be. Or if he'll even make one at all.

Hollister Boy lingers by the group, making my heart beat a little bit faster. I peer down at his name badge. Oscar. *Yep, classic hot guy name.*

Henry turns his attention to me. "And you must be Eliza."

"That's…me," I manage to get out with some pep. He shakes my hand and it's like being struck by lightning – or what I imagine that would feel like anyway. He's literally buzzing with energy, which is a little jarring at first, but it quickly rubs off.

"Our queen of Halloween!"

"You bet." I've never said "you bet" before in my life. I don't even think it makes sense. To be honest, I would have agreed with whatever he said. Anything's better than "drama school reject".

"Glad we're going to have you here for that." He turns to Oscar, who's just a little bit taller than him. "Harvey, any advice for our newbies?"

Harvey? But his badge…

"It's like you always say: if we're happy, the guests are happy," he imparts in a professional yet charming tone I didn't hear this morning.

"Exactly. So if there's anything we can do to help you get settled in, just let us know."

It'd be easy to shrug that off as something he only says to be nice, yet I can't help but feel like he means it.

"Anyway, team, I gotta run." *The Magic Roundabout must be calling.* "But great meeting you both. Welcome aboard."

"Harvey, have you met your buddy yet?" Maddison sets up our introduction. "This is—"

"Eliza." He offers out his hand. "Nice to put a name to a face."

There's an intensity to him that makes me feel like I'm drowning. I try my hardest not to blush as his giant hand squeezes mine. "Likewise."

"Don't you mean 'face to a name'?" Maddison tries to correct him.

He barely controls his smirk. "No. No, I don't."

22

THREE

"What if they ask me something I don't know the answer to?" I fret.

"Just be honest." Oscar must sense my fear because he quickly adds, "You're allowed to be new."

I'm comforted by this and his easy smile.

I refuse to call Oscar "Harvey". That's his surname, as it turns out. I had to endure enough corporate wankers out-macho-ing each other on a daily basis thinking it made them "cool" to call people everything other than their first name, which it definitely *didn't*. I'm certainly not about to start down that same path here.

We're on meet-and-greet duty tonight, which I'm told is "more about being a friendly face on the ship than Wiki-pedia", but I'm not convinced. We've been bombarded with questions since our shift started, none of which even occurred to me as something I'd need to know the answer to. Though Oscar never seems to tire of repeating the same replies, talking to every passenger like he's known them for years, to the point even *I* start to believe he has. There's a twinkle in his eye that shines brighter each time he helps someone, and it's captivating.

I expected to be more of a silent observer on a shadowing shift, seen and not heard, but Oscar makes a significant effort to introduce me and includes me in each new encounter despite barely knowing me himself. It's nice to be allowed to engage. In my last job, I was just dragged around big conferences and trade shows like an accessory. I think Tinky Winky's handbag was about as useful as I ever was. More so, if anything.

Oscar looks at his watch and there's a shift in his approachability. "Right, time to start getting people to the theatre."

We finally free ourselves from the barrage of guests and start walking slowly towards the front – no, *the bow* – of the ship.

"There are two performances tonight that we need to split those interested evenly between. Otherwise, we risk overwhelming catering or exceeding the auditorium's capacity," he explains.

On our way, Oscar continues chatting to people, casually asking if they're seeing this performance or the next one and prompting them to make a choice about their evening plans, until we're standing by the open doors to the theatre welcoming everyone in. Oscar leans over to ask quietly, "Are you hungry?"

"Yeah, I can be." I've completely lost my appetite, but if I skip a meal, I don't know how much time will pass before I have an opportunity to eat again.

An usher comes along to close the doors, leaving us standing alone in the empty foyer. My heart sinks a little when I realise we aren't sticking around to watch the show.

Obviously, we aren't. We're here to work. Remember your place, Eliza.

"Want to see the opening number?" he offers.

"Really?" I respond a bit too brightly.

"Sure. I'd say we could watch the whole thing, but this is the best time to get dinner."

Hope overflows at his words, but I don't know him well enough to insist.

"Come on." He pulls on the heavy door, and we sneak into the darkness, finding a spot at the back to stand in.

I feel the music in my chest and my heart begins to glow. I've seen "Mamma Mia" in the West End more times than I dare to count. I can't resist mouthing the lyrics to "Honey, Honey" as I stare starry-eyed at the stage. The performers are beyond talented. Of course, my dream was to be up there, but I'm okay with where I've ended up, even if it is plan B. I clap with the audience at the end of the song and look up at Oscar, ready to leave, but he's already looking at me.

How long has he been looking at me?

"We can stay if you'd like."

"No, it's okay. We should eat something," I urge, not wanting to take his kindness for granted. I'm grateful to have even seen this much.

Oscar waits long enough for me to change my mind but guides us out when I don't. He heads up the stairs in front of the foyer instead of down.

"I thought we were getting dinner?"

"We are," he replies with a hint of mischief and just enough authority that I won't question him further.

I catch myself in the reflection of a large mirror on the midway platform between floors. I thought I'd look a bit frumpy when I first saw my evening uniform, but it's surprisingly flattering. I'm in a baby-blue blazer, a matching knee-length skirt, and a white blouse with a pointed but professional neckline, with modestly heeled white shoes finishing off the look. I look a bit like a flight attendant but without the scarf. I'm usually a sucker for men in suits, but having seen Oscar in almost nothing this morning, I can't say his attire tonight is affecting me as much as it normally would. I need to burn that image out of my brain.

We arrive at the guest buffet dining area and take turns hovering our hands under the sanitiser dispenser by the entrance.

"Are we allowed in here?" I query, rubbing the gel into my palms.

"Of course. Perks of the job." He grabs a tray and a plate and starts making his selection, so I follow suit.

We find a table by the window and sit opposite one another. Now that his host front has softened, I'm struggling to look him in the eye. Still pink with embarrassment over this morning's fiasco, I seek comfort in the view out the window. Despite the blackened sky, I can just about make out the waves tumbling alongside us.

"Good first day?" Oscar's gravelly voice commands my attention.

"Aside from making some terrible first impressions, yeah, it's been pretty good so far."

"I wouldn't worry yourself. First impressions are overrated anyway." The corner of his mouth curls up as he cuts up his food.

"Did you know this morning? About being buddied up with me."

"Not straight away. I knew I was training someone from England. Wasn't hard to put two and two together."

"Brilliant. Didn't fancy saying something at the time?" I quiz him with an abashed smile.

"I mean, I was caught a little off-guard, what with you breaking into my room like that."

Our eyes lock, and the faint twitch of his lips makes my insides quiver. I shove my attraction aside and cringe at the memory.

"I didn't think you'd have appreciated it."

"I think you might be right."

We laugh off the awkwardness and the ice begins to break. Though ice breaking is the last thing I want to think about while I'm here.

"You're a theatre nerd then," Oscar asks.

"Is it that obvious?" I reply coyly.

"Don't worry – so am I."

Relief rushes through me. Only now do I realise how often I've apologised for my passion. Stuck in an office job in a completely unrelated line of work for the past year, I felt like a traitor confessing my heart lay somewhere else.

"Did you go to drama school too?" he asks.

"No, though not for lack of trying," I admit with a strained laugh, the sting of rejection still fresh from the last few years of auditions. I couldn't even hack it this year. I gave them all my mum's email address instead of mine because if it were bad news I didn't want to know about it. The hope I had just a few months ago when, unlike before, I got through to the final rounds. The disappointment when all the acquaintances I'd made then announced their acceptance or refusal in various group chats and I had no update to give them. I don't regret not broadening my applications though. There are only three schools I want to go to, and if I'm not right for them I don't want to go.

Were. There *were* only three schools I *wanted* to go to.

"It's not all it's cracked up to be." I know he's saying it to make me feel better, but it doesn't change how much I wish I could have gone.

"So, how come you aren't on that stage?"

"I used to be."

"Oh. What changed?"

"Wasn't for me." His tight-lipped smile feels familiar. I take the hint not to dig for the *why*, but I'm filled with the need to know.

"What was the last show you did?"

"'Grease.' On Deity, actually – my last ship."

"Nice. Let me guess… Kenickie?"

"Danny."

"Oh shit." I can't hide my amazement. In an instant, I'm insurmountably more attracted to him than I was this morning, which I didn't quite think was possible. He's a *leading man*. The hottest kind of guy there is in the industry. And out of it. "Wait, sorry, you're…" I take a second to get my thoughts together. "You'd really rather be doing this?"

"Like I said, it wasn't for me." He shrugs.

I can't deny I thought being a host was a direct result of a failed career on stage, but if someone with training and experience behind them is working the same role as me, maybe I'm not doing as badly as I thought.

"Anyway, enough about me. Where's home?"

"I've been in London for a few years, but I grew up in Arundel."

Oscar's entire expression changes, his attention snapping up from his plate to me. "You're kidding."

"Why? Where are you from?"

"Brighton."

I almost don't believe him.

"Fancy that, coming all this way and meeting someone from round the corner."

28

"It's just going to be one disappointment after another, isn't it?" I jest, and something lightens between us. He's still a stranger and I'm still a million miles from home, but I take comfort in our commonality, hopeful the *excitement*-induced knot in my stomach will soon untie itself.

After dinner, Oscar and I return to our duties. Growing surer of myself, I attempt to answer some of the guests' questions, regurgitating key phrases I heard earlier while Oscar holds back and lets me run with it. I have to say, it feels really good to be this involved.

Valentina approaches us outside the theatre and helps welcome people in. "Some of us are headed to the crew bar. Join us when you're done," she says when there's a brief lull.

I have a sneaking suspicion she's overcompensating for her earlier coldness. I look to Oscar, unsure of what social plans our schedule allows for.

"We'll be there," he pledges, and her eyes narrow inquisitively.

"Good. See you there." She saunters off, and we guide the last few guests inside.

I know being sociable tonight is the best thing for me, but I'm desperate to watch the show.

"There'll be a thousand chances to see it, I promise." Oscar's hand hovers over my shoulder.

What? Oh. I've glazed over while gazing longingly at the stage, hindering the usher from closing the door. I apologise and step aside with no choice but to follow Oscar like a lost duckling being dragged away from the pond where it just learnt to swim.

The crew bar is probably the closest I'll ever get to a

student union. From what I've heard, they're basically the same: cheap booze, familiar faces, and an extensive curriculum of events to keep people distracted from the fact they're stuck here for the foreseeable. I sensibly opt for a soda and lime. I'm a lightweight at the best of times – and a horny drunk at the worst – and my first day is not when I want everyone to find that out. Or ever if I can help it. Scanning the room, I spot Tom laughing and joking with the team as if he's been here for months, not minutes.

I wish I had that confidence. Regardless of what I've done in the past, I eventually seem to embarrass whoever's introducing me. The problem is, I don't know what makes a better first impression. Should I go for the slow burn and eke out my personality over the next few weeks in the hope people's curiosity will keep them interested, or do I go in all guns blazing, full entertainer mode and unapologetically myself? The problem with that option, though, is that I haven't felt like myself for such a long time now I'm not even sure how to act like it. *For God's sake.* I thought I had this all figured out, but now it's happening I'm second-guessing myself.

Snap out of it, Eliza. You're not a pathetic little tagalong. You earned your space here like everyone else.

As we walk over to the table, my shoulders drop, relaxing in the heartiness of the reception the others give us. Oscar introduces me to everyone, most of whom I've already met today, but I'm grateful for the reminder of people's names. The only one I haven't met is Oscar's roommate, Obi. Valentina was right – he does look like he eats rainbows for breakfast. He waves cheerfully from where he's sitting, his smile bright. There are more entertainment staff on a table nearby, but their names are rattled off so quickly I barely catch them.

Tom pats the empty seat he's saved next to him, and I

split off from Oscar to take it. We've only been apart for a few hours, but there's already so much to catch up on. He revels in the aftermath of an evidently juicy game of Mr and Mrs he and Maddison hosted, making me excited to run it with Oscar next week.

Tom's roommate, Daniel, stands up and clears his throat. "To our new arrivals."

The others join him in raising their drinks. I repeat his words quietly to Tom as if he needs a translator.

"Shut up." He laughs back, elbowing me in the ribs.

"Welcome to the family."

We all clink our glasses together. It's official: I survived my first day and I'm part of a team that actually wants me.

"And now that I have everyone's attention…" He pauses while everyone groans as if they've heard the same Christmas cracker joke two years too many. "We need to decide what we're doing for the talent show."

Tom and I watch on as the others jeer like MPs in parliament, shouting out suggestion after suggestion – but of all the loud voices at the table, Daniel's seems to be the loudest.

"Whatever it is, it has to be better than the actors. The same Britney track was on a loop in the gym earlier, so I think we're in trouble," Obi warns.

"Tom, Eliza, any ideas?" Daniel tries to include us.

"Sorry, what's this?" I ask.

"On Friday there's a little competition between some of the departments," Oscar elaborates from the other side of the table.

"Little?" Valentina scoffs. "Harvey, I don't think we're talking about the same thing."

He sinks in defeat as his plan to play it down fails.

Why does no one call him by his first name?

"All the departments get involved," Maddison adds.

"Medics, sports staff, chefs, engineers, beauticians – you name it, they're competing."

"Awesome! What kind of things do people do?" Tom looks like he's about to fall out of his seat with excitement.

"Songs, dances, skits, parodies. There was even magic last time. Anything you like – it just needs to be better than the *professionals*." From Valentina's air quotes I pick up on some not-so-subtle hints at a rivalry.

"Obi here did a one-man rendition of 'Bohemian Rhapsody' in its entirety last time," Daniel boasts proudly, putting his arm around him and squeezing tightly.

"*With* an interpretive dance!" Obi says, holding his finger up to emphasise the point.

"And he was robbed!" Maddison exclaims.

A commotion breaks out on the table as they cheer in agreement, doing impressions of certain performance highlights. It's sweet how supportive they are of each other.

"What if they did it?" Maddison suggests, nudging her head in our direction.

"On their own?" Daniel debates with her as if we aren't here.

"Yeah, trial by fire, see what they're made of," Valentina encourages.

"I'm in if you're in," Tom commits tenaciously.

"Yeah, definitely!" I match his vigour, but it takes some effort. I love performing, so why does this feel so daunting?

"Okay! What skills are we bringing to the table? Dancing?" Daniel interrogates.

I nod, but Tom shakes his head.

"Singing?"

I nod again, and Tom shakes his head faster.

"Let's try this another way. Tom, what do *you* suggest?"

His earlier courage dwindles as he ponders.

"Don't overthink it. Just say the first thing that comes to you."

Tom gasps. "We could do a lip-synch battle! That could be fun."

"Good starting point. Eliza, suggestions?"

"I love musicals." For the first time in forever, I decide to be bold with my opinion. "We could lip-synch a song from a musical?"

"We can work with that. Team, put your heads together. What are some good musical duos?"

"Ooh, J.D. and Veronica!" I trill at the very thought of my favourite musical, "Heathers", only to be met by a wall of blank expressions. All except Oscar, who smiles at the mention, bobbing his head in approval.

"Elphaba and Glinda," Obi chimes in, completely dismissing my suggestion.

"Who are *they*?" Tom's face scrunches up at the strange-sounding names.

"You haven't seen 'Wicked'?" I gawp at him, but he just shrugs.

"What about Audrey and Seymour?" Oscar proposes.

"You're going too niche, babe." Obi puts him down gently.

"Brad and Janet?" I mumble with shrivelling conviction.

"The excursion team did 'Rocky Horror' last time," Maddison sighs.

I suck in my lips, silencing myself to prevent any further rejection.

"What about 'Grease'?" Oscar puts forwards.

The team eye up me and Tom in consideration.

"Look at them – they'd be perfect for it."

Tom and I briefly study one another. Our hair colours are presumably the driving force of our typecasting.

"Everyone in agreement say 'aye'." Daniel rallies, prompting a ripple of unanimous "ayes" from around the table. "That's settled then."

I catch Oscar's eyes twinkling again.

"Don't fuck it up," Valentina spurs us on.

Another idea comes to me, but I decide not to share it.

The next hour or so flies by as the team fill us in on everything we should know about surviving the contract, divulging embarrassing anecdotes from their own first weeks to put us at ease, and it certainly helps. I was expecting to be drilled with all sorts of questions about our lives before the ship, but with no shortage of time to get to know us, tonight seems to be all about making us feel at home.

Tom eventually excuses himself to unpack. The fact he's comfortable enough in himself to leave a social situation is admirable. His roommate drinks up and goes with him, and it dawns on me I won't have that luxury tonight. Nevertheless, I take his exit as an excuse to tear myself away from the group too. They kindly wave me off and wish me a good night, though I wish they'd offer me some help with finding my room. I could use that more than anything else right now.

Where's Hoggle when you need him?

When I enter my room, a profound emptiness knees me in the stomach. The cabin's bare, with no character or charm, completely bereft of any colour or personal touches. I thought the last thing I'd be when I came aboard was lonely, but now the feeling's unignorable. I should be relieved – people would kill to have a room to themselves on here, as evidenced by the jealous reactions I got when I mentioned it earlier. And surely it's better not to have a roommate than to be stuck with a bad one. But that hollow feeling I thought would disappear when I arrived has only become greater.

The door crashes behind me and brings me back to reality.

I look for my phone to settle the instinctive need to distract myself until I remember I put it in the safe earlier and that's probably where it's best kept. It's not like I can use it for anything vaguely comforting without forking out money on internet access anyway. And probably not even then.

Once showered and wearing something comfier, I push my exhaustion away and begin to unpack, convincing myself the room will feel homier once I've put my stamp on it. But before I get the chance to stew over which of the empty cabinets to claim as my own, there's a knock at the door.

"Thought you might like some company," Maddison offers.

I welcome her in, touched by her thoughtfulness. "Thanks. I'm not really sure where to start."

"Lucky for you, I'm an expert."

She isn't wrong; it's like having Marie Kondo in my room. If Marie Kondo were nosy and Texan, that is. Maddison picks the optimal storage spaces quickly, giving peculiar but valid reasons for all her choices. It's also great to hear all about ship life from someone who's been here for a while. The YouTube videos I watched before I left were beyond helpful, but Maddison's a lot more honest about things than the people who had to filter their experiences and opinions to prevent potential defamation lawsuits from their employers. I have to set aside my weird germaphobe quirk of her being on my bed in "outdoor clothes" while she makes me a nest up on the top bunk with sheets that smell like home and the fairy lights I bought after seeing them in a cabin tour vlog. She moves on to the finishing touches, sticking my photos to the wall with my star-shaped magnets.

I scowl when I see the photo I deliberately removed from the collection my sister put together for me. It was taken at Latitude Festival a few years ago, the summer I turned eighteen. My arms are wrapped around Tara and *Kate*, who stand either side of me with their hands in the air, cheery smiles on all three of our faces. Just from looking at the picture, I swear I can smell that overpoweringly sweet dry shampoo in our floral headband–decorated hair. I told Sarah there was no way in *hell* I was putting a picture of that bitch up on my wall, but she argued I needed more photos that made it seem like I had friends. I disagreed, but it looks like she had the final say.

That was the last summer before everything changed. The three of us moved to London together, Tara and Kate going to our top choice of drama school and me taking an unexpected gap year with the plan to work and re-audition for the following year. What's that saying? *The best-laid plans of mice and men often go to shit.* Yeah, that sounds about right.

"Question," Maddison says, putting up a photo from a family holiday. "Are you single?"

"Why? You interested?"

"No, just curious." She's up to something and she sucks at hiding it. All it takes is a raise of an eyebrow for her to crack. "Fine. I think someone's into you, that's all."

"I've only been here a day!"

"That's like a week on here."

"That's still not very long," I protest, but she dismisses my comment. "You can put down your arrow – I'm not available."

"Who's the lucky…person?"

"Oh, no, I'm single. Straight and single, but I'm not getting involved."

"Don't you at least wanna know who it is?"

"Nope."

Yes.

Maddison stares at me open-mouthed. Clearly, her gossip is seldom refused.

"What? I'm here to work."

"That's what everyone says. Give it a week."

"A week won't change my mind. No good ever comes from a workplace romance."

Maddison tilts her head, surveying me.

"Sure, I might be dusting off the cobwebs as soon as this contract ends, but until then, my legs are staying firmly closed."

"All right, I'll keep it to myself."

I can see how much this pains her. She's waiting for me to give in, and luckily, just as my defiance begins to wane, there's another knock at the door. To my secret delight, it's Oscar. He's holding my clothes in the same folded pile I left them in on his desk earlier.

"I thought you might need these back." He hands them over, our fingers brushing in the exchange and sending a small ripple through me.

I let the heavy door rest on my foot. "I completely forgot. Thank you."

"You getting settled in okay?" There's a softness in his voice and care on his face as he leans against the doorframe.

"Yeah, almost there, thanks."

"Hi, Harvey!" Maddison calls out from the top bunk, causing him to tense a little. I open the door all the way so they can see each other.

"Glad you're not alone. I'll leave you to it."

"Don't leave on my account," Maddison insists, her tone full of mischief.

"Breakfast at eight?" He ignores her with a puckish eye roll.

"Sure. See you there." When the door shuts, I turn back to find Maddison unintentionally impersonating a glitching android.

"Care to tell me why Harvey has your clothes?"

"I'd prefer to keep that private." I refuse only because I know it'll wind her up. Leaving her to speculate, I busy myself with ferrying the rest of my toiletries into the bathroom.

"So, what were you doin' before you came here?"

"I was a personal assistant," I say with an inflection as if answering her question with a question. I notice the anticipation wilt in her eyes.

"Oh. I thought you might have done somethin'…"

"More entertaining?"

"Spookier."

"Ah, I used to work at The Cellar."

I'm greeted by the same animated reaction I get from everyone when I reveal I worked at London's top scare attraction. You wouldn't think a job that calls for you to scare and scream at guests would lead to a position as a chirpy entertainment host, but somehow I managed to twist my cover letter to promote how well I maintain my composure while being constantly screamed at. It sounds miserable to describe it like that, but working at The Cellar was the best job ever. That was probably the only time in the past few years I've been happy. Or at least it was until—

"No way! That's awesome. We did a haunted house for the guests last year and it was *awful*. Maybe you can get involved with this year's one."

"Yeah, that would be cool." I quash my hopes before I get carried away. I highly doubt they'd let me give my creative input into anything. "How about you – what were you doing before cruising?"

"I came straight from college. And that I only did to get away from home and start thinkin' for myself."

I'm kind of flattered by Maddison's openness. Maybe

she's like this with everyone, but I appreciate it nonetheless. "Was it not...?"

"I was an only child, homeschooled by strict, religious parents. I ain't ever goin' back," she reveals but grins despite it all.

I've known loneliness when surrounded by people – more often than not, people who claimed to be my friends – but through it all I've always had my family. To not even have your family's support... I can't imagine how dark Maddison's lows must have been. But here she is, bright as a button, reaching out to me to protect me from that feeling. For that, I want to cling to her and never let go.

"So you found your thing here?"

"Oh, absolutely. Nothin' beats this."

We share a warm smile. She's going to be a good influence on me, I can tell.

"So, scare actin' – that's different from personal assistin'. Why the shift?"

There it is: the question I was dreading being asked the most. I avoid her eye and put away the last few things from my case. She's shared with me, so it's only right for me to do the same. But I came here for a fresh start, excited to have a clean slate. Somewhere no one knows what a colossal loser I am.

"Just needed a change." I keep my tone light, pretending there's nothing more to it than that. It doesn't sit right, but I need to at least give myself a chance to start over.

Once my suitcase is empty, I put the jeans I got back from Oscar in there. No chance in hell I'll wear those again. It's way too hot for that nonsense. I zip up and flatten down my holdall as small as it will go and shove it under the bottom bunk. Then, thanking Maddison profusely for keeping me company, I give her a hug good night, find my iPad, and stick on an episode of "The Office" I've seen a thousand times to fill the silence.

I'm not even under the covers before I'm ripping Kate out of the picture of us from Latitude. Tara got too busy to keep in touch, but I know if I saw her tomorrow it'd be like no time had passed at all. Kate, on the other hand… Enough time will never have passed for me to forget what happened.

When I lie back on my pillow, I feel something odd inside it. Maybe Maddison missed a photo. I sit up and find the culprit. There's a little purple envelope in my pillowcase with my name written on it. I already know it's another one of my sister's surprises, and I'm glad Maddison left it for me to discover where it was planted.

Inside the envelope is a letter and a photo, on the back of which reads:

Can't wait to meet you in March!

I turn it around and discover it's a baby scan. My heart thumps as I scramble to open the letter.

Dear Auntie Eliza,

You're officially the first person we've told! Now I know you're going to want to break your "first week no phone" rule and call me, but just hang in there, Lize. We're telling everyone else on Sunday at Mum's birthday lunch (the table's booked for 1 p.m. UK time), so if you're free to FaceTime us then, it'd be so good to see you.

Have the best time out there! We're all so proud of you.

Love Sarah, Simon, and Bump x

. . .

I breathe in the smell of my bedsheets and tears stream effortlessly down my cheeks. A small sob leaves my tight throat as I process the news. I'm both overcome with happiness for Sarah and in complete and utter despair at being sequestered from her.

Calming myself down, I use a spare magnetic star to stick the picture of my nibling to the wall beside me. *See you in six months, little one.*

FOUR

I spend most of breakfast wrestling with my eyelids, barely acknowledging the granola and yoghurt I'm slowly shovelling into my mouth. I try to engage with the others, but there's a certain level of energy you need to keep up with them that I just don't have. It would be like entering the motorway on a mobility scooter.

A foot taps mine twice under the table. I look up to find the perpetrator. Oscar's watching me with concern etched in his brow. I perk up quickly, nervous he's not the only one who's noticed my distance.

"Want some tea?"

"Yeah, that's a good idea. I couldn't find any earlier." I look back at the serving area to see a very obviously placed coffee machine with a stand of colourful teabags next to it. *Idiot.* "Can I get you anything?"

"I'll come with you." Oscar walks with me over to the tea station. "Jet lag or rough night?" He tears open a packet and pops the teabag into a mug before handing it to me.

"Maybe both. I kept waking up confused and had to remind myself where I was." I press the button for hot water.

"Ah, that's no fun. There's time for a nap this afternoon if you need it."

I bounce the teabag by the string before pushing my mug against the dispenser on the milk machine. *Should I really trust milk from a machine?*

"But my advice is to push through the day if you can. You'll sleep better tonight and wake up tomorrow feeling human again."

"Noted. Thanks." I stare at my mug, perplexed. The steam doesn't smell right. It's not like an off-milk smell; it's almost citrusy.

"Oh, it's Earl Grey. Not a fan?"

Earl Grey tea is the worst thing I've ever put in my mouth, and I've made some bad choices where that's concerned… It's deceitful and deserves no place in my life. It disguises itself as a refreshing beverage and then poisons you with its horrible aftertaste. Come to think of it, Earl Grey would be a good name for my ex. That's probably the politest thing I've called him since we broke up. I digress. My point is, Earl Grey tea will never be as good as traditional tea. If it were a millennial, it would no doubt spend its days comparing itself to other teas online before ultimately being diagnosed with imposter syndrome.

"No, it's okay. Don't want it to go to waste." My polite-ness has always brought me suffering, but waste has always brought suffering to the planet, so this is the lesser of two evils.

"It won't." He puts his teabag, which he hadn't yet opened, back into the box on the stand and exchanges it for a *normal* one before checking in with me for approval.

"Whose first choice is Earl Grey though?" I ask accusingly.

"Mine. Shouldn't it be?"

"No."

"Why's that?"

"It's – and please know I don't use this term lightly – *minging*."

He chuckles. "Is that so?"

"Mm-hmm."

A smirk appears on his cheek while he swaps our mugs over. I thank him, and we head back to the table.

"Call yourself a Brit." I can't help but mock him under my breath.

His grin widens midway through taking an impatient sip from his mug and he catches my eye out of the corner of his. I'm ashamed to admit it but I think I'd now willingly douse myself in the putrid stuff if it meant he'd put his lips against me.

If the tea didn't wake me up, having our drill sergeant of a safety officer shout "ABANDON SHIP!" at the top of his lungs over a megaphone certainly does. Fully clothed and donning our life jackets, the other new recruits and I jump into the indoor pool and start swimming over to the line of life rafts that look like floating tents. Too many people seem to be going for the first one, already forming a queue to get in, so I decide to swim to the next one along. As I approach, I notice a few people struggling, perhaps not necessarily the strongest swimmers, though these jackets do make everything harder. If I were in the sea, I'd obviously be glad to have it help me withstand a good pummelling from the relentless waves, but in a pool it's nothing other than a hindrance.

I decide to be a team player and go to the third and final life raft on the furthest side of the pool at the deep end. I hoick myself up and crawl inside it, immediately looking out to see who I can help up. No one else has made it down to this end yet. Perhaps instead of being commended for my thoughtfulness, I'll be berated for tiring myself out and theoretically risking my life. Was this part of the test?

Tom's exhausted face emerges from around the side of the second raft, and I can't help but giggle to myself when I see the state of him.

"Like to make it hard for yourself, don't you, Elizabeth?" he puffs, flailing around, his life jacket making a worthy attempt at swallowing him whole.

"What are you doing?" I shout.

"I wasn't made for the water!"

"Then what are you doing on a *ship*?"

"Hurry up, Parks!" the sergeant yells at Tom.

The splashes become rampant as Tom's limbs get more urgent. He tries to clamber up into the life raft but can't get the purchase he needs.

"Want help?"

"No." He slips and disappears with another big splash. "Yes."

"Get your knee up!" I instruct over the chaos. I grab onto him and his life jacket and pull roughly as he thrusts himself out of the water. Overcome with momentum, he propels forwards as I fall backwards, resulting in him landing on top of me like a beached whale. I let out an almighty huff as all the air is forcibly removed from my lungs.

He scurries on his knees to zip up the pod and visibly relaxes once we're sealed in. When he looks back, I'm still collapsed in the middle of the raft, purposely sticking out my tongue, playing dead.

"Oh no, gonna have to start CPR! What's that stand for again? Oh yeah, Crush Person Repeatedly." Tom throws himself on top of me, our life jackets making it feel like we're in those padded wrestler suits you get at fairs.

"I'm alive! I'm alive!" I cry, and we erupt with laughter as he rolls off me.

We lie there on our backs staring up at the pointed roof until we compose ourselves. Then we turn our heads towards one another, and for a short moment, being alone together in this private pod is exhilarating.

"So let me get this straight. You don't like dancing and you don't like swimming. Next you'll say you have a phobia of boats," I tease.

"Now you mention it…"

"Tom!"

"I'm totally kidding." His eyes widen and he looks away sharply.

"Did you even read the job description before coming here?"

"I wanted to be *on* the water, not *in* it!"

Instead of taking a nap in the time between lunch and our retreat back to the crew centre for more training, Tom and I head to the gym to start rehearsing for the talent show. We agreed on the song "You're The One That I Want" because we both know it well enough not to worry about learning the lip-synch in the short time we have. Due to Tom's limited tolerance for dance, we focus on making the routine more character-driven with only a few very basic moves. There's no denying comedy comes naturally to him; he throws out a bunch of ideas that help to energise our performance, and which will definitely get us a few laughs.

Just as I hit "play" on the speakers for the last time and

turn back to Tom, Oscar walks into the gym in his workout gear. Apprehension engulfs me, and it takes everything to block him out and get through the song. I'm really proud of what we've managed to put together in such a short space of time, so why am I uncomfortable with being watched?

"Looking good, guys!" he praises, and I find I've suddenly gone shy. He's literally the expert on these characters, this song – this whole routine even – and I dread to know what he *really* thinks of our act. If it's shit, he doesn't let on.

"So, any advice?" Tom asks. It may have been a mistake telling him about Oscar's experience – he's now fixated on impressing him.

"It's really good. You're both natural performers – that's obvious."

"But..." Tom pushes, and I wish he wouldn't. I'm not sure I can handle criticism, no matter how constructive.

"'Grease' is a classic. Everyone knows it," Oscar states. "Why not make it something no one's seen before? You should know better than anyone, Tom, that the best comedy comes from the unexpected. Feel free to ignore me, but with these things, it's always better to play to your strengths."

Tom and I look to each other for a big idea, but nothing springs to mind.

At least not yet.

This evening's activity is a pub quiz, which is a welcome tonic after spending the afternoon discussing various topics from lost-child procedures to what to do if we discover a deceased passenger. I thought it was a myth that cruise ships had morgues, but no, turns out they do.

Because people die on board.

Often enough that they need to have a morgue.

It doesn't take long for other crew members to greet me and Oscar as we pass through the ship, all only calling him by his surname.

"Please don't tell me this is a last name–only kind of place, because I'm not sure I'll last if it is," I groan.

"Why? You have a great last name."

I scrunch up my face in disdain.

"But no, just me and maybe one or two others," he assures me.

"Do you like it?"

"I don't have much of a choice."

Before I can ask why, a frail-looking lady approaches us needing help finding her activity.

"You all right to wait here?" Oscar asks me. "I won't be a minute."

They shuffle away at her pace, and I instinctively start patting my pockets in search of my phone until I remember it's still locked away. I hate that that's my reflex to being left alone. I'm hoping this job will knock that habit out of me. Instead I take the opportunity to watch the sunset through the huge window beside me. It's so beautiful out here. This beats any heavily edited *#GoldenHour* snaps I could have seen on my screen.

I wait for what feels like an eternity before looking down at my watch. He's already been gone for ten minutes, which seems a little too long just to escort someone. I hold out for another five minutes, but when there's still no sign of him, I start to debate whether I misheard "wait here" as "meet me there". Maybe he got caught up helping someone else on the way back. Maybe the woman tripped over and he's taking her to the medical centre. Or maybe she died suddenly. Apparently, that isn't out of the question on here, and I imagine holding onto Oscar's muscular arm for support is enough to increase anyone's heart rate a dangerous amount.

Now fully trained in handling these situations and expecting the worst, I decide to follow in the direction they left, which leads me outside through a glass door to the pool at the front of the ship. It's way quieter than when I last saw it at the Sail Away Party, though still pretty busy.

"Oscar?" I call out timidly. I clear my throat and try again, and then one more time, as if I'm summoning Bloody Mary in the girls' bathroom mirrors at school.

Out of nowhere, a swarm of crew rush over to me and start looking over the edge of the ship. "Where are they?" a crew member asks me urgently.

"I don't know – I'm looking for him."

Someone grabs a life ring from the side of the ship without taking their eyes off the water.

What is going on?

"Where did he fall from?"

I freeze in confusion and fear. It wasn't Mary I summoned; it was a bloody *army*. Everyone is desperately searching the water below. Someone runs towards an emergency phone on the wall behind me, almost knocking into Oscar, who rushes over having seen the commotion.

"Did someone fall in the water?" he asks, his face stony with severity.

"No. I don't know. I was just looking for you and this happened." I stretch out my arms, showcasing the disarray around me.

"False alarm, everyone!" he bellows to the concerned onlookers who take some more convincing before they retreat.

I apologise profusely, though I'm still not sure what for.

"Sorry. Her activity was on the other side of the ship," Oscar explains, but I'm too startled to respond. He places his hands gently on my shoulders and looks at me intently. "You okay?"

Well, that depends. Would you constitute almost causing a ship-wide emergency on my second day, and having that tingly feeling in my bowels like I could have an emergency of my own at any minute, as being okay? "What just happened?" Is all I can say.

"I should have told you. People call me Harvey because my first name, which we're never going to shout on an open deck ever again..." – he coerces confirmation from me, and I nod my head slowly – "on some cruise ships means 'man overboard'," he says in a hushed tone.

"Shit. I'm so sorry."

"It's okay. It's my fault – I should have told you." He squeezes my shoulders before letting go.

"Wait. I thought that was a code blue?"

"Yes, officially it is. But there are crew on here who've worked with other cruise lines and know it as something different, so we just don't say it."

"Got it. What an unfortunate coincidence."

"Tell me about it."

"Harvey it is," I say with mild contempt.

"All right, my surname isn't *that* bad," he protests, and I smirk. "Right, we need to get a shift on, Chapman, because we are *very* late."

For a brief second, I feel like I'm back in London. They've done a great job of turning this bar into the perfect replica of a traditional British pub, nailing every detail down to a T, from the dingy, beer-soaked patterned carpet, to the slot machine in the corner, to the high ratio of balding, middle-aged men.

The guests don't seem at all inconvenienced by our tardiness, though I reckon Oscar could walk in, scream vile profanities and leave and they'd still be pleased to see him. That's hot-guy privilege for you. He kicks off the quiz by announcing the prizes, which infuses the room with a buzz of competition. I'm excited to see my first actual activity. The meet-and-greet was enjoyable, but it was much less structured than this appears to be.

Oscar reads out a few questions, and I relax into what should be a fun night. He moves the microphone away from his mouth to ask me, "You recovered?"

"I think so."

"Good." He hands over the microphone and the tablet with the questions on it. "Off you go."

"Really?" I chirp in disbelief.

"Really." He laughs with a nod of his head.

I give myself a chance to read the next question and then go for it.

Oscar uses a clicker to run through the slideshow full of music intros, pictures, and videos throughout the quiz, leaving me to focus on hosting and interacting with the guests. There's something unsettling about walking around the pub with all this authority, but I like it. I'm so used to being the most insignificant person in the room that I almost forgot how good it feels to be centre stage.

"I've got it!" Tom bursts into my room at 8 a.m., before my pupils even have the chance to acclimatise to the light, let alone keep up with the way he's bouncing around.

"Good morning," I rasp sarcastically.

"Elizabeth, we don't have time for these British pleasantries you insist upon," he mocks in a terrible attempt at an English accent.

"Why are you here, Tom?"

"I know how we can make our act different."

I wait for him to elaborate.

"When we were brainstorming the other day, my idea got, like, split in half, and I think the thing that was cut is what could help us win."

"Right?"

"Lip-synch *battle*. We should be competing, one-upping each other or something. It's a love song – no one would expect us to hate each other."

"All right, you might be onto something there."

"Wanna try it out?"

"Sure." He gets his phone out and starts scrolling to find the song.

"What, *now*?"

"Yeah, I don't have long before I need to meet Maddison."

I stare at him dreary-eyed.

"Look alive, Elizabeth."

I use my arms to hold my boobs down while I jump on the spot to shake myself awake, ready to give his big idea a go. And fair play to him, this really is a fun twist. His enthusiasm for us to succeed inspires me to get creative too. I mark out some good places to add fake slaps, shoves, and even hair-pulling, and we somehow end up tussling on the floor, fighting to be the one on top for the final line. When the song finishes, I appear to have won our little game. I'm straddling him, my hands on his chest feeling the rise and fall of his now shortened breath.

"That was so good!" he cheers as he throws his arms back like a starfish.

"I think we've got this in the bag. Good work, you." I pat his chest, quickly realising sitting on top of him in my skimpy pyjamas probably isn't the wisest thing.

"No, good work, *you*."

His hand lightly grips my bare thigh just above my knee. *Don't focus on how good that feels.*

"I just thought we'd be a bit feisty or something, but you added the aggression, and I love it!"

"Teamwork."

We high-five so hard my palm stings, and the way his eyes scan my body on top of his ignites something dangerous. *Get up. Just get up. Stop seeing how long you can push this physical boundary you've surpassed and get the fuck up!*

But it feels *so good.*

The knock at the door immediately throws water over the fire.

"Hey, I managed to get you a few costume bits from Wardrobe's store last night." Oscar hands over two leather jackets, a yellow cardigan, and a long yellow skirt with a petticoat. "I wasn't sure if you were going for the all-black finale look or a more classic Sandy costume."

"Sweet! Thanks, man." Tom comes to the door and the smallest hint of surprise flashes across Oscar's face. It wouldn't be hard to jump to a certain conclusion about what he's doing in my room. We're both out of breath, Tom's hair is all over the place, and I might as well be in my underwear.

Oscar's expression turns stoic. "Oh, sorry. I'll see you at breakfast. Let me know if they fit okay," he says politely and walks away, leaving a fresh wave of shame to wash over me. I want to chase after him and proclaim our innocence, but I refrain from doing so because a) I'm not all that innocent, and b) any declaration of such innocence would almost definitely fall on closed ears.

FIVE

The rest of Wednesday is agonising, to say the least. I spend – or should I say "waste"? – the entire day paranoid rumours about Tom's appearance in my room are spreading around the ship like wildfire. I'm convinced that before long, everyone will be labelling me as some loose-legged hussy, while Tom, on the other hand, will probably get propelled to a new social standing. Despite denying that I care what people think of me, there are certainly some black spots, particularly where my romantic liaisons are concerned.

I'd like to think I can trust Oscar not to be a gossipmonger. He seems like a good guy, and despite being well-known on the ship, he's somewhat on the edge of the social scene, so I doubt it's something that would come up in conversation. But I've been wrong about people before. To play it safe, I decide it's best I keep my distance from Tom, but it makes for a particularly dull day. In retrospect, I may be risking our chances of having a well-polished routine for Friday night by refusing to rehearse with him again.

I go to bed berating myself for having this "main character mentality" that makes me stupidly assume I'm interesting enough for people to fritter away their time talking about me. I'm a nobody.

But hey, at least the jet lag's gone.

In an attempt to shake off these bad vibes and start my day right, I drag myself to the gym for a quick run on the treadmill, feeling better almost instantly. I mean, it's impossible not to perk up when show tunes are blasting through my headphones.

Just as I'm about to hit my distance goal, a group of alarmingly loud and attractive people, some of whom I vaguely recognise from the opening number of "Mamma Mia", walk in and start retrieving chairs from a storage cupboard, placing them in a very specific formation. Intrigue keeps me running just a little longer to find out what they're up to. It's like I'm being blessed with a gift from the talent-show Gods. When one of the group connects their phone to the speakers and a Britney track plays throughout the room, I make no attempt to pretend I'm not watching.

"We're fucked. Completely fucked," I declare as I stride into Tom's room, instantly pacing back and forth, tiny beads of sweat still clinging to my hairline. I was hoping Daniel would be about to vouch for us should someone see me barging in, but unfortunately for me, he's already up and out. But this discovery is too important not to share.

"Good morning, Elizabeth. How are you?" Sarcastic pep is rich in his tone.

"We need to scrap our entire routine. They're going to wipe the floor with us!"

"Whoa, slow down."

In my competitive haze, I completely failed to acknowledge he's only wearing boxers. Very tight black boxers. *Jesus Christ.* I quickly shift my attention from him, but there's more than a slim chance he caught me looking.

"I think the problem is we're not sexy enough," I continue, though Tom and his toned physique aren't helping me validate my point. "We're doing a school play, and they're doing bloomin' 'Magic Mike'!"

"Who are?"

"The actors."

His eyes widen as urgency finally takes hold of him. "Show me."

I get him to sit on his desk chair in the middle of the room after deciding the easiest section to repeat is the part where the guys are sitting down as the girls dance around them. Using Tom's phone, I find Britney's "I'm a Slave 4 U" (poor girl's been crying out for help since the Noughties) and skip to the chorus. I replicate what I saw – the body rolls, hair flicks, and provocative positions - completely lost in my short-term memory, only to register too late I've essentially given him a lap dance. Except he's the one in his undies, and I'm the hysterical clammy one who instigated this interaction.

His face is just inches away from mine and my eyes are raptly locked onto his. Our groins might as well be made of magnets because here I am, yet again, straddling him inappropriately. Except this time there's no interruption. His gaze shifts past me, and I follow it to the mirror behind me on the inside of his open wardrobe door, catching his eye in the reflection. From this angle, it looks like he isn't wearing anything.

Good lord.

"I think we're sexy enough." His voice is soft and tempting in my ear. I look back at him but don't dare to say anything in response. I begin to pulse in all the right places where we touch. The longer we stare at each other, the hungrier my body gets, and the more impatient my growing lust. All it would take is a tilt of my hips and he'd be mine.

Eliza, don't do this. No funny business – that was the deal.

"So, any big ideas?" I disturb the heavy silence, ignoring his hand on the top of my thigh, his restless fingertips skimming the Lycra barrier over my skin.

I want him. Fuck my rules. Fuck everything. *I want him.*

"Just one," he whispers. His left hand reaches for the side of my neck, his thumb resting against my cheek, and the other slides up from my thigh to my waist to pull me into him.

Elizabeth!

"Tom."

"Mmm?" Our lips are so tantalisingly close that mine buzz from his hum. I wish I could engorge myself on his mouthwash-rinsed lips, but if word got out that I'd been intimate with someone – not just someone, but a *coworker* – after only knowing them for three days, I could never come back from that. I could never escape it either.

"I meant about the act," I say quickly. *I hate myself.*

"Oh." He freezes. Then words tumble out of him. "Yeah. Uhh… Yes." He releases his gentle grip on me and puts his hands up in polite surrender, allowing me to get off him.

"Sorry," I say softly.

"No, are you kidding? Don't be sorry. *I'm* sorry. I thought… No. Uhh… The act."

"We can talk about it later. If you want?"

"Yeah. Let's do that."

I hurry out the door and race back to my room, hoping no one sees me and reads into my flustered state. *Shut up. No one cares about you, Eliza.* Great, so there are still no improvements on our act, I'll have to spend another day avoiding Tom, and now I'm horny and have no time to deal with it.

Clawing off my sweaty gym clothes, I find it unbelievable Tom found this appealing. Are his standards really that low, or does he have some kind of sweat kink?

I stick an episode of "Drag Race" on to drown out my overthinking spiral and hop in the shower. What was it Oscar said? "Play to our strengths." Well, the actors are certainly playing to theirs, being all model-like and – if the rumours are anything to go by – grinding on just about everything. Tom's strength is being funny twenty-four-seven, but what's mine? Hating myself? Terrible self-control? Letting down everyone around me? Yes, that's it, I can see it now: *"And the winner is…Eliza Chapman with her special talent 'severe disappointment'!"*

Give me a gun.

I'm a genius. (I think.) This could be my best idea ever. (Or just another in a long line of deluded thoughts.) Either way, I'm running with it now.

I've spent every break I've had today messing around with our track on GarageBand, which has been very helpful in my quest to avoid Tom at all costs. Two birds, one stone and all that. God, do we need someone to chaperone our rehearsals now? I don't trust us to be alone together. Or rather, I don't trust myself to repel his magnetism when it inevitably pulls me in again.

Noticing the time, I force myself to stop working on the song and quickly get ready for this evening's formal night. Regardless of the activity, black tie is compulsory for us and the guests, and I'm really looking forward to dressing up having spent the past four days in either my PE kit or the rigid flight attendant getup. I bought a few options with me, but eventually I settle on a tight baby-pink off-the-shoulder dress that rests just below the knee. I select my favourite necklace and my white closed-toe heels, not forgetting to transfer my name badge from my day clothes before I head out the door.

Oscar, Maddison, Tom, and I are attending a cocktail party for the ship's VIP members, which Maddison described earlier as "a wedding reception hosted at a care home", so I don't hold out much hope for an adrenaline-filled evening.

My blonde hair tickles the bare skin on my back as I walk to meet the others outside Maddison's room. I'm only a few minutes late, but I push to walk a little faster than I'm comfortable with in these shoes. Seeing Tom down the hall in a fitted tux like he's just stepped off a red carpet is the last thing I need right now. It takes all my strength to slap away the giddiness that flutters through me for the briefest of seconds. I was worried I'd be overdressed for the event, but I'm relieved to see Maddison in a vibrant orange maxi dress that perfectly complements her sunny disposition.

"Eliza! Where've you been hidin' that body of yours?" she calls out, causing the boys to turn in my direction. I dip my head in embarrassment, unsure of what to do with the attention. "Stunnin', ain't she, boys?"

They both make noises of polite enthusiasm.

Please make it stop.

"You all look incredible," I say back. *Great work, Eliza. Compliments are always more genuine if you stare at the ground the entire time.*

"You like stars, don't ya?"

I look up to find Maddison staring at the delicate chain with a tiny silver star resting on my chest. My eyebrows crinkle. Weird conclusion to make from that alone, but she's not wrong.

"Your magnets, the fairy lights…"

"Your tattoo," Oscar adds.

How on earth does he know about—? Of course, my first day. Guess he got a good peek at the tiny minimalist galaxy on my ribcage – among other things, I'm sure.

"You mentioned it the other day," he lies, and I don't let myself react to Tom and Maddison's eyes darting between us.

"Oh yeah. I guess I do. Can't even remember the last time I saw real ones though." Concern sweeps over Maddison as if I'm alluding to a traumatic childhood spent locked in a basement. "Light pollution in the city," I clarify, desperate to move on.

The evening feels pretty similar to mine and Oscar's duties on my first night here, but there's a much more relaxed atmosphere tonight. I'm learning a certain chaos naturally ensues on embarkation day that evidently settles as the week goes on. With no need to herd people places, we can take the time to really get to know the passengers. It's nice, actually.

Insistent upon some girl time, Maddison demands Oscar swap with her tonight. They couldn't have more different approaches to their jobs if they tried. She's a lot chattier than Oscar, and certainly more tongue-in-cheek, but everyone we speak to loves her.

In a gap between schmoozing, she and I slip off to the bathroom, passing a small crowd crying with laughter as we go. Tom's at the centre of it, completely in his element. I wish he were boring. I wish his personality let him down so it would give me just one turn-off I could fixate on. But unfortunately for me, he's perfect. Though maybe this "full of life" quality I like about him so much is, in actual fact, just part and parcel of being an American. Maybe I fancy all Americans. Mmm, sweeping generalisations – those will help me quash this teeny-tiny crush.

"Tom's fun, ain't he?" Maddison pipes up between the cubicles in the staff bathroom.

"Yeah," I reply, careful not to sound too enthusiastic.

"Boy, am I glad to have a break from him tonight though. He makes me laugh so much my cheeks hurt."

"Same." He causes me physical pain. I'll remember that next time I'm drawn to his light like a mosquito to a trap. Though I bet that little shock, the ultimate burst of heat, would feel fucking amazing.

"Y'all seem to be gettin' on well."

Without seeing her, it's hard to know if she's digging for something. Though knowing her even just a little, I suspect she is.

"Yeah, no. We just click, I guess."

Maddison and I reunite at the sink, and she studies me in the mirror while we wash our hands.

"Fucked yet?"

"What? No! Why? Is that what people are saying?"

Real subtle, Lize.

"So you haven't fucked?"

"No!"

"'Cos just then you acted like ya had."

"I haven't. Has someone said that?"

"No, but would ya?"

"Never."

"Okay, well, now I *know* you're lyin'. And don't even try to tell me you're not." She points a finger at me sternly, instantly shutting me up.

"Would *you*?" I throw the question back, hoping she'll feel just as cornered.

"Absolutely."

Well, that backfired.

"Have you *seen* him?" she says, walking over to the automatic dryer. I'm hit with an image of them together and I don't like it.

"Are you going to?" I ask.

"Eh, I like my men a little taller."

I don't let my relief show. Tom isn't short by any means, but Maddison's tall, putting her at the same height as him – or taller with heels on.

"Don't sweat – he's all yours." She winks at me. "You know he's never had a girlfriend?"

"What, *ever*?"

She nods with wide eyes as if saying "I know, right?". "You could be his first."

"I don't like him like that," I shout over the whoosh of the dryer.

She just teases me by mouthing, "I can't hear you," back.

I give up and use the dryer next to her. Once it times out, her voice returns to normal.

"You don't have to be coy about things like that on here. Everybody does it."

I'm not a prude by any stretch, nor am I a stranger to casual sex, but sleeping with a coworker is an absolute no-no. I can't risk it becoming anything more than physical, and in a place like this, it would be impossible to get the space I'd need to keep myself emotionally distant.

I grumble at her before shifting the conversation in another direction. "Tell me about your conquests. I want to live vicariously through you."

Without hesitation she recounts her most recent sordid

tale in a hushed whisper as we return to the room and mooch over to the bar, getting ourselves another drink. Prosecco in hand, Maddison observes the room with her back to the bar while I wait for my lemonade.

"Interestin'," she muses like a detective on the brink of a discovery. When I look at her, it's hard to miss the mischievous grin on her face.

"What?"

"Nothin'. Well, it ain't *nothin'*, but you told me to keep a certain somethin' to myself."

I scan the room to find whatever she's referring to.

"It's not there anymore."

"What was it?"

She shakes her head.

"Oh, go on. Please?"

"Fine. Someone was…admirin' the back of your dress, that's all." Maddison takes a smug sip of her drink.

"This dress was a mistake."

"No, don't be like that. Enjoy it while you're the hot new piece."

"I don't want to be the hot new *anything*."

We resume a slow meander around the room. A moving target is surely less enticing. Though now I think about it, having my back to the bar was the safest spot. *Shit.* Too late now.

"You're seriously tellin' me that if someone single, smokin' hot, and definitely into you made a move, you'd turn 'em down?"

"Yup," I stubbornly decree with no trace of a lie. I've been tried and tested now. I know I would.

"Turn down who?" Tom's voice approaching from behind makes my stomach drop.

"Nobody," I squeak.

"Everybody," Maddison corrects without missing a beat.

I can't bring myself to look at Tom, so I focus instead on acting as normal as I can.

"Oh no," Oscar sighs, his eyes fixed on the other side of the room.

Maddison whips her head and immediately tenses up like a bank teller in a robbery. Without shifting her focus, she paws for Tom's arm, grips the fabric of his sleeve, and yanks him away. The only thing that stands out is an old guy who seems to have sought fashion advice from Toad of Toad Hall.

"What's going on?"

"No time to explain." Oscar bolts to the doors that lead outside, and I instinctively follow. With haste, he strides along the partially lit deck, heading towards the back – *stern* – of the ship and up some steps.

"Where are we going?"

"There's something I want to show you."

"Can't it wait?"

"No. That guy was about thirty seconds away from faking a dizzy spell."

"Right…"

We walk along another deck for a few paces and head up another set of steps.

"Shouldn't we help?"

"Trust me, you don't want to be there when it happens. Every cruise, often more than once, he puts on this whole charade around female members of staff so they'll pander to him."

"Oh. Ew."

The public-friendly steps gradually get narrower and steeper the higher up the ship we get. These heels were not designed for this. Neither was this tight dress, which is rapidly rising up my thigh.

"You see, to some men, any attention is a win for them. They don't care how they get it." Our ascent continues. "And it's particularly prevalent in men who spend a lot of time at sea. Guests and crew alike."

"Well, now I feel rather naïve following you to God knows where in the black of night, all because you want to *show me something*."

He chuckles. "Don't worry, it's not me I've brought you up here to pay attention to."

We arrive at what I'm hoping is the last level and he extends his hand to help me down two little steps to a small sunken area of decking, so out of the way and basic I don't imagine anyone bothers to come here. To my right, there's a large, bench-height metal storage container, and to my left, curved railings provide a good place to lean and look out over the stern of the ship to the now closed pool. In the daytime, it's a loud and hectic waterpark, but at night, it's a peaceful blur of colours.

"Didn't have you down as a skiver, Harvey."

He's as unsettled at my use of his surname as I am. My mouth physically rejects it.

"Blagh, no. Can't do it."

He grins. "We're not skiving. We have some business to attend to."

Judging by the only times in my life I've heard that, I'm either about to be told off, ravaged, or spanked. And despite my appalling self-esteem, temporary vow of chastity, and low pain threshold, I'd let him do all three to me.

Pull yourself together, woman. One guy at a time. Please.

"Look up."

I oblige sceptically, my face softening in an instant upon seeing the starlit sky. He's managed to devise the kindest gesture out of a passing comment. There's a faint tinge of the sunset still resting on the horizon long after the sun's disappearance, and all I can hear is the water lapping against the side of the boat and faint echoes of people talking by the pool far below us. It's a thing of meditation videos.

"Thank you," I say, unsure of how long my trance lasted.

That's when I see he's not been as transfixed as me. Or perhaps he was, but not on the same thing. His gorgeous blue eyes are exploring my face. Again. I can't let him make a habit of stealing glances whenever I'm distracted, but am I going to do anything to stop him? Absolutely not. Purple and blue lights dance delicately across his face, his eyes shining even brighter than usual.

"This here is the best spot on the ship."

"Mmm, bit of a hidden gem. Though surely if it were the best, everyone would be out here."

"Well, that's a matter of opinion."

"So in your opinion, why is it?"

"This is the one place you can actually get some time to yourself that isn't stuck in your cabin."

"Sounds like a good place to think."

"Exactly."

I'm dying to know what he thinks about. He's so quiet and reserved all the time. It'd be easy to assume that's just who he is, but there's something I can't quite put my finger on that makes me suspect there's a side to him he doesn't let people see.

"But this secret spot is only for thinking."

"And stargazing?"

"Yes, that too. Tell anyone else on the crew about it and it'll become just another hookup spot."

"My lips are sealed," I promise. "So this is your hookup spot?"

"God no."

"Thank goodness for that. I'm not sure how much further I can run in these heels."

"Yeah, sorry about that." A smirk appears his cheek.

"When do you think – and this is in no way all I'm here for – but…when might I get the chance to get off the ship?"

"Wow, just four days in and already asking to leave. I see how it is."

"No, no! I didn't mean––"

His hard expression breaks, and I remind myself to loosen up a little. "We should be able to sometime next week. This week's just so full-on with your training. Don't worry, I'll get you off as soon as I can."

"What an offer."

"Not like…" He exhales in defeat at his poor choice of words before allowing himself to laugh with me.

Stop flirting, Eliza.

"There's something you can sign up for, actually, to assist on excursions. You'll get to do things like quad-bike trails, kayaking, horseback riding – that kind of thing. All for free, I should add. It's really good fun."

"Is this one of the ships that go to that beach with the swimming pigs?" My veins vibrate with possibility.

"It is, but––"

"So I might get to swim with pigs?"

"Ah, now that is a particularly coveted spot. It's very rare someone not on the excursion team goes, so I wouldn't get your––"

"Rarely. So not never?"

"There are a lot of really fun days out to be had, just *maybe* not with swimming pigs."

"Can't believe I'm going to swim with pigs."

He shakes his head at me and smiles.

The smell of talcum powder and an intense soapy perfume assaults my nostrils upon our return to the party. Toady's slumped over in a chair being tended to by two female servers, one monitoring his pulse and the other loudly asking him to drink some water. Oscar flashes me an "I told you so" grimace and rushes to rescue the latest victims without a second thought. It's incredible how quickly the man recovers once the *objects* of his affection disappear.

When the night wraps up, Oscar and I decide to grab a quick drink at the crew bar. Tom and Maddison disappeared a while ago, so I'm hoping we won't run into them, but of course we do. You can't avoid anyone on here for very long.

Maddison takes Oscar off to get drinks, leaving me and Tom to stand like lemons by a high-top table, half avoiding eye contact, half unable to look away. The music's so loud I doubt we'd hear each other even if we did want to talk. And I validate my silence with that for a bit – but deep down I know I owe him an apology, so I summon the courage to speak first.

"I'm sorry," we both say over one another, which makes us laugh awkwardly.

He comes closer, his lips up against my ear. "I misread the signs."

I try to correct him and tell him I gave him those signs whether I intended to or not, but he keeps talking.

"Can we go back to being friends?"

I relinquish my attempt to explain. He doesn't seem to want to talk about it more than he has to. "Yes, please. It's been so boring without you."

"Tell me about it."

The frost around us warms and my body loosens up again.

"You look great, by the way. If I can say that? That colour really suits you."

"Thank you." I blush.

We stare at each other for just too long. Whatever tension there was between us hasn't gone. Far from it. It's just retreated from screaming in our faces to sitting on our shoes like a toddler throwing a tantrum. And if my experience from binge-watching "Supernanny" is anything to go by, I know that no toddler quits until they get what they want.

"So I had an idea today, for the show."

"Oh yeah?"

"Oscar dropped off the Danny and Sandy wigs earlier," I say into his ear, "in case we wanted them for the Night at the Movies thing tomorrow." The wigs are these horrifically shiny, synthetic, drowned rat–looking things that have probably been worn and sweated in by a hundred people. Apparently, silly wigs and over-the-top costumes are highly encouraged for guests, and even more so for the entertainment crew.

"Awesome."

"I've decided to go with the yellow skirt."

"Cool." He nods, but he's clearly not fussed either way.

"But I'm not going to wear it."

His forehead crumples dubiously.

"You are," I reveal. His face is always alive with expression, but for the first time, I can't read it. "Are you a fan of 'Ru Paul's Drag Race'?"

He lights up, and I do too, with a smile so sneaky you'd only see it on someone plotting the ultimate Parent Trap-style ruse.

SIX

"'Spank me harder, Daddy.' Is that your final answer?" I ask the girl dressed as a Ghostbuster onstage with me. She can't be much older than me, and she has definitely been making the most of her all-inclusive drinks package.

"Sure is," she confirms, leaning into the small microphone on the glittery game-show podium.

"All right, let's take a look at the screen. Oscar, is the catchphrase 'Spank me harder, Daddy'? No, funnily enough, the answer we were looking for was, in fact, 'Give yourself a pat on the back', but I like where your mind took you, Becky."

I appear to have successfully disassociated my way through the day. I vaguely remember breakfast, then sometime later a belly flop contest, but every time I relaxed, another bloody entertainment team member asked if I was ready for tonight, forcing me to visualise being called onto the stage with Tom, which in turn caused my chest to pound with panic and my memory to fog over again. When did I get into costume? And what possessed me to put this God-awful itchy wig on when my hair is already the perfect colour and length for Sandy?

Oscar's a sight for sore eyes, dressed up as Marty McFly from "Back to the Future". He opted to go without a wig, instead pushing some styling wax through his blonde hair so it sits in his usual relaxed quiff. He looks like a sexed-up version of the original, as if he's just stepped onto the set of some porn parody. *Bareback to the Future?* Now that I would pay to see.

Stop being a pervert.

Typically, the pair dressed as Danny and Sandy would be working on something together, but Tom is in an entirely different part of the ship looking just as mismatched from his mentor as I do. He's in a T-Birds jacket, and Maddison's dressed as a gender-blind Doc Brown.

We're particularly disappointing duos for the guests this evening, firstly because we're only worth half a blot each on the Character Bingo sheets that were made for them as part of "Movie Night Madness", and secondly because I don't exactly recall a film where Marty McFly and Sandy ride off into the sky in a car their partner spent too much time working on.

Actually, I think we've nailed it.

People have been popping in and out of the theatre all night, either shouting "Bingo!" or sighing loudly and leaving. At least I hope that's why they keep leaving.

"Give it up for Becky from Boston, everyone!" I announce, prompting the hundred-and-something–strong crowd to clap and cheer as she makes her way back to her seat. "No one give her a pat on the back for her efforts though – she'll be severely disappointed."

I hand the mic over to Oscar to wrap up the game, though he has to take a second to compose himself after the mayhem that's just ensued. He's been in a fit of laughter for the whole of the last round, eventually needing to wipe actual tears away from his eyes.

I check my watch in between every guest I make small talk with on their way out, but time seems to be moving at half-speed. Tom and Maddison should be here any minute now. Maddison's meant to be swapping out with me to take over packing up so Tom and I can go and get ready. With Tom's secret drag transformation, we're going to need all the time we can get.

I look up and see Oscar staring expectantly at me. "Hmm?"

"I said they loved you out there. You're a natural," he repeats.

"What can I say? I watched a lot of 'Catchphrase' as a kid."

"I haven't laughed like that in a long time."

"Every ship needs a Becky."

"No, you. You're hilarious."

Oh. I only batted off what others were giving me; it's not like I have any good material up my sleeve.

"Keep it up."

I take the compliment and let the warm glow of praise rush over me.

The queue of guests dies down, so Oscar and I head back to the stage to start packing away. There isn't too much left to do as the AV team and stage crew take care of all the technical bits. There are just a few props and leftover prizes to ferry backstage.

"Are you cold?" Oscar asks.

"No, boiling."

He stares at me with concern, and it's only then I notice my teeth are chattering.

"Just adrenaline, I think."

"You nervous about tonight?"

Petrified, but I mustn't show weakness. "Nah, I'm all right." I chew my bottom lip, eating my lie, and walk away from him.

"Chapman?" he calls out, and when I don't stop, all it takes is a few strides for him to be in front of me, preventing me from going back through the curtain to get more things. "Deep breath," he orders.

We breathe in and out together, but my body stays tense. He holds my arms to keep me steady.

"Ignore everyone else – just have fun up there. Whatever you guys do will be great."

I nod and force an unconvincing smile. I can't look at him. My eyes sting all of a sudden.

Get a grip, woman.

"Hey, come here." He wraps his arms around me, but I barely manage to stretch around his bulky Marty McFly puffer jacket. We share a small giggle, and he pulls the jacket out wide. "Come on – get in."

I slip my hands inside and along the denim jacket he has on underneath, then I rest my head against his chest and focus on his heartbeat, controlling my breathing to match his. God, he smells *so* good. He holds me just tight enough, squeezing me tighter whenever a shiver passes through me. He rests his head on mine, and eventually I relax, all the tension in my muscles drifting away. I didn't realise how much I'd missed hugs. My family hugged me goodbye, but aside from that, I honestly can't remember the last time I had a proper hug.

I should care about someone seeing us, but I don't. Right now, this is all I want to think about. Just us behind the curtain in almost complete darkness – other than the thin strip of light coming in through the small gap where the tabs don't quite meet.

A sudden cascade of "Bingo!" alerts us to Tom and Maddison's arrival. The perfect domino effect, each one setting off the other. Oscar loosens his arms around me but doesn't let go completely. He looks into my eyes.

"Break a leg, Chapman. I'll see you down there."

Tom and I pelt down to my room, rushing to avoid being bombarded by people completing their Bingo sheets. Throwing open the door, we get to work. Tom dumps a bag of makeup on the desk.

"Crikey, where did you get all this?"

"Maddison."

"You didn't tell her, did you?"

"Course not. Top-secret."

We peel off our wigs in unison, sighing with relief as we tend to our itches. He shrugs off his leather jacket and lays it over the back of the chair. I copy him, doing the same with my cardigan. I take off my name badge and fling it onto the desk. He crosses his arms in front of him and begins to take off his T-shirt but stops dead before he even reveals so much as his belly button.

"Well? Don't look!" he whines.

We both laugh, and I spin around so we're standing back to back. He holds the T-shirt out to his side. I unbutton my blouse and hold it out too, and we take the shirts in our free hands like a conveyer belt. We've learnt our lesson about seeing one another barely clothed. But when the bare skin of his back touches mine for just a second, heat courses through me. I put his top on and take off my skirt, holding it out for him.

"Do you need my pants?" Tom asks.

"Ew, no. Why would I need your pants?"

"Oh. So you've got pants?"

"Yes, I've got pants."

He turns around and I flinch, making myself as small as possible while still standing up. He quickly spins away again.

The penny finally drops.

"*You* meant trousers. *I* meant… Ah, Jesus Christ, it's been a long day. Yes, I need your *trousers*."

He holds them out for me to take. They looked loose on Tom, but he's far slimmer than me. I'm curvy, blessed with an ample bottom and thick thighs, so they fit more like skinny jeans on me. With our costume swap done, and sensing no risk of mounting one another for the time being, we safely turn around to face each other again.

We work quickly to securely fasten the new wigs to our scalps and get most of Tom's makeup done. He studies the pack of fake eyelashes with terror. I kneel beside him, apply the glue to the lashes, and wait for them to get tacky.

"Close your eyes," I instruct before carefully applying them. "Keep them closed."

He sits there so peacefully, without a trace of nerves or toxic masculinity in him. Seeing a man so secure in himself is so damn hot.

Nope. We're over this.

"Okay, you should be good now."

"How do I look?"

"Like a drag queen," I say as if the words sparkle.

We missed the start of the night, but we're last on in the running order, so we sneak into the back of the crew bar and hope to attract as little attention as possible. If someone talks to us, the whole reveal is ruined. It doesn't help that Tom's several inches taller than me, but hopefully, people will assume there are heels involved and won't look down at the trainers on his feet. We *should* look like we're in the same costumes as before and not stand out as anything different from the other costumed people in the bar. Most people probably won't even know we're competing.

Tom's wrapped a large yellow silk handkerchief around his head and put on some big white sunglasses so he looks like Audrey Hepburn out on a drive in a convertible. I've put on sunglasses too and popped the collar of my T-Birds jacket to mask my face as best I can. With the jacket being however many men's sizes too big, it almost completely swamps me – something that comes in handy when covering up any evidence I have boobs. Meanwhile, Tom stuffed a bralette I lent him with as many socks as he could, ready to throw them at me as part of the routine. We're taking this way too seriously, but we're both so eager to impress the team that neither of us can rein it in.

Housekeeping don't miss the opportunity to strut their stuff to Cardi B's "WAP". Buckets and mops included, obviously. One of the chefs brings a portable hot plate on stage and does pancake art – something he clearly has a knack for but doesn't get the chance to showcase all too often. Then two of the bar staff showcase their mixology skills, which is… Let's just say it's a good thing we have buckets and mops on standby.

When the actors perform, we know we're in trouble. Everyone goes mental for them. As if they weren't at enough of an advantage, what with being professional dancers, they also have the most outspoken and confident cheerleaders in the room.

"Shit, you weren't kidding," Tom remarks.

I don't say anything; fear has rendered me speechless.

Tom reaches for the hand hanging loosely by my side. "We got this."

When we're called onto the stage and push our way through the crowd, everything slows down. My pulse drums in my ears, and my throat burns with what feels like acid. Mistaking me for Tom, Daniel gives me an encouraging whack on the shoulder, so firm it almost knocks me over. I step up and tread the boards of the small stage, my energy completely shifting the second I do. We take our positions facing the back of the stage, and I can't help but smile. We peer over at one another, suddenly ready to show everyone what we're made of. Adrenaline rushes through me and I love the way it feels.

It's showtime.

Ru Paul's famous voiceover starts our track: *"Two queens stand before me…"* Tom takes off his sunglasses and tosses them to the side of the stage in the two bass-filled beats I added. People are already screaming. They have no idea what they're in for. *"The time has come…for you to lip-synch…for your* life!*"* In another two beats, I pop my collar down and shift my weight into a new pose. *"Good luck, and* don't *fuck it up."*

The entertainment team don't hold back their excitement. I can barely hear the start of the music, but I've rehearsed this moment in my head more times than I care to count. I confidently spin around bang on cue to lip-synch the first line, the music turning up louder to compete with the noise. Behind the shining lights, it's hard to see much, but as I step forwards I catch a glimpse of Maddison, her mouth wide open. The anticipation of Tom's reveal builds more with every second.

It's a good thing the music's now as loud as it is because the screams that occur when Tom turns around are unbeliev-able. Their encouragement spurs us on to heighten everything. Nothing is too big, too over-the-top, or too outrageous. This is by far the best we've ever run through it, and I already know whatever the result, I'll be ecstatic just to have performed.

The more we push and shove each other out of the way, the more people laugh. I was so scared this idea would flop, but it's excelling. My body is electric. I'm not fearful or anxious anymore; I'm *alive*. The stage has always been where I've felt most at home – I've just never been able to call it that for very long. And now I'm here, I never want to leave.

Ru Paul's voiceover wraps up the act: *"Shantay you both stay."* And then we lip-synch the final line.

The room erupts. Everyone is whistling, whooping, and applauding us – the actors too. It's nice to see the rivalry is only surface-level. I can't help but laugh with relief that all our hard work paid off.

Tom and I celebrate together, panting and smiling, soaking up the praise before stepping down off the small plat-form hand in hand. The entertainment team swarm us in a huge huddle. Oscar throws his arms out and wraps us both up in a bear hug, Maddison bundling us from behind.

"Y'all smashed it!" she screams in my ear.

We break apart, and Maddison steals Tom away.

Oscar squeezes me so tightly my feet leave the ground. "Chapman! Who are you? That was incredible!" This is the most vocal he's been since I got here, and I can't believe I'm the cause of it. He returns me to the floor, and for a second I swear I'm immune to gravity. He holds me by my shoulders like he knows if he lets go there's a good chance I might float away. "*You're* incredible." He looks down at me with so much pride my heart goes into orbit.

When the crew activities manager steps onstage to announce the prizes, my stomach drops. Tom and I reunite, wrapping our arms around one another's waist. The rest of the team gather behind us, shaking us as each department gets placed.

"In third place, winning themselves a free drink at the bar…it's the horticulture team!"

Three topless lads bounce their way onto the stage uninvited like rowdy football hooligans. They're covered from head to toe in soil, and I can't help but think we missed one hell of a performance.

After allowing them to bask in their glory, the small but commanding crew activities manager takes back control of the room. "I don't think any of us will ever look at an orchid the same way, so thanks for that."

The quick rise and fall of laughter vibrates on my back from Oscar and Obi, who are pressed up behind me.

The room's anticipation has hit its peak. It's between us and the actors.

"This is usually the part where I say it was tough to decide, but I'mma be real with y'all: there was only one clear winner here tonight. I think I speak for everyone when I say I am *shook*. I want to live inside their heads because it must be fun as hell in there!"

"Yes! We've done it, lads!" Daniel whispers behind us, clutching our shoulders, but I don't let my hopes rise yet.

"In second place, winning a free drink and one hour of free Wi-Fi, it's…"

The room thunders as hands drum on tables and feet stamp all around us. I think I might be sick.

"The theatre team! Meaning in first place, winning free drinks, an hour of free Wi-Fi, a meal at Coral's, *and* this cute li'l trophy…it's the entertainment team!"

We did it!

I'm deafened by the outcry behind us, and to add to the

disorientation, Tom and I are rattled around like almost empty ketchup bottles. Stevie Wonder's "Signed, Sealed, Delivered" plays as we're shoved back onstage to collect our prizes. We pose modestly for photos with our tiny plastic trophy, and I take a second to enjoy this feeling before our evening descends into chaos, making a note for the future that none of my anxious premonitions came true and I really must stop giving them so much weight.

Tom takes my hand and insists we do a little curtsy together before we hop down off the stage and rejoin our crew.

I feel like a celebrity. Being so new here, I'm unbelievably grateful the others got us to do this. It's suddenly as if everyone knows who we are, and if they don't, they want to. Oscar introduces me to some of the actors who – I'm embarrassed to admit – I was kind of terrified of before now. But our win has definitely helped level the playing field a bit in my head. We slowly drift apart, pulled by the currents of different conversations into smaller groups. Every now and then I catch him looking over at me, more like he's keeping an eye on me in case I get swept away than because he's checking me out. I should be so lucky.

Tom's a changed man. He's willingly on the dance floor, boogying away with some of the others. I took my wig off hours ago, but he's kept his on. He really does look incredible in drag.

It's a while longer until I finally get the chance to regroup with Oscar. At the bar, I melt into his side, and he holds me without hesitation, continuing his conversation with an American guy dressed like Maverick from "Top Gun". I sip the last few drops of my drink through a paper straw, enjoying the way his voice rumbles against me. His friend jumps into action when a bartender becomes free, leaning over and placing his order. He turns back to me.

"What you drinking, champ?"

I shake my head. "Just water, please."

It takes some convincing, but he finally orders just that.

"Alcohol is stronger at sea," I say to Oscar, leaning across him to plonk my empty plastic cup up on the bar. "Fact."

He chuckles at my declaration. "I don't think that's right."

"Is." I look up at him while leaning on his chest, his arms loosely draped around my lower back.

"How you feeling?"

"Fuzzy," I admit, much to his amusement. "I've only had two." It feels important to state considering there's a strict alcohol limit for crew members. It's more about your tolerance than the actual units consumed, but my tolerance is abysmal.

"Two?" His eyes widen. "You eaten much today?"

I think back, but my brain has wiped the day from existence – or never let it exist in there in the first place. Did I have lunch and forget, or did I just not have lunch?

Because I'm taking too long to answer, he shouts to his friend to get some chips and leads me over to a high-top table to get us out of the way of the queue forming behind us. I make myself at home on a stool, my legs merrily dangling from it. Oscar pulls another stool up in front of me, his legs resting firmly on the ground, and in an instant, the Friday night ruckus around us disappears. His legs close in around mine, not quite touching them, but my body is on high alert, hopeful for the chance they might.

"Did we do you proud?" I lean forwards to ask, making a significant effort to be heard over the music. My addiction to the now familiar smell of his aftershave becomes even greater with every second that passes.

His hand ever so gently touches my knee as he responds. "You certainly did. Given me a run for my money, that's for sure."

Our cheeks hover close together. Hearing his voice so near, his breath on my ear and neck, makes goose bumps dance across my skin.

"I'd love to see you perform one day." I pull back just a little, wanting to see his eyes so he can see the hope in mine.

"One day," he promises.

I'll hold him to that.

We sit quietly in a dangerous game of chicken, neither of us willing to be the first to look away. His fingertips don't leave my knee, and I think I might die if they do.

"I've had fun this week." My stomach flutters as I test the water. *Don't do it.*

"Good."

I lose the game and my eyes drop down his body for a split second, returning almost instantly. I know it won't go unnoticed, but I don't care. I want him to see it. I've been checking him out all week whenever his back has been turned; it's only fair he sees me this once.

"With you, I mean." My eyes plant firmly on his. *Stop, Eliza. You're tipsy and he's your mentor.*

"Really?" He dodges my attempt to flirt, but it's disbelief on his face, not avoidance. "Don't feel like you're stuck with me?"

Why on earth would I think that? I shake my head. "No," I say resolutely.

With a small nod of his head, he straightens again, the cracks in his self-esteem filling back in. "Good. I've had fun this week too." He makes no secret of flashing his eyes down my body and back up again. "With you, I mean." His left cheek rises where he firmly holds in his smile.

Holy shit.

Our bubble pops with all the hollers from the dance floor. We both turn to see some kind of dance battle going on – or at least that's what I'm watching. Oscar's lost in thought, his attention solely on Tom.

"We were just rehearsing the other morning."

Oscar looks back at me, his expression soft.

"Just in case you thought…"

He smiles kindly as our drinks are slammed down on our table, followed by the rustle of a packet of crisps that land by me. I look at them with a confused frown, casting my eyes to Oscar and waiting for him to react, but he doesn't.

Jesus Christ, it's happened again. Twice in one night. *Seriously?* You'd think I would have cottoned on to all the strange Americanisms by now.

Disappointed but still grateful, I thank his friend and take a big gulp of water. The warmth from Oscar's fingers on my knee disappears, and I take a deep breath, scared it might be my last. He opens the bag for me, tearing along the seam down the side and leaving it on the table, all the while smirking at my mix-up.

"You'll get used to it." He returns his hands to his lap, the backs of his long fingers just lightly brushing my knee.

My lungs relax again. I take a "chip", my pout quickly vanishing when the salt and vinegar hits my tongue.

One crisp remains in the packet. Oscar and I are in an unspoken battle of manners only Brits can turn into flirtation.

The entertainment team eventually seek us out, handing

over shots that are precariously balanced between their fingers. As good as the midnight snack was, it hasn't sobered me up. Those drinks I was given had to have been doubles – a round of shots could topple me. But then Oscar winks at me and I know I'm safe.

Daniel leads everyone in a toast to me and Tom. I raise my glass to go with the crowd but don't participate. While they're all busy downing their drinks, Oscar throws his back, swaps his empty shot glass for mine, and takes a second. He shuts his eyes hard and breathes out sharply as it burns his throat.

"I knew there was a reason I stopped doing shots. Who picked these?" Oscar looks around for the culprit.

I tip my head down to the lonely crisp, both of us knowing it's exactly what he needs to get the taste out of his mouth. He rolls his eyes and reluctantly takes it, causing a smug smile to break out on my lips.

For no reason other than wanting to touch him, I hook my fingers through his and raise his hand, pretending to check his watch.

"Oh shit, is that the time?" Maddison says over my shoulder.

I didn't even read the ticking hands, and quite honestly, I wasn't going to. It's a quarter to two in the morning. *Good grief.*

"They're gonna kick us out soon. Where we goin' next?" *Next?*

"What about Eliza's?" Tom pipes up. "She's got no roommate – there's tons of space compared to mine or yours."

"Great idea!"

No, Maddison, terrible idea. I don't want a bunch of drunk people I barely know in my bedroom. Unfortunately, she and Tom scurry away to spread the news before I have a chance to protest it.

The trepidation must be apparent on my face because Oscar leans in closer, his hand firm on my thigh. "Don't worry, I'll keep everyone in check."

I shiver as his warm voice rings in my ears once again.

"I'll be back in a sec." He gets up and walks away, my legs noticing his absence.

Fine. Okay. It's happening. Party back at mine. Why am I stressing? I used to like parties. Flashbacks to my twentieth hit me like a double-decker bus. Me, abandoned in a theatre. Her, ditching me for another party. The humiliation of having all my flaws pointed out in front of the only people I had left. Losing my best friends, my home, and my social scene all in one go. And after I'd already lost everything else too. No party can ever be worse than that one, so I'm safe, right?

I feel better knowing Oscar will be there. He's visited my room plenty of times this week but is yet to cross the threshold. Excitement flurries through me at the idea of him in my space, snooping like I did in his. Seeing pictures and little glimpses into my life, searching for answers to the questions he might have wondered about but never asked.

Oh God, he's going to think I'm a right slob if he sees the state Tom and I left it in.

I get up and make for the bar to tell him I'll see him there, but he collects two pint-sized glasses of water from the bartender and insists upon helping.

We track down Tom and Maddison on the way out, asking them to stall so I'll have time to quickly pack up our things and hide anything vaguely personal, embarrassing, or valuable. While I make a start on bundling rogue clothes, makeup, and personal effects into the unused cupboards, Oscar sets the mood, turning off the main lights so we're left with just the glow of the fairy lights. The room's instantly more inviting, if a little intimate.

I can tell he wants to be helpful but is too polite to rifle through my things and bung them any old place. Not that there's any logic to what I'm doing – I'm just grabbing and shoving at this point.

"No dog pics to coo over, I'm afraid." I make light conversation, pretending to ignore the fact we're alone in my almost dark bedroom together.

"Dog pics? Oh, right. Had a browse then?"

"Just a bit." I swear I see the memory of me undressing in his room derail his train of thought. "Cute surfing picture."

"Liked that one, did you?"

I ignore his teasing. "Do you go a lot?"

"I did growing up. It was more my sister's hobby than mine. I only went to spot her and keep her company. Mostly I was just made to take photos for her followers." He sighs, pretending it bothered him, but his gentle smile says he'd do anything for her.

Is there even a bad bone in his body?

"It's hard being so generous with your time, isn't it?"

"Absolute torture."

I can't stop smiling, glad I'm finally getting to see a more playful side to him. I shove the last of the mess away and take a breath, scanning the room to be sure I didn't miss anything.

"Now, I should warn you…" His tone becomes more serious as he takes a step towards me. The backs of my thighs brush the desk as I steady myself. "Some of these parties can get a little…wild."

"Ahh, so the rumours are true." Yes, I've heard about cruise orgies. No, I don't plan to participate.

He laughs with me. "I'm just saying if it gets too much, we can call it, okay?"

"Okay." The comfort of his offer is fleeting. I never thought I'd feel more pressure from potentially cancelling an orgy than potentially hosting one.

"How about we make a secret code and as soon as you've had enough, tell me with that, and I'll shut it down so you don't have to?"

"Yeah, okay. What's the secret code?"

"I don't know. Maybe tap my foot with yours or something."

"So you're a foot guy?"

He rolls his eyes and tries not to smile. "No."

"But what if you're all the way on the other side of the room?"

We take a quick look around and laugh as we remind ourselves just how small my cabin is.

"Then I'll just have to stay close by."

My heart thumps so hard I'm certain he can hear it. I want to know what his hands feel like on my skin, what his lips taste like, what sounds he makes when he's being satisfied. I lean back against the desk and crane my neck up more to see him. His focus drops to my lips and back up to my eyes, but he doesn't move. Wanting but waiting. The quiet Oscar I thought I was getting to know is suddenly powerful and dominant, and he hasn't even lifted a finger. He just watches me. Is he waiting for me to make a move, or is he not sure if he wants to make one?

I know I shouldn't. I know this will come back to bite me. I gave myself rules to follow. But I don't want to follow them. Cautiously, I place my hand on his shirt. He doesn't flinch away or tell me to stop, so I squeeze my hand into a fist and pull him closer. Our faces are now just inches apart. He still doesn't make a move, but his eyes darken exponentially.

Burn the rule book.

There's a loud knock on the door, and our breaths hitch.

Fuck off. Nobody's home.

His eyes close tight, breaking the spell we've been under. Maybe if we stay still they'll go away. But Oscar slowly rises to his full height, the disappointment evident on his face as he looks down at me.

"You ready?"

I nod, still unable to get any words out.

Stepping back, Oscar pulls his body away from mine, his hand gently nudging me to get the door when my legs don't move. I feel weak, like a newborn giraffe, dropped from a great height and forced up onto my toothpick legs, when all I want is a bit more attention from the beautiful giant standing over me.

Am I still tipsy or just drunk on lust?

There's another knock, more urgent this time. I open the door to see Tom – breathing like he just ran a marathon – and Maddison standing there with a whole squad of people behind them, most of whom I recognise now but don't really know. Surely we won't all fit in this room? Nevertheless, bodies pile in carrying their leftover drinks, and I spiral into a panic, scared about the mess this'll make and wishing I could go back ten seconds to pause time forever.

A hand on my wrist brings me back to reality.

"Come sit." Oscar guides me over to the lower bunk, placing the plastic glass of water he got me into my hands. He sits down by the ladder but rests forwards, too tall to sit under the top bunk. I sit to his left.

Tom and Maddison join us, sandwiching me between the boys. I pretend I'm not flustered from what just happened – or almost happened – but I think Tom might be onto me. He's asked me if I'm okay twice already and is all but glaring at Oscar with more than a hint of suspicion.

There are too many people to count. Just a mass of limbs moving about, finding a place to hover, however uncomfortably. Someone's brought a Bluetooth speaker, music already playing from it, and is that…a box of *condoms*? I look at Oscar and lead his eyes back to the box. He sighs as if at a loss for words.

"Call it naïve optimism."

My eyes almost bulge out of my head. I should be salvaging the remains of my rule book from the fire I just threw it into, but I know full well there's nothing in there that could prepare me for this.

I'm on my own now.

SEVEN

HR would have a field day if they knew what went on in these cabins after dark. Everyone's tipsy, hyped up from the competition, and horny. Really, *really* horny. From the tension alone I'm certain there's some kind of sex bomb in this room, and it's only a matter of time before it detonates. Though there's more than a slim chance I could be projecting.

Obi and Maddison seem to be masterminding something while everyone else makes themselves a little *too* comfortable. Luckily, Oscar's here to stop anyone from climbing up onto my bunk. I might be instilled with a newfound confidence from our win, but that doesn't mean I'm brave enough to tell people they can't hook up in my bed.

"Buddy up!" Obi commands as he grabs the arm of some guy he's clearly had his eye on.

Oscar places a protective hand on my knee instantly, and Tom touches the small of my back not a second later, but neither of them look at me. Instead their gazes are fixed harshly on one another, locked in a silent exchange. I consider saying something, making a choice about who I want to be with for whatever is about to happen, but I can't bring myself to speak.

Someone calls Tom's name, forcing the three of us to look at her. My eyes trail all the way up her long legs and athletic body to the hopeful expression on her blemish-free face. It doesn't escape my attention I couldn't look less glamorous than her right now if I tried. She's drop-dead gorgeous and dressed as Harley Quinn. Of course she is. The ultimate pick-me–girl costume. I've never seen her before, and I wish I could have kept it that way.

The hand on my back disappears, and straight away I wish "drop-dead" meant exactly that. But I knew he'd go. Boys always run as soon as something shinier comes along.

No, that's not fair. While I'm spending all this time judging her, Tom's waiting for me to make a decision, and I've said nothing.

Valentina's paired up with a soil-covered gardener, and Maddison's with one of the sports staff jocks. Daniel's sitting alone on the desk swinging his legs but looking pretty happy about it.

"Face your partner," Maddison instructs.

Oscar and I get up and negotiate a space within the other bodies. It's impossible to avoid brushing shoulders with the people around us. How the hell has everyone fit in here? This must be some kind of record. Oscar stands just in front of the bunk bed, and I stand opposite him so my back is facing the room.

"Y'all know how to play Mr and Mrs by now, don't you?" she asks.

Okay, party games. I can handle this.

"But we ain't holdin' shoes above our heads, are we?"

There's a chorus of "Hell no!" and "No, ma'am!" in response.

"Nope. We're gettin' naked, baby!"

Come again?

Sex party games. Right, I guess this is really happening. I don't have to stay. I can just leave. Or wait outside, I guess. And for a second I think I will, but then I look up and see Oscar with his honey-coloured hair, chiselled jawline, and ocean-blue eyes focused solely on me, and I feel like a book he stumbled across in a shop. I've somehow enticed him with my cover; he's skimmed over the blurb and made me his, and now all I can hope is that I'll live up to his expectations. He promised to look after me, and I want to give him the opportunity to prove he will. So I'm staying. I want to stay. For now. When they start waving their willies around, I'll reassess.

"I'm gonna ask a question, and whoever it's the most accurate for gets an item of clothin' removed by their partner."

A mix of apprehension and arousal rushes through me. Oscar's jaw pulses with the clenching of his teeth.

"So if I asked 'who's the tallest?', the shortest person would…" Maddison pauses, waiting for us to take action.

I stand on my tiptoes and take hold of the top of Oscar's red puffer jacket. My hands feel their way down his bulky arms as I slip it off. He watches me with a certain steadiness, the bubble quickly surrounding us again. I swallow hard as it dawns on me I might be about to see *all* of him. Though I think there's a higher chance of me having a heart attack than seeing this game through to the end. Either way, it's safe to say this game will be my undoing.

"We don't have to play," Oscar says, piercing me with his eyes.

"Do you want to?" *Please don't be having second thoughts.*

He hesitates but then nods ever so slightly. "We can always st—"

"I know my limit." I cut him off with feigned self-assurance. I have zero bloody clue what my limit is, but he doesn't need to know that. I've entered uncharted territory, and I'll be damned if I jump ship now.

"Obi, you're up." Maddison relinquishes control of the game.

"Who's the funniest?" he asks.

Oscar gets to his knees and takes one of my shoes off.

"See? Foot guy."

He cracks a smile. "See? Funny."

"Both shoes and socks count as one layer, people. Come on now – we're not in high school anymore," Obi clarifies.

I help Oscar by shifting my balance until the coarse carpet scratches my feet.

"Who's the best performer?" a new voice asks.

Despite my protest, Oscar takes my leather jacket off. Even though I've never seen him perform properly, he's professionally trained and he's done huge UK tours – obviously, he's better than me.

"Who's been here the longest?"

I take off his footwear.

"Who's better at their job?"

I take off his denim jacket.

"Who's the kinkiest?"

I eye him up and down and then beckon him to strip me.

"What makes you so sure?" His tone is curious but laced with seduction.

"Dunno. There's just something about you that screams *vanilla*." I emphasise the word with my hands as if I'm announcing the title of Hollywood's next big movie franchise.

"One minute I have a foot fetish, the next I don't—"

"So you *do* have a foot fetish?"

He quickly resigns and reaches for the front of my jeans. "What's your kink then?"

The buzz of my zip going down slowly makes my core tingle. Blindsided by my alcohol-infused courage, I whisper my reply into his ear when he moves closer, his thumbs skimming the skin of my hips as they hook themselves inside the waistband of my trousers. He bites his bottom lip just a little, closes his eyes, and takes a deep breath, composing himself before wrestling to get the tight, restrictive fabric over my bum. Every nerve ending comes to life in his wake.

My black thong exposes more of me than either of us were prepared for, and when he towers above me again, I revel in watching him fail miserably at looking unflustered.

"Who's the sexiest?"

I paw at the buttons on Oscar's shirt while he attempts to take off my T-shirt.

"Nuh-uh. Veto." I shake my head.

Hold on, he thinks I'm sexy? Sexier than him*? He's having a laugh.*

"No, you can't just—"

"Veto," I say firmer, reaching up to push the fabric over his massive shoulders. Making no effort to hide my interest, I study his impeccably sculpted body and every tiny freckle as if I'm mapping out my very own constellation. I don't even bother to fake embarrassment at being caught in a daze when the next question is asked.

"Who's the most generous in bed?"

Oscar and I are at a stalemate. I know exactly what I bring to the table, but as for him, who can say? I'm not budging yet. He raises an eyebrow and shakes his head slowly. A sudden vision of his face buried between my legs makes me weak.

"Veto." His voice is so devious it's almost a growl.

Lord have mercy.

I unbutton his trousers, and as I move them down his muscular legs, I make a point of resting on my knees to help him out of them. The intense eye contact he's maintained up until this point only breaks to save himself any embarrassment. With his attention momentarily off me, I sneak a peek at his boxers and my breath catches in my throat. *Holy shit. Is he smuggling a salami down there?* He places his hand out for me to use as I return to my feet, my legs requiring the extra support to hold me up as lightheadedness almost gets the better of me.

"Who's given the most hand jobs?"

Oscar waits for me to insist with a nod before he lifts off my T-shirt. He takes his turn to study me, and I will myself not to crumble. Why did he wait before taking my top off? It should be obvious by now I'm not a twenty-one-year-old virgin. Unless… Is he maybe a little bit bi? Or perhaps he had an experimental phase at drama school. And there I was thinking he couldn't get any hotter.

"Who is the horniest right now?"

We're both in our underwear. If it's him, he's naked, but the alternative leaves me topless.

"Come on then." I encourage him to strip me, but he doesn't move. He's hesitant, clearly wrestling with something in his head. He looks behind me then leans in close, his fingers toying with the clasp of my bra. My body stays strong and composed, but internally I'm screaming.

Take it off. Please, God, take it off.

His soft skin presses up against mine as he puts his lips to my ear. "I'm afraid I've hit my limit, Chapman."

His whisper makes me tremble. For the first time since we started playing, I look back and reacquaint myself with all the people around us I successfully tuned out. I know this isn't rejection; it's chivalry. I'm sure I'll thank him for this in the morning. But right now, *thanking* him is the last thing on my mind.

"Never have I ever…had sex on a cruise ship!" Daniel declares with gusto from somewhere within the throng of barely dressed bodies scattered about the place. There are slightly less of us now as "the horn" got the better of a few pairs after the last game, which has given us all some well-needed breathing room

Tom, Oscar, Maddison, and I stand in the four corners of the room waiting with our best poker faces while the remaining party-goers rowdily place their bets on who they think the statement is true for. Most guess Oscar and Maddison. Two dancers stand near Tom, and just one person stands by me.

What with us being the two newest arrivals, the others are using this opportunity to find out everything they can about me and Tom. After an encouraging elbow from Valentina, Maddison stepped up to the firing line as well, supposedly to support her buddy, Tom – but they looked far too happy when that meant Oscar had to play for me.

Oscar and Maddison step forwards. The people near them cheer and retreat a few paces back into the middle, while those who backed Tom and me groan and sit out. Our aim is to reveal a bunch of raunchy details about ourselves, but everyone else's aim is to be the last person standing. It's a bit like "Million Pound Drop". Though "Million Pound *Slut* Drop" feels more appropriate. It has to be said, when alcohol consumption is limited, people sure know how to get creative with party games.

Tom asked me for makeup wipes earlier, and I'd say I'm disappointed he's no longer in drag, but I won't turn my nose up at an opportunity to see him in just his boxers again. I keep catching him checking me out. Heat radiates through me every time I do. He's gotten more brazen about it, flashing that cheeky grin of his whenever I notice him. I decide not to hold back either. I thought I saw a tattoo on his bicep the other day, but I didn't get a chance to look properly. Upon closer inspection I think it's a superhero logo, or a few merged together, with vibrant colours splattered over it like flecks of paint. Perhaps it's a Marvel-themed something or other I don't quite get the reference to.

"Never have I ever had someone walk in on me during sex," another person says.

Votes are placed, the others all step forwards, and the few people who backed me are forced to sit out.

"Doors have locks, you know," I remind them.

"Just wait until you have to share a room," Valentina warns me with an expression like she's still haunted by the experience.

"Never have I ever jerked off while my roommate was in." Tom takes his turn, not so subtly working out the cabin-mate etiquette.

Oscar steps forwards bashfully; Maddison with less embarrassment.

"What?" Valentina and Obi scream at them.

"Oh, like y'all haven't!" Maddison claps back.

They both retire from the argument.

"Never have I ever been choked," Oscar states, staring me dead in the eye with a devilish smirk.

Bastard. I shared my kink in confidence.

So he does still want to play.

People split themselves between Maddison and me, but I'm the only one who steps forwards, significantly reducing the pool of contestants.

Obi gasps my name after guessing wrong. "I should have known! It's always the quiet ones."

"Never have I ever...had a threesome," someone else proclaims.

Memories of my experimental encounter with a couple I met online invade my thoughts. My smile must give me away as barely anyone has to sit out when only Oscar and I step forwards. Tom and Oscar raise their eyebrows at me. I raise mine back, particularly at Oscar. Clearly, he's not as vanilla as I thought.

"What we sayin' here? Two girls? Two guys?" Maddison asks us both, hungry for details, but neither of us divulge any information, choosing instead to wind her up with our silence. "Fine. Never have I ever been attracted to someone in this room."

Once the votes are locked in, I step forwards even though I told myself not to. *Fuck.* Thankfully, I'm not alone. Maddison, Valentina, and Obi scan the three of us, all looking absolutely delighted. I refuse to look at either of the boys in a bid to play it cool, but my cheeks warm under the stares coming from every corner of the room.

"Never have I ever kissed someone on this ship." Maddison's eyes dance between us all as if she's on the cusp of a great discovery. Tom's eyes are on me too.

"Do you mean someone currently on this ship or, like, since each of you arrived?" Valentina asks, making sure no one – namely Oscar, I assume – can hide behind semantics.

"Umm...I guess since we arrived," Maddison decides.

The two people left remaining stand in front of Maddison.

They bicker, and one sidesteps over to Oscar to make things more interesting. I don't want to look at Oscar, and I can't bring myself to look at Tom for more than a split second, aware this is probably rubbing salt in the wound I made. Instead I pin my eyes on Maddison, who steps forwards. Her voter celebrates. I eventually look back over to Tom, whose eyes briefly dart between Oscar and me. He seems relieved by the lack of confession.

"Harvey, you're meant to step forwards when you've done something."

"I know."

While worrying about the boys, I completely missed the fact only Maddison stepped forwards.

"Bullshit. You have not gone four months without kissing someone," one of the jocks heckles.

Oscar nods like it's no big deal.

"How?"

His hesitation makes sense now. He needed to be sure.

"I guess the opportunity never presented itself." When his eyes catch mine, my insides do somersaults. I refuse to believe he's not had the opportunity. I mean, *look at him*! People must be throwing themselves at him on the daily. I should know, I'm one of those people.

"Well, if you actually came to one of these parties before, you might have got lucky," Valentina comments.

Surely this isn't the first party he's attended on here. Why only now?

He shrugs off the judgement, looking entirely unbothered.

"Wait – he stepped forwards on that 'fancying someone in this room' one," Obi notes. "Kiss them!"

"Yes! Kiss them!" People cheer.

Oscar glares at Obi. "Yeah, I'm not going to do that."

Chants break out around the room. Oscar takes a deep

breath, patiently waiting for them all to tire themselves out with no sign he'll even consider giving in to the peer pressure, and I like him even more for it.

"All right, all right, leave him alone." Maddison steps in to save him. "Eliza, Tom, you're ship virgins too, so let's make this fun."

Tom, Oscar, and I check in with one another, anxious for what's about to come.

"Everyone up. Lights out."

Someone clicks the fairy lights off, plunging the already dimly lit cabin into total darkness. Giddiness fills the air as everyone starts drifting closer together.

"For this next game, there's one rule, and one rule only. No talkin'," Maddison explains. "*None.* This is about keepin' our identities a secret. This applies now and after tonight. If I hear so much as a *peep* 'bout this tomorrow, I'll lose my shit," she warns, making people giggle. "Ladies, move around. Y'all can use your hands to help you, but fellas, keep yours to yourselves, please."

Little titters break out around the room, but they're quickly silenced. I squeeze through the cluster of bodies, but it doesn't take long until I can't distinguish between people at all. It's just a sea of skin – some firm, some soft, some warm, some…wet? *Ew.*

"Now, fellas, move around. Again, hands to yourselves – there'll be plenty of time for that in a minute."

They're certainly more brash in their movements. I'm knocked about like a pinball, every accidental shove disorientating and disarming me. I squeak when my foot gets trodden on by what feels like a herd of elephants.

"Find the closest person to you…and do what comes naturally."

Clammy hands are quick to grasp me, claiming me as

theirs. I tense up instantly, his unwelcome touch snaking all over my waist. No, not even snaking – *slugging*. Everything about him is slimy, and I want out.

"No, thank you," I whisper definitively, pushing against him with all my might. Though I don't need to; he lets me go without a struggle. I make my hasty getaway as the music is turned up enough to block out the horrendous slurping noises that have already begun. But only just.

I slam into the desk, bashing my knee and hip hard against the side. I cry out in pain, but before I can recover, someone crashes into me from behind, the impact bending me over into a precarious position, causing another squeak to escape. Large hands involuntarily brace themselves on my hips, but they're quick to leave. I can't help but quietly laugh to myself.

He takes hold of my hand and moves it with his, patting the desk behind me twice as if suggesting I sit there. So I do, not letting go of him. The darkness is disorientating; my eyes are wide open, but I can't see him, not even a shadow. I clutch my knee with my free hand, searching for a bump or a graze where it hurts. His other hand feels its way down from my shoulder until it finds my fingers. Then his thumb lightly circles the area I'm soothing.

The heat of his body in front of me disappears, and the next thing I know, his lips are pressing against my knee. I puddle at the sweetness of the gesture. When I sense him standing up straight again, his fingers stay with mine. I chance it and move them up to my hip where it also hurts, just above my knickers, rubbing in tiny circles and hoping he'll take the hint.

He does.

As the pulse between my legs instantly deepens, I feel the upwards curve of his lips where he grins against me. I guide his fingertips up along my stomach, between my breasts, and round to my neck, and his lips follow. Each kiss is softer and more tantalising than the last, his tongue barely making contact, but it's all I can focus on. I touch my lips, and when he kisses me the world stops spinning.

It's just one kiss, but it's enough to make me sure nothing will ever feel as good as this.

We break apart and pause to gauge the other's reaction. Who could this be? I know two people who I'd like it to be. He's too broad to be Tom, and Tom would smell and taste like makeup wipes, which this guy doesn't. Could it be Oscar? I'm so turned on by the thought I might explode.

He holds my face close, his strong fingers almost massaging the base of my skull. I slide one hand up his bare chest to find his jaw. His cheeks rise under my thumb, which makes me smile back. We eagerly let our mouths meet again and it's like finding water in a desert; we're both parched for one another and immensely grateful for the salvation.

I part my legs, inviting him to stand in between them. His hips align with mine and our mouths open, allowing just enough space to brush the tips of our tongues against each other's. I shiver with pleasure, finding his waist and gripping tightly to pull him into me, then wrapping my legs around him. When his firmness presses up against my core I can no longer control myself.

Slut mode activated.

His hand on the side of my face pulls me in closer, his tongue pushing deeper with each new wave. A small groan escapes him, and I lose it. Our kisses get faster and heavier. My body craves him – and apparently, his feels the same. His other hand begins to wander down my waist, then my thighs, and back up again, squeezing my curves like he's overcome with desire. I suck his bottom lip, lightly grazing it with my teeth.

No, this isn't Oscar. He wouldn't be so bold, not even in the dark.

Whoever this is, we're starving for one another, like two teenagers going at it in a nightclub bathroom, not even knowing the other's name or if we'll ever see them again but unable to focus on anything other than pleasure-seeking. *Fuck.* I don't know how much time is left, but every second gained with him is another second lost.

If I don't find out who he is, I will never forgive myself.

I might be shot for this, but it's worth the risk. Tearing myself apart from him, I move my lips closer to his ear. "Who are you?" I whisper.

He plants light kisses on my cheek, moving down to my neck.

"Please," I sigh.

"Can't."

It's one word, but it's enough to determine he's American.

Our lips return to one another's. Now I need to find something else – *anything* else – that will help me identify him later. Any jewellery? Or a watch? Yes. He's wearing a watch. What else? My fingertips trail along his body under the guise of teasing him until they find purchase at the waistband of his boxers. I slowly let my fingers run along where his skin meets the fabric. If they're a brand, maybe I can trace the stitching. *God, this is some real MI5 shit.* I fight with myself to stay in the moment and just enjoy it for what it is, but I also can't let a lead – no matter how bizarre – slip away. I compromise by letting one hand slide all over his rock-hard torso while the other tries its luck at learning underwear brail.

As the music dies down, I ache with the reluctance to stop.

"Okay, everyone, I think we should quit there before we get too carried away."

Maddison's voice tears our lips apart. I rest my forehead against his chest and sigh.

"Mix yourselves up again, no talkin' 'til I say so."

His name. I just want his name. He starts to move away, but I grip his hand tighter, not letting him leave me just yet. I fumble around on the desk, hoping it's exactly where I left it when I tidied earlier. *Yes.* The rounded metal is cold on my fingers. *Yes.* I place my name badge in his palm. He doesn't question it; he closes his fingers around it and brings my hand up to his lips to kiss it before walking away. I take it as his promise he'll return it to me. Then I hop down off the desk and dizzy myself once again.

Though he can't be more than a metre or so apart from me, he already feels oceans away.

I was incredibly wrong to think I could come here and avoid any and all romance. Incredibly *stupid*, in fact. Because now I've had a taste of the fruit I forbade myself from, there's no going back.

EIGHT

Like a caveman having just narrowly avoided meeting my grizzly end with a lion, all I can think about now is shagging every person in the near vicinity to keep my legacy alive.

Blindfolded, grabbed, and dragged into the bathroom, stumbling into the arms of somebody else equally as bewildered, I may have just been gifted the opportunity.

The door slams shut behind us.

"Seven minutes starting...*now*!" shouts someone from outside.

I take off my blindfold, but darkness still cloaks my vision. My hands cautiously get my bearings of the body in front of me, and he does the same, stroking and squeezing me in all the right places. He plants slow kisses up my neck, and I whimper, overwhelmed with agonising want.

"Elizabeth?"

"Tom?"

He recoils and clears his throat to compose himself. "I'm so sorry."

Why is he sorry?

"I didn't mean to— I didn't know it was— I wouldn't have—"

He doesn't want me is what he's saying.

"We can go if you want?" I offer.

"No, no, I feel like I've hardly seen you all night."

He's actually seen an awful lot of me tonight, but I don't bother to correct him.

"Unless you want to go?" he says.

"Let's stay."

"Okay."

"Okay."

The tension clings in the air like thick smoke, making it hard to breathe. I wish he still wanted me.

"We could play a different game," Tom suggests.

"Sure."

A few more quiet seconds tick by. "Get in the shower."

"What?"

"Get in the shower." His feet pad on the linoleum as he takes a few steps away from me.

"Am I going to get wet?" Or *wetter*, I could say.

"*Elizabeth*!" he scoffs like I'm being too forward.

"Thomas…"

"Your chances are high."

Noted. I feel around behind me for the door, sweep my hand until I find the lock, and then twist it shut.

"What are you doing?"

"Taking off my undies," I say casually.

His silence speaks for him, but this isn't a seduction tactic.

"What? I don't want to sit in wet knickers for the rest of the night."

"Good point." There's movement on his side of the bathroom, and I imagine fabric sliding down his body. "I'm on the edge of the shower. Get over here."

I don't know how to without our very naked bodies colliding, but I slowly tiptoe towards his voice, bracing my hands in front of me. I stop and step away when I touch his skin.

"Sorry."

He reaches back and takes my hand, standing me beside him so we're shoulder to shoulder. The throbbing of my clit betrays my attempt to have only platonic feelings for him.

"So, what do we do now?"

He leans forwards, and after a few pats against the wall, the shower turns on. Ice-cold speckles hit me from the waterfall in front of us.

"Tom, that's arctic!"

"Exactly! I don't know about you, but I need a cold shower."

"That isn't a game!"

"Course it is – I just haven't told you the rules yet."

Dread and a little excitement surge through me.

"Because you're still a complete mystery to me, let's take turns to make an assumption about the other person, and if we're wrong, we get pushed in."

Oh God.

"I'm gonna put my hand on your back, okay?"

"Yep."

He very carefully places his hand on the small of my back, where it never should have left. I respectfully hate that my feelings aren't reciprocated anymore. Crossing my arm under his, I hold him too, the water taunting us.

"You first," I insist.

"You've thought about fucking Harvey at least once tonight."

Christ, he isn't messing about. "No, I haven't," I say, too shy to admit I definitely have, but also wanting to test his lie-detection skills.

All of a sudden I'm nudged forwards into the water. I squeal, the sting of the cold freezing every flight instinct I have. He's laughing at me, so I find his hand and pull him in too. Tom shrieks. Both of us giggle as we squirm away from the water like kids playing with a garden hose on a summer afternoon. We stand back on the edge catching the breath the shock took away from us.

"That isn't fair. Play by the rules, Elizabeth."

"Why did you think I was lying?"

"Because even *I've* thought about fucking him and I'm straight as an arrow, so *you* definitely have."

"Well, now I'm thinking about the two of you fucking."

"In your dreams."

"Oh, it will be."

"Only if he's bottom."

I laugh at him while fighting every debilitating shiver.

His hand brushes my bum while returning to the spot on my lower back. "Shit, sorry. Your turn."

"You've done anal," I guess.

He pushes me in. *Wrong.* I scream again, but this time I jump away from the stream as quickly as I can.

"My accent turns you on."

There's smugness in his voice. He knows damn well it does. I don't push him in. Defying all logic, I feel warm again.

"Only because it's novel. Its charm will wear off soon."

"So I'm charming?"

I push him in, my quick thinking immediately disarming him.

"Fine, fine. You get two now."

"You're circumcised."

He doesn't push me in.

"You're Jewish?"

He still doesn't push me in, and I can't help but snicker.

"Don't laugh!"

"Sorry. I've just never seen one like that before, in person."

"Seriously?"

"Seriously. It's super rare in the UK. Like, only if there's a medical condition or your parents are sadists."

"There are a lot of health benefits to getting it removed."

"Nope. I'm not falling for your anti-foreskin propaganda."

He laughs.

Frankly, I'm just glad I've breezed over the fact all I can think about is his dick right now. I wonder if it's hard...

"You won't fool around with a coworker."

That feels oddly specific... Nice of Maddison to share. Up until a few hours ago, I was sure of a different answer. Now, however... I push him in. He gasps, but for once he doesn't make a fuss. When he returns, he lays his hand on my waist. So was he just respecting my boundaries a minute ago?

"You've thought about fucking me at least once since we met." My words come out unintentionally hoarse.

He doesn't push me in, and my heart hammers faster. It may as well be made of tinder at this point; it's just one strike of flint away from igniting.

"You wouldn't stop me if I tried." The playfulness disappears from his tone. It's not a statement; it's a question.

I don't push him.

Everything happens so quickly. His grip on me tightens and his body reaches forwards. The shower cuts off. He takes a step into it and pulls me with him. Tom's soft lips meet mine, cold from the water. One of his hands cradles my cheek as his tongue dares to lick mine. I moan softly into his mouth, my puckered nipples touching his chest just barely as I try to pull him closer. He refuses with a quick, "Mm-mm." Why not? Oh. *Oh.* So that's why his other hand isn't holding me; it's too busy keeping a certain part of himself away.

The slow push and pull of our lips drives me wild. But when he moves onto my neck, I can't hold back another sigh of pleasure. I think we both now regret stopping this before.

"Fuck. I'm so wet, Tom."

He purrs almost like he's in pain. "I wanna taste you so bad."

A shout from outside sends reality crashing down. "Time's up!"

Neither of us move.

"This isn't over." He kisses me once more, our lips dragging as we pull away again. "Now go find your panties," he orders, and I giggle.

Panties. Such a stupid word.

I hunt in the dark for my towel, quickly dry myself off, and hand it to him before seeking out my underwear. When we're both decent, we bravely return to the bedroom. Everyone's standing in a circle. A few people turn to look at us with sly smiles, their minds clearly reeling, wondering what we got up to without their prying eyes on us. I'm grateful for the dim light; I don't want what feels like a hundred semistrangers in my room to see how flushed my cheeks are or question why my hair is soaking wet.

I look back at Tom, not expecting the rush of heat that suddenly hits me when his eyes find mine. I shift my focus down his body to where his hands are not-so-casually positioned to cover the strain of his boxers. I catch his eye once more, and we share a smirk.

People break apart to let us join the circle, their attention turning back to the other side of the room. The bottom bunk is occupied by some girl grinding her hips furiously on some guy. She's making out with him as if he's in a coma and her saliva is life support. My deodorant is on the floor, pointing to the guy on the bed, so I take an educated guess that we've moved on to Spin the Bottle. I look around the room to find Oscar and my heart sinks when I don't see him.

Please tell me he left. Please.

People count down from five until the girl eventually clambers off. The guy sits up. Bile rises in my throat as the bitter hand of karma chokes me.

Oscar runs a hand through his hair, not rising to the attention people give him. Some of the guys punch his arms jovially in celebration of him finally getting some action, but he keeps his eyes on the ground. When he finally stands up, he returns to his spot in the circle, looking up to train his gaze on me.

He didn't want this. *Any* of this.

I deserve everything I feel. I can't expect more cake when my mouth is already full. The bottle keeps spinning, but I pay it no attention. Until, that is, Oscar steps forwards to spin it. I keep my eyes down, not prepared to watch him play tonsil tennis again. But then the bottle lands on me. I ignore the excited calls of my name. I can't do it. I don't want to. I know what I just did in the bathroom hurt Oscar, but if I kiss him now, I'll only hurt Tom.

"I'm pretty sure that landed on Tom," I say with absolute certainty.

Tom's eyes almost pop out of his head. It's his own fault – he gave me the idea. Looking over at Oscar, he appears to relax. He's game.

"You sure about that?" Tom retorts, his voice a pitch higher than before.

"Sorry, what was it you said just now…? 'I've thought about fucking him, but only if he's bottom.'"

The room sides with me. Oscar's eyes widen and blink slowly, accepting the compliment.

"Now, that's been taken wildly out of context." Tom tries to defend himself, but it's no use; the mob's turned its attention on him now. He reluctantly relishes his joke being used against him. He's going to do it. I know he will. Because if I've learnt anything about him this week, it's that he can't back away from a challenge. Especially not when there's a crowd to please.

Sucking in his cheeks to hide a smile, he turns his attention to Oscar. "Come on then, Harvey." He steps into the middle of the circle, shrill shrieks breaking out all around him.

Oscar moves in too, and when Tom's nerves grind him to a halt, Oscar takes control, lightly touching Tom's waist.

"I'm so nervous!" Tom says breathlessly as an aside, fanning his face with his hand.

Never misses an opportunity to play the room, that boy.

"Don't be," Oscar reassures him.

Tom quietly swoons. Their faces get closer together. Oscar places a hand on the side of Tom's neck, his thumb resting on his cheek.

"Is this okay?"

Tom barely whispers his consent before clearing his throat and saying it again in a deeper, manlier voice. Oscar's different with him. He's confident, unflustered.

"Good," Oscar says before his lips come down on Tom's.

The room goes berserk. Tom's eyes squeeze shut and his body tenses but quickly eases once the initial fear of discomfort is over. He kisses Oscar back, placing his hands on his almost-bare body to hold him closer. The kisses become more passionate as they both play up to the reaction of the room.

New fantasy unlocked.

The countdown begins, and I'm pretty sure I just saw a tongue. Tom places a hand on Oscar's bum and gives it a quick squeeze to gain back some form of control, but we all know he has none. That's evident in his startled expression when they break apart.

"And here I was thinking I was straight," Tom jokes, getting a good laugh out of us all.

"Sexuality's a spectrum," Oscar rasps with all the confidence in the world.

Obi and a few of the male actors raise a hand in the air, clicking like they're at some spoken word poetry night.

"Yeah, I see that now. Well, I'm definitely Harvey-sexual. Fuck!" Tom walks away from our side of the room, insisting he go where Oscar was to give him a full lap to recover.

Oscar fills the now-empty spot to my left. His skin brushes mine and I don't miss his quick side glance at me, silently communicating what feels like a thank-you.

The bottle continues to spin, but I can't concentrate. My head is a mess. That solution only solved the short-term problem; I've still complicated both my friendships with the boys tonight, and I need a second to work out what I want. Just before it's my turn to spin, I tap Oscar's foot, drawing his attention.

"Can we play a new game? I think we've had enough of this. I mean, I don't know about anyone else, but this game has peaked for me," Oscar says quickly. He winks at Tom, who makes a show of blushing like a schoolgirl.

Someone stands up and heads to the speaker in the corner of the room. They lean down but don't retrieve the speaker;

instead they reveal the box of condoms they brought in earlier.

"Nope." Oscar shuts him down.

"Don't you even wanna hear what the game is?"

"Nope. I've got a better one."

The party-goers cling to his every word, utterly enthralled he's getting involved.

He turns to me. "Have you got paper and a pen?"

I nod and head to my desk drawer. Turning to a blank page in my notebook, I hand it to him and he tears out a page, ripping it into smaller pieces.

"Girls and gays, write your room numbers on a piece of paper. Once you've done that, or while you're waiting, find your room key and nothing else." He picks up the Indiana Jones fedora that was on the floor and starts collecting the scraps of paper into it.

"Oh, we know where we're going," Obi says to Oscar when he tries to split the gays into two groups.

"And if you want to join us, Harvey, you're more than welcome to," one of them pipes up.

"I'll bear that in mind." Oscar continues collecting numbers with an amused smile. He places his palm out for mine and then shifts the hat into that hand too, the brim covering up my slip. I like seeing this sneaky side of him.

Once he's got all the girls' room numbers, he opens the door, propping his body against it to allow the light to stream in from the corridor. "Off you go, ladies." He smiles. "Don't worry about those," he insists when they start searching for their clothes.

The entertainment team stare at him in disbelief, but no one argues further. The girls and gays congregate just outside the room, looking to one another for reassurance that if they run the others will too. The rest of us inside count them down from three, and they all dash off, squealing quietly as they streak down the hall. We hang our heads out the door to watch them disappear. When they're all out of sight, we retreat into the room.

"Gangbang anyone?" I joke in the brief silence.

When the laughter kicks in a split second later, I'm more than a little relieved it landed. My focus shifts quickly between Tom and Oscar, and I bask in their amusement, wanting it more than anyone else's.

"All right, chaps, pick a number." Oscar jostles the hat in the middle of the group. They all lean in and pick one out.

"Harvey, have you got a number?" Tom asks over the various mutters and swaps going on between the others.

"Right here." He flashes my folded scrap of paper at him.

When I look back at Tom, he isn't smiling anymore.

The guys gear up for the countdown, riling each other up before they all start running down the hall in their pants. Everyone, that is, except for Tom, who hovers at the back of the pack.

"After you." He gestures to Oscar to step out of the room and run to his destination.

"No, I insist, after you."

Tom waits for a beat as the last few guys run off, confirming his suspicions that Oscar isn't going anywhere. He looks back at me, attempting to read me like he's checking if I'm okay. I give him a tiny nod. His lips form a harsh line.

"Night, Eliza." His Adam's apple bobs as he swallows.

"Night," I reply, my voice small.

He doesn't bother looking at Oscar again before he leaves. The door swings closed and slams behind him.

He didn't call me Elizabeth.

"You all right?" Oscar's question holds me back from whatever shame spiral I was about to endure.

"Yeah, just knackered. You?"

"Mm-hmm. Hasn't quite been the night I thought it was going to be."

You can say that again. I feel awful. He only came to look after me, and I didn't look after him.

"Do I even want to know what the time is?"

He looks at his watch. If I hadn't already checked every male body in the room for watches, I might find that simple action more revelatory. The ship is like a bleedin' time-telling convention; every guy except Tom was wearing one (because "it just didn't feel like Sandy"). Plus, he's not American. So I'm no closer to finding my mystery man. Why didn't I study it – the shape, the size, the bumps? I'll just have to be patient.

"Um…" He winces. "Not nearly five."

"Christ." I look around at the mess left in the room and sigh. It's a sea of discarded costumes and cups. This is going to take a while to clean up.

"You got a bin bag?" Oscar asks.

I lift the current one out of its place and find the roll underneath it, tearing one off for him. He fans it out and starts putting clothes in it. I collect all the cups and empty any remnants in the sink, stacking them together to take back to the bar tomorrow morning.

Nope. *This* morning.

When we're done, we shuffle on our feet waiting for the other to speak first. I would, but I have no idea what to say.

"I should get myself to bed," he says finally.

"Me too. Thanks for this." I point to my now tidy room.

He puts his clothes back on while I pretend I'm not look-ing, opens the door, and hangs the bin bag on the outside handle for people to collect their belongings later.

He knows all the tricks, doesn't he?

"I'll come get you for breakfast?"

"Sure." I wait for him to leave, but he lingers as if there's something he wants to say but he isn't sure how.

"They're just party games. Don't read too much into them." His lips don't quite break into a smile.

I mirror his expression and nod, taking his comment on board.

"Good night, Chapman."

"Good night."

NINE

Today is a "hair up" kind of day. An "extra concealer under the eyes" kind of day. A "please don't ask too much of me" kind of day.

In my horny haze, I forgot name badges are compulsory to wear on shift, which means Oscar has to take me to get a replacement after everyone sees through my "I'm sure it will turn up soon" act almost immediately.

Mortifying.

Thankfully, the few activities we run are pretty quiet as the majority of passengers are off exploring the port. The Sail Away Party upon their return must look like a zombie apocalypse, though, with most of us hanging out of our arses and/or relying solely on caffeine to make up for severe sleep deprivation.

Despite receiving a lot of attention after the success of last night's talent show, unfortunately, the day comes and goes without the romantic badge-returning ceremony I was hoping for. But at long last, I'm showered and tucked up in bed, not caring one bit that the others are definitely going "out" tonight. Oscar wants an early night, which gives me a free pass to have one too. I say "early" as if it isn't already gone ten. I have every intention of staying up for a while and chilling out on my own for once, but I barely make it through the opening credits of "The Office" before my eyelids are too heavy to keep open.

Help! My eyes don't work. Why are there railings around my bed and fabric caging me in? *Where am I? Is this a hospital bed?*

Realisation hits. I take a big breath in and out to steady my racing heart.

I'm okay.

My teeth feel weird. Fuzzy. Gross – I forgot to brush them. It must be the middle of the night. I follow the muffled voices of the overly familiar Dunder Mifflin employees coming from somewhere under my duvet and tap to see the clock in the corner of the screen. 11.30 p.m. Good. More sleep for me. But first: teeth.

I throw off the cover and fling myself down the ladder, shuffling my feet all the way to the bathroom in the dark. The very instant mint tingles on my tongue, there's an unwelcome knock at the door. I wait and cross my fingers in the hope whoever it is just got the wrong room, but they knock again.

Ugh.

Not bothering to interrupt my brushing, I traipse over to answer it, squinting as the harsh light behind the two figures burns my retinas. Eventually, I make out a dolled-up Valentina and Maddison, who stand there silently judging me.

"Nope." Valentina tugs the toothbrush out of my mouth and pushes past me.

"What?" I garble, following her to the bathroom to spit, granting Maddison the opportunity to also enter uninvited.

"You're *not* spendin' the night locked away in your room," Maddison huffs, slapping the light switch on.

I recoil like a vampire in the sun when I return to the room. "Wasn't last night enough? How are you not exhausted?" I protest, but they ignore me, choosing instead to raid my wardrobe. Looking for Narnia, by the sound of it. The hangers scream as they're slid across the rail. Maddison pulls out various items, presenting them to Valentina for approval. "It's just Saturday night."

They look at me like I've told them I have twelve nipples and rainbow pubes.

"Put this on." Valentina shoves the approved outfit into my arms. Neither of them turn away until they see me cave.

They put me in my skintight lilac spaghetti-strap dress, the one Sarah insisted she lend me because she thought it'd be cute for the beach, but which I had no intention of ever wearing. Maybe no one will see me.

The bar is heaving with people and only illuminated by the colourful lights that pulse along to the music. My chest vibrates with each thump of the bass. We head over to the bar to order ourselves drinks, and I scan the room. Without meaning to, I've looked for Tom in every room I've entered today, and around every corner I've turned, nerves wracked each time I saw a not-quite-six-foot brunette, and then disappointment extinguishing the optimism when it wasn't him.

"What happened after we left last night?" Maddison quizzes me.

"What do you mean?" I play dumb, but they don't buy

my naivety. "You first. Wait – did you have two guys come to your room?"

Maddison nods with the biggest grin on her face.

"Did the four of you…?"

"She went to theirs." Valentina tips her head at Maddison.

"Theirs. Plural?"

Maddison nods again, so giddy she might explode. "I had a threesome!"

I laugh at her excitement. "Congrats! How was it?"

"A lotta work, honestly."

"I can imagine. Did you not want to get in on that?" I ask Valentina.

"Period," she grunts, but she doesn't look all that disappointed.

"So…who stayed back at yours?"

"Oscar."

"Yes! I knew it! He was giving you some serious fuck-me eyes all night. What happened? Tell me everything!" She sizzles with impatience.

"He helped me tidy up and then left."

They study me, waiting for a micro-expression to expose a lie, but eventually Maddison sighs with defeat.

"I told you nothing would happen," Valentina says, leaning back with her elbows against the bar. "Who did you fuck last night, Tom?"

Huh?

I follow her line of sight, startling when I see him, nervousness flurrying through me. I'm not really sure where we stand after how the party ended, and now I'm anxious to hear the answer to her question – the one I hadn't dared to think there'd even be an answer to.

It takes him a second to shake away the abruptness of it.

"No one." He casts a cursory glance my way and then back to her.

"What do you want?"

"Daniel sent me to get shots." He looks back, and through the ocean of bouncing bodies I spot a table on the other side of the room, where Obi and Daniel sit waving at us like a pair of old ladies saying "cooee!".

"Of course he did," Valentina mutters.

Tom's eyes meet mine again and he smiles. "Hey."

My heart skips a little. It's a different kind of "hey" from the "night" he gave me. A good kind of "hey". An "I'm happy you're here" kind of "hey". And suddenly I'm happy I'm here too.

"Hey," I reply, my voice smaller than expected.

"Bye, Tom." Valentina stares him down until he retreats.

Good to know I'm not the only one who's a little petrified of her.

Maddison gasps the second he's out of earshot. "Please tell me what went down durin' your seven minutes in heaven. He won't tell me nothin'."

"Because nothing happened." If he wants to keep a secret between us, then so do I. And to be honest, even if he didn't, I still wouldn't say anything.

"No, enough of this *nothin'* business. I heard screamin' and ya'll came out soakin' wet," she presses.

The bartender interrupts us, and I lose myself briefly in the memory of his lips on mine. His bare skin so nearly up against me. I get a sudden drop in my stomach as if I'm on a rollercoaster.

"Go on – we got these." Valentina jerks her chin over to the table. "And quit smiling. She'll only ask more questions," she says while Maddison's distracted.

I bite down on my lip, wiping off the smirk that accidentally crept its way onto my face, and escape as instructed. I catch up to Tom and reach for his arm. He stops, warms at my presence, and continues muscling his way through the crowd. Any worry I had about losing him last night disappears as he gallantly leads the way.

We make ourselves comfortable, the girls arriving not long after us with our drinks and a paddle of six shots.

"Well done on a successful quest, lassies! Where was our lost damsel?"

My eyes flick to Tom with confusion. What in the "Runescape" is he on about?

"I'll explain later," he whispers to me.

"She was about to go to sleep." Maddison outs me.

"I *was* asleep before you turned up."

The boys look at me like that's the most adorable thing they've ever heard.

"Don't you guys ever do that thing where you, you know, lie down and close your eyes?" I ask.

"Oh, we lie down plenty," Obi assures me, high-fiving Maddison without looking, making his meaning very clear.

Daniel grabs a shot, stands up, and holds it out in front of him with authority. "Challenge!" he shouts. The others copy him like this is normal, so I follow along, all of us now standing with our shots outstretched. "Your challenge, should you choose to accept it…" His thick Glaswegian accent projects around the table.

I look to the girls for a little more explanation.

"We boycotted his 'Dungeons and Dragons' nights. Just go with it," Maddison whispers in my ear.

"Obi. Thou must not…dance on the tables this merry eve," Daniel orders.

"Challenge!" Obi chants, raising his shot higher before knocking it back.

"Fair maiden Maddison, thou must not…"

"Gossip," Valentina orders.

"Me? Never!" Maddison says playfully. "Challenge!" she shouts and seals her fate with a shot.

"Veracious Valentina. Thou shalt…"

"Smile. All night," Obi pipes up.

"Challenge!" she says with her final frown of the evening, flashing a pearly-white fake smile after drinking.

"Daniel, thou shalt not…get white-boy wasted," Obi suggests.

"'Tis a heavy cross, but I shall carry it with honour. Challenge!" He drinks and slams his glass down on the table. "Eliza, our sleeping beauty, thou shalt join the congregation and say yes to every opportunity presented henceforth, else I fear we'll have a Harvey Junior in our midst."

"I don't think he'll be making a junior anytime soon," Tom quips, and the others giggle.

"And Sir Thomas, no wisecracks must ye lip-smack. Harvey may be unlike our kind, but he still be one of our own. Now, are ye quest virgins up to the test?"

"Speaking of virgins…" Obi teases.

Daniel raises an eyebrow his way.

"What? You said he couldn't, not me."

"Challenge!" Tom and I shout in unison and take our shots.

"Huzzah!" Daniel cries, and we all echo him.

It's quite possible I'm still asleep.

Two drinks later and I'm as good as drunk. Again. But I think I can finally admit I'm a little bit obsessed with Tom. I'm hooked on his every word, never knowing what he's going to come out with next. Everything about him is interesting. Every joke is hilarious. Every story is captivating. I want to be wherever he is, and if he's not here, I'm counting down the minutes until he's back.

We sit close together, my bare legs daring to press against his jeans under the table. "So you know what I'm thinking about right now?" I ask him, my mind coming alive at the possibility.

"Yes, as a psych-majoring college dropout, I'm fully qualified to read body language with one hundred percent accuracy."

"Go on then – tell me!"

"All right. First I need your hand." He opens his on the table and I place mine inside it, my whole body fizzing like a firework with a lit fuse as he tightens his hold. "Then I need to look into your eyes." As his chocolate gaze settles on mine, I think I finally understand Augustus Gloop; the river tempts me in, and I instantly know I'd do anything for a taste. "Hmm, yes. I see luck in your future."

"Oh, shove off. You're a psychologist, not a psychic."

"Okay, okay. You're thinking…you're glad you came out tonight."

I endeavour to keep a straight face, but he's right.

"You're a little bit tipsy even though you haven't actually finished your second drink yet."

I bite my numb lip to mask my smile.

"And…you're a little bit turned on."

The jig's up.

"I didn't need to see your face for that – your legs are doing more than enough talking."

"Sorry." I bashfully retreat.

"No, don't take them away. I like it." He smiles, slipping

his hand under the table and pulling my legs back against his. His hand stays there, keeping me close.

"Anything else?" My eyebrow quirks up and my smile widens.

He narrows his eyes and inches closer, and then he gasps suddenly. "Elizabeth! Not here." He looks around as if everyone else can read my thoughts too. "So dirty!"

I can't stop giggling. If only he knew exactly how dirty my thoughts are right now. "My turn, my turn. I wanna see if I can read you."

"Well, okay, but it takes an awful lot of bullshit. I'm not sure you've got it in you."

"But I've had such an excellent teacher."

His smile is intoxicating.

I take his hand with both of mine, his other one staying under the table drawing circles on my knee with his thumb. "You're thinking…how lucky you are to have made such a great friend already."

He grins in amusement.

"You're thinking about taking up a professional career in dance after last night's performance…"

He pouts. "'Fraid not, but don't beat yourself up. It takes years of training to get to where I am."

"Wait – something's coming to me." I mock a vision. "Hmm, that *is* interesting."

"What?"

"Really? Wow, Tom, I'm flattered."

"What?" His excitement builds with every second I tease him.

"It seems you also can't stop thinking about last night."

My words linger in the air with the dropped gauntlet, and I lose myself in want. I long for his lips to catch mine, for my hunger to be satiated.

"You're right. I've been fantasising about that kiss all day." He picks up the metaphorical glove. "Those soft lips, big hands, and that tiny bit of stubble grazing my chin."

I tickle with laughter. "Wisecrack! That was a wisecrack!" I point at him to get the others to all witness him losing the game.

"No, no, it wasn't, I swear!" He wrestles to restrain my accusing finger, giggling with me as he does. Good God, that *giggle*. Our hands end up under the table, his holding mine down onto my legs. I stop my struggle only until I feel him relax, and then I whip my hands away and hold his against me.

"So you were thinking about him?"

His face stills with hesitation. "Yep." He commits to his joke.

"So you're into guys?"

"No, I'm definitely not into guys."

"It's okay if you are. More guys should be bi."

"Oh, I agree, but this guy only likes women." He spreads his fingers along my skin, his hand higher up on my thigh than it was a second ago.

I raise my chin to make my lips more accessible. "Prove it."

"Eliza!" Maddison grabs my shoulder. "Let's go dance!"

Of all the people who could have possibly cockblocked me tonight, she was last on my list. Maddison would do well to study body language herself.

"I'll be there in a minute," I say, turning back to Tom to sew back up the tension between us.

His hand reinstates itself on my thigh.

"But it's *my song*!" she pleads, Valentina beside her also imploring me to join them with her counterfeit smile.

Whose song is "Africa" by Toto? A *dubstep* version at

that. I give her *the look*, but she gives me one of her own back.

"I promise I'll be there in a sec."

"Challenge," Valentina presses.

"Oooh, she's gonna lose…" Tom teases me.

I sigh, full of indignation. Tom gives me a firm squeeze under the table and releases me.

Fine.

The girls take my arm, and we form a chain with Obi, pushing our way through the crowd to the dance floor.

"You'll thank me later," Maddison says, her sickly-sweet tone having completely evaporated.

What's that *supposed to mean?*

Looking back at my suspicious face, she goes on. "You said no coworkers."

But *she* was the one who— Ugh, whatever. I look at Tom as he leans back in the chair next to Daniel. His eyes are glued to me, the slightest hint of a smirk on his face as he drops his line of sight all the way down my body and back up again.

This isn't over.

Maddison knows me better than I know myself. It was absolutely the right call to stop me from snogging Tom's face off in front of everyone.

Because I wouldn't have been able to stop.

I swear only a minute passes between my head hitting the pillow and the chime of my alarm going off, each trill making my brain ripple with pain. Why couldn't I have just lost the game? How hard would it have been to say no to the drinks that were handed to me all night? Or for Tom to have asked me to leave with him instead of amusing himself with my obvious displeasure at the guys grinding themselves against me. And why did I set my alarm so early? It's only eight.

My call home!

With great caution, I get my uniform on, tidy myself up, and open the safe. I thought retrieving my phone for the first time would be more ceremonious than this, but I'm too tired to care. Though I'd feel a lot worse had I not dug out a vitamin C tablet before bed and chugged several pints of water in between alcoholic offerings. For the first time this morning, the threat of nausea becomes real as I remember the one suitor the others refused for me...

"Who's gay for pay?"

"Obi! I said 'single for the stay'! He has a wife at home but DOESN'T THINK IT'S WORTH MENTIONIN'!" *Maddison shouts, hoping to be heard by him as he sulks off. He doesn't even try to defend himself. "Don't worry, I reached out. She's havin' way more fun without him."*

I stand there speechless, attempting to swallow the disgust, but it sits so uncomfortably I want to vomit. It was very nearly a full circle moment but in the worst way – because this time I would have been the villain.

With almost a full battery and an hour's worth of free Wi-Fi to use, I set myself up in the little spot outside that Oscar showed me at the top of the ship. It's the prime location for my first call home. It's out of the way, quiet, and has the perfect view to show off to Lawrence.

Paranoid about incurring hefty data roaming fees, I keep airplane mode on and just log in to the Wi-Fi. A little buzz goes through me in anticipation of the dopamine hit as I brace myself for the influx of notifications. I head to my favourite contacts and prepare to call Sarah, holding off for just another few seconds for those alerts, but nothing pings up. Maybe the Wi-Fi's so slow I have to open the apps individually. I'll do it after the call – I'm already running a little late. I hit Sarah's name and wait for her to answer. I guess the plan is for me to sit there on a video call like I'm part of the meal and she'll make her big announcement when she's ready. I can't believe my sister's going to have a baby!

"Nelly! How's the circus?"

It never takes long for my brother to push my buttons, but this is a new record. He made several Nelly the Elephant references when I handed in my notice, despite my constant reminders that Nelly ran away *from* the circus, not *to* it. Clearly, it never got through that thick skull of his.

"Hilarious. Where's Sarah?"

"Toilet. Said she wasn't feeling well. Must be the new perfume Dad got Mum for her birthday."

"Oi!" Dad huffs in the background.

Lawrence turns the phone around to show Dad shaking his head as he cuts up his roast beef. "But at least he got her something."

"Lawrence, stop it," Mum scolds him. "I got the flowers you sent me, darling, thank you. That was very kind," she says to the screen, her knife and fork hovering over her plate.

I'm glad they got there okay. I made sure to order them before I left, but part of me feared something would go wrong with the order and I'd be powerless to amend it.

"Hi, Mum! Happy birthday!" I stick my neck out like I'm hoping to be more visible to her.

"Not like you to be so organised, Lizzie."

Ah yes, the incompetency jabs. How I've missed those.

"Funnily enough, when you're not working for an obnoxious little worm, it's pretty easy." I know I should be more grateful for everything he did for me when I was struggling to get work, but he made my life hell from the second I walked through his office door.

"How is it, sweetheart?" Mum asks.

"It's awesome! There was a talent show on Friday, which my friend and I won. Everyone's super nice. I'm having a lot of fun." I rattle off a few of the events and activities I've been doing this week, waiting to be interrupted by excitement, but I'm not. There's only silence.

"Hello?"

The words "poor connection" appear onscreen.

"What was that, love? We lost you," Dad's soft voice calls out.

"Which bit did you hear?"

"Awesome! Super! You've been Americanised already. You'll be slinging a gun in no time if you're not careful."

I roll my eyes at Lawrence.

"Ready to pack your trunk yet?" he pokes.

"You wish. Everything falling apart without me?"

"Thriving, actually. Your replacement has links with all sorts of high-flyers around the city, so business has never been better."

"Ugh, no one cares, Lawrence. Hey, get off my phone!" The image jiggles around until I see Sarah grinning from ear to ear. Oh, it's so good to see her. "Eliza!" she squeals. "You found my letter then?"

"I did!"

The screen freezes again. I get intermittent bursts of her talking, but I can't quite make out what she's saying. For a second I see a pixelated blur of Simon, and then he's gone. I keep smiling, waiting for the internet to catch up.

"Oh, there you are. We're just about to give Mum her present," she says in a knowing tone. The picture shakes some more, accompanied by clattering and clanking. I think she's propping me up against the condiments.

Sarah's always been a career girl, but a broody one at that. And since she beat her five-year work plan in about three, now the lead developer on— Oh God, what was it? She's told me so many times, but it's IT jargon I don't understand. Either way, she's *really* good at what she does and clearly, the rest of her timeline has shifted up too.

She passes Mum a small gift bag, which Mum stares at for a while. A long while. What is she doing?

Poor connection.

Oh God, not now! I swear I'm seconds away from skipping my phone like a stone on the water.

The connection kicks in again, but all I get are freeze frames. Mum holding a Baby-gro, hugging Sarah and Simon. Dad wiping away tears. Lawrence is too close to the camera to see, but I get little snippets of his stupid voice every now and then. I keep smiling, so happy for her good news, but I feel like an outside observer to something that's bringing everyone else together. Reality dawns that this isn't going to be the only milestone or special occasion I'll miss while I'm here. Life back home is continuing on without me and there's nothing I can do about it.

The call cuts off.

No, no, no.

I quickly call back, but the signal is so bad I don't even get to say goodbye before it drops again. If I keep calling, I'll only be interrupting their special moment.

My thumb instinctively taps on WhatsApp, hoping maybe some messages will fly in once I give it the chance to connect, but there's still nothing. I refresh my last Google search – "What are the odds of a cruise ship sinking?" – and it loads a little slowly, but it works. So I have internet; I just have no messages. I open Instagram, hoping for more luck there.

I swipe the screen down to refresh it. No DMs. No notifications that aren't useless spam from people I don't care about posting things I don't care about. Nothing.

At the top of my feed is a post by Tara. She's on tour with "Waitress" right now, understudying for Dawn, and from the looks of things she got to go on last night. There's a slightly blurry video of her curtain call taken from the wings, her smile the widest I've ever seen it, her dark red curls shining even brighter under the stage lights. I feel so much pride I could burst. *She made it.* I remember going to see a soiree in her first year of drama school. She sang "When He Sees Me" and I got tingles all over my skin. She was born to play that role. The jealousy only kicks in when I swipe across to see a picture of Kate hugging her at stage door. *Why is she still friends with that psycho?*

Quickly scrolling down my feed, a post by one of my old Cellar friends, Mae, pops up. She, Liv, and I used to be inseparable. Anytime we all had a shift together was a good day – we were always giggling and causing trouble. Even outside of work, we got up to all sorts. Mae was too disorganised to keep a diary and Liv loved spontaneous plans, so they were always up for anything. Which worked out great when Tara was busy with her new boyfriend and Kate started excluding me from such events as dinner parties in my own home with people from her course I knew well enough to consider my friends too. The photo is of Mae and Liv out for dinner with a big group of smiling faces posing along the table behind them. The caption reads, "Dinner with my favourite ghosts and ghouls."

I thought we were real friends, but when I had no choice but to quit, Mae and Liv quickly forgot about me. I know friends of convenience exist, but I didn't think I was that to them. Though looking back, I guess I was.

Why am I always the one who gets left out?

It was nice of Maddison and Valentina to drag me out last night, but let's face it: they're the actual friends here, and I'm just a third wheel they'll drop eventually.

I recognise every single person in the photo. More fake friends. But what makes anger burn my insides like poison is when I zoom in on the couple at the end of the table. It's *him*. He has his arm around *her*. This is so fucking backwards. *I* should be in that photo. *He* should have quit in shame. *He* should have been ostracised by our entire friendship group. *He* deserves to have trudged through the past year like I have.

I turn off my phone and sit in silence, hearing nothing but the waves crashing against the side of the ship. Any homesickness I had after my failed call with the family has quickly vanished. I never want to go home. I was right. There's nothing left for me there.

I send a congratulations and happy birthday message on the family WhatsApp chat, which delivers no problem before I turn off my phone. I go back to my room and lock it up in the safe, confident I'll have no desire to get it out again until I leave.

It should feel harder to hide my upset from the guests and find the energy for today's activities, but I'm worryingly proficient at pretending everything's fine. Oscar smartly chooses not to dig any deeper when I say as much, but he stares at me more than usual, like he's waiting to catch my mask when it falls.

As soon as we're done for the day I slip off to my room. I

don't have the appetite for dinner; I just want to be alone. There are so many people here it's suffocating, and unsurprisingly, I don't escape unnoticed.

"Elizabeth! There you are. Have you been hiding from me? I haven't seen you all day." Tom jogs over to where I'm hovering outside my door.

"Damn, you found me." I pretend to play with him, but it comes out flat and humourless. "Good day?" I'm not in the mood for small talk, but going through the motions keeps other people comfortable, so for that reason I persist. He won't want to know me like this. No one ever does.

"Yeah, great, thanks. Oh my God, you should have been by the surfing simulator today. Some guy totally wiped out—"

I act as if I'm amused by his story, but I don't even hear him.

"...ass out, running after his shorts."

I puff out a fake chuckle, hoping he buys it.

"Oh, your call home! How was that?"

I nod and smile. "Really nice."

"Yeah?"

"Yeah, it was, um..." I'm suddenly reminded of the fact none of my family said they missed me and not a single friend had texted to check in because I don't have any.

Don't cry, Eliza. Not yet.

My bottom lip betrays me. I fight hard to keep the smile on my face, but after a day of wrestling with my emotions, my defences finally collapse.

TEN

TOM

I have a superpower. And like all superpowers, I only got it after suffering a life-altering tragedy. Four years ago, I discovered I have the ability to make someone smile even when their entire world has gone dark.

She's hiding behind her adorable bangs, but I can still see those big blue eyes just enough to tell their usual shimmer has gone. This is a look I know well, and I need to act now before…

Too late. Devastating tears fall down her cheeks. Without thinking, I pull her into me so tight I feel her lips trembling against my shoulder. It's like hugging a statue for a while, her body rigid with tension from everything she's holding in, but she isn't fighting me, so I keep my arms wrapped around her until she eventually hugs me back. A small sob lands on my chest, and I squeeze her even harder.

I thought I was destined to be numb forever, and I was kind of okay with keeping it that way. It sure was better than feeling what everyone around me was feeling. But from the second I got here, it's as if a switch has been flicked; all my emotions have been coming back. Desire, joy, nerves, and now pain. I was certain I could never experience more of that, but now I'm learning I was wrong. Very wrong. Is it this place that's changing me, or is it her?

I stroke her hair to find it's a million times softer than I thought it would be. Our bodies sway a little while I make a plan to find whoever hurt her like this and avenge her.

Footsteps approach in the distance, and I keep my eye on the corner, annoyed but not surprised when Harvey appears from around it. It's clear he came to see her – his room is in the other direction. Is he responsible for this? Has he come to apologise? If I weren't so desperate to keep holding her in my arms, I'd confront him. He stops in his tracks when he sees us.

FRIDAY NIGHT

Maddison, Valentina, and Obi's jaws hit the floor as they watch him leave the bar with her.

"Don't worry, she's got a thing about coworkers," Maddison slurs in my ear, noticing my eyes fixed on the door. "She won't let that happen."

My relief that maybe she didn't reject me before, only my working relationship with her, is quickly overshadowed by the guilt I tried anything at all. Before I can even sit with that feeling, something else consumes me: the protective urge to save her from the discomfort if he were to try something now.

"What if the party went somewhere else instead?" Obi suggests with a gleeful smirk. He knows his roommate might be about to get some action.

I can't round up people fast enough.

. . .

She doesn't know any different – her head's still tucked into my chest. Harvey's brow crinkles with concern, and he locks eyes with me like he's asking if she's okay or if I've got this. I give him a faint nod, still not confident he isn't the perpetrator, and after taking another look at her, he walks back the way he came. He clearly knew something was up. Did something happen today? Is she homesick? Or is she still upset about that married guy last night? She didn't do anything wrong. He danced with her for all of ten seconds before the others pulled her away. She tried to go, but we didn't let her. I even braved the dance floor to fend off any more assholes for her, but she wasn't quite the same after that.

She pulls away from me. "Sorry." Her fingers sweep away the tiny droplets, nervously laughing it off.

"Don't be sorry."

She swipes her hand against my chest. "I made your shirt all wet."

"I've got more." I ease her worry. "What's up?"

"Honestly, it's nothing. I'm fine."

"Missing home?"

"No. I thought I would, but…" She takes a deep breath and thinks for a second. "I miss my sister and my parents, I guess. My brother… Ugh, it's hard to miss him."

Glad I'm not the only one who couldn't be happier to see the back of their brother. I stay quiet and wait for her fill the silence. Talking is good.

"I don't know. If anything, I feel nothing. Which somehow feels worse."

Oh, Queenie. She's been this ray of light since day one, but looking at her now, all I see are storm clouds. I should have spotted this sooner. It's always the ones who seem like they've got it all together who are hurting the most.

"Ah God, that sounds so dramatic. I don't mean—"

"No, I get it." The more I get to know people on this ship, the more I'm learning I'm not the only one running away from something. "Are you doing anything now?"

"I was just going to grab a shower and call it a day."

I can't let her be alone right now – not with all this noise in her head. "Okay, how about you shower, and I'll head to the library and pick out some movies, maybe even grab some snacks from the commissary…?"

Even though she's rolling her eyes in disapproval, she smiles, and suddenly everything gets brighter. "Stop calling it that – we're not in prison."

"Fine. What would you call it, a *tuck shop*?" I mock in a British accent. There were always a small handful of rich English kids at summer camp coining the weirdest phrases, and I'm glad I made an effort to remember some of them.

She's trying not to laugh but failing.

"Anyway. I'll swing by and stock up on supplies for a midnight snack. Sound good?"

"I'm okay, I promise."

"Yeah, you will be. Because you'll be watching movies with me all night," I persist.

She takes a deep breath, knowing she isn't getting rid of me, but her protests stop, so I know she's happy about it.

"Any requests?"

She shakes her head.

"What, not even Skittles?"

The tip of her tongue pokes out the corner of her mouth. I reach into my pocket and hand her a half-eaten packet I've been waiting to share with her all day. I've learnt to keep a stash on me at all times after I offered her some of the "rare ones" on our first day and she squealed with excitement as she guessed each flavour. I quickly became addicted to seeing her face light up like that.

"I'll get us some more."

I wake up to the curtains of Eliza's spare bunk being swung open, some girl being thrown on top of me, and Daniel piling on top of us.

What the *fuck* is Daniel doing in here? Even though I've had a night free of his snoring, this immediately makes putting up with that seem tolerable.

The petite pixie-looking girl squeals and leaps up again, Daniel quickly following. It takes me a second to work out where I recognise her from, but I eventually connect the dots to the photos by Daniel's bed. His long-lost girlfriend has finally arrived and Eliza's got herself a roommate, I guess.

They awkwardly make their escape back to our room, leaving me homeless for at least the next thirty minutes. Who am I kidding? He hasn't seen her in months – it'll be safe in five. Even so, I have no intention of rushing over there.

As soon as the door shuts behind them, Eliza's reading light clicks on.

"Tom?" she whispers, and I stick my head out of the bunk to look up at her peering down at me.

"Hey," I whisper back. I'm not sure why since it's just the two of us in here now.

"What was that all about?"

"You have a roommate."

She looks as disappointed as I feel.

"You okay?"

She nods with a sweet smile before sitting up and patting the end of her bed as if she's summoning a puppy. And damn, if I don't allow myself to be summoned. Leaving the warmth of my borrowed bed, I scale the ladder and perch on the end of hers, stealing the bottom of the sheets to cover my almost bare body. I dangle my legs over the side of the bed where the gap for the ladder is and her tiny feet wriggle their way onto my lap.

"You sleep okay down there?" she asks.

"Mmm, that was actually the first good night's sleep I've had since I got here."

"I wouldn't get used to it. I doubt you'll be getting any more for a while."

I groan. "Oh, please, Your Highness, *please* let me move into Buckingham Palace with you. I promise I'll be good," I beg like some well-mannered orphan boy living rough on the streets of London. I have no idea where that reference came from, but I'm sure it was something I was forced to watch as a kid.

"Darling, please. Buckingham's just for show. It's all about Windsor."

I giggle with her, more than pleased to see she's cheered up.

Hopefully last night was as fun for her as it was for me. I wasn't sure which movies she'd like so I picked my favourites and then a few I'd never seen before. Though as soon as I heard she'd never seen a Marvel film all the alternatives went outta the window. We did blind taste tests of every flavour of Skittle, and she thought I'd spent a fortune because she's apparently only ever seen these packets in the over-priced candy stores on Oxford Street. Then she proceeded to tell me all about some conspiracy theory she came up with after having only seen one season of "Ozark". She also said she'd show me around London if I ever visited. She doesn't know it yet, but that's an offer I'm going to take her up on the second I get the chance.

My powers worked a treat. That is until I suggested I

should go once I saw it was way past midnight – only because I thought I was overstaying my forced welcome, not because I actually wanted to. That was when I knew she was just as happy to have me there as I was to be there.

"What's she like? Daniel's girlfriend."

"Probably a cute nerd like him. I think he said she works in one of the makeup stores along the boardwalk."

She hums thoughtfully. "Speaking of girlfriends…"

I roll my head to look at her, knowing full well Maddison must have told on me. I want to tell Eliza the real reason I've never had one. With her, I feel like I could and it would be okay. But for the first time in I don't even know how long, I don't have to be the guy with the sick dad or the guy whose dad just died. I'm just me. And for now, I'm going to keep it that way.

"Guess I just never met the right girl." I shrug.

Maddison and I make our way back from the muster drill in eerie silence.

I like Maddison. She's a ball of energy and a real chatterbox, which is why her zipped lips are making me anxious. When we pass through one of the crew doors and head down an empty flight of stairs, she finally speaks up.

"Where were you last night? I came by to get you for breakfast, but you weren't there."

"I was with Eliza."

"Two girls in one weekend? I wonder what Polly will think."

Fuck. How does she know about her?

"Girls talk, Tom." She answers my unasked question when it takes me too long to reply.

So much for wanting to preserve the privacy of someone who clearly doesn't care about mine... I could try to deny it, but I know for a fact Maddison won't buy it. And unfortunately, my next outburst is enough of a confession anyway.

"You're throwing a lotta stones for someone living in a glass house," I say, realising too late I've done myself no favours. I'm not saying it to shame her about what she got up to on Friday; I'm just embarrassed as hell about what I did.

I fucked up.

Jealousy: 1. Good life choices: 0.

I should've gone back to my room. I would have had just as much fun there as I did with Polly. Which is to say I had none. Nothing personal – I just don't feel anything with women anymore. I actually don't think I've ever known what it's like to be *intimate* with someone. Even the word feels alien to me. I go through the motions, pretend I had a good time, and leave as soon as I can. And yet after just one kiss with Eliza, having to leave her – and maybe more to the point, leave her *with him* – sent me into a tailspin.

Then to hear nothing happened... I'm such a jackass.

I've experienced Eliza's restraint firsthand. I should've known she wasn't going to fuck the first person who showed interest. Unlike me. This place was supposed to be a fresh start, and I ruined it.

"Nothing happened with Eliza. It wasn't like that."

"What was it like then?" She pulls on another door at the bottom of the staircase and insists I step through first, which I do in order to buy myself every second possible to think before I speak.

"We just hung out and watched movies."

"Oh, so y'all Netflix-and-chilled?" She acts like she's caught me.

"No. Not everything is about sex, Maddison," I remind her.

"I'll believe *that* when I see it." She peers at me through the corner of her suspicious eyes.

"She needed a friend, that's all. I slept on the bottom bunk, for the record. Just ask Daniel – he and his girlfriend gave us an early-morning wake-up call."

"Give it time. No one can last a whole contract. Unless you're Harvey, apparently."

"Yeah, what's his deal?" I latch onto the change of subject like a fish on a line, both because I have a lot of unanswered questions about Harvey, but also because I'm not willing to unpack what she means by "give it time". "How is someone that friendly to guests, yet so distant to us?"

"I honestly have no clue. He doesn't let anyone in. I love him though. He works hard and looks out for everyone, a lotta the time in ways most people wouldn't even notice." She stops in the middle of the hall. "You know, I once heard a rumour. Whisperin's…" She's itching to tell me but stops herself. "No, I shouldn't spread this. I have zero evidence." She keeps walking.

"Hell no, you gotta tell me now." I'll take any dirt on this guy I can get.

"Fine." She stops again.

Well, that didn't take a lot of convincing.

Maddison lowers her voice. "There was a bartender on here who left like a week after Harvey and I started. Apparently, he knew Harvey from his last contract and told me he used to be a *real* party animal."

Interesting. I struggle to believe it though. He's got a stick so far up his ass he could be a corndog.

"And then he left! And by the time I had questions, there was no one to ask. I really wanna believe it, but then I take one look at him and know he's not that guy. I just can't see it. I've never seen him let loose. And I want to *so* badly!"

Me too, Maddison. Me too.

Racing down the I-95 – otherwise known as the main crew hallway – I make my getaway from the others in the bar and go in search of the other "sardines".

I hear her before I see her.

"Where are you going?" Without stopping, I grab her hand and pull her along behind me.

The echo of her giggle through the halls and the smell of her sweet perfume decorating the air rushing around us send a shiver through my body. I love how she doesn't wait for the answer and follows anyway, excited for whatever adventure I'm about to take her on.

Going off my hunch, I dart into the gym on our right. My shoulder pushes on the solid door, stalling our momentum. I catch Eliza when she falls onto my chest and hold her steady by the waist as we drift back into the room. In a dangerous slow-motion second, I see us fumbling with each other's clothes, suffocating in kisses. But I blink and the vision disappears. Something in her eyes tells me she saw it too though.

I head to the storage closet, knowing it's tightly packed with spare kit and chairs, which makes it the perfect space to hide in. The current occupants jump when I open the door before bunching up to make room for us to fit in with them. Eliza, though confused, enters the dark closet with me, and I reach past her to close the door again.

"What's going on?" she whispers to me.

"Sardines."

"Oh, well, why didn't you say!" Sarcasm makes her voice sparkle.

I wish I could tell her how much her sense of humour amuses me. When someone in the back shushes her, I want to smite them for even daring to shut her up.

"What the fuck is Sardines?" Her feisty words tickle my neck.

"Hide-and-seek, but we all hide together. Last one to find us loses. That okay with you, Queenie?"

"One more question. Why?"

"I've been banned from my room for...the foreseeable."

The door swings open, making all of us suck in a sharp breath. Everyone except Eliza. Nothing ever scares her. Our sardine school shifts to accommodate them, and that keeps happening for a while, a voice counting down how many players are left to find us with each new arrival.

I wrap my arm around Eliza protectively as the closet fills up and up and up. Her hands rest against my chest until she slides them around to my back. We settle into a hug, her head resting on my shoulder. It's dark in here, and even when the door swings open, letting the light in, there are too many bodies all crammed together to make our embrace look like anything other than a competitive necessity.

I don't know when it started, but her slow, scratching fingers find their way to my skin. My whole body breaks out in goose bumps at her touch, and with her being pressed up so hard against me there's no question she'll know exactly how much I like it if a part of me presses back harder. Everything will be fine so long as I don't think about the shower...

Great. Now I'm thinking about the shower.

My pants get tighter, but I refuse to give in to my intrusive thoughts. Even now, with her nails digging in that little bit harder. She knows. And she's making sure I know she does.

The door swings open for the last time this round, our final seeker now the lone Sardine. He gets a head start to hide, and people drift out of the closet one by one to seek him out. But even as more room becomes available, Eliza doesn't distance herself from me. Following in her footsteps, I dare to move my hands down her back until, in a bold play, they find the back pocket of her pants, waiting for a rejection that never comes.

Such a good ass.

One of her hands slips away from my back. I panic for a second that she's pulling away, but the opposite happens. She slips her hand into my pocket too. I squeeze her ass and her body writhes against mine. Her other hand, still on my back, tugs at my shirt. I'm not sure I'm gonna be able to wait for these final few people to get out before my needs take over.

She steps away when we become too obvious, and even though she's right to do so, I wish she wouldn't.

"You guys go. I'll catch Eliza up on the rules," I pledge to the last two sardines while they count down to their escape. These final few minutes of small talk have been agonising. I just want a moment alone with Eliza – is that too much to ask?

Not a second passes before my lips are on hers, devouring her, after the door shuts behind them. Her hands pull my neck closer, fingers tangling themselves in my hair. A small moan escapes her cotton-candy–flavoured lips between breaths that makes my dick throb. I sigh against her mouth. She giggles and pulls away from me, heading to the door.

"Hey, where are you going?"

"To play Sardines. Where else would I be going, Thomas?" Her voice twinkles with suggestion.

"I have a few ideas."

"Mmm. It's going to take some real convincing to make me forfeit my new favourite game." She pushes open the door and looks back with a playful smirk like a predator playing with its prey. "What are the rules?"

"This deck only. No cabins."

"Shame."

From the way her eyebrow twitches, I know her mind is filling itself with filth at the prospect of hiding in a cabin with me right now.

"Are you not joining me?"

"I think we both know I'm gonna need a minute," I reply.

Her eyes drop down to my pants, a smug grin tugging on her pink lips. There's fire in her eyes when they return to mine. "Don't be too long."

Watching her walk away adds a few more critical seconds to my wait time.

It isn't hard to track down the other players when I'm finally able to liberate myself. I overhear laughter coming from the library, only to find them all either smooshed under a mountain of beanbags, planking on top of shelves, or even *inside* the couch with the huge cushions positioned on their laps and in front of their chests. It's a lot of effort to then not even bother tucking their hands and legs in or burying their heads out of sight. It reminds me of the part in "Alice in Wonderland" when she outgrows the house.

A hand grabs my arm and tugs me behind a bookcase. Obi and a few of the actors are tucked up together.

"Who's left?" I ask when I can't see her.

"Just Eliza now," Obi replies.

An aggressive "shh" interrupts us. Approaching footsteps echo from the hall and then pause. My heart pounds a little harder at the prospect of being found, even more so knowing it's her. The footsteps restart, but they sound like they're walking away. Snickers break out around the room before someone calls out her name, everyone craning their necks to see her reaction.

When she steps into the library, her shoulders shrug with a deep breath, silently scolding herself for not bothering to inspect the room just now. "Bloody hell. I thought you actually had to *hide*, not just lurk in the corner of a room!"

Everyone laughs with her and begins to retreat from their spots.

"I was like, there's nowhere to hide in there. No *way* would they be that obvious."

She's so cute when she's pretending to be annoyed.

"Off you go, Little Britain. Last round," Obi hurries her.

She turns to go, but her feet don't move. She looks back. "You will come find me, right? I'm not going to be, like, abandoned waiting in some tiny cupboard alone for the rest of the night, am I?" Her eyes narrow with suspicion, but in them I see a hint of the loneliness I saw last night.

I'm just about to sweep her up in my arms and go with her when Maddison brushes past me, taking her by the hand. "Course, silly! But just to be positive, I'll join ya. I got too much dirt on these guys for 'em to even *think* about ditchin' us – ain't that right?" she threatens the room.

Maddison isn't capable of being malicious, and I know better than to believe she's as confident as she comes across. Deep down she's so scared of not being a part of a social scene again that she's *become* the social scene.

"Clock's ticking, ladies!" Obi says, spurring them both to hurry down the hall.

After a short head start, I follow next. I knew where they were going as soon as Maddison stepped forwards. She's made no secret of telling me who she's caught hooking up with whom in whatever room we've entered – not that she's into that sort of thing, apparently; she just loves a scandal. The only room she still hasn't discovered people in is the first place I look: the classroom. I find them just as they sneak into the storeroom, much to Maddison's frustration.

The three of us pile into the room, and in the dark, I dare to take Eliza's hand in mine. My dick instantly grows hard again. *What's gotten into me?* While waiting to be found, we make whispered conversation with Maddison as our fingers play with each other's.

The classroom door opens, and we fall silent.

"Yeah, I'm sure. She's obsessed with this room!" Valentina says before the storeroom door bursts open. Clearly, I'm not the only one Maddison overshares with. Behind Valentina's silhouette is another.

"There is *not* enough room in here for everyone," Obi complains before they both get in anyway.

He's right. The five of us can barely fit in here as it is, let alone when more soon follow. Eliza's up against the back wall, and all I want is to pin her against it and lose myself in her mouth again, but I keep my lust under control.

She shows less restraint.

With the others distracted talking about how great this hiding place is, Eliza's free hand sneaks up my shirt and her soft fingertips trail all over my skin. I lean down slightly and press my cheek against hers, breathing in the scent that lingers in her hair and on her neck the way I've been wanting to. I let go of her hand, unable to cope with the finger-fucking, and hold her waist, squeezing the perfect curve of it.

The door opens so suddenly I jump. Two of the actors force their way in, and we have no choice but to get even closer together. I turn Eliza away from me because I know I won't be able to stop myself from kissing her if we have to spend another second face-to-face. What I forget to consider, though, is how impossible it is to behave when her perfect ass is pressed up against my front. We could just about get a few inches away from each other if we tried.

But let's be honest, neither of us is trying.

She arches back, deliberately pushing her butt into me, and there's definitely no hiding my hard-on from her anymore. I tighten my grip on her waist as she grinds against me.

I get more excited each time the door opens with new players. My chest is now pressed firmly into Eliza's back, and I can't get enough of the sensation of her slowly wiggling against me. She takes my right hand off her hip and leads it around to her stomach before guiding it up and letting go. There's no doubt what she's after. My fingers skim over her tight T-shirt, swirling light circles on her nipples. Her shirt's just thin enough that I can feel the excited pebbles already waiting for me.

I lower my hand, and both of them then take great pleasure in sliding up the inside her clothes. Her skin is so soft it's as if she's made of silk. I squeeze her firmly over her bra. She squeaks, and we both freeze.

Shit.

"Ow, that's my foot! Budge up a bit, will you?" she covers quickly.

"Sorry! I've got Maddison's elbow digging into me." I pretend to fuss, but I'm told to shut up by everyone else immediately.

I think it worked.

I rub her nipples firmer through the fabric before taking both hands and pulling it down, freeing her incredible tits. I press my face into her neck and sink my teeth into her while squeezing. I almost want to make her squeak again.

Her body weakens with pleasure, but then her hand pulls one of mine down her stomach and dares me to go further. *Fuck.* She's so much naughtier than I thought she'd be, and I'd love to see just how far we can push this in here. But after teasing me like she did in the gym, I'm not giving in so easily.

I slip my hand inside the waistband of her pants but only graze my fingertips along her thighs, every now and then toying with the elastic of her panties but never giving my physical attention to what she wants. The same can't be said of me mentally. The longer I tease her, the more she writhes against me in frustration, but that only makes me pinch her nipples harder with my other hand.

Her patience – which was hanging on by a thread – finally comes loose, and she reaches behind her, taking hold of me through my pants. Her thumb lightly swipes over where I throb again and again, hypnotising me, and just as I'm about to cave and give her everything she wants, the door opens for the final time.

Game over.

"All right, Tom, this was fun, but can we drink now?" one of the many entertainment staff I dragged into this before they could even order a drink earlier asks.

"Yeah. He's gotta be done by now, right?" I reply, pretending *that's* the reason we're still playing this game. The space around me begins to free up as everyone files into the main classroom, and reluctantly, I separate my body from Eliza's.

Eliza's usually icy blue eyes are almost entirely black, her pupils looking like the dark side of the moon when we get to my cabin door.

"So what does the Queen make of Sardines then?" I ask, fetching the room key out of my back pocket.

"It was okay." She shrugs, acting indifferent. "Don't see what all the fuss is about."

"Mmm, I hear it's very popular among the peasants' children. I should have known that was beneath you. I'll work harder to impress you next time, ma'am." I grin so hard my cheeks hurt.

Her eyes drop down to the key in my hands. "You going to bed?"

"Mm-hmm. Unless you'd prefer I didn't?" I challenge. It hasn't gone unnoticed that so far she's only ever been able to tell me what she wants in the dark. I need her to be braver if this is going to go any further. Even if it means living with a permanent ache in my balls.

Please tell me not to go in there. Please grab the collar of my shirt and drag me to your room. Please look at me and tell me you want me the way I want you.

She takes a deep breath. "Night then." Her tight smile tells me she's disappointed, but why can't those same lips tell me that explicitly? Enthusiastic consent – that's all I'm looking for here.

"Night, Queenie."

"Oh, is that name sticking then?"

"Sure is."

She rolls her eyes the way she always does, with a smile that says "I like it", and sets off for her room.

I touch the key to the reader, waiting for the green flash and the beep. Nothing could prepare me for the sight I'm greeted with when I push open the door. A startled yelp leaps from my lungs, and any trace of swelling in my pants instantly diminishes.

Daniel's sweaty ass is on full display as he thrusts into the squealing woman underneath him. I recoil back into the hall as quickly as I can, hearing their shocked screams too and spotting Eliza looking back at me curiously.

"My bad!" I shout through the door, my hand holding it open just an inch so I can listen out for the scrape of the curtain on the bottom bunk as they cover themselves up.

Eliza tips her head to the side, gesturing I go with her, and if I had more power over my situation I'd continue to press her for a verbal invitation. But I'm in no position to negotiate now.

I knock on the door. "Can I just grab my toothbrush?"

"Sure, pal!" Daniel calls out. Averting my eyes just in case, I waste no time grabbing my toothbrush and picking up the clothes I'll need for tomorrow before rushing back out of the room. The slapping of skin on skin eases up but never fully stops all the while I'm in there.

"I'm happy for you, man," I say as I open the door and step out.

"I'm happy for me too," Daniel shouts back through the closing door.

I catch up to Eliza, who isn't hiding her satisfaction with the situation. "Scarred for life?" she asks.

"You have no idea."

We walk the rest of the way in weighted silence, my mind racing with all the possibilities of what might happen when we're alone.

"What's that smile for?" I ask when we get to her door.

She taps her card against the scanner. "I don't think Daniel and Gwen are the only ones who are going to have a sleepless night."

I'll take it.

Bursting through the door, I claim her. Her lips part to allow my tongue between them. I throw my things on the desk, freeing up my hands to feel every inch of her body. She claws at my shirt, and I tear myself away from her only to take it off and help her out of hers too. She groans softly as we overwhelm each other with kisses, and I groan too from the sensation of her skin against mine. She tugs on the front of my pants, fumbling with the zipper until they come loose. I free my legs of them as she removes her bra, her gorgeous blonde hair falling back down and covering her nipples.

For just a second we stare at each other, panting. Her eyes grow wide when she sees how close I am to bursting outta my boxers. She's so dang cute.

Brushing her hair to the side, I kiss her neck, doing everything in my power not to mark her. But shit, I could cover her in hickies. Unable to hold back any longer, I move my way down, taking her nipple in my mouth and indulging her – and myself – in warm, wet kisses. My hand takes the other, pinching the firmed nub. The squeak returns, but this time she doesn't silence herself. I moan against her delicate flesh before swapping to her other breast. She slips off her pants and I help her out of them, urgently returning my lips to hers.

Eliza strokes me over my boxers, and for a second I think I might pass out from excitement. "Do you have a condom?" she asks between kisses.

I hide my surprise by grazing her bottom lip with my teeth. I wasn't expecting her to want that tonight – or at all, if I'm really honest. From that smile in the hallway, I was hopeful for a makeout session and maybe some dry humping if I was really lucky. But sex? I mean, *yes, please.* Though part of me is scared to rush this. I'm scared she'll regret breaking that rule she came here ready to live by.

"Not on me. Do you?" I say into her lips.

She falters, her eyes peering up into mine with nothing other than disappointment.

Ah.

"I didn't…um. I wasn't planning to…"

"It's okay," I reassure her. This is a good thing. As much as I'm *dying* to know what she feels like wrapped around me, to please her in ways I hope she'll remember for the rest of her life, it's all happening too fast. "We don't have to—"

"Don't even *think* about suggesting we don't use one," she bites. It's the first time I've seen her stern and it's hot as hell.

"Whoa! Nope. Not what I was going to say," I correct her quickly, and she relaxes again. We both take a deep breath. I tuck a lock of hair behind her ear and hold her close, planting a kiss on her stressed forehead. "I was going to say…we don't have to do that tonight."

She nods in a slight daze. "Would you want to, if we had—?"

"Elizabeth, you have no idea how bad I want you."

Her eyes darken again.

"But I don't want to rush this. I want *you* to be sure you want this."

"I do. I really do." She nods eagerly, and I giggle while I kiss her again.

She eventually pulls away, the playfulness returning to her eyes before she walks into the bathroom. The sound of running water makes my pulse beat harder. She comes back into view, her eyes shining like diamonds as she runs her fingers over her pink panties. "You want to help me out of these?"

I catch my breath, instantly under her spell, and drift over to her. My eyes are locked on hers as my thumbs hook themselves in the soft material, sliding them down with ease. When they fall to the floor I can't help but look down at her body.

"Coming in, or would you prefer to watch?"

My brain is too scrambled to reply coherently. "Yes."

She grins and takes a scrunchie from beside the sink, tying her hair up in a messy bun before stepping under the stream, making sure to keep her head out of the way.

I take my time to admire her, watching on as warm water cascades down her slender body. Droplets bounce off her collarbone and over her beautiful tits. Her small waist is accentuated even more by the curve of her hips. I linger too long on the womanly V between her legs, but when I eventually drag my eyes away, it doesn't feel like long enough.

When I return my gaze to her eyes, I'm glad to learn the leering wasn't one-sided. I bask in her attention, almost losing my mind when her eyes drop to my crotch and her teeth instinctively bite her bottom lip. She raises her eyes to mine, looking back down and returning back up quickly. And though it's a silent request, I will gladly accept it.

I remove my boxers, grateful to finally be free of the restriction as I spring out of them. Her breaths become shallower as she watches me. I join her, my hands quick to wander up her sides.

Don't rush. I want to savour every minute.

Her hands slide up my now wet chest. She kisses me, water covering us both. Her lips are so fucking perfect and she tastes so damn sweet.

"We never should've left this shower," I say, and she sighs in agreement.

I grab her ass and press her body up against me, my stiffness poking us both in the stomach. She breaks away and her fingers trace down my body again, running teasing lines along the dips in my pelvis. She takes me in her small hands, and I shudder as she strokes me, but when she stops I open my eyes to notice a crinkle in her brow.

"You okay?"

Her lack of immediate response panics me. *Too soon.* I should've stayed in the bedroom. She's freaking out. I've rushed her even while giving it my best shot at slowing things down.

"It's okay, we can stop," I tell her quickly. "Let's stop."

"No, it's not that. Unless you actually want to stop."

"What is it?"

"I just…um…" She looks down at where she's cautiously wrapped around me. Her shoulders push forwards, going shy, her breasts squeezing together as she does.

Oh.

I suddenly remember what she said at the party. She's not used to guys like me. Jeez, the thought of being her first *anything* is so fucking hot.

"I don't know what feels good." Her voice is timid but husky with lust.

"Want me to show you?"

She nods.

I bring my palm to my mouth to wet it before rubbing the tip in circles and sliding my hand down and up my shaft. She wets her hand too and holds me again, sliding over the tip while she studies my face.

"Is that not too sensitive?"

I shake my head at her caring face and amaze myself with the groan I make when both her hands begin to stroke me. I take her face in my hands and kiss her deeply. As her grip gets firmer, my lips involuntarily fall away from hers to gasp at her quickening pace. She makes me weak. That devilish grin of hers has come back, and desire roars inside. It physically pains me to slow her down, but I can't let myself go this soon.

"Not yet." I take her wrists gently, requesting her release.

I hold her and continue to kiss her, warm water soaking

our lips. I allow my hands to move down her back, squeezing her round ass tightly. She giggles against my lips when a garbled sound of appreciation is all I can give her. I love making people laugh, but hers is the only one I care about.

Slipping my hands between us, I run the backs of my fingers over the exposed skin between her legs and watch her. I want her to want this too. Her eyes open when she realises I've paused. She nods with a smile before biting her lip and moaning softly when my fingers slide along the line of her pussy. She's slick, and not from the shower.

I bring my hand up to my mouth and suck my fingers, humming with enjoyment as I do. Heaven. This is what heaven tastes like. She swallows hard at the sight. I return my fingers back to her and watch for the hitch in her breath when I find her sensitive spot. I circle my middle finger against her swollen clit, and she whimpers even though I'm barely applying any pressure.

Eliza takes me in her hands again, and even as she struggles to stay upright from my teasing, her strokes make my head spin.

"More. *Please*," she whispers, her eyes looking up at me as if I'm the only person in the world who can help her.

My cock throbs at her plea, and I press the slightest bit firmer. "Like this?"

"Mm-hmm. There," she groans softly, and all of a sudden her eyes widen and her voice is strong. "*There*. Fuck, don't stop, Tom. Please don't…" Her voice wavers again, her hands wrapping tighter around me as she begins to unravel. God only knows how, but I find the strength to focus on her even while immense pressure builds within me. I stay consistent, desperate to give her what she wants. "*Tom*," she gasps, her whole body tensing as if she's just about to fall.

And then her eyes shut tight and her brow creases deeper,

her teeth sinking into her bottom lip until it turns white. She shudders in waves, which only makes her grip on me fucking mind-blowing. Without a doubt, she is the hottest thing I have ever witnessed.

She works me faster. Fuck. I thought she didn't know what to do with a guy like me, but this is *unreal*.

"I'm gonna…" is all I manage to say before spilling onto her skin. When I open my eyes, she's beaming her perfect little grin back at me, seemingly getting as much joy out of watching me come as I did watching her.

I pull her into me to kiss her smiling lips before reaching for the body wash to clean her up. Her slippery skin is all too much to handle. I need to see her come again.

Just as I touch her, she screams, but sadly not because of me this time. Ice-cold water rains down on us, and we both jump out from under the downpour. I rush to turn off the tap. Her nipples tighten and she shivers while she catches her breath. We laugh like we did the other night, and my heart is the fullest it's felt in years.

"Come on – let's get you warm," I say, reaching for a towel to wrap her up in. Once I've put it over her shoulders, she stretches her arms wide and bundles me in with her, pressing her lips to mine.

I could kiss this girl all night.

And I do.

I've never been the type to stick around. In high school, it was because I knew it was Bobby the girls really wanted; I only ever got his castoffs. I was the scrawnier twin, the goofier twin, the star of the football team's twin. Girls would settle for me, so I never settled for them.

Then, in college, even after I started hitting the gym, I couldn't face going on dates. I never wanted to burden someone with the sadness of my home life. I couldn't get to know anyone without dragging all my baggage along with me. Plus, I didn't want to waste what little time I had left with Dad on some chick who would only leave me once she figured out I wasn't the good-time guy I pretended to be.

I don't have to pretend with Eliza. On day one she barely knew me, but she helped me. I was so far outta my comfort zone, but she made it comfortable. That's how Dad always said he could cope with the cancer, even at its worst, because having Mom there made everything comfortable.

He's the real reason I'm here. No matter how much I denied it, he knew deep down I was holding back from living the life I would be if he weren't sick. I didn't take a year off to travel with my friends. I didn't go to my dream college. I wanted to be nearby in case there was an emergency. But I could pursue my other passion. I'd perform my stand-up routines to him and his pals in their hospital beds and then show them all the videos after I performed them to a crowd so they could hear how every joke landed on the night. They were who I was really hoping to entertain. I didn't care what a room full of strangers thought of my jokes; so long as it made Dad and the other patients laugh, that was all that mattered.

One day when I went to visit him, he sat me down with his friend who told me all about his life as a cruise ship entertainer. Dad said that was what I should be doing, not some dumb course I didn't care about. I really wanted to care. I really tried to. I knew studying psychology and eventually becoming a therapist was how I could do what I was good at: making people happy.

"But would it make *you* happy, son?"

For the need of one stable thing in my life, I ignored his advice and stuck out college for a while longer, finding joy in my regular gigs at college bars, but not much else. It took some time for the world to start spinning again after Dad died, and even when it did, I felt as if I was standing still. But I knew exactly what I had to do to start moving again. Entertain. I dropped outta college and spent my days writing jokes and my nights playing the local circuit. It might've made me *happy*, but after a few months, it made me poor as hell. That was when I applied for a job here.

I never used to believe in signs, but something aligned in mine and Eliza's lives for us to end up on the same ship, working in the same department, starting on the same day. Dad promised he'd look out for me, and I can't help but think her appearance in my life has something to do with him.

She wakes up with the same fear I've had ever since I got here. Except for this morning. Her body – completely naked except for some cute panties that can't contain her ass – is tangled up with mine in this narrow bed. The stress leaves her; she appears comforted by my presence. And her smile – *that smile* – shines as bright as ever.

"Morning," she says, nuzzling her lips into the sheets.

"You sleep okay?" I ask, and she nods, burying her head more. "Why are you hiding from me?"

"I've got morning breath."

"Don't care."

"You should."

"I want it." I pester her cheek with kisses. "Gimme your morning breath. I want it." I finally find her lips, and the tightness of them quickly relaxes.

She overpowers me, and the next thing I know, her warm thighs are straddling me. I run my hands along them before giving my favourite part of her body a firm squeeze. Her breasts fall over me, moving freely as she starts to slowly grind her hips against my already firm dick. Eliza leans in, kissing my cheek, my earlobe, and my neck.

"Fancy a trip over to your room?" she purrs.

"I think there'd be several complaints to HR if I went anywhere with this rock-hard *weapon* right now."

She bursts out laughing.

"Someone in a hurry?" I taunt her.

She stops moving and lets out an adorable grumble. "Want."

"Mmm, well, now I've seen how hot you are when you want something, I might just make you wait *even* longer."

She pouts and carries on grinding on me. *Fuck.*

"How about we take a trip to a pharmacy on port today and get you stocked up? Or...there's always the commissary when it opens."

Her eyes widen like she'd die of embarrassment.

"Pharmacy it is."

Her rhythm picks up, and from the friction coupled with her pleasing sighs, it's hard to think about anything else. I twist onto my side to make enough room for her to lie down. My fingers tease her lightly through her panties. She's already so wet. I pull the soft cotton to the side, and it isn't long before my finger enters her, her soft moans warming my neck. Her pussy is so sensitive to my touch it barely takes any time for her to shatter.

She kisses me hard on her comedown.

"You know what you've done now, though, don't you?" she asks, her breathing irregular.

"What's that?"

"You've just made me want more."

ELEVEN

ELIZA

I don't know what it is, but being around Tom makes me want to let loose again. I didn't notice how uptight and closed off to everything I'd become until I met him. It's been so long since I had any fun I honestly forgot how good it felt. How good a lot of other things felt. And no, not just sexy things, but the way he wanted to be around me the other night even though I clearly wasn't going to be good company. No one's ever wanted to look after me before.

I know it's probably stupid to, but I trust him.

You also thought you could trust Twatface, and look how that turned out.

I'm next to Oscar filling up a bowl with granola when two girls approach the opposite side of the circular island. My body tenses when I recognise one of them from the party in my room. The delightful Harley Quinn. A small pang of jealousy pounds in my chest, but I force myself to ignore it. Especially since while Tom was undressing her in that game, I was undressing someone else. Plus, she didn't just have the night with Tom that I did.

"You've been in an awfully good mood lately, Polly," the girl I don't recognise says to her.

"I got a delivery on Friday," she replies.

A daring look lights up the other girl's eyes. "What did you order?"

"It was a substantial package."

"Express delivery?"

Polly smirks. "No, it took its time to arrive."

"Sign here if you're satisfied with the service you received." The curious friend holds out her hand, and Polly signs the girl's palm with her finger.

Hiding my amusement at their postal euphemisms, I trade places with Oscar beside me and quietly make up a small bowl of fresh fruit.

"Would you like to sign up for a subscription service to have this package delivered to you on a regular basis?"

"Absolutely. I'm seeing him tonight as a matter of fact."

The friend squeals with excitement. "And finally, would you recommend the service to a friend?"

"No, back off! He's mine!" Polly snaps like she's joking, but it's as clear as day she means it.

"Oh, go on then, you tease. Who's the mailman?"

Polly looks up to where Oscar and I are. I quickly avert my gaze and pretend I'm not listening. She whispers something I don't manage to catch.

"What! Tom?"

"Shh!" Polly's eyes flick to mine under her lashes for the briefest of seconds, and all the blood in my veins sears me.

"Crikey! Well done, girl. He is *fit*."

My cheeks flush hot with humiliation and my fingers tremble as I pick up my tray and, on unsteady legs, find a table. I feel sick. How could I have been so fucking stupid? Of course he lied. Everyone fucking lies. Here I was thinking

166

he was special, but really, he's just a two-timing prick like every other guy I fall for.

Idiot. Idiot. *Idiot*.

Oscar calls my name like it's not the first time he's tried to get my attention. "Tea?"

I nod, but I'm going to need something stronger to get through today.

I toy with the idea of not getting off the ship this afternoon, but the alternative is sitting alone in my room feeling sorry for myself, and the last place I want to be right now is my room. To think I was so excited this morning knowing my sheets would smell like him. Not only that, I was planning to be twisting them with him all night.

Now I just want to burn them.

I've been dying to go exploring ever since I got here, and I'm not going to let some love rat ruin my first day out.

The only redeeming thought was that Oscar and I could break away from Maddison and Tithead Tom, with or without the others, and enjoy the afternoon together. But he's had to stay behind for some meeting, so I'm stuck with them. And now I think about it, maybe that was wishful thinking anyway. It's not like Oscar and I have hung out much socially outside of working hours. I doubt he even considers me a friend. Why would he? Things haven't exactly been all that comfortable between us after what happened on Friday. He's been perfectly professional, but that's just it: *professional*.

I can't blame him though. One minute he was almost kissing me, and the next I was in a shower *actually* kissing someone else. He probably hates me as much as I hate Tithead. What was I thinking?

Well, I wasn't. That's the problem.

I engross myself in deep conversation with Daniel about board games until we all reach a cafe just so I don't have to talk to Tom. A huge "free Wi-Fi" vinyl sticker decorates the window of a small cafe not far from where the ship's docked. Everyone begins to head inside, but I hold back. I don't want to call home, and I certainly don't want to be in close quarters with Tom right now. In the hope of sneaking off unnoticed, I keep walking down the street.

"Elizabeth?"

Fuck. Off. Tithead.

I keep walking away pretending I didn't hear him, but he calls out again, and on his third attempt I have no choice but to give in. I turn back to him, poker-faced. He's jogging over. I hope he trips.

"You not coming in?"

I shake my head. "Nah, gonna go find the pharmacy," I lie.

A boyish grin slides across his face, and I want to drag him there so I can scrub it off with the roughest loofah I can find. "Really can't wait, huh?"

Can't wait to never see you again, yeah.

"Come grab a shake real quick and I'll go with you after. Maddison hasn't stopped talking about this place. I won't hear the end of it if I don't check it out."

"No, it's okay. I've got to pick up a few bits anyway," I lie again, hoping the mere hint of shopping for toiletries is enough to deter him – and thankfully, it is.

"Okay. We're gonna hit the beach after, I think. You'll come find us?"

"Mm-hmm." I nod, forcing the tiniest smile I can muster, and instantly I know I haven't fooled him.

Good. Let him stew in it.

"What drinks y'all want?" Maddison hangs out of the cafe door to shout over to us.

Saved by the belle.

"Just a minute," he shouts back. He tries to read me, and I hate it. "Everything okay?"

Don't pretend to give a shit now. If you really cared, you wouldn't be leading on two girls at once.

"Yeah." I inflect my voice to make it sound like I'm confused about his concern.

He doesn't look the slightest bit convinced.

"Eliza," he whispers, taking hold of my waist, but I twist out of his grip when Maddison shouts over to us again. He turns back to her, and I use this as my opportunity to escape.

"See you later," I say before hurrying off, hoping he won't stop me again because I can't stand the sight of him, but most importantly, so he can't see the tears that have started rolling down my cheeks.

I don't know how long I've been walking for by the time I come to what seems like the endpoint of the beach. Large boulders block my path, and I turn back to check I can still see the ship behind me – which I can, of course, even in the distance. It's not exactly hard to miss.

I take in the view: clear blue skies, even clearer water, sand so clean it's almost white, and luscious greenery growing freely all around me. There's not a shred of imperfection in sight. I should be overwhelmed with a sense of awe and immense gratitude to be in this perfect postcard of paradise, but instead I'm too furious to care. With Tom, sure, but more so with myself. I had *one* rule. I was meant to stick to it and I didn't, and I got hurt.

I have no friends to reach out to back home for a distraction. My sister has much more important things to spend her time on than me, and it's not something I can talk to the other members of my family about. Any friends I thought I'd made here are probably all laughing behind my back in my absence. *Not that I care.* I'm fine on my own.

Fine, she says, sitting on a rock so hot it's burning her arse. I hug my knees and sob into them like a child.

Things were meant to be better here. I promised myself they would be. Turns out my promises mean about as much as I do to Tom.

I don't expect him to have wifed himself off to me after a week. Friday was a mess. *I* was a mess. I was being pulled in three different directions, but *as soon as* I made that choice with him during Seven Minutes in Heaven, I put everything else on pause. I didn't pick up where Oscar and I left off before the party – not when an entire room full of people were screaming at me to, and not even when we were alone and could have done whatever we wanted to without people knowing. No, I waited. I waited until I was sure of my feelings before I did anything else because fooling around with more than one person while they think – no, they're *told* – they're the only one is deceitful and cruel and wrong.

Serves me right for thinking I could trust someone again.

With more makeup applied to my pink and puffy face than usual, and with my uniform on, I swing mindlessly out of my room only to slam into a wall of muscle before the door even clicks shut behind me.

"Whoa." Oscar steadies himself and catches me from stumbling back. "Good timing." He chuckles as he recovers from the shock, and even though I'm dead inside, I feel a little less miserable just for hearing his laugh again.

We begin making our way through the corridors and upstairs to the main pool deck.

"Did you have a nice time off the ship?"

"I did, thanks. How was your meeting?"

"Good, actually. Shame I couldn't show you around though. There's an amazing ice cream stand about halfway down the beach I wanted to take you to. Did you see it?"

I didn't. That's not to say I didn't pass it. I'm now thinking about what I did see, but nothing springs to mind because I spent most of the time with my head down. What a stupid thing to do.

"Don't think so."

"Bet Maddison made you all get smoothies at that internet cafe instead."

"Yep." I force a sarcastic "how did you know?" face.

"Shocker," he jokes.

We reach the main deck and loiter, waiting for the Sail Away Party to start.

"You look like you've caught the sun though," he says.

"Do I?"

"Yeah." His soft eyes study my face. "Your cheeks are a bit pink."

It's definitely not from sunburn, but I don't correct him. "I'll get some aftersun on that later then."

I work hard to keep us away from everyone else when they start to emerge, avoiding eye contact at all costs. But that doesn't stop Maddison from strutting over and pulling me to one side.

"Wanna tell me what's goin' on with you and Tom?"

"Nothing's going on."

"I saw that hand on your waist, missy. Plus, he spent all

afternoon lookin' out for ya. I'm not here to judge – I just wanna know you're okay."

"Never better."

"Oh, so you ditched our day out for nothin'?"

I stumble while thinking of an answer.

She pushes an impatient breath out through her nose. "Lemme guess, you liked him, he told ya he's already slept with someone, and now—"

"Wait – you knew?"

"Why d'ya think I cockblocked you so hard on Saturday? Sorry, I should've told ya I took Challenge too seriously."

I sigh, realising how dumb I must have looked.

"I'm in a million different inner circles. It's not your fault you didn't know."

I know; it's his. *Because he told us he didn't fuck anyone.*

My heart feels like it's been stamped on. He had sex with her – what, half an hour after kissing me in the shower? That hurts me all over again. What the *actual* fuck? I'm so stupid to have thought that meant anything. Did the nights afterwards mean nothing to him either?

"You know, slut-shaming's really not in these days."

"I'm not— That's not why I— He can sleep with whoever he wants."

"Really?"

"Of course he can." I look out over the water. "He just can't lie and lead us both on at the same time," I mutter.

"That just don't make sense. He's *so* into you."

"He's really into her too. She said she's got plans with him tonight."

"Oh, Tom. Whatcha doin'?"

My cheeks ache from the fake smile that's been glued to my face for the past half an hour. I have every intention of disappearing before the gang congregates, but being buddied up with Schmoozey McGee over here has hindered that plan. I smile sweetly by Oscar's side as he makes meaningless chit-chat with a couple I've never seen before but may as well have. I'm not even two weeks in and already the passengers are starting to look the same.

We break away from them and make it as far as the crew staircase before I hear my name echoing off the walls above us.

Tom.

"Eliza, wait up."

He used my real name again. Good – he's panicking.

Oscar slows down behind me, but I have no intention of stopping. Before I can turn down the next flight, I catch sight of Tom, his legs moving a mile a minute to catch me.

"Hey."

"Hey," I say flatly as I keep descending, making him walk with me.

"Where did you go earlier?"

Excellent. Oscar's just caught me in a lie.

"Just for a walk."

"You said you'd come back."

"I lost track of time." I keep walking away, but he jogs down a few steps ahead of me and blocks my – and subsequently Oscar's – path.

"I was worried about you." He looks up at Oscar as if *he's* the one interrupting us.

"I'll come grab you for dinner," Oscar offers politely before continuing down the stairs. I want to scream, "Please don't leave me alone with him!" but, unsurprisingly, I don't.

Tom looks at me seriously while all that goes through me

is unadulterated loathing. Ugh, why am I even wasting time on someone who doesn't know who Elphaba is?

"Is everything okay?"

Don't give me this shit. You know what you're doing. "Why wouldn't it be?" The jig is up. Time to come clean, grovel, *beg* me to understand.

"I'm not sure, but I feel like you're mad at me."

I don't reply. I just blink and wait for him to confess as other people pass us.

"If this is about last night—"

I flinch, painfully aware we aren't in the privacy of a cabin right now.

He lowers his voice. "Or this morning…"

"Can we just forget it?" I go to walk past him, but he doesn't let me, so now I'm just one step above him, our eyes finally level, providing the perfect spot for me to watch as the hurt creases his face.

He stutters as he pieces things together. "Eliza, if I did anything that made you uncomfortable—"

"No. That's not what this is about."

"Then what is it about?" His arms leave his sides briefly with the question.

Why do boys always make you spell it out to them? Is it because they're too busy flicking through an entire encyclopedia of their wrongdoings and they're scared to confess to something you haven't caught them doing yet? Or are they just that obtuse? Some simple self-reflection should make it abundantly obvious. *Retrace your steps back to when you thought you could get away with this. Come on, Tom – you can do it.*

"What time do you finish tonight?" I bait him.

"Nine, I think." He fumbles to get the schedule out of his

pocket when I don't reply to his vague answer. "Yeah, 9.15 p.m."

"Shall we meet up then?"

"Okay." He's still on edge, but there's the slightest shift in his stance that tells me he's relieved.

"Sure?"

"Yeah."

"So are you cancelling on her or meeting up with her afterwards?"

He crumples up his face with supposed confusion. "Who?"

"Polly."

Watching the penny drop is unbelievably satisfying.

"Eliza, I can explain."

"Don't bother. I won't believe you." I sidestep past him and stride down the steps without looking back.

For the first time today, he doesn't follow me.

TWELVE

OSCAR

Not hungry, she says. Tough. I'm not leaving without her.

"That's okay, just come with me so I don't have to eat alone. I'm gonna go upstairs. Not in the mood for curry tonight." Not true – curry night's my favourite, but I'm not about to let her starve because she doesn't want to bump into a certain someone. I don't know the details, but it doesn't take a genius to piece things together.

Though the same can't be said for her. One minute I think I've got her sussed out, and the next she's flipping my entire perception on its head.

There's a timidness to her – I notice it in the way she stands by my side, either waiting obediently for instruction or bracing herself for feedback. She's careful not to speak until she's spoken to – something I'm hoping to drum out of her, because when she speaks, everybody wants to listen. And yet for all that shyness, when she steps onto a stage or gets a microphone, it's as if a switch flicks and she shines.

Her talent for on-the-spot observational comedy is enviable. She knows exactly how to work a room. I've watched so many people try, but they just end up making one person the butt of every joke and it quickly gets uncomfortable to watch. But Eliza has this way of including everyone and making them feel like they're part of it.

I've made a point of talking to guests far more than I usually would because everyone wants to shower her with compliments. Even when I'm not with her, the regular passengers come up to me to tell me how lovely she is.

I want nothing more than for her to believe in herself, because everybody else does.

I almost didn't recognise her on Friday. Unexpected costume aside, that performance she pulled off was so different from what I was expecting. It was outstanding. But I think that's her – the real her. If she lets herself be. They could have played it safe, but instead they went against the grain to show us all what they could do. It takes a lot of courage to do that.

"I've had fun with you this week."

She'll never know how much it meant to hear those words. I thought it was going to be harder to restrain myself when I first joined the ship, but it wasn't. Advances were made, but it was easy to refuse them. And then she said that.

Even though it stung hearing their squeals from the bathroom at the party and watching her need him on Sunday and not me, I honestly thought it was for the best. Tom's a nice guy, and I didn't want to complicate the trainer/trainee dynamic between me and Eliza. Though, unfortunately, he's just like every other new starter: overwhelmed and lonely, which in turn manifests as horny and stupid. I can hardly judge. I just wish he didn't have to involve her.

The food upstairs is irresistible, and I'm glad to see it doesn't take long for Eliza to relinquish her hunger strike. It isn't hard to find a private spot in the dining area at this time of night when there's so much else for the guests to be doing besides eating.

"What's your dream role?" she asks.

Despite having spent plenty of time together, we've not had much time to talk properly. It's all been about the ship or the basic getting-to-know-you questions. Anything past that and we always end up getting interrupted, either by guests or the others and their antics.

"Elder Price, 'Book of Mormon' or…J.D., 'Heathers'."

"That's a bit of a shift." She studies me, her initial shock waning. "Yeah, I could see that, actually."

"Yeah?"

"Mmm, you've got that 'mysterious and brooding' thing going on."

"Mysterious and brooding?" No wonder she doesn't feel like she can open up to me.

"Oh, is that not what you were going for? Because you're nailing it." The playful glimmer returns to her eyes.

"Not quite, but it's better than half the things people call me on here, so I'll take it."

"What do people call you?"

"If you don't know by now, I'm sure you'll find out soon enough."

"Ooh, mysterious." She quirks a smile, and I can't help smiling back.

"What's *your* dream role?"

"Well, now mine's gonna sound like I'm trying to impress you."

"Are you?"

"Li'l bit, but not enough to change my answer."

"Appreciate the honesty. Go on then."

"Veronica, 'Heathers'."

To kiss her and have a script to hide behind. *Hmm.* Why

did we have to get interrupted on Friday? It's all I've been able to think about since.

"I'm not one for type-casting, but you'd be a very good Veronica."

"Right? I mean, I'm basically her already. Socially awkward, tick. Terrible taste in friends and men, tick." Her cheeks flush as if she spoke without thinking, as if this is a conversation she's had before, which is highly possible given this is a favourite topic of conversation for us luvvies, and it makes me now certain of two things: Tom was a terrible choice; and he isn't the first guy to hurt her. As for her friends? I don't like this one bit. "And I look great in blue." She tucks an imaginary lock of hair behind her ear with the fake boast, which makes me laugh.

"Incredibly accurate. I'll give my old agent a call, set up a meeting."

"Fantastic. I'll be waiting for the call."

"Though I should let you know, they have a strict 'no method acting' policy."

"Really? Damn. I was just about to start committing a string of murders against the people who've crossed me."

"Best get hiding those Ich Lüge bullets you brought on with you."

"And the drain cleaner."

We laugh for a while and the mood lightens. This is one of the first times she's treated me more like a peer than her superior – which I'm not, for the record. But the way she stiffens around me and pauses to think before she speaks, she clearly sees me as someone who's judging or assessing her. And yes, I'll be asked to give my opinion at the end of training, but seeing as I'm responsible for her success, it'll only reflect badly on me if I don't think she's good at her job. Not that I'll be saying anything close to that when the time comes.

"You okay?" I ask and immediately scold myself for doing so in case she tenses up again. But if she's just lost the one person she thought she could talk to here, I need to work harder now more than ever to show her I'm here for her. It's not because I want to pry. I hope she knows that.

She takes a deep breath. "Yeah." She sighs and nods, not going into any more detail but not denying anything or shutting me out either. She presses her lips together tightly.

"Don't be too hard on yourself. No one else will be."

She smiles with appreciation and takes a sip of tea, instantly frowning at the taste of the Earl Grey that was long overdue. Since her first morning, it's become a daily battle to wind the other up with the wrong tea. Not that I have anything against normal tea, I just pretend to because I like seeing the joy she gets from being sneaky. Though it goes without saying I made her English Breakfast this morning.

"What's wrong with you, boy?" She tuts.

"Forgot. I'll remember next time." I won't. Our tea wars are my favourite part of the day.

After dropping Eliza back to her room, I head down the hall to mine. It's refreshing spending time with her, especially after giving her space these past few days. The other entertainment staff are great, but it's hard work keeping up with them at times. They don't get me, and I'm okay with that. There are days I don't get this new me either.

Acting made me self-centred. For too long I walked around thinking I was God's gift. If I could go back and never take that role in "Grease", I would in an instant.

That show was my undoing.

People treated me differently just because I was the

leading man. The cast, the guests, the other crew. The brown-nosing was constant, and the worst part was I believed it all. I got home and didn't understand why there wasn't a queue of directors booking me for their next show. I blamed my agent, harassed them into getting me auditions, and then turned down the ones I thought were beneath me. Safe to say Mum was appalled with my attitude; she said I was turning into my dad, which should have been the wake-up call I needed, but I was too stubborn to listen. Instead it took the humiliation of being rejected for all the leading parts I went for and only getting callbacks for the chorus – if I was lucky – for me to see how entitled I'd become, and I hated myself. So I did the only thing I knew how. I ran back to Mum to get her to put me back together again like the pathetic idiot I was. I tasked her with my emotional labour because I couldn't take enough responsibility to do it myself. I learnt from that – big time.

It took a while to work out what I wanted to do next. It wasn't as if I could move out. I was meant to be flush with cash considering I'd had six months of no rent, no bills, and no food costs, but I'd spent pretty much everything I'd earned at the bar or on big days out with my castmates. I didn't want to wait tables until I landed my next big break. Partially because my ego couldn't take it – though it deserved it – but mostly because I didn't think I wanted a big break anymore. I'd already had it and I'd turned into a monster.

Months went by while I hunted for all kinds of jobs, not once letting myself genuinely consider the other jobs available to me on ships, but it was all I kept coming back to. I love cruising, even if I take the acting gig away from it. It's a way for me to be by the sea but not to stay stuck in my hometown. Plus, I can put my degree to good use in a different capacity. Understandably, Mum was sceptical, but I promised her things would be different. And sure, I've not quite got it right this time – for the opposite reason – but it's a definite improvement.

"Harvey!" one of the few people who's never stopped inviting me to things, despite me never turning up to them, calls out.

I take two steps back to look down the adjacent corridor and find Obi scribbling something on the crew message board with Valentina. "What's this?" I ask, walking over to them.

"Scavenger sign-ups." Obi's eyes light up with devious excitement.

"You going for it?"

"Oh, hell no, honey!"

I look at the sheet and my heart thumps hard when I see he's already put Eliza's name down. "Have you asked her about this?"

"We'll tell her later."

"Is that a good idea?"

Scavenger isn't something to sign up for lightly. But he ignores me, leaning in to write another name.

"Who else are you putting down?"

"Tom."

I slap my hand on the sheet. "No," I say more forcefully than intended.

Both of them stare at me in shock, and if I could, I'd stare at me too. I've never voiced my opinion like that here. A suspicious look passes between them. They're going to read into this, aren't they?

"You need at least one person who knows the game," I say to cover for my outburst.

"Thank you! This is what I've been saying." Unbelievably, Valentina takes my side.

"Ugh. Fine. Who then? *Harvey*?" Obi suggests sarcastically to her as if I'm not here.

"No, he's as stiff as a dead guy. No offence. We need someone who's going to get stuck in, not be too polite to do anything."

"I did it on Deity."

The mention of my last ship's name gets their attention.

"And we won," I add in case that wasn't enough.

They both look gobsmacked. And I don't blame them. Why am I trying so hard to prove myself? I've never cared before now.

"Well, fuck. Kept that quiet."

"I don't think I even know you anymore." Obi shakes his head at me in a daze. "So you'll do it?"

"Okay."

"What, *really*?"

"Sure, and I'm going to tell her exactly what it is that you two have signed her up for in the morning so she can make an informed decision."

"Oh yeah? And how's that gonna go? 'Hey, Eliza, last night I signed us up to a gameshow where we'll almost instantly be stripped down to our underwear and made to dry hump each other all night. Valentina and Obi tried to sign someone else up, but I insisted I do it with you.'"

I grind my teeth.

"Or will it be more, 'Valentina and Obi tried to sign you up for the event of the season, but I denied you that opportunity because I'm" – Obi places a hand on his chest and looks at Valentina, pretending to be confused – "*jealous*'? That's what's happening, isn't it, V? I'm not making that up."

"Yep, that sounds about right," she agrees.

They've got me over a barrel, and they know it.

"Leave it to us, Harvey. We'll tell her what she needs to know. If you go in there *asking* her, she'll be too embarrassed to say she wants to do it. You want her to want it, don't you?"

I gulp, still trying to figure a way out of this. And failing. "For the record, I think this is a very bad idea."

For the past few months, I've been determined to stay out of trouble. I've shut myself away and focused on work. Until last week it was easy. But after this next Friday night, it's going to be almost impossible.

"How was the interview yesterday, darling?" Mum's voice has a weird way of making me miserable with homesickness while comforting me at the same time.

I sit up in bed, running a hand through my hair. "Yeah, it went really well, thanks."

"When do you find out?"

"Couple of weeks, I imagine."

"If anyone deserves it, love, it's you."

"I don't know about that."

"Oh, Oscar. Would it kill you to believe in yourself for five minutes?"

"I can't be too sure."

Mum sighs. "Keep me posted."

"Will do."

"Photo stream's been good lately." She changes the subject. "Nan's always telling me what you're up to like I don't see it too."

"I know. She even tells *me*." Nan comments on every single picture I post on the shared album. Usually something about what a handsome young chap I'm growing up to be, quickly followed by my sister, Gemma, saying something to the contrary. It's a nice way to keep in touch. I should have done it on my first ship, but I was too caught up in it all to share anything. We do so much every day and go to so many beautiful places, I felt selfish not sharing it with them all – especially now Nan can't really get out and about anymore.

Weekly calls to Mum are also part of the "don't be a bellend" plan we came up with. Seeing how abandoned she felt when I got back from my first contract was awful. It wasn't the "my boy's all grown-up now" kind of abandoned either; I had well and truly ignored her for six whole months as if I were too important now to check in back home. Like a bellend.

"Who was that girl next to you in the last photo?"

Here we go. "Which photo?"

"You were all dressed up like movie stars."

"What, Maddison?"

"Ahh, so you do like her."

"Mum, we've been over this. I don't have a thing for Maddison."

"I know who Maddison is, you daft bugger. I'm not talking about her. I mean the adorable little blonde you have your arm wrapped around."

Ah.

"Pretending she doesn't exist as a form of deception is the oldest trick in the book."

I couldn't pretend she doesn't exist even if I tried. And I wouldn't want to try.

I laugh it off. "I've known her for a week."

"Your great-grandmother was married and pregnant with Nan inside a few months of meeting my grandad."

"Yes, but sex before marriage was frowned upon back then, and they were just a couple of horny teenagers."

"Oscar!"

"Just saying."

"All right, smarty pants. She looks like one of the nice ones, that's all."

"Yes, she's nice," I admit, causing her to coo. "Mum, please. I'm keeping my head down like we talked about."

"I know, darling. I just hate the idea of you being lonely out there."

"I'm doing okay, I promise."

Eliza makes a break for her room after dinner.

"Nope, we're not done just yet."

Her eyes fill with dread thinking there's another activity to run.

"Not work-related, don't worry," I assure her.

She eases but remains confused.

"Come on." I walk away knowing she'll follow.

"Where are we going?"

"You'll see."

"Not mysterious *my arse*," she mumbles.

"What was that?" I ask, both of us knowing full well I heard her.

"Nothing!" She smiles sweetly, and I fight back a smile of my own.

Every Wednesday, I and a few of the actors and dancers get together and play around with songs from various musical theatre shows. I remember how fed up everyone would get singing the same songs and doing the same dance routines for months on end on the various jobs I've done, but we never did anything about it. So when I got here and saw the actors going as stir-crazy as I once did, I thought this would be a fun idea. Plus, it's nice for me to dip my toe in every now and then.

I open the door to the rehearsal studio and wait for Eliza to step inside before me, but she freezes.

"What is this?"

"Come sing with us."

She may as well have just coiled up like a hedgehog. "You're joking right?"

I shake my head, confused. I thought she'd like this.

"But I'm not as good as them."

"Doesn't matter." I smile at her. I want to tell her she's wrong, but I've never heard her sing, and if I'm going to give compliments, they have to be genuine. Another bad habit from my past I've shaken off.

"Do they know I'm coming?"

"They do now."

She looks into the room again to see everyone's friendly eyes on us. "I don't want to impose," she whispers.

"You're not." And with that, I walk in. "Hope you don't mind – I brought a guest."

I was intimidated by them at first too, so I know exactly what she's thinking. Full-blown imposter syndrome. I felt embarrassed to come here as an entertainer and not a member of the cast before quickly realising how much more fulfilling and rewarding this job can be.

She eventually steps into the room, and I watch as she relaxes in the warm welcome. That's already a win in my book.

We all gather around the piano, where Max runs us through a vocal warm-up.

Max was the one I went to when I first had the idea for these meet-ups. He used to teach singing and piano lessons full-time around his auditions and knows almost every show tune by heart like some kind of musical prodigy. Without him, these nights wouldn't be what they are.

Eliza's hiding with me at the back of the group,

attempting to take up as little space as physically possible. More so than usual.

"Right, who wants to sing what?" Max asks.

"I've got something," I volunteer. I want to lead by example for Eliza and hope she steps up to the task like she does when we're working. I want her to see how supportive this room is, and more than anything, I want to hear her sing.

I opt for "Waving Through A Window" from "Dear Evan Hansen". A song all about feeling like an outsider, not fitting in where you think you should. I want her to know that I see her. No matter what's going through her head right now, she's allowed to be in this room.

Some weeks it feels like I'm living Wednesday to Wednesday, waiting for these nights to remind me I'm part of something good here. And then she came on board. Maybe it's because I know I'm helping her find her feet, or maybe it's just her, but I'm living for every day now.

The others, all by the mirrored wall in front of me, start singing the chorus line, harmonising against the traditional scores because they can, and it warms my heart when Eliza joins in. When the song finishes, everyone claps and cheers, but all I focus on is Eliza. She's looking around and smiling and I know it's working. Someone else steps up to sing their song, and the session flows like it always does.

"Do you want to have a go?" I ask her between songs. So much time has passed and she's yet to put herself forwards.

"I'm okay just watching."

"That wasn't my question." I smile to charm the real answer out of her.

She nods almost apologetically.

"Do you have a song?"

She nods again, more sure of herself.

When Sophie finishes her song from "Six", I step

forwards to hold the space. I encourage Eliza towards the piano to tell Max what she wants to sing with a tip of my head. As she walks out, the room comes alive with encouragement, and I couldn't be more grateful to my friends.

"Eliza, we only have one rule here: you can sing from any musical you want, *but*…if you pick 'Mamma Mia', we'll all walk out," Max jokes with her.

She brightens and agrees before leaning over to tell him what she wants to sing. At that same moment, I get butterflies.

"Can we skip the dialoguey bit and just go straight in?"

"You got it!"

She takes her place in the middle of the room and tries to calm herself discreetly. It's my fault she's nervous – I've thrown her into the lion's den. But it's no different from how I've run every activity with her. Give her a second to scope it out and then she's in control. She can do this.

The piano starts, and it's an intro I recognise straight away despite Max freestyling around what's just been cut out. *"Heathers"*. Eliza looks right at me with a knowing smile. She's trying to impress me.

She picked "Fight For Me". It's the song where Veronica sees J.D. for the first time. He's in a fight with the jocks and she instantly falls for him, wanting nothing more than for him to fight for her and protect her from the horrors of high school.

A shiver goes down my spine when she starts to sing. Her voice is gorgeous. There's a quality to it that's unlike any of the others in the room. We've all had our voices fine-tuned by vocal coaches to make sure we can blend into any chorus line and sing songs the way people expect to hear them. But hers is untamed and unique. Whether she means to or not, she makes the song completely her own.

I tear my eyes away from her to look around. Everyone is focused on her. They would be polite no matter what came out of her mouth because they're nice like that, but real amazement is written across every face in the room. Yet she can't see them. She's looking through us, past us – not even at herself in the mirror, just somewhere else. That or she's closing her eyes. I believe every word she's singing and I know she does, but there's a disconnect.

When was the last time she sang for someone?

I feel for her. Drama school auditions are brutal. I was one of the lucky ones, and I know that now. How many times was she told she wasn't good enough? How long has she been carrying around that judgement? I'm going to make it my mission for her to know she's more than good enough.

Her voice is strong; it hits every big note effortlessly. We sing the chorus line like we've done with everyone else, and I hope she hears how good she sounds with us.

The room explodes with applause. I'm so happy she got up there and gave it a go. She pulls an arm across herself and pinches her elbow, unsure what to do with all the attention. She deserves every second of it. When she looks at me I'm clapping and beaming my proudest smile. She blushes, and for a second I see her stop batting away the praise people are giving her.

She retreats back to the comfort of the group. She's one of us now.

"What a voice!" Max is well and truly taken aback by her. "Where did you learn to belt like that?" He looks at her with admiration. "Sorry, I need more. Eliza, come back here. Harvey too – I need to hear you together or else I won't sleep all week."

I wrap my arm around her shoulder tightly and bring her back into the centre of the room.

"'Seventeen'!" someone shouts at us. Another "Heathers" track.

"Yes! Exactly what I was going to ask. Thank you!" Max gushes. "But…we know you can sing now, so you don't need to worry about that for this one."

She looks at him, confused.

"Instead I want you to focus on acting. Connect with us, Harvey, that mosquito over there – I don't care, just be present."

This is why Max and I get on so well: we seem to have the exact same thoughts half the time, and he always knows the perfect way to express them.

"You're not skipping the dialoguey bit this time. Get angry with him. Fight with him. Feel it."

She nods, accepting her assignment.

It's hard work getting into character when I'm this happy, but it's worth it to get to play one of my dream roles with her. Sure, it's just one song, but I'll take whatever I can get.

Mysterious. Brooding. But what about the kiss? *Come on, Oscar, focus.*

As expected, she takes Max's notes on board and lets me have it. She's in the scene, and I'm immediately transported with her. We start on opposite sides of the floor and slowly come together as the mood changes from teenage angst to a declaration of love. Her voice harmonises with mine so perfectly I forget where we are.

I've heard this song a thousand times and sung it in the shower a thousand more, but only now does it sound new.

I hold the upstage side of her face gently. She responds to my touch by placing her hand on my chest. Our eyes lock as the lyrics imply, and it's as if no one else exists anymore. It's just me and her. During my too-many-to-count performances of "Grease", I never felt this with the girl playing Sandy, but one song with Eliza and I'm falling head over heels. Does she feel this too? It isn't okay for professional actors to read into these scenes. But then again, I'm not a professional anymore.

I want her to hear the lyrics and know it's me saying it to her, not J.D.

The short musical break where J.D. and Veronica usually kiss is coming up. Should we? No. I won't. I can't. But *fuck*, do I want to.

I resist, instead holding her gaze as she looks up at me as intensely as I look down at her. Her grip is tight on my T-shirt. I continue to take stage directions from the lyrics and embrace her. She settles against my chest and then pulls back just a little to look up at me, my arms still around her, but loosely. I bring my forehead to hers. I never want this song to end. I want to bottle this feeling and drink it forever.

In the four months we've been running this group, I've never quite witnessed a reaction like this. Everyone's screaming, swooning, clutching onto one another doe-eyed. Someone's wiping away tears, though most likely they've just had a hard week and it's released itself in an odd way.

"All right, we're done. Nothing's going to top that tonight, I'm afraid." Max closes the lid to the piano and gets up from his stool.

The group agree, sweeping Eliza up into the middle of them all as they leave for the bar. I hang back and walk with Max.

"What the hell is she doing hiding that voice?"

"I wish I knew."

I know one thing for certain though, I won't let her hide it anymore.

THIRTEEN

ELIZA

"I don't care how feral it gets tonight, the rules still apply here. Regardless of what they bribe you with – and trust me, they'll try – don't get involved. Just hang in there a few more hours and it'll be your turn to play," Jerry, the tubby and extremely camp activities manager from LA, briefs us backstage.

There are loads of us from entertainment working on tonight's guest activity, Scavenger, and hundreds of guests are piling into the arena-style venue as we speak. We've each been given laminated sheets with large numbers on: one to twelve, excluding six and nine to avoid confusion, apparently.

"No matter how innocent it may seem, in this game things can quickly snowball. Any inappropriate behaviour with a guest will land you in *hot* water. Do I make myself clear?"

"Yes, Jerry," we all reply.

"Ugh, thank God that's out of the way. Now let's go have some fun!"

Everyone cheers and runs after him as he pushes through the curtains to the side of a giant projector screen. Beyonce's "Crazy in Love" plays and colourful lights bounce around the room. Oscar takes my hand, jogging us over to our side of the stage. I say stage – it's supposedly a dance floor, but to me it looks more like a jazzy basketball court. He lets go of me, drops his number, and starts hyping up the crowd, getting them to dance along to the music, and I follow his lead.

Jerry warms up the audience before introducing Henry, who bounds into the spotlight fitted with a wireless headset mic so he's hands-free. One of the ship's AV crew follows him with a large camera resting on their shoulder, the live feed streaming directly onto the projector screen at the back of the "stage".

"Good evening, folks and welcome to Scavenger, the best adult treasure hunt around! There are three rules and three rules only tonight. No kids, no Karens, and no questioning your marriage. What happens in Scavenger stays in Scavenger, am I right?"

I look around the room full of laughing faces and spot a few parents shooing their early teenage kids out of the venue.

He splits up the room into ten sections and then asks for two volunteers from each group to make their way down to the stage. Oscar opens the waist-height gate, letting our guests onto the floor.

"These are your Scavengers! I'm gonna be asking them to track down all sorts of things, and they'll need your help to find them. Scavengers, everything I ask for will be in this room. And if your team don't have it, nab it! When you have what I'm looking for, you need to come to me with your team number and item as fast as you can. First team gets five points, the next four, three, two, and then everyone after that gets one point. The faster you are, the more points you get. And what do points win?"

"Prizes!" all of us shout back. We use the now well-known catchphrase during most of our activities.

He does a test run, asking the Scavengers for their team number and a room key. The music turns up and everything gets more frenzied. One of my Scavengers fumbles in their pockets and the other snatches the laminated number four from my hands before racing towards Henry. He calls the team numbers out in the order he sees them: "Two! Ten! Four! Seven!" Jerry scribbles down points at his desk in the corner of the court, and I cheer my team on when they return.

The requests started simple: a candy bar, a woman with a nose ring, a man with sunburn. But decorum was soon abandoned…

Turns out this is less of a scavenger hunt, more a horny rendition of "The Hokey Cokey". The players run back and forth, fulfilling bizarre requests for the best part of an hour, and the room is alive with crazed merriment.

My team ultimately places fifth. Tom's team win, much to his delight. Thankfully, he's out of my direct line of sight for most of the night.

It's been hard to avoid him since Tuesday, but somehow our interactions have consisted only of passing each other in the halls or when Oscar and I join the group for meals just as they have to leave. I thought he would have had the balls to apologise by now, but that was clearly wishful thinking.

"Us next." I beam up at Oscar.

"Indeed. Look, it's not too late to—"

"Oscar, I swear to God."

Oscar gave me plenty of opportunity to bow out of playing tonight, but the others said this was the first time he'd agreed to participate in a crew activity and that I was to do everything I could to make sure he didn't back out. I promised I would, not realising quite how much work it would be.

"All right, all right, I'll stop. I just want you to know exactly what you've signed up for."

"I do." I turn back to scan the room. "It looks fun."

"Yeah, but—"

"Come on!" Maddison appears and takes me by the wrist. "No time to waste." She and Valentina drag me off before Oscar can finish. "Obi, sort him out, will ya?" she calls out as we pass him.

I feel like Cinderella being styled by singing mice. If you interpret slagging off my entire wardrobe as singing. Maddison picks out her sexiest underwear set for me to wear because apparently mine isn't pretty enough. In my defence, when I packed I wasn't going for pretty; I was going for practical. So I'm now in an "easy-peel" outfit consisting of stretchy black velvet trousers that cling a little too tightly to my bum and flare out at the ankles and a baggy but cropped baby-pink jumper. When I tried to protest I'd get too hot, they just told me I wouldn't be in it for long, which only made me hotter.

"Take this." Maddison hands me a bottle lid full of mouthwash, which I throw back like a shot and swirl around my mouth. "Think Harvey's gonna bail?"

I spit into the sink. "I hope not."

"I bet you don't."

I ignore Valentina's offhand comment. "I'm not sure what he's so worried about. It's not *that* bad."

The girls stay quiet, but I catch them looking at one another.

"What?"

They resist elaborating for all of ten seconds because it

takes nothing at all for Maddison to break. "The guests' game is pretty tame compared to ours."

"Right…"

"Our version is *filthy*," she gushes like a kid telling a ghost story.

"How filthy?" *And why is this the first I'm hearing about it?*

"About as filthy as HR let us get away with," Valentina mutters under her breath.

"Who are kept outta the room!" Maddison almost sings, flashing the widest smile I've ever seen.

"One piece of advice: don't take your underwear off."

"What?"

"Just don't do it. We've got you covered."

They open up their clutch bags and present the contents like magician's assistants. Clean knickers, lipstick, condoms, and a fluffy pair of handcuffs.

What the hell have I got myself into?

OSCAR

"You don't want to play?" Obi asks while I look for a change of clothes.

"No, I do."

"Then what's the problem? Is it Eliza? You not feeling that? Are you blind? I'm not that way inclined, but that girl is…" He makes an "okay" sign with his hand, which is his way of saying something is too good for words. It was accurate when he was talking about the menu at Coral's, and it's accurate now.

"I'm meant to be looking after her. I don't want her to

feel…" I sigh. "If I cross a line tonight – which we both know has happened to people in this game before – I will never forgive myself." And it's true. I couldn't forgive myself knowing she'd either have to silently suffer through the next few weeks until I left or speak up – and good on her if she did, but I could lose everything I've worked for.

"Did that happen when you played before?"

"No."

"So what's the problem?"

"I just need to keep out of trouble, that's all." I walk away from him and into the bathroom to freshen up, hoping to avoid any further questions.

"Harvey, is there something you're not telling me?"

I lock eyes with him in the mirror above the sink, and from his expression alone, I know he won't let me out of this room if I don't come clean. I put my aftershave back down on the shelf and breathe a heavy sigh. "You can't spread this around."

He throws his arms out wide. "Do I look like Maddison?"

I wanted to keep this quiet in case I don't get it, but I need to give him some perspective so I can get real advice. "I'm up for activities manager."

"Shit, really? This early?"

I shrug to downplay it, perching on the end of our desk. "Job came up. I had to push Jerry hard to even consider me."

He glazes over as if he's thinking something through. "So you mean to say all this time you've been locking yourself away in here and avoided messing around with the rest of us, it was because you thought if you had *fun* you wouldn't get the job?"

Well, it sounds stupid when he says it like that.

"Oh, Harvey. My poor little lost boy. An activities manager is about being the master of fun, and I mean this with all the love in the world: you're kind of the master of boring."

I know people call me boring here. And I'm fine with it, or at least I keep telling myself I am. I've started to wear it like a badge of honour, as if it means I'm a better person than I was before, when in actual fact, I've just swapped one bad reputation for another.

"You know Jerry's the one who comes up with the tasks, right? If anything, you *refusing* to join in is what will lose you that job."

He's got a point.

"Can you honestly tell me you're happy here?"

I look down at my hands.

"Then it's time to shake things up a bit. No more hiding in the background, Oscar Harvey."

ELIZA

The entertainment team aren't messing about. I'm taken to the bar where Oscar and I are force-fed shots, which all just taste like mouthwash. Then, with our throats burning and our bloodstreams sufficiently tainted, we all head back up to the arena, where the guests have cleared out and crew members are starting to pile in. Our gang commandeers the front row of seats behind us, handing over more potent drinks to keep us buzzed while we wait for the game to start.

"Good luck, you two." Jerry hands us the number five with a smirk and continues on to the pair next to us.

Oscar has a new energy about him. He seems calmer, more certain of himself. It can't just be the booze; we had the same amount, and he's three times the size of me.

"You look nice."

Was that a hint of flirtation in his eyes?

"Thanks. Take a good look now. Apparently, I won't be wearing it for long, so…" *I see your flirt and I raise you suggestive imagery.*

"What exactly have they told you?"

"Originally, they described it as a sexy treasure hunt, and understandably I didn't really know what that meant, but I think I have a better idea now."

"That's pretty spot-on, actually. Just promise me something?"

"Yeah?"

"If there's anything you don't want to do, you'll tell me."

"I'll tell you." I bite down hard on my bottom lip so as not to give away just how much I love it when he's protective. "But *you* have to promise to stop worrying about me and just let loose for once. *Please.*"

"Deal."

Music blares, colourful stage lights spin, and the auditorium lights dim as the air fills with excited screams. Electric apprehension rushes through me. I've not quite comprehended the reality of what's about to happen. Somehow, I'm expected to endure an hour of playing raunchy games with possibly – no, not possibly: *definitely* – the hottest man I've ever laid eyes upon and not pass out. I look back for moral support and see all the entertainment team, actors, dancers, and theatre staff cheering us on from their seats, which rake right up to the top of the room. Tom flashes me a reserved but encouraging smile. I almost smile back.

Henry runs through the rules again, and I think I might burst with anticipation. "The first thing I need is your team number and…a tied-up Scavenger."

Maddison faffs around in her bag, struggling to free the

fluffy handcuffs because they're caught on all the underwear and other bizarre objects she's crammed in there, and time is ticking fast.

"Tie! I need a tie!" I shout to the team.

Valentina yanks one from the neck of an officer on team four who doesn't put up much of a fight, and in a matter of seconds I've made a pair of hoops for Oscar's wrists to slip through. I watch the shock hit his face when the loose and unsuspecting hoops tighten with one slick pull, his wrists slamming together. I wrap the leftover tie around the gap between his hands and tie a final knot before pulling him like a dog on a lead with our number and run to Henry. We get the full five points and our team erupts.

"Where on earth did you learn how to do that?"

"Oh, I'm sorry, do I not look like how you'd picture someone with a bondage kink?"

"Not quite."

"Good. I don't have one. That's all I know how to do."

I love surprising him, having him look at me like I'm some puzzle to solve. Just when he thinks he knows me, I throw something else in there to confuse him.

We watch on as all the other teams improvise with ties, belts, and even shoelaces. All opting to tie up the female Scavenger, I should add.

"Scavengers! I need ten shirts."

Oscar and I strip off immediately and collect the shirts that are flung at us from all directions. While counting them up, clothes continue to fall on the gang's heads as they're chucked down from the top of the stalls. When I turn to Oscar, I briefly forget how to breathe. I'm lost in his bare skin. His abs. His biceps. How does a man as sweet as him with looks like that even exist? Some days I swear I feel lucky just because he knows my name.

He snaps me out of my trance by dragging me by the hand towards Henry, shouting, "Run!" at me over and over again.

Maddison's bra is all beauty over function; my boobs aren't big by any means, but they can barely be contained. Regardless, I hold myself down and soldier on. I'm not sure how many points we scored, but it definitely wasn't a lot.

"You've got something just here." He touches the corner of his mouth with concern.

I mirror him and touch my lips, feeling nothing.

"Oh, sorry, just thought I saw a bit of drool," he mocks.

"Fuck off." I swat his arm, giggling with embarrassment.

"Ten pairs of pants."

Pants?

I demand the girls open their purses and hand over the bajillion pairs of knickers inside, but they just shake their heads with evil grins.

"Trousers, Elizabeth!" Tom shouts at me over the chaos, throwing his pair over to Oscar.

Fine.

I strip off my trousers, leaving me in just Maddison's underwear, and take the team number from a half-naked Oscar, whose arms are full and eyes are stuck staring at my behind, and we run forwards. We only get one point, which I know is entirely my fault, so I have to work hard to be quicker next time. On our way back, I tap the corner of my lips to mock Oscar as he did me, which earns me a sly smile.

We're given no time to put on clothes before the next task is given.

"I need our Scavengers…in the man's favourite sex position."

"Let's go, Mr Whippy. It's obviously missionary."

"Come here, trouble." He scoops me up in his arms so our (almost) bare chests are against each other's. He runs with me, and I can't stop laughing, wrapping my arms tightly around his neck and clutching our number. When we get to Henry, he slips his arms under my legs to gain even more control of my body.

"This Neapolitan enough for you?"

"I'm more of a mint chocolate chip girl."

He dares to rock me ever so slightly, my softness bouncing against the front of him so perfectly I go weak. A wave of horniness takes over and the pulse between my legs practically thumps at the now very real image of Oscar having his way with me.

"Okay, okay, I'm converted," I proclaim. Any more rocking and I might not be able to stop myself from jumping his bones right here.

His laugh is so naughty it's almost sinister. I think I love him.

I don't even hear our number called, but he retreats, still holding me in his arms like the strongman he is. God knows what the other teams are up to. At this point, they may as well not even be here.

Henry's over by Jerry's table holding up a small yellow packet. "There are a few parts to this one, so listen closely. First, I need a Scavenger with one of these on their tongue, no sucking."

I run forwards without conferring with Oscar, my hands firmly bracing my boobs. I regret running when I recognise the packet. Nevertheless, I tear it open and place the sweet on my stuck-out tongue, my entire face shrivelling up at the instant sting of sourness that infects my tastebuds. Henry calls our team number first, and it's an agonising wait for the other teams to catch up.

"Remaining Scavengers, stand in front of your teammates."

The others swarm over to us, and once they're in place we get our next instruction.

"I need to see lips on lips."

What?

Oscar's soft lips press gently against mine.

"Now, without letting your mouths separate, finish the sweet."

All I can hear is screaming. Oscar's large hand cups my neck, his thumb resting against my cheek, and he's kissing me.

He's kissing me! We're kissing! Fucking yes!

The hard sweet passes back and forth between our mouths, our tongues doing their best to dissolve it. He holds me close to him. The sourness disappears suddenly and the sweeter inner layer is ours to enjoy, and *fuck me*, am I enjoying it. His technique isn't rough or fast, but gentle and seductive.

I hear numbers being called already. They must have chewed it. *Cheats!* Stuff it – I'm making no move to call them out. I open my eyes, wanting to quickly take stock of the hottest guy in the world making out with me. That's when I notice we're the last ones left.

"All right, you two, time's ticking."

Oscar's hand leaves my back and I feel his wrist flick as if to say, "Who cares?" He picks me up again and slowly carries me off, not letting our lips part for even a second. The noise from our side of the room isn't even real; a whole hoard of guys are shouting, "Who, who, who," like barking dogs. We giggle and keep making out. When he eventually puts me down, he doesn't go for the glory and play up to the others' celebrations like I thought he might. He holds my gaze and smiles back at me as bright as anything.

I feel like I've just taken his virginity.

He chews the rest of the sweet, leans over to Obi, and takes a sip of his drink as the sour sherbet centre kicks in.

"How do you *still* have it?" Obi asks.

"You know me, not one to rush things." He winks at me.

I think Maddison and Valentina might break. Who is this guy and what's he done with Oscar? He's so confident. Just when I didn't think he could get any sexier.

"Bonus points are up for grabs here, kids. I need a Scavenger with a hickey. *Nowhere visible*, I hasten to add. Bonus point for the team with the kinkiest place."

We flounder for a second. I wouldn't even know where to kiss him that I'd get enough traction to leave a mark. He's all muscle.

"Show me where!" he requests.

"Dealer's choice!" I shout back over the noise.

He gets onto his knees in front of me, and before I know it, my left leg is flung over his shoulder and his lips are planted on the inside of my thigh. I squeal as he sucks my skin and lean back on the railings for balance. It tickles, and I love it. The way he looks up at me corrupts my mind with a million unsavoury thoughts.

Before I'm ready for him to stop, he does, assesses his work, throws me over his shoulder, and carries me to Henry. Apparently, my little legs no longer travel at a sufficient enough speed. We present my love bite before I have a chance to feel weird about flashing my groin at a very senior member of staff I don't know all that well – though I think we went past the point of no return a long time ago – and wait to see if we've snagged the bonus point.

Nope. The Scavenger on team two got one on her *actual* boob.

"I need the Scavengers in the lady's favourite sex position."

My turn to steer this ship. I run with Oscar, snatching the number from him.

"On your knees behind me," I instruct as we run, and I fall to my knees when we get there, lining up with him and leaning forwards just a bit. His hands instinctively grab my hips. "Your hands!" I shout over the noise.

"Where?"

"Take a guess," I dare him, because all of a sudden being fast feels way less important than the fun I can have toying with him.

He closes his eyes and breathes deeply as if he might break. Then he places one hand lightly around my neck.

I finally hold up the number, leaning into his hand and seizing the opportunity to get my own back by bouncing into him, feeling the outline of him through his boxers. He takes my hair by the roots and pulls me closer to him with the perfect amount of force. My back straightens and presses firmly against his chest.

"You are so bad," he growls into my ear.

"Wrong. I'm a good girl," I purr into his, turning his eyes wild.

Yep. That's it. I'm going to fuck him tonight. I *need* to fuck him tonight. Our team is *screaming*.

Jerry brings ten chairs onto the floor, spacing them all out in a line. He places small blue bottles on the chairs.

"I need a man sitting on one of these chairs, covered in sunscreen. I want him to look like a pornstar at a bukkake gangbang."

Could've done without the image, but I guess I know exactly what we need to do.

We rush towards the chairs. He sits, and I start squeezing the bottle with all my might. With sun cream covering his chest, arms, and legs, he holds our number high.

"Now, without the men standing up, and without either of you using your hands, completely rub in the sunscreen."

"Pony" by Genuine plays and the onlookers lose their minds at our hijinks. Guess there's nothing else to do except grind on him like there's no tomorrow. I sit on his lap and my body writhes against his, the smell of holidays and beaches floating in the air. He hardens beneath me, which only spurs me on more.

"You're killing me, Chapman."

Once my back's got what I can only guess is an even coat, I stand up and straddle him. Pressing my chest into his, sliding up and down. His hand grips my bum and assists my motion on his lap. My eyes are locked on his, basking in his full attention.

"Remember, no hands, folks."

He removes his hand and looks awfully tortured about it, but then he uses his forearms to rub the sun cream into my back.

"Glad you didn't drop out now?"

His only reply is a tortured growl.

Eventually, I hold our number high, my back against Oscar's chest again. There's no way we've rid our bodies of any evidence of sun cream, but any more grinding and we'll be playing a very different game.

"Next, I need a man without an erection," Henry says, and the room bursts out with laughter as none of the men hold their number up.

Oscar rests his elbow on the arm of his chair, burying his forehead into his hand.

"Help is on the way, dear!" Daniel hops the barrier and charges towards us quoting Mrs Doubtfire's iconic line. Oscar hands him the number, and Daniel presents himself to Henry, patting his crotch as if to prove it, which scores us top points.

"What are you doing to me?" Oscar mutters just loud enough for me to hear.

I smirk at him. "I've done nothing yet."

He presses his teeth into his knuckles, fighting to maintain his composure.

OSCAR

Our hard-earned – poor choice of words – third-place medal hangs from her neck. She's stolen my shirt, only done up one or two buttons in the middle, and put her tight trousers back on. From the way she snatched the shirt from me when I tried to put it on, I got the sense it wasn't to cover herself up, but to stop me from covering myself.

I haven't left her side all evening. Partly because the minute I turned my back, she was surrounded by half the men on this damn ship making her all sorts of offers for the evening and it became clear she needed a bodyguard. But mostly because I don't want to be anywhere else.

I can't help but notice Tom didn't follow us when we all moved to the bar, and I wonder if that's why Eliza's more relaxed now than she has been for the past few days. When the dust settles, I'll get them talking again, but until then, I want her to enjoy this high she's riding.

She's sucking on the straw of the ice-cold water I got her

and staring up at me with those bright blue eyes. There's a whole room of people wanting her attention, and somehow I've got it. She stands on her tiptoes to speak to me, and I lean down closer for her.

"I want to know something." She shouts to be heard over the music, but there's mischief in her tone.

I place my hands on her waist and pull her away from the speaker right above us so we can talk. Then I loosen my grip but find I can't let go completely.

"What's actually your favourite sex position?"

"Are you accusing me of lying, Chapman?"

She nods. "Because I picked on you."

"Yeah, you did, didn't you?" I want to taste that smirk on her lips, but I need to remember why I mustn't . "That's…top three."

She arches her eyebrow with jubilant curiosity and her fingertips skate over my bare stomach as she waits for an expansion on my answer, no longer looking like my new nervous trainee. I don't know how she hasn't worked it out yet, but around her, I'm like a spider, far more nervous of her power over me than she could possibly be of mine.

I play along, tucking my hands inside the loose shirt so I can stroke her soft skin, and lean in close to her ear. "That position…but with you underneath me."

"Me?" She pretends she's caught me out and this isn't the game she's playing.

I don't correct myself; instead I hold her challenging gaze firmly until her resilience cracks.

"Why that one?"

I can't help but sigh with amusement. As if feeling incredible isn't a good enough answer. "Because, Chapman, if I'm going to be intimate with you, I'm going to make sure I can watch you enjoy it." I squeeze her waist and stare at her pointedly.

Her eyes drop to my lips for a split second. Yeah, I've won this round.

I shouldn't be doing this. I'm clinging onto the cliff's edge of "just flirting" by my fingertips, and I don't know how to bring myself back from it, nor if I even want to.

"And the other?"

The fragility in her voice wills me to risk replying. "Remember how you got that love bite?"

The cliff starts to crumble above me as her eyes widen with understanding that it isn't her thigh I want my lips on. Her chest starts to rise and fall faster. "That's not, like…a *sex* position though," she stutters, weakly arguing in an attempt to get yet another position out of me.

"I think there are a lot of lesbians out there who'd disagree." The best advice I ever got from my queer friends back home: "make love like lesbians without a sex toy". Christ, what I'd give to watch Eliza fall apart on my tongue. "Say, 'Sorry, lesbians'."

"Sorry, lesbians," she repeats.

"Good girl."

Yeah, that's done it. Her eyes are bliss-filled as if she's floating on a cloud and I'm the wind keeping her up.

"Gosh, is that the time? I should really get to bed."

Oh, is this the game we're playing now? She hasn't looked away from me, and even if she did, there's no clock in here and neither of us have our watches on or our phones with us. I reach into my back pocket to retrieve her room key, which I've been keeping safe, and hold it out for her to take.

I can't go back to her room. She's capable of handling this tension on her own. I know *I* will be the second I get back to my cabin.

She looks down at the key card, her tongue tracing her plump lips, and then she looks back up at me, a smile brushing the corner of her mouth. She ignores it and walks away from me, and now I'm the one on the cloud caught up in her sweet breeze as I follow her out of the bar and down the hall.

I'm only walking her back. I won't go inside. I will resist no matter what it takes. We've done this journey plenty of times before. Tonight is no different.

Neither of us is watching where we're going. My eyes are glued to hers, and she seems to be struggling with a similar affliction until we round the corner. Then she stops in her tracks, a breath catching in her throat, and I look ahead too, following her line of sight.

Shit.

"This was a mistake." Tom, who's clearly been sitting outside her door for a while, gets up and takes off past us.

She calls after him, her previously smiling eyes now full of worry and guilt.

"I'll sort this," I reassure her and follow after him. I don't give her time to argue with me. He's going to be mad, and I'm not letting him take it out on her.

"I don't wanna talk to you." He strides down the corridor trying to evade me.

"I know what that looked like. I was just walking her back."

"Bullshit."

"I'm not going to come between you." He stops dead and faces me. He was upset before, but now he's *pissed*. He steps closer to me, squaring up, stone-faced. "I'm not talking about this with you."

"Tom. We're going to be on here for a long time. You can't fall out with everyone."

"Watch me." He opens his door sharply, the clunk of metal punctuating his words with aggression.

I catch the door.

"Back off," he warns.

I hold the door open and stay in the doorway. "I'm not letting you ostracise yourself. I don't know what happened, but—"

"But nothing. It's none of your business."

"No, it's not. But *this*," – his anger –"this is my business. You can't let your temper flare on here."

"Why do you care?"

"Because I've been where you are. I know what this is, and I want to help."

"I don't need your help. As if some magic pep talk from you will solve anything. You're so fake!"

I step into the room, letting the door close behind me so no one else will hear the commotion.

"I've got you all figured out. This whole thing of yours is an act. You play the nice-guy card until you get what you want, and then you'll hurt her just like I did. I'm impulsive and stupid, but you, you're smarter. You knew exactly what you were signing her up for tonight. You just wanted to get your hands on her and pretend you had nothing to do with it. I'm glad I waited for her, because even though I was there to straighten things out, you came along and proved me right, so thanks for that."

"I'm glad you were there too."

"What the fuck does that even mean? Why are you so calm? Why aren't you defending yourself?"

"If that's what you think of me, I can't change that. But for the record, Obi and Valentina signed her up and gave her a pretty good idea of what to expect. I signed myself up *impulsively*. I guess I wanted to prove something to them, I don't know. I have been begging her all week not to play but *she* wanted to. Ask her – ask anyone. I did not go into that game willingly."

He falls silent.

"If I can give you just one piece of advice I wish I was given when I started…"

He looks at me, eyes on fire but waiting.

"Don't fuck your friends."

"What, so you can?"

My gaze on him hardens.

"That's what you were about to do, though, right?"

"I was walking her back."

"Don't treat me like I'm stupid, Harvey."

"I'll admit, tonight messed with my head, but I wouldn't have mixed her up in that." If I'd made it to her door, there would have been so much temptation, but I wouldn't have gone inside. I would have stopped myself.

"Easy to say now."

I shake my head, tired of him trying to get a rise out of me. "Nope, that's a rule I take very seriously."

"Why?" he snaps, but I can see he actually wants to hear the answer.

"Because…this place, it's…a minefield. We all turn up expecting to immediately understand this unconventional new lifestyle, working all hours under the sun, too busy to think straight but so overstimulated that everything becomes boring, insufferably lonely, while at the same time we're not able to move for people. Everyone's single, pretending to be single, or about to be single, and sex loses all meaning. Here it's just a pastime. The lines between coworkers, crushes, and friends with benefits are practically non-existent, but friend-ships – *real* friendships – are hard to come by. You never know who you can really open up to on here, so when you find someone you think you just might be able to, don't compromise it."

His anger is dwindling. His breathing is slower. He's listening.

"If you want to patch things up with Eliza, I'll help you. Just…accept her reaction. Let her be angry. She's hurting, but she'll come round. She's working things out on here too, don't forget."

For a while he says nothing, and eventually I decide to leave and let him process whatever he needs to now he's calmer.

"Is she your friend?" he calls over my shoulder, the open door in my hand. I feel the weight of the question and don't answer until I'm certain.

"Yes."

FOURTEEN

ELIZA

Whoever thought a breakfast rave at 9 a.m. on a Saturday morning was a cute idea deserves to be shot. My head is pounding, and every staff member Oscar and I passed on the way here gave us some kind of knowing look. I want to curl up in a ball and die.

Though, unfortunately, hangxiety is the least of my problems this morning.

I nurse the biggest cup of tea I can get my hands on and shadow Oscar as he judges Musical Pancake Flipping (who comes up with this shit?). The guests are given real pancakes and Fisher Price frying pans and are made to dance *and* flip pancakes simultaneously *in the dark*. Then if they're moving when the music stops, or if the pancake drops, they're out. It's absolute carnage.

Despite my many bribes for dead silence and a round of sleeping lions, the DJ – whom I affectionately name "DJ Sausage" after he tricks me into sneaking him an unholy amount of chipolatas while he pretends to consider my request – is still blasting the most aggressive dancehall anthems known to man.

I should have resisted the booze last night, but after the girls confessed what I'd really been signed up for, I knew it'd be the only cure for my sudden onset of nerves. So there I was, a horny drunk – though still technically sober enough not to be fired – playing whatever the hell Scavenger was with the finest specimen of a man I've ever seen. It's no wonder all sense went out the window.

A pancake princess is crowned, and Oscar ushers the ravers over to another part of the venue to dance while the cleaners rush in to tackle the blobs of cooked batter that have been splattered all over the floor. Too uncomfortable to stand back and watch them tidy a mess we're responsible for, and not having any pep left in me to join Oscar and the partying guests, I make myself useful. Pinching a dustpan and brush from the cleaning trolley, I get on my knees and start sweeping up the mess, counting my lucky stars it's just batter and not a mush of syrupy berries and powdered sugar too.

As the floor becomes sufficiently less edible – though the infuriating pulse of lights in here makes it too hard to tell for sure – a pair of large white trainers appear in front of me. My eyes slowly trail up the body before me, taking note of the heaving chest and raw desire etched on his face. Oscar's professional mask slips for just a second, but I'm confident his brain is running rampant with a similar train of thought to mine.

He likes seeing me on my knees.

And I like being on them.

Fuck, I have enough to deal with today already without being this horny too.

He offers me a hand up, his eyes slipping to the purple bruise on the inside of my thigh when my shorts ride up. When I'm at my full height, just a few inches apart from him, there's no missing the hungry clench of his jaw. Neither of us speak, but his voice is loud and clear in my head.

"If I'm going to be intimate with you, I'm going to make sure I can watch you enjoy it."

Double fuck.

Clearing his throat, he takes the dustpan from me to throw the pancakes into the bin along with any residual unfulfilled lust from last night. I dust off my knees and, in a daze, go in search of the nearest sanitiser dispenser, hoping there's a way to inject it straight into my brain to clean my filthy mind. A long, fully clothed hug wasn't quite what I envisioned receiving when we left the bar, but I should be grateful to Tom for once again keeping me on my path of celibacy after spending all week facing the consequences of straying from it. "Should" being the operative word.

I'm just horny. That's all this is. Scavenger chewed me up, spat me out, and made me crave things I know would only be bad for me. Just like how my hangover is making me crave an entire stack of pancakes, a basket of pastries, and every crispy corner of the leftover hash browns. It has nothing to do with how, for the first time in a long time, I recognised myself this week, all because Oscar got me to sing with him. And it definitely has nothing to do with what happened to me when he sang. He was acting – of course he was. But he could have picked any song, yet he chose one about wanting to be seen.

And I saw him.

I need to get it into my thick skull that having uninhibited, spontaneous, and passionate sex with Oscar last night would have complicated everything more so than it already is. I tried casual sex back home and it only made me lonelier than I was beforehand. Not to mention a vibrating piece of rubber could give me more satisfaction than those hookups ever did. And

I've tried mixing work and romance and it well and truly ruined my life.

So what do I really want with Oscar?

Uninhibited, spontaneous, and passionate sex and a committed relationship with no consequences. Obviously.

Stop.

"Can't take my eyes off you for one second this morning," Oscar says, his voice amused and gruff.

Shit. My hand's still outstretched under the sanitiser dispenser and my palm's now dripping with gel, the smell of hospitals assaulting my nose. He laughs at me and immediately finds a solution to my problem. Tangling his large hands with mine, he steals the excess and uses it for himself. It's not just his touch that leaves me breathless, but the way he's looking at how my hand fits in his. This must be every germaphobe's wet dream.

"Do you have any plans for your long break later?"

Is he asking me out, or is he hoping to remove the spanner that was thrown in our works last night and instead put *his* spanner in *my* works? Oh, Lord Jesus, just smite me down already. I shouldn't want that. I *know* I shouldn't, but I can't help myself.

"Not currently."

"I'll see when Tom's free. It'd be good for you two to talk."

Well, I completely misread those signals.

It's horrendous being at the centre of all this drama. Oscar doesn't go into detail about what was said between them, only that Tom wants to make things right. I wanted to have it out last night, but Oscar thought it would be best to wait until today, when we'd both have clear heads. Yeah, as if my head was ever going to be clear after the night I had, alcohol consumption aside.

If this were the real world, I would have blocked him and moved on, but I can't do that here.

He fucked up, there's no doubt about it. *However*, seeing him sitting by my door wanting to make things up to me…it made me want to give him a chance to explain. Even now, Twatface has never apologised for what he did. It's not exactly a high bar to jump, but if Tom apologising is what it takes to remove this acidic ache in my stomach the anger towards him has caused, I'm willing to listen.

In the dying embers of the day, I take myself out to the running track, the meeting point arranged by Oscar and Maddison, to find Tom waiting anxiously there for me. The track's relatively deserted at this time of day, most people either in their rooms getting ready for the evening or soaking up the last hour or so of the sun by the pool, but an older couple stroll past us as I get to Tom, so we pace slowly in the other direction until we're out of earshot.

"I'm so sorry, Eliza."

I look over at him, the burnt orange sunset painted on his troubled face, and instantly I no longer want to see him as the guy who hurt me, but as the guy who comforted me when I was upset.

"I'd just like to set the record straight. I wasn't playing you. I never had plans with her."

"Then why did she say—?"

"I was hosting some after-dark pool party that night. She was lifeguarding. That is the *only* reason I could think she would say that. I didn't know she'd be working on it. I had no intention of…*seeing* her again. And to put everything on the table, she tried to shoot her shot, but I said no."

Oh.

Oh God. I really blew this out of proportion, didn't I?

"I don't talk about this kinda stuff with anyone, not just you. I don't think it's fair on the other person to share something private. Plus, I regretted it. A lot. Especially when I heard you and Harvey didn't..." He sighs, and it's clear he's been beating himself up over this. "I should have told you. I know I screwed up, but I—"

"It's okay."

I should have known he wouldn't hurt me on purpose. But since Twatface, my default is to always assume the worst in someone. I get why Tom lied when Valentina asked. I've played that moment over in my head a lot. Talk about being put on the spot.

"I'm sorry too."

"You have nothing to—"

"It wasn't fair of me to shut you out like that," I interrupt. "I should have come to you directly. I was being childish, acting like you'd betrayed me after ten years of marriage or something." My exaggeration gets a laugh out of him. "I really wish I'd handled it differently because you didn't deserve that."

We round the corner at the stern of the ship, and upon seeing no one else around, Tom stops walking and pulls me in for a hug, causing all the tension that was stacked like bricks in my chest to be knocked down. Up until now, I could barely breathe. I wrap my arms around him, and we relax in our shared relief.

"I've really missed you, Elizabeth."

"I've really missed you too." Emotion clutches at my throat.

"We'll get it right one of these days." He pulls away from me and smiles optimistically while I struggle to fight off the pangs of guilt that stab me in the chest for being so unkind to him. "Think we should stop taking our clothes off together. That might help."

I giggle, already feeling lighter. How does he do that? He always knows exactly the right thing to say to cheer me up. "And no more communal showers," I add.

He sighs, his eyes fluttering back and forth between both of mine.

"Now you're just thinking about the shower, aren't you?"

"Yep."

And so am I. It's the curse of the pink elephant.

"We're so good at this friendship thing."

"So good. You frcc now?"

"Yeah."

"Good. We're going to the arcade."

"Why?"

"Because if there's one thing I know for sure, it's that my competitive streak is the most unattractive thing about me. Prepare to get the ick, Elizabeth."

There must be something in the water. I thought Wednesday was meant to be hump day. but turns out it's actually Monday. I'm brushing my teeth without a care in the world when Gwen and Daniel burst through the doors flinging clothes around like confetti. I've seen Gwen having sex more times than I've actually spoken to her – which until now was only something I could say about pornstars. Despite reminding them of my existence, being the exhibitionists they are, they continue on their "quest for enlightenment", as Daniel would probably say – ew – leaving me with two choices: stand there and watch or flee immediately.

Unsurprisingly, I choose the latter.

Like Mary and Joseph, I go off in search of refuge. I trundle down the hall to the girls' room, only to be met by a noise-cancelling headphone–wearing Valentina, music blasting through the earphones as she peels them off to talk to me. Upon hearing Maddison's sighs from behind her curtain, it becomes immediately clear Valentina is far more tolerant of her roommate than I ever will be of mine.

Oscar and Obi's room is next on my route, followed by Tom's when there's no answer, though this is a real last resort. Our friendship has certainly been patched up, but I wasn't quite prepared to test the credibility of the ick just yet. Thankfully, I don't have to as he doesn't answer either. To my frustration, my search for peace continues.

The library seems like a good choice until I see four fumbling feet poking over the edge of a sofa, so I'm left with no other choice than to head to the bar. Though calmer than the weekend, it's still bustling and loud. I find an empty table in the corner and bury my head into my folded arms on the table. I'm so exhausted from the past couple of days that for a minute or two I think I might be able to sleep here for a bit until Gwen and Daniel tire themselves out.

"Interesting place to take a nap, Chapman." Oscar stirs me from my sleepy haze.

"Daniel and Gwen's bits are gonna wear down to nubs if they're not careful."

Oscar chuckles. "Let's get you to bed."

"But I'm homeless." I pout.

"Well, lucky for you, Obi won't be back tonight. He left with his special friend a second ago, so I'll take his bunk, and you can take mine."

It might be the only option I have, but it's certainly a good one.

"Sheets were clean on this morning."

"What about… What are you doing here?"

He points over to Max on the other side of the dimly lit room. He's shifting his chair up to sit with the rest of the actors. "I do have one other friend besides you," he toys with me.

"Don't let me stop you. I'm fine," I say through a yawn.

"Mmm, sure you are. Come on."

"But Max…" I don't know why I'm resisting, but I feel like I should at least try to.

"I've already said good night to him."

I stick my arm out in the air and wait for him to pull me up, my body lazy like a rag doll.

While Oscar brushes his teeth, I clamber out of my trackie bottoms and pull my jumper over my head, leaving me in just my knickers and an elastic bralette. Then I scale the ladder and make myself at home in his bed. Just thinking about him sleeping here makes me a little too excited, but it's exactly those kinds of thoughts I need to ignore if I want to avoid a repeat of the Tom situation.

The ripple of his muscles when he peels off his T-shirt makes me question my resolve. It's a sight I've had the pleasure of seeing a number of times now, but I don't think I'll ever get used to it.

He passes me up a bottle of water, turns his reading light on, and switches the main light off. I pull my curtain across and lie down, hearing the fabric of his trousers sliding down his legs.

Good grief.

We make small talk about what tomorrow's got in store

for us before wishing each other a good night, and though I was too tired to even walk here, I now find myself struggling to sleep at all.

"What's that noise, Chapman?"

I stiffen. "What noise?"

He waits a second before replying. "It's stopped now, sorry."

I relax again.

"There – that noise."

"Oh. I wiggle my legs to get to sleep sometimes. Sorry, I'll stop."

"Don't stop on my account. I was just curious."

I attempt to settle down without wiggling for a minute, but trying not to do it only makes me want to do it even more. I finally give in, feeling instantly comforted.

"You're like a little cricket." I hear the smile in his voice as he mocks me.

"Just don't ask me to be your conscience."

I'm not sure what the time is when the cabin door clatters open and closed, but it's definitely not morning. The bath-room extractor fan starts whirring, and the door closes gently and locks. There's a sigh below me, followed by a duvet rustling. I sneak my head out of the curtain to see what's going on, but it's pitch-black except for the small slither of light coming from under the bathroom door.

"Oscar?" I whisper.

"Hey," he whispers back, his voice no longer under me.

"Is that Obi?"

"Yeah. He never normally comes back."

"Come up here. I'll go. I'm sure they've tired themselves out by now."

"No, it's okay. I'll sleep…here." I'm not sure where "here" is, but I'm assuming the desk or the chair. Or the floor.

Oh God.

"Oscar, get up here. I'll go."

"I'm not gonna make you leave."

"I'm not gonna let you sleep on the floor."

He takes a deep breath and eventually starts climbing the ladder. I pat around the bed for my clothes before remembering I discarded them somewhere on the desk. In the dark, our bodies knock against one another as I shuffle down the bed.

"Eliza, you're not even dressed."

"I have clothes, I just can't— Ow!" I hit my funny bone against the side of the bed while descending the ladder, which stuns me momentarily. "They're down here somewhere."

The bathroom lock twists open and I panic, retreating straight back up the ladder again, safely hidden away behind the curtain. I'll wait for Obi to pass out and then I'll make my escape.

Oscar finds my hand and gives it a squeeze, holding me while I perch at the end of the bed. When the coast is clear, I attempt to set off, but Oscar's firm grip stops me.

I'd like to think we can trust Obi not to blab, and it's not like we've been up to anything remotely gossip-worthy, but I'm sure both of us would rather not be caught in the same bed together knowing full well any denial of promiscuity would only incriminate us further.

Oscar lightly pulls me closer to where he is by the pillow, and I make no more effort to refuse. The bed's narrow and Oscar's bulk takes up most of it, but lying on our sides, with me as the little spoon, we manage to Tetris our limbs so we're not *quite* touching. It doesn't escape my notice he's only in his Calvin Kleins. With his bare skin just centimetres away from mine, all I can think of is what almost was the night after Scavenger. But he's being respectful, so I in turn must do the same.

Suddenly, Oscar places a firm hand on my bare thigh and I forget how to breathe.

Please.

But his hand doesn't wander; his fingers don't stroke me. Ah, I was cricketing again. Is he worried about the noise I'm making or—?

Oh my.

Just the slightest shift back with my hips tells me everything I need to know. Oscar has a thing for Jiminy. I place my hand over his. I've heard his message: I need to stop. So I'm still. So still everything aches and itches with a need to move.

I'm never going to get back to sleep like this.

I slide my arm out of the duvet and pat it down behind me, creating a padded barrier between my bum and good ol' Pinocchio Pants. The quick breath of a tired laugh lands on my shoulder. I find his hand and pull it over the covers, wrapping it around my body. He interlocks his fingers with mine and settles down, both of our bodies finally relaxing, my insect instincts safe to take over again. He nuzzles his face into my hair as my thumb slowly strokes his.

I don't remember when I stopped.

OSCAR

Despite only having one half of a single mattress, I have the best night's sleep since I got here. Or very possibly longer.

I quietly curse Obi's alarm as it disturbs Eliza. I place a comforting hand on her arm, which is now wrapped around my waist, as her head lifts off my chest. My pulse trips over itself when she eases back against me. For a second, I thought she was scared of where she was, realising and regretting. But that's not the case at all.

With Obi's reading light brightening the room behind my curtain, I'm able to watch her gentle features fight off the drowsiness. Tipping her head up to me, she smiles, and I know she's adding a mark to her tally of the number of times she's caught me staring. I'm not even pretending not to anymore. She has the most expressive face of anyone I've ever known, and I'm utterly addicted to working out what she's thinking. Seeing things through her eyes has changed my perspective on so many things already.

I tuck a shorter strand of her hair behind her ear, then find I'm unable to stop myself from sweeping my fingers over it once more. She leans into my touch, encouraging me to do it again and again, until I'm stroking her. I have no idea how much or how little time we have until Obi leaves, but I intend to make the most of every second I can get with her in this silent haven.

She swirls her fingers over my skin like a paintbrush to a canvas, her eyes following them closely as they come up to the side of my face. She runs her small hand against my rough stubble, smiling as it tickles her fingertips. I turn my head towards them and nip her playfully with my teeth.

An innocent move I now realise has cost us greatly.

Her eyes drop to my lips. *She's my friend*, I remind myself, but the way we're now looking at each other is anything other than friendly. Her bare leg brushes against mine as she stretches, making the strain in my boxers just that little bit more difficult to conceal. I don't mean to hum, but now it's happened I have to commit to it and make it sound like a yawn.

"Morning, Harvs."

"Morning. What happened to you last night?"

"Ugh, he wriggled too much. You have no idea how annoying that is."

"I can imagine," I sympathise, which earns me a scowl from Eliza.

"Sorry if I woke you."

"No need to apologise." I give Eliza a pointed squeeze.

"You showering first, or am I?"

If he showers, Eliza will leave. Or she might not, and then we'll be alone and I *will not* be able to ignore the way she's carving her nails along the hard lines of my torso. But if I shower, she'll be stuck in my bed for a while longer, and I'll have dealt with my...affliction, and the urgency I'm overcome with right now will have tapered off enough to get her out the door without me needing to stick my hand down the front of her knickers.

"I'll go, if that's all right."

Eliza deflates with disappointment. There's no missing it, but this is for the best.

I roll to the side, sliding her delicious body off me. Hovering over her for just a second too long, I twitch with need.

Shower. Now.

I shuffle down the bed, adjust myself under the covers, and climb down. Obi eyes me suspiciously as I head over to the bathroom. He looks up at my bunk and then back to me. I shake my head, pretending I don't know what he's implying. He turns his attention over to the desk, which Eliza's clothes are decorating in such a way that it looks like they were ripped off in a hurry. His impatient gaze draws back over to me.

Busted.

I shake my head seriously, not letting him get carried away with his assumptions. He pulls his lips together tightly, eyes twinkling. I fire him one last warning look not to bother her before I lock myself in.

Shower on. Underwear off. Inconspicuous travel bottle, now half-full of lube, squeezed into my palm. The relief is instant.

I knew alone time with my hand was going to be the only action I'd see on here, but I barely touched myself until two weeks ago. Now it's constant.

Does she touch herself thinking of me too? Is she doing it now, seeing just how much she can get away with in her hiding spot? I wouldn't put it past her – she's got a naughty streak, and I will spend every waking second thinking about it because this can only ever exist in my head.

Sun-creamed skin writhing against me. Sweetly sour tongue. One hand around her neck, the other tugging her hair. Stubble-grazing and teeth. She likes it rough. She plays innocent, but the reality is the opposite.

On your knees. Mouth open. Eyes on me. Deeper. Good girl.

Fuck. Fuck. *Fuck.*

FIFTEEN

ELIZA

Obi smiles too much when I sit opposite him and Valentina at breakfast. He knows. And he knows I know he knows, but I won't give him the satisfaction of an explanation.

"He's just talking to Jerry," Obi says when I cast my eyes around the room for Oscar.

I place the second mug of tea next to me and don't let my anticipation to see him again show. His cheeks were flushed when he got out of the shower, and from the look in his eyes when he saw me getting dressed, it wasn't the heat of the shower that did that to him. He might be frustratingly respect-ful, but he isn't a saint.

Obi's been eyeing up the queue for omelettes since I got here and finally makes his move, leaving me to eat in stony silence opposite Valentina. Any attempts at small talk are quickly shut down, so I instead decide to appreciate the one bit of quiet I'll probably get today.

It's short-lived.

A bunch of the actors walk past singing my name like the line from Hamilton. Sophie, who's coincidentally playing

Sophie in "Mamma Mia", stops at our table, letting the others walk on ahead.

"You joining us again this week?" she asks me.

I'm invited?

I sense Valentina's icy gaze boring into me. I know they're our fiercest rivals for all sorts of extracurricular activities, but I'm allowed to be friends with them outside of that, right?

"Yeah, I'd love to."

"Perfect. Do you tap?"

"Yes. Not got any shoes with me though."

I completely abandoned the tap classes I used to attend after my second year of failed drama school applications. They clearly weren't getting me anywhere, so there was no point in wasting more money on them. Though later, I did think about restarting them again to make something of a day otherwise wasted in an office, but each time I tried to go, my stupid brother and his stupid company had some *stupid* out-of-hours drama, and it felt like a sign from the universe not to even bother. So I didn't.

"No stress. I'll pinch some spares from Wardrobe. I'm thinking 'Book of Mormon''s 'Turn It Off' or basically anything from '42nd Street'. You got a preference?"

"Oh, two votes for 'Book of Mormon', definitely."

"Awesome!" She looks over at Valentina. "Hey, V."

"Hey," she says sheepishly.

Valentina sheepish?

"How's the painting going?"

"It's getting there."

Painting? I saw a pot of brushes on top of a metal tin of watercolour paints in the girls' room the other day but assumed they were Maddison's. If I knew Valentina was creatively inclined, I would have guessed she was into cross-stitch or knitting – you know, something where the tool doubles up as a weapon.

"You'll have to show me when it's done."

Valentina smiles, but it's like a *real* smile, not her fake guest smile or her "I'm secretly thinking of all the places to hide your body" smile.

"You going to the pool party on Friday?"

"Yeah, absolutely!"

That's one phrase I never thought I'd hear come out of her mouth unless followed by "disgusting" or "not".

"Cool." Sophie's bright eyes linger on Valentina.

"Cool," Valentina repeats back. She's going to run out of her yearly quota for smiling any second if she's not careful.

"Guess I'll see you there. Have a nice day, V!"

"You too," Valentina replies.

I wait until Sophie's gone before quizzing Valentina, her face already returned to the ice I'm used to.

"What was that?"

"Shut up."

"Did you just have a stroke?"

"Shut up."

"Has Valentina got a soft spot for someone?"

"No!" Her face pinkens.

"I didn't think she'd be your type. Not because she's a she, but, you know, she's perky, bubbly. Says things like 'have a nice day…*V*'," I tease.

"If you tell anyone about this I'll kill you."

"My lips are sealed."

She's quiet for a minute. "It's probably just a phase," she mumbles, taking a bite of her toast. "I've slept with a bunch of guys, so…it's not like I'm gay."

It upsets me to hear her dismiss her feelings like that. That's something she's heard from some repugnant homophobe, but she's repeating it as if it's the truth. I have no intention of letting her invalidate herself like that. Plus, the term "slept with" rings a few alarm bells. It doesn't sound particularly loving or enjoyable. I've just seen her entire aura shift for one cute girl, which makes me think this tough-girl act of hers is exactly that. I wonder how much happier she could be if she were brave enough to accept the truth.

"It's not just a phase, though, is it?" I say, my tone no longer playful.

She doesn't reply, but when Obi rejoins us, her glance at me over the table isn't as harsh as it once was.

My heart skips a beat when Oscar walks through the door. He does a quick scan of the usual tables we frequent and smiles when he catches my eye, heading straight over. There's a definite pep in his step. A secret grin on his face. It's the first time I've seen him like this, and he looks... happy. Have I not seen him truly happy until now? Is it because of me? God, I hope it is.

He arrives at the table but doesn't sit down.

"Someone's in a good mood. Sleep well?" Obi asks with a deviously pointed inflection.

"Eliza." Oscar ignores Obi completely. "The excursion today, something's come up that I need to be here for, so someone else is going in my place. Are you okay to go without me? I don't want you to miss out."

"Yeah, no problem," I say confidently. Nothing I can't handle. It's just a bus tour – what could possibly go wrong?

"Be an excursion escort," he said. "It'll be fun," he said. Yeah, right. Packing twenty-something clammy, middle- to old-age passengers onto a minibus with no functioning windows and a broken air-con unit in over thirty-degree heat is *real* magical. I think being an actual escort would be more pleasurable than this.

I've been truly blessed with a seat next to Mrs Dove, the passenger who ranked lowest on the same "I get the most travel sick" fight I used to have with my siblings to bag the seat up front. I never won then, and I'm definitely not winning now. She's one of the regular passengers and a text-book hypochondriac. She describes every single one of her ailments in graphic detail – not that I ask her to – and I can't remember the last time I said a word that wasn't a consider-ately toned "oh".

I don't even know what we're doing out here. I think this was meant to be a tour of various landmarks around the island, but so far we've only seen some oddly shaped rocks that supposedly, if you squint hard enough, look like two people fucking. And then after that we saw a waterfall, which in hindsight was beautiful, but at the time I was too distracted hatching a plan to successfully waterboard myself in it so I wouldn't have to endure the next hour of "guess which body part of mine hasn't oozed in the past six months".

Each time we pile back onto the minibus, I swear the roads get even more winds in them.

"Here we are, folks!" the driver announces, and I join the guests in an excited peek out the windows, but there's nothing noteworthy to see. I'm looking for a landmark, a quaint little hut famous to all the locals for that one dish they do so well, but there's nothing. "Just look at those views."

Oh, good. So we've come all the way to the top of a cliff we could see from the bottom at the start of the trip, just to see the view of the bottom of the cliff from the top. How thrilling.

A kind man offers to open the sliding door when he sees

me struggling, yanking it like some desperate loon, but I insist on wrestling with it myself so no one can get off before me. This cliff is my final stop, and I want a running start.

"Get your cameras out!" Oscar's stand-in advises.

Fabulous. I must remind myself to add "professional photographer" to my CV. The queue for me has already formed as people hand me their relic phones with cameras so blurry I could take pictures of my bare arsehole with them and they wouldn't know the difference. Or at least their family members wouldn't when the slideshow came out, but Patty and Mike from Michigan would have that image burned onto their retinas forever: me, bent over, taking a picture of my arsehole on the top of a cliff in broad daylight with their beloved camera phone. That would seriously redefine the meaning of honey*moon*.

Looks like the minibus has had the same idea as me upon our return and has completely lost the will to carry on. Thirty minutes of map-flapping sticky skin later, the driver finally manages to flag down the only passing vehicle to give us a jumpstart.

"Unfortunately, we're going to have to head straight back to the ship as we're cutting it too tight for time to see the rest of the sights," the other escort says. She promises partial refunds to the guests, and we get back on the road. Maybe things are starting to look up for me after all.

I spoke too soon.

Not long into our descent down the island, Mrs Dove goes quiet. *Peace at last.* But I must've forgotten they say it's silent in the eye of a hurricane. I should have known better than to relax. I should have known something wasn't right the second she began rifling frantically through her purse.

"Have you lost something?" I ask, pretending to care.

She shakes her head, white as a sheet with panic in her

235

eyes, before hot vomit spills out of her mouth, directly onto me.

Didn't think to lean over and do it on the floor? Nope. Straight onto me.

"I'm so sorr—" More hot vomit spews out of her.

Turn away, woman!

I shouldn't have expected anything less from Mrs Dove. Classic attention-seeking behaviour. She just *has* to make sure *everybody* knows that *she* gets the most travel sick. Those front-seat fakers are starting to look pretty smug right now. *Just wait until I give you all a nice big cuddle.*

And as if that wasn't enough, someone on the row behind me begins to puke too, but thankfully they have the foresight to use the little paper bag housing the postcard and tacky keyring they just bought at Lovers' Rock.

We had all the time in the world to look at a shitting waterfall, but of course, right when we need it the most, we have no time to stop and let the passengers empty themselves on one of the finest bushes the Caribbean has to offer. Instead, we all have to endure the next forty-five minutes of *actual hell* while almost every passenger falls victim to the chunder chain. Any hope this driver had of earning a good tip today went straight out the nonfunctional window the second that decision was made.

By some miracle, the contents of my stomach stay in place, but not comfortably, and after smearing the contents of *Mrs Dove's* stomach around my body with the *one* wet wipe she so kindly pinched off some other passenger, I feel I'm ready to take on the world. In a mass homicide kind of way, not in a #Girlboss kind of way. I smell like three different types of sanitiser I'll never be able to use again without wanting to top myself in a Pavlovian response.

We only just make it back to the ship in time for embarkation, and it's safe to say I'm done with cruising. Forever? Possibly. But definitely for today. There's sick in my shoe and it squelches between my toes as I walk down the hallway out of breath after running to the gangway to get them to stay open for the stragglers.

"What happened to *you*?" Just from Maddison's tone, I can tell she's gawping at me in alarm. Tom's standing by her side. Good. So glad he's getting a shot of this too.

I avoid making eye contact with either of them. "I don't want to talk about it."

"Aren't you coming to the Sail Away Party?" she asks.

"Fuck the Sail Away Party."

Fuck it right up the arse.

First I shower in my clothes. Then, once I can be *sure* there are no secret chunklets of spew left on them, I strip and throw them in the sink – ready to be incinerated in the hottest wash imaginable – before scrubbing my skin to within an inch of its life.

Freezing-cold water rains down on me. *No, no, no, please not now, for fuck's sake!* I jump out of the way of the stream, shampoo bubbles spilling down my shower gel–covered body. I hold my hand under the stream, waiting for the warmth to return. And I wait. *And I wait.* I should have thrown myself off that cliff when I had the chance. I give up and scream in frustration.

There's a knock at the door.

Fuck. Off.

I snatch my towel off the hanger, fling it around myself, and whip the door open, shooting daggers at the person on the other side of it. Oscar's eyes open wide before pitying me.

"News travels fast," I snap. I don't mean for the words to be so sharp, but I have no capacity for manners anymore.

"I'm so sorry."

"You should be," I sulk, stomping over to my desk, not necessarily inviting him in but not telling him to go.

"How are you…coping?" he asks nervously.

"I'm not going to dignify such a pointless question with an answer," I spurn half-jokingly.

I can't tell if Oscar looks amused or scared. Bubbles keep trickling down from my hair, covering my body, and even though I couldn't feel less sexy if I tried, Oscar still looks at me like I am.

"Have I been fired for no-showing? Please say yes."

We were warned back at the start of the contract that failing to show up for a shift would result in a strike against our name. Well then, strike me down! See if I care!

"I think everyone will agree these are exceptional circum-stances."

"Nothing about this feels exceptional."

He considers his words carefully before speaking again. "Shall I leave you to your shower?"

"No point. Hot water cut out, and no matter how long I'm in there I'm never going to feel clean again."

"Oh, Chapman," he says, doing his best not to laugh. "Where are your clothes?"

I point towards the bathroom sink.

He walks over to the bin, lifts the current bag into the air, and finds a spare one underneath it. Protecting his hands with the bag, he scoops my clothes into them as if they're a steaming pile of dog shit.

"I'll get these cleaned for you. The hot water's on a timer, so give it ten minutes and it should be back up again. See you at dinner."

"Thank you," I mumble.

He gives me one last sympathetic glance and goes, leaving me with nothing better to do than spend the next ten minutes wallowing.

When I'm as squeaky clean as I'm going to get without peeling off a layer of skin, I put on my comfiest tracksuit bottoms and jumper and head to dinner. Almost all of the others are there, and before I can even sit down with my dinner they're giving me a round of applause.

"Get fucked," I say playfully.

"So…what happened?" Obi's teetering on a knife's edge.

"Two words: Mrs Dove."

The gang heave a collective sigh. I decline to say any more than that so we can all get through our meal in peace, and I thank God it isn't stew on the menu tonight.

The ship is always full of the sweetest people. Or so I thought.

While cohosting a volleyball tournament with the sports staff on our sand court, I see a whole new side to some of the passengers, and they are *feral.* I never would have expected it from a bunch of women who, just hours before, were in a flower decorating class. There's a brief minute where I actually fear for someone's life, but Oscar expertly defuses the situation with the charm that comes so naturally to him. The way they all cling to his every word like he's the Messiah is hilarious. Though that's one second coming I'd pay very close attention to.

I clock one woman letting her hair down and putting lipstick on as soon as she sees he's running the event, and another tightening her bikini top to give her cleavage that extra pop. All are welcome to play, yet it seems to only be the ladies who participate, their loved ones made to sit on the sidelines and cheer them on.

One of the long-term cruisers, Mrs Whiteside, takes a bit of a tumble, claiming she was pushed, but if you ask me, she leapt to the ground just so Oscar would sweep her up and tend to her. She swoons while he carries her "Baywatch"-style over to the lounger next to her husband, who barely even looks up from his crossword. The lack of concern he exhibits says to me this is a regular farce of hers, yet Oscar smiles courteously and calls over a lifeguard to ice her ankle. She's less keen on that idea, but Oscar promises to check on her afterwards. About ten minutes later, she tries to return back to the game, which Oscar denies her the pleasure of because he "couldn't bear to see her get seriously hurt". She reluctantly retreats, proceeding to watch him with her little hawk eyes for the rest of the tournament.

It's nice to be back with Oscar again. This week I've officially started running the activities I've been trained in either alone or with the others, not as a trainee or under supervision, but as an equal, and it's amazing. Tom and I have even hosted some things together that either got far too competitive or resulted in debilitating laughter for us and the participating passengers.

With all this entertaining, hosting, and getting to know the guests, it's like I'm back at The Cellar again before everything happened. The best part is, after my shift is over, I don't have to spend the next forty-five minutes pressed up against miserable strangers, giving the businesspeople of London accidental lap dances on the tube. No siree, I get to watch the sunset on the horizon with my friends. And when I go to bed, I don't dread waking up like I did when I was working for

Lawrence; instead I'm excited, as if the next day can't come quick enough.

Spending time with people other than Oscar has helped me see things a bit clearer too. There's no denying he and I have a very close bond, and for the most part that's just friendship. But then there are these moments that seem to leave as quickly as they arrive, where no amount of reasoning with myself can stop me from wanting him.

I care about Oscar a lot. That's what this jumble of feelings I have for him really comes down to. He's helped me find my voice where so many people tried to tell me it wasn't worth listening to, and from the few bits I've heard from the others about how different he's been these past few weeks, I think perhaps I've helped him too.

People can say what they like about working on a cruise ship, but the crew welfare team know how to keep us entertained. The indoor pool has been closed off to the passengers and transformed into a space that could rival one of Budapest's best sparties. Without the daylight pouring in from the curved atrium ceiling and glass walls, it's like a completely different room. The last time I was here, Tom and I were learning how not to die, but fingers crossed we won't have to put any of our life-saving skills to the test tonight.

The room's buzzing with people in swimwear and beach attire. DJ Sausage has his decks set up on the other side of the room, moving party lights radiating from his booth and every corner of the room courtesy of the theatre technicians.

Oscar and I finished earlier than the rest of the gang, and there's a notable lack of chaos here in their absence. They shouldn't be far behind, though, and the actors' show will be over soon, so it won't be long until we're surrounded by familiar faces again.

Since Scavenger I've been teetotal and determined to keep it that way, but after the week I've had, I bloody deserve a drink. Plus, it's the first and maybe only time frozen strawberry daiquiris are on the menu and I simply cannot resist. *Just one*, I promise myself. Oscar gets the same, and we head off in search of two sun loungers to claim as our own. The way his board shorts tighten up around his thighs when he sits down almost kills me.

"So, Mrs Whiteside. She's…a character." I bite back my smirk.

Oscar inhales slowly. "She is quite a persistent little madam, yes. Today was nothing."

"Seriously?"

"Seriously. She once asked me to rub her sun cream in."

"Gross."

"Not to mention highly inappropriate."

"And did you?"

"God no. I politely declined and suggested maybe her husband help her."

"Wait – he was there?"

"Oh yeah, right next to her."

"Jesus. What a woman. Did he have much to say about it?"

"I think that was the first time he's touched her in a long time."

"Aww, well, when you say it like that, I can't blame her for trying to get a bit of action from a strapping young guy like you."

"Strapping, huh?"

I giggle. "Oh, piss off – you know you look like a model."

Oscar blushes and sips his drink in an attempt to hide that big grin of his.

"So, who else do I need to keep my eyes on?"

Oscar has me in stitches, filling me in on the antics of the other regular passengers: the couple he's caught in compromising positions on more than one occasion; the wannabe Hugh Hefner who has a different female companion on every trip; and the fight he had to break up when jealousy got the better of a pair of swinging virgins. It's not until my straw sucks up nothing that I remember where we are. The music has been turned up considerably and the room is way more crowded than before, though there's still no sign of our lot.

"Come on." I stand up and lift my dress over my head, revealing my bikini. It's white with cute colourful dinosaurs all over it. I may or may not have stolen the trick of that lady earlier and tied the top a little too tight to make my very average-sized boobs look like they're bursting out of the cups. Though I didn't have to do anything to the bottoms to make them cling to me the way they are.

If I ever turned up to a work event back home in what's now essentially a thong, I'd be causing quite the scene. But then again, context is everything.

My hair falls back on my shoulders and I drop my dress on the sun lounger. I catch Oscar's wandering eyes and leave him to enjoy the view just a second more before interrupting him.

"When you're quite done, I'll be in the pool." I strut off.

A topless Oscar joins me at my side, and I can't help but tease him some more. Stumbling, I grab onto his forearm to steady myself, making a sharp wince as I do.

"Shit." I freeze, raising my ankle off the ground.

Oscar springs into action, getting to his knees and resting my hands on his shoulders for balance while he inspects it.

"What have you done?" The compassion in his eyes as he looks up at me is enough to make anyone weak.

"I think I twisted it."

He gently palpates my ankle in his hands and tries to move it.

"Oscar," I say with a pained brow and gritted teeth.

"Yeah?"

"Could you just…"

He stops to look up at me again.

"Rub my sun cream in?" I bite my lip hard but can't hide my devious grin.

"That's it," he says, and before I have a chance to stop him, he throws me over his shoulder with ease, making me squeal in delight. "You're going in!"

I demand he let me go, kicking my legs and feebly pounding my fists on his back, but really, I want him to hold me forever. He marches us over to the deep end until he's stopped by a whistle and his surname being shouted forcefully behind us. Then he puts me down by the edge and apologises to the lifeguard for being *that* guy. But as soon as their back is turned, his hand is on my side, giving me an almighty shove. I shriek and fall into the water, just managing to grab his hand and pull him in with me. I let go as soon as we sink, immediately swimming to freedom. I struggle not to inhale water while I fight back my laughter.

The whistle blows again, getting our attention. The lifeguard raises a stern eyebrow at Oscar before leaving us be.

"You're the worst!" I declare, splashing water at him.

He runs his long fingers through his wet hair. "That all you got, Chapman?"

I sweep my arm across the surface, an impressive wave cascading over him.

"Oh, you're on."

"You'll have to catch me first." I swim as fast as I can over to the corner and try to hoick myself out of the pool, but his strong arm wraps around my waist and pulls me back down.

"Caught you." His low voice drips with seduction.

I spin around to face him, my skin skimming against his hand under the water where he holds me up, his other hand holding onto the side of the pool. I wrap my legs tightly around his waist, pulling him closer. "You sure about that?" I say, my lips just inches apart from his.

It's not only the air that suddenly feels thick. With every slow kick of his legs, he rubs against me, his definite firmness pressing exactly where my body wants it. The silence between us grows inexplicably loud.

I was so determined not to repeat what happened with Twatface here that I naively failed to consider quite how intricately entangled work and personal lives are in a place like this. It's not possible to separate one from the other without completely sacrificing any and all social interactions in your downtime.

And I didn't come all this way to be a hermit.

His focus drops to my lips, and mine does the same to his. Excitement pools in my belly. He squeezes me tighter. Our noses brush as we remove whatever space is left between us.

The whistle sounds again just as his lip grazes mine, yanking Oscar's attention away from me – but this time it's not us they're scolding. Despite that, Oscar clears his throat and pulls back, his eyes darting around the dark room. I let my legs fall away from him and reach out to hold the side as my support goes.

Now there are two lifeguards on my hit list.

"Sorry," he says under his breath, frowning like he's punishing himself.

Here comes the jumble again.

I don't understand. Why does he keep letting himself get close to me and then immediately put this barrier up? Is it something I'm doing? Something I've done?

Or maybe he doesn't want to be seen with me. Just like Twatface. Just like Kate. He hid me from Obi. He didn't want to do Scavenger. And now this. What the fuck is so wrong with me that people can only tolerate my existence for so long? Am I really *that* repulsive or weird? Is that why I repel everyone away? Or does being around me feel like a chore?

He's too polite to tell me he's embarrassed or whatever his problem is, so I make it easy for him. I push off the side and go to swim away to the steps. Except he reaches out, catching my arm. His grip holds strong, easily overpowering my momentum and pulling me back into the corner.

"Please don't go," he whispers.

I hold myself against the side, my mind too busy making sense of the mixed signals to reroute my escape path or hide every single one of my thoughts from showing on my face.

"Don't cry," he begs softly.

"It's just the chlorine."

He stares at me and my reddening eyes, seeing right through my lie.

"I don't know what you want." My words come out defeated and small. There's a rapid banging in my chest, and every single one of my muscles goes numb under his intense stare.

"You." He clears his throat. "I want you," he admits with confidence. Confidence I would have believed if it didn't dissolve a second later. "But I can't." He shakes his head with shame.

"Why?" I deserve to know that much.

"It's unprofessional. Of *me*, not… And I—"

"Why do you need to be professional?"

I don't mean to quiz him, but he's not making any sense, talking so ambiguously he might as well be speaking in riddles. I look around at the room of scantily clad crew. Us *nearly* kissing is definitely not the most improper thing happening right now. I watch as worry lines crease his forehead and he takes a deep breath.

"I used to be very…different." He can't look me in the eye, but he's ready to talk, so patiently I wait. "I wasn't good. I was selfish. Arrogant," he says as if the words are poisonous. "I didn't consider others before I acted, and I didn't much care about them afterwards either. I'm not that guy now. I've worked very hard not to be, but…wanting you scares me." His eyes lock onto mine. "I don't trust that feeling yet. And I don't know how to."

Wow. Here I was making this about me, my past, my demons – *yet again* – all while completely failing to see he's fighting demons of his own.

"So you were just like every other bloke before they grew up then?" I say – not to diminish his feelings, but because he's being too hard on himself. This guy right here is unequivocally *not* a bad person. He's so gentle and quiet he couldn't hurt a fly. He is a good person – almost to a fault, according to the girls – and I won't listen to him putting himself down like that. "You deserve to have nice things, Oscar."

The cracks of relief on his face are palpable.

"I'm not saying I'm that nice thing, but I'm not *not* saying that either…" This gets me a chuckle. "But if you don't eventually reward yourself for this mansformation, what are you doing it for?"

He smiles, and for a while that's all we do, tread water and smile.

"Thank you, Chapman."

"So I scare you, huh?"

He chuckles again.

"What, a five-foot-nothing person like me intimidates a giant like you?"

"I didn't mean—" He tries to defend himself.

"I've scared a lot of people. Don't go thinking you're special."

"Oof, don't lump me in with everyone else."

"I'll do what I want with you," I joke, and he heaves a loaded sigh. "I think I've found a loophole in your reformed bad-boy plan."

"Oh yeah?"

"Party games." Memories of the afterparty and Scavenger flood my mind, and now they're flooding his too. "You want to play one with me now?"

He arches his eyebrow at me. It's a yes, but he doesn't want to admit it.

"You said it yourself, they're just party games. Not something to read into."

He puts all his time into helping others – especially me these past few weeks – and it's high time I help him now. This is what he needs. He needs to learn that letting go and having fun isn't a crime. And if that is within the confines of some game, then so be it.

"What did you have in mind?"

"Truth or Dare."

"That's asking for trouble."

"Good. I like trouble. It's fine if I'm the one being selfish, right?"

He gives me a grateful smile, and I look around before wrapping my legs round him again, careful not to pull his top half closer. His hand ends up back under my thigh to support me, so my grip on the side isn't quite so imperative. Thankfully, it's dim enough in here that no one can see what's going on under the surface.

"This okay?"

He nods, and we let ourselves enjoy the closeness again.

"Truth or dare, Oscar Harvey?"

"Truth."

"Are you bi?"

There's the slightest hesitation before he answers. "Yes. It doesn't mean I'm—"

"I know what it means," I reassure him. Though I've not experienced it myself, I know exactly what small-minded opinions might have been thrown his way. He isn't greedy, promiscuous, or undecided, and *it isn't a phase*. His attraction just isn't limited by gender. "In which case, I'm sorry about the other week."

He doesn't follow my meaning.

"I enjoyed watching you kiss another man. A lot. I fetishised you and I should feel bad about it."

"But you don't?"

"Nope. *So hot*."

A sly grin breaks out on his face and his grip tightens as my hips roll against him just once. "Truth or dare, Chapman?"

"Dare."

"Tell me a secret."

"That sounds an awful lot like a truth to me."

"Would you prefer I dare you to skinny dip?" he challenges.

My face must show my dread because he grins. "Fess up."

I chew on my bottom lip as I think about it. "I've completed Pornhub." Though I've never been shy about enjoying porn, I've never quite admitted to what extent. It could probably be classed as an addiction, but with no physical consequences, why stop?

His eyes are on me but drifting all over my face as if he's picturing what I get up to when I'm alone, wondering how pleasure changes my features. "And how are you coping being cut off from it here?"

"I came prepared." I roll my hips again.

He raises his eyebrow at my double entendre. "And if I stole that iPad of yours, what would I find?" His eyes go dark, and just like that, he's the Big Bad Wolf and I'm Little Red Riding *Something*.

"Bit of this, bit of that," I tease him.

"What's your go-to?"

"Depends on my mood."

There's a frustrated grumble in his throat that vibrates through me. He looks at me dangerously as if to say, "Don't test me." But I want to. I want to push him right to the edge and be the one holding his shirt as he dangles over it.

"What's it to you?"

"Tell me," he growls, squeezing me hard.

"Teacher-student," I say because admitting it's really master-servant would send me over the edge with him. I don't miss his purposely slow and controlled grind against me as he draws the parallel between our relationship. "Truth or dare?"

"Truth."

"Tell me what you think about in the shower."

Pensively, he sucks in his cheeks, realising he didn't get away with it the other morning. "I think about a lot of things."

"Such as…?"

"What you're like in bed."

Fuck. "Oh yeah?" I try immensely hard to play it cool.

"Mmm. Some days I think you might be the slow and gentle type. Other days…I think you might be the opposite."

"Truth."

"Which is it?"

"The opposite. Not like 'Fifty Shades' or anything, but maybe ten shades."

"What's that ten – the pain or the control?"

"Control." There's no doubt that was the answer he was hoping for. Our laps grind together harder while he grumbles to himself.

"Dare," he demands before I can even ask.

"I dare you to…slide your fingers right here." I drag my fingers inside my bikini top.

He lowers me further into the water, the surface up to my chin, and after some internal deliberation, he discreetly slips two long fingers inside the fabric. Taking me by surprise, he pinches and pulls my nipple between them, just enough to elicit a gasp from me.

"God, I bet you look so pretty when you come."

"Maybe you'll find out one day." I sink my teeth into my bottom lip to keep my excitement at bay. "Dare," I request.

"Let me take you on a date."

Of all the things he could have asked for right now, he picked that. Yeah, there's no way I'm falling for this douchebag past malarkey. He's fucking adorable.

"Where?"

"Well, if we were back home, I'd take you to dinner, we'd see a show, and then we'd go for an evening stroll by the sea."

He didn't even say "back to mine". Yep, he's one of the good ones.

"Would you look at that – we can do all of those things here too."

Oscar hums, knowing exactly what he's asking for.

"Sounds like you've put a lot of thought into it."

"I have."

"Would it end in a kiss?"

He takes a deep breath as if he's considering it. "We'll have to see if you earn one or not."

"I'd have to earn it? Not sure I want to go if there's no kissing."

"You'll do as you're told, Chapman," he purrs into my ear.

"Yes, sir."

TOM

What the fuck is he doing?

I knew it. I knew he was a fake piece of shit.

"What's got your panties all bunched up?" Maddison forces a drink into my hand when I don't look away. Her eyes follow mine to the far corner of the pool. She gasps, slapping Obi's arm just as he reaches for his cocktail from the bar.

"Hey! Careful!"

She continues to slap him.

"What is it, woman? Oh!" The two of them exchange high-pitched noises behind me that perfectly complement the boiling of my blood.

"I'm going over there." I need to save her from him.

"No, you are *not*." Obi grabs my arm and holds me back.

"What we looking at?" Valentina stands beside me sucking on her straw.

I tear my eyes away for a second to find hers and lead them back.

"So?"

"He said he didn't like her."

"And you bought it? Aren't you, like, a psych major or something? Even *I* know that's bullshit."

That's the last time I trust a word that comes outta that asshole's mouth.

"Come on, kids, let's leave them be." Obi ushers us like a principal on a field trip, keeping us a safe distance from the pool. "Heads down, heads down," he instructs just before we pass them, but he spins himself so he's always got a good view.

I don't take my eyes off Harvey for a second, burning holes into his smug face. Eliza's giggle shoots through me.

We pile onto some loungers and I make sure I have a front-row seat. I'll give him enough rope to hang himself with – then he'll have no more lies to hide behind.

Go on, make a move. *I dare you.*

"Tom, my man, got something to ask you." Daniel bundles onto the lounger next to me. "You seen Eliza around? Need to speak to her too."

Before I can reply, he clocks them in the pool.

"Eliza!" he bellows.

"Daniel!" the others sigh.

"What?"

I love the guy, but *boy*, does he need to learn to read social cues.

Harvey notices their spectators. Eliza's head comes up over the side and her eyes widen. Daniel waves her over, and Harvey lets her out of the muscular jail he'd trapped her in. She swims over to the metal steps and all the air leaves my lungs. Jeez, she looks incredible. She grabs her towel from a few loungers over and clutches it to her chest, dabbing at her wet skin before heading over.

"Put your tongue away." Maddison elbows me.

I make room for Eliza to sit next to me. It doesn't escape my notice Harvey's slower to exit the pool than she is.

"I wanted to apologise. Gwen and I haven't exactly been great roommates to either of you," Daniel starts, and for some reason, he keeps flicking his eyes over to Harvey behind us. "Now, I can't promise we're going to get any better, but I thought there might be another way around this. How would you guys feel about swapping rooms? That way, you both might be able to sleep again."

"Great idea," I say instantly.

"Is it?" Eliza and Maddison blurt out.

Absolutely. Not having to put up with the snoring or the sighing *and* cockblocking that son of a bitch behind me? It's the perfect solution.

This was everything *but* the perfect solution. Sharing a room with Eliza is *torture*. We've been getting on so well this week, and we're still getting on well after three nights of roommating. I just hugely underestimated how over her I was. Everything about her turns me on. The way she hums when she's getting ready, how she looks in the morning after she puts her makeup on, how she looks *before* she puts her makeup on, and that noise – *oh, that noise* – she makes when she tastes her favourite Skittle. Fuck, what I wouldn't give to hear that forever.

She doesn't even have to be in the room; her perfume lingering in the air gives me an instant hard-on the second I get in. And if all that weren't bad enough, every time I open the drawer I used to have in my old room, expecting to find my underwear, I find hers instead.

I thought I wasn't sleeping before, but now I'm an insomniac.

The only consolidation is that I'm doing my duty of keeping her away from Harvey.

Speaking of which, why aren't they in the bar with us?

SIXTEEN

OSCAR

One more minute and then I'm calling it.

I got here early. Too early. But I've been running out of time since we met. Tonight was about making the most of what little is left, but the auditorium's almost full, the show's about to start, and she's nowhere to be seen.

She's not coming. Of course she's not coming. I *dared* her to date me. Because I'm a bellend.

I shouldn't have even asked her, but I couldn't resist the loophole she granted me. I'm nothing but a hypocrite. Though I guess tonight she's my date, not my friend. Just another loophole to exploit, it seems. Being rejected is only the start of what I deserve.

When I look at this objectively, I'm backsliding. I'm no better of a person than I used to be. But behind the scenes, it feels different than before.

As my last morsel of hope evaporates, I spot her in the crowd coming up the stairs and a wave of calm washes over me. Her lips twist into a perfect smile upon seeing me, and mine do the same in turn.

She came. And she dressed up. *For me.*

Tight, white, blue flowers. Straps so thin I could snap them in my hurry to undress her. But I won't allow the opportunity to arise.

I run my hand through my hair and smooth down my over-ironed shirt. Too much time to kill at all the moments I don't want it. Should I go in for a hug, a kiss on the cheek, or just let her arrive like I do when we're working? Hug. It's informal but more than normal. Plus, I can't pass up an opportunity to touch her – not since the pool party.

"Sorry," she pants. "Got stopped by, like, a million people."

I'm frozen still, not brave enough to make the move. But to my relief, she stands on her tiptoes and reaches up for me. Thawed, I hug her back, though I can't help but hum my amusement. She's still small even in heels. Still has to arch that slender neck of hers to meet my eye. The sighs she'd emit if only I could put my lips there. *Hmm…*

"I was starting to think I'd been stood up," I say, not letting my tone give away the truth in the statement.

"Dare's a dare." She shrugs her bare shoulders with a playful grin so I know not to take her words seriously. But a part of me still does.

We head into the auditorium and look around the balcony at the last few pairs of seats available. I leave the choice to her. If this is just a dare or some game we're playing, she'll pick somewhere near the front. Visible. Friendly. But if it is a date, she'll want to sit further back, out of the way. Somewhere without too many prying eyes.

Shit, I'm acting like a teenager on a cinema date. Though that's the only frame of reference I have. Embarrassing really. She's expecting a man, and I've only just learnt how to be one.

With one questioning look up at me, she heads to the back

row. Somehow, my chest relaxes despite the quickening thump inside my ribcage. I follow on a few steps behind, envying her dress and how it clings to her hips as they sway side to side.

"It's rude to stare, Oscar," she reprimands without even needing to look back.

I'm so nervous I've resorted to leering at her instead of complimenting her. Excellent.

"It's a very nice dress."

"Oh, is that what you were looking at?" She gives me the side-eye and nestles her body in the blue velvet seat.

"No wonder it took you so long to get here." I nod my head while looking at her name badge, hoping she won't work out how my gaze landed on it in the first place. "You don't need to wear that tonight – you're off the clock." We should be taking full advantage of not yet being recognisable out of uniform to many of the new guests. It's not often we get the chance to blend in.

She stares down at it, looking troubled. Her attempt to take it off turns quickly into fighting with it. "Ugh, this thing is too stiff. Honestly, it takes me forever every day to—"

"Let me," I offer, and she surrenders her struggle.

I slip my fingertips cautiously down the front of her dress. Her skin is soft and warm against the backs of my knuckles. No bra. Nothing to stop me from making her gasp again. She watches me closely while I watch my hands, careful not to prick her with the pin. Catching her eye is a mistake. She taunts me to tease her like I did before. However, if relinquishing control is what she wants, she doesn't call the shots anymore. I do.

If the room weren't so crowded I'd pull the delicate fabric further from her chest and take a peek.

But the room is crowded.

I clear my throat, my mind along with it, and hand the badge to her. She holds it awkwardly, not sure where to put it.

"No pockets."

"Ah, the patriarchy," I sigh with a gentle shake of my fist.

"Can you keep hold of it?" She passes it back to me just as the houselights go down and the room quietens. "I'll only lose it," she mumbles.

"Like you lost your last one?" I whisper back.

"Shh." She squeezes my arm with untamed excitement when the band starts, and I can't fight off my disappointment when she lets go.

No. We're on a date and I want to hold her. I find her hand on her thigh and interlock it with mine before I can talk myself out of it.

I'm allowed nice things.

She looks up at me with the sweetest smile, only looking away when the show begins.

We used to have guinea pigs that would jump uncontrollably when they were happy, typically when we moved them onto fresh grass or gave them their favourite vegetables. "Popcorning", I think it's called. I've noticed Eliza does something similar. And it's not just how her legs wiggle when she's falling asleep – it's when any strong emotion grips her. As if her body can't contain everything she's feeling.

I was looking forward to watching her mouth along, shiver when a ballad got the better of her, or tap her tiny feet on the floor to the music. But she doesn't mouth along, she doesn't vibrate with excitement, and her tiny feet don't tap. In fact, the longer the show goes on, the less she glows. She catches me looking over at her more than once and sticks a smile back on her face, but it's not real.

She claps at the end of every song, finding my hand again between them, and cheers for our friends as they take their bows. But by the end, she's an entirely different person from the one I came in with.

I sneak us around the crowd and through a staff-only passageway that leads us outside for our walk. It's a beautiful night, but she's looking down at the ground and not up at the stars like I imagined she would.

"The show was really good. Thanks for taking me." She lifts her head to smile at me then drops it back down to the floor.

"Everything okay?"

"Mm-hmm. Sorry, just tired."

I want to ask her what she's thinking, but I don't know how to without prying. *Please let me in, Eliza.*

"I wish I could do what they do," she says as quiet as a mouse. "Like, I wish I was good enough to have made it to where they are."

Oh, Chapman. I know drama school never worked out for her. I've witnessed firsthand how long it's taken her to find her confidence again, and every week at our Wednesday meet-ups I see her start to believe that maybe she isn't so bad after all. She idolised the gang when she got here, to the point she was terrified of them, but now they're her peers. And over the past ninety minutes, she's put them right back on that pedestal again.

If only she could see what the rest of us do.

"I know everything happens for a reason and all that, and I really do love this job, don't get me wrong. It's just—"

"It's plan B."

"Yeah." She nods slowly, her cheeks dimpling, but not from smiling.

"It can take some people years to get into drama school."

"I know. Trust me, if anyone was the poster girl for 'if at first you don't succeed', you're lookin' at her. But when your dream schools reject you for a third time, it's probably time to take the hint."

Three times? That can't be right. Are they deaf? Blind?

"Eliza, you're seriously talented."

"I'm not so sure."

"Mm-mm, none of that. You are. I don't say things I don't mean."

She smiles, beginning to hold her head higher. "Do you miss it? Being up there."

"Sometimes."

"And other times?"

"I remember how fake it all was."

She stops walking for a second to look up at me before continuing. She wasn't expecting that answer. "What do you mean?"

"The first week of any new show was always great...then the autopilot kicks in and everything just blurs into one. Did you ever feel like that at The Cellar?"

She takes a second to recall. "There'd be times where I'd be getting into costume and have no idea how I was going to get through the shift, like if I was having a bad day or something. But as soon as it started, I was in it. I got to switch off from everything else and just have fun with the audiences. By the end of the day, I'd always have forgotten what it was I was worrying about."

"Sounds like a good job."

"It really was."

"Why did you leave?"

Her eyes drop back down to the ground, and I instantly regret the question. Though I've wanted to many times, I've never asked her before. I hate it when people press me for the reason I'm not performing anymore, but I just can't go another day leaving this many of her stones unturned.

She sighs. "A messy breakup of sorts."

"What happened?" The words are out before I can stop them. "If you don't mind me asking."

The longer the silence stretches on, the worse I feel for asking her to relive what's clearly an uncomfortable memory.

"We were together for almost two years. It wasn't perfect, but I kept telling myself 'love isn't meant to be easy' because I'd seen it on some inspirational post on Instagram or whatever. Stupid, I know, but I was eighteen/nineteen and incredibly basic."

I laugh at her self-awareness.

"Some other Cellar friends and I were putting on a show at The Vaults Festival. It was this immersive horror thing, and we managed to get an amazing slot as a regular instalment for a fair chunk of it. Anyway, I dropped my shifts right down and spent most of my time writing, rehearsing, learning lines, and all that. We didn't see much of each other, but it wasn't a biggie. He kept saying he was going to book a ticket for the show, but there was always an excuse why he couldn't – waiting for payday, he'll do it when he gets home, he's just waiting to hear back about some big audition and needs to keep his diary free. Somehow *I* was the one being unreasonable when opening night came and went and I dared to get upset because he still hadn't booked."

I can't help grinding my molars. *Manipulative wanker.*

"He *eventually* came to see it…only because that was the night everyone else from The Cellar was going and he didn't want to miss out on the social." She rolls her eyes, but humorously. I don't know how she's keeping it so light. Nothing she's said so far is okay. "It was one of those shows where the audience had free rein of the space and chose their own adventure. I remember him going around in a small group with one of the new girls. I didn't think much of it at the time – or maybe I did, but I pretended I wasn't the jealous type because that felt like the 'in' thing to do. I didn't know her that well. Still don't."

A storm is brewing inside of me. My body is hot and tight with unease. I don't like where this is going.

"Then, an embarrassingly long time after the show had finished and I was back, I worked out that they'd been shagging each other from the second I cut my hours."

What she's saying is devastatingly sad, but her entire energy couldn't be further from it. She walks tall, stating facts as if they're nothing. She could be telling me about her last trip to Tesco with the tone she's using. Casual. Emotionless. That's what makes this even harder to hear.

"Honestly, as shit as it was, what sucked the most was that everybody else knew and yet no one told me."

How could anyone even *think* about betraying her?

"Despite his 'you never had time for me anymore's"— *Still found a way to make it her fault, I see*—"and many grovelling pleas to give him another chance, I told him to do one. But it was clear neither Twatface nor she had any intention of leaving a well-paid, regular acting job, and I couldn't face staying there and seeing them every day. Nor could I face the people who claimed to be my friends but had zero loyalty when it came down to it. Of course I get not wanting to get involved or whatever, but I know full well they had no problem sticking their noses in to get the gossip. So, yeah, I quit."

"I'm so sorry you had to go through that." I wrack my

brain for something else to say, a piece of wisdom or something helpful, but nothing can undo what happened or make that pain go away. This wasn't what she was fretting over earlier, and I've just reminded her of it. I'm the worst date ever.

She shrugs. "Character building, innit." Her lips make a tight smile.

I want to take her in my arms and never let her go. If I could blow an impenetrable bubble around her so no one could hurt her again, I would in a heartbeat.

"What did you do after that?"

"Um… I was lost for a while. Nowhere I wanted to be wanted me because I hadn't gone to drama school. And I missed that year of auditions because, well, I was happy with my life at the time I needed to get my applications in, and having already been rejected twice, I thought it just wasn't meant to be. I was living with my best friends, who I'd known since Stagecoach, but we…grew apart, I guess you could say, so I just had to hit the reset button. My parents thought it was best I take a break from the acting scene for a while and convinced my brother to offer me a job so I could stay in London, because moving back home would have felt like failure at the time. Not that it is – I just wasn't ready to give up *everything* all at once, you know? So I became his PA, which was…a waking nightmare. And usually I'm the one giving people nightmares, so I finally got a taste of my own medicine," she jokes. "That shitty job was all the motivation I needed to apply again this year, and when I didn't get in, I decided it was time to give up on the first half of my 'be a performer on a cruise ship' dream and focus on the second half."

"And here you are." I'm overcome with amazement. She learnt to be strong on her own because there was no one there to fight for her. They say it's not about the fall, it's about the recovery, and *God*, does she make the recovery seem so possible.

"Sorry, talking about myself. Wh—"

"I asked you to," I cut her off. I'm not ready to close the window I've opened into her life, so I don't let her peek through mine.

An easy smile curls her lips, and we come to a stop at the front of the ship. I lean back with my elbows on the railings, look up, and wait for her to do the same. I can feel the warmth of her hand just inches from mine. I wait for the voices to kick in and tell me it would be wrong to touch her, but they don't come. I stretch my pinkie finger out until I find hers. A tiny hum rings through her, and she latches onto me. Out of the corner of my eye I watch her stargaze, peace settling in.

"I do wonder where I'd be now if I hadn't quit," she says after a while. "Obviously, at the time it felt like the only option, but what if I just rode it out?"

"Sometimes we can get caught up in the what-ifs and lose sight of all the great things that have happened because of the choices we made."

"You're right. I could do with being more resilient though. Or getting a thicker skin."

"You're a lot tougher than you give yourself credit for, Chapman."

She glances over at me, half-smiling, then back to the sky. "But I let a stupid *boy* ruin something I loved." There's anger in her – there must be, but she doesn't show it. She can't hide the hurt, though, and it kills me. "I always quit when things get tough, and I hate myself for it."

"Don't be so hard on yourself."

Did she not hear anything she just said? Things didn't just

"get tough"; her whole world crumbled, and she had no choice but to either go down with it or reinvent herself.

Holding onto the tips of her fingers, I stiffen and step away from the railing, my focus trained on her. She straightens under my stare.

"I think you did exactly the right thing. You should be proud you had the courage to walk away from something that wasn't good for you. You protected yourself. I know so many people who would have stayed and given him chance after chance, spending the next few months or years of their lives just talking about what they *should* do, never actually acting on it. I swear sometimes people just stay for the drama. But you didn't. It takes an incredibly strong person to move on from something like that."

She smiles up at me, not quite believing it, but thankful to have heard it. The deck is clear enough of guests that I decide to chance it and pull her hand up to my mouth to kiss it hard before holding it by my side. I keep it there as we begin to walk again. Fuck passengers seeing us – Eliza needs to know someone's on her side. And that someone is *me*.

On the one hand, I wish I knew her back then so I could spare her from… What did she call him? Twatface and his atrocious behaviour. But on the other hand, I'm so glad we've only just met. I would have been just as bad for her. Not *to* her – definitely not – but…not good enough. I look back at my past and I'm disgusted with myself more times than I'm not, but for some reason, Eliza seems to believe in me. She's inspired me tonight to stop wasting time on the fall and instead focus on the recovery.

We walk for a little longer before Eliza's heels get the better of her and we head inside. Anguish twists my stomach. When this date ends, she's going back to her cabin. Back to Tom. He'll be the one who might have to help her out of this dress, not me. Can't even risk a good-night kiss outside her door. I don't want a repeat of what happened the last time I walked her back late. And he's almost guaranteed to be there now.

A room swap was the only solution. Asking Daniel to be more considerate with his nighttime activities got me nowhere. *"Can't make any promises, but we'll certainly try."* Having witnessed both Eliza and Tom space out on multiple occasions since Gwen got here, I couldn't sit back and watch them suffer in silence any longer. Their friendship seemed like it was in a stable enough place to risk the proximity, and besides, if he was in there, it was a surefire way to keep me out. Of course, I didn't know how much I'd regret that decision until *after* I spoke to Daniel.

Just as we get below deck, an idea comes to me that could help her as much as me. I lead us to the bar, buy her a drink like a good date should, and instead of taking her over to our own private table, I sit us down with the actors. She's more than worthy of sitting at this table, and I won't stop proving it to her until she believes it.

"Are we doing a haunted house this year?" I ask Jerry, desperate to change the subject. It's not often I get to talk to him outside of activities, so I should be grateful Obi dragged him over here from the omelette station in an attempt to big me up. But would it hurt him to be more subtle about it? I haven't heard back about the second interview yet. They say no news is good news, but to me, it says they need more time to interview other candidates because the ones they've seen so far aren't what they're looking for.

"We sure are! Henry and I are actually meeting later this week to talk about it."

"What's the theme?" Eliza perks up.

I purposely asked him about something she could get involved in too, and I'm glad she is.

"Halloween," he answers like he didn't really understand her question.

She cocks her head but decides not to press further.

"I think we should do somethin' different with it this year," Maddison says. I always forget she was on this ship for her last contract too, hence how she's been a fountain of knowledge from day one.

"What was wrong with it last year?" he questions, but Maddison keeps staring at him as if to say, "What *wasn't* wrong with last year?" "Ouch, okay. What do you suggest we do?"

She shrugs, crunching on her toast. "I dunno. Ask Eliza – she's the expert."

He turns his attention back to Eliza, realising he may have dismissed her too soon, and something seems to click. "You worked at The Cellar, right?"

She nods in the middle of a sip of tea, narrowing her eyes and slipping me a mean stare. I won the fight over who got to make it this morning. And I've been mixing things up. Keeping her on her toes. So worth it for that glare.

"So tell me, what do you think of this?" He pulls out his phone and proudly proceeds to show her a YouTube video he uploaded of a walkthrough from last year's haunted house. She watches it intently, making various polite noises of interest but keeping a stoic poker face. I know exactly what that means. It's the same face she made when Mrs Dove cornered her and complained about her infected ingrown toenails in explicit detail. This was before the minibus incident, of course – she hasn't bothered us at all since then. Eliza hates it, and she's doing her best not to say exactly that.

"Cool. I bet the kids really enjoyed that."

Oh no. Collectively, we all wince, and she sees her mistake.

"Oh God, no, I meant… I didn't…"

We all giggle at her faux pas, including Jerry, which makes her ease up a little and laugh too.

"Let me start that again. Is this for all ages?"

"It is. I have a feeling that's not the right answer though."

"Did you have a kid time and an adult time?"

"Nope, just everyone all the time," Maddison pipes up in a sing-songy tone as if she also knew it was a terrible system.

Eliza bares her teeth, and it reminds me of the cringe emoji. Jerry doesn't need any more convincing that he needs her help.

"What would you do differently?"

She looks at me for reassurance, which I give her in the form of a small nod. "Well, firstly, what's scary for kids isn't scary for adults. I don't think that's a shock."

Jerry looks a little embarrassed, but there's a curious smile playing on his lips.

"But what's happening in this video is just jump scares. One or two times, great. But it gets old fast. People probably left there on the same adrenaline level they came in with. You need to have a variety of scares because what works for one person doesn't always work for another. Maybe have some stalkers, a claustrophobia tunnel, a story to set the scene." She's gone, her eyes sparkling as her mind runs a mile a minute. "Ooh, quick question. Did people laugh a lot?"

"No, of course not. It's a haunted house – people shouldn't be laughing." He guffaws, looking around the table for support, but Eliza has us all hooked on her every word.

She presses her lips together, willing herself not to respond.

"Go on, say it."

"The only enjoyment that comes from being scared is being able to laugh about it immediately afterwards."

He looks at her perplexed.

"Could I show you another video?"

He hands her his phone. She quickly types something into the YouTube search bar, taps something, and hands it back over to Jerry, gesturing for everyone else to watch too.

We all get up from our seats and huddle around him while she sits and watches us patiently from the other side of the table. The video reminds me of a hazard perception test: we're in a car driving along a country road. We watch and we wait, none of us sure why after a while because nothing's happening. The camera slowly pans down to a hand changing radio stations, then suddenly it whips back up again, revealing the face of an angry clown with pointed teeth and bright yellow eyes in the windshield at the same time as a piercing scream erupts from the speaker. All of us flinch. Maddison and Obi shriek and clutch each other instinctively. Jerry and I make noises I'm pretty sure neither of us have ever made before. And then we laugh, really belly laugh, at how stupid we must have looked. As we do, the relief settles in. I've never noticed that before.

"Okay, I'm sold. Where are you on Friday at three?"

She reaches into her pocket for her printed schedule. I look at mine too in case we're doing something together and I can cover it. "I will be…halfway through darts," she says, her excitement deflating.

Voices start coming out of Jerry's radio.

"I'm free. I'll finish it up for you," I offer.

"Are you sure?" She looks at me with so much hope.

"Yeah, no problem."

"Excellent. Thank you, Harvey. Eliza, think you could prepare a few ideas? I'm sure Henry will be just as excited as I am to hear them." Jerry smiles and prepares himself to leave.

"Sure."

"I'll see you then. Have a good day, everyone."

It's not until he's put his tray away and left the room that we all puff out the breath we were holding.

"Holy shit, a meetin' with Jerry *and* Henry! That's a big deal, girl," Maddison chimes.

Eliza's breathing is all out of sorts. She's vibrating as if she could supernova at any second. This. This exact emotion is my favourite of hers. I'd give anything to watch her blow their minds in that meeting, because I have no doubt she will.

SEVENTEEN

OSCAR

The venue fills up with guests ahead of Battle of the Sexes, a rowdy competition where men and women go head-to-head partaking in ridiculous tasks to determine which is the better sex. It's not exactly progressive, but it makes for excellent viewing.

This afternoon I'm working with Tom, which both of us seem equally as pleased about. Though, his dirty looks have subsided as the week's gone on. I would have addressed it by now if I knew how to explain I'm not doing what he's accusing me of. One fake date. That's it. And it didn't even end in a kiss like she wanted it to. Like *I* wanted it to. But he won't see it like that.

There's one last activity to train her in tonight, and then it will be luck of the draw as to which things we get to do together. If it wouldn't affect her reputation with the company, I'd suggest she needs more help in some areas and that training should continue for a bit longer. Six weeks longer, to be exact.

After dumping the kit bags down, we start laying out

props around the space, and I work hard to keep my thoughts in check as memories from Scavenger rise to the surface. I place a cone in the spot we kissed. Another where I made her scream with my mouth between her legs. Another where I developed a fetish for sun cream. *Hmm.*

"I never said thank you." Tom interrupts my daydream.

Thank you?

"For talking to Daniel," he clarifies.

"How's that working out?"

"I no longer get up more tired than I was the night before, so yeah, all good. Although—" He shakes his head, stopping himself from saying whatever he was about to.

"What?"

He gives in after I refuse to ignore it. "She wriggles *so* much. Like, Monday, I thought I'd actually have to restrain her."

I busy myself to hide my smile. My little cricket got all excited after our date. "Guess you can't have everything."

"Yeah, it's either that or a live sex show, so can't complain."

We focus for a second to check we've lined everything up evenly for one of the tasks.

"Why did you do it though? I thought I'd be the last person you'd want her to share a room with."

"It wasn't good for either of you. And you guys are good now, right? With everything…"

He nods. "Well, thanks."

We share a small smile and get to setting up the prize table.

"Wanna make this interesting?" he asks.

"Like a bet? Sure." What's the worst that could happen?

"So if my ladies win…"

"Oh, so I'm doing the chaps, am I?"

"Well, you have such a way with them I assumed you'd want to."

"Still thinking about that kiss, are we?" I quiz him. It was a good kiss – for a straight guy – so long as I kept telling myself I couldn't taste Eliza's candy-floss lip balm on him.

"It keeps me awake at night," he says flatly.

"So if your ladies win…"

He thinks for a second. "Break the rules."

What's he up to?

"And I don't mean put your nametag on the wrong side or chew gum. It has to be more obvious than that."

"Right, okay."

"By the end of the day," he adds quickly as if a lightbulb has illuminated above his head.

"Do you have something specific in mind?"

"Not really. Just be spontaneous for once. Do something you shouldn't. I don't care."

"Okay. And if the men win…you get to ask me one question and I have to give you the one-hundred-percent honest answer."

Curiosity, or maybe suspicion, takes over his features, but he doesn't object. I need him to want me to win, because I really don't want to lose my job.

Tom, now finished with work for the day, watches me like a stage manager guarding a props table. After crowning his ladies champion, he doesn't leave my side. Including when I go to the bathroom *just in case* my rule break involves illegal substances and my back passage. Seriously? He said break the rules, not the *law*.

He's taken a seat up on the balcony overlooking the stage in the large cabaret lounge for Big Band Bingo. Eliza hasn't spotted him just yet, and I'm hoping it stays that way. I'm not sure what he's expecting me to do here of all places – or at all, for that matter – but I'll let him waste his time.

I introduce Eliza to the band once she's back from handing out blotters. I know the pianist, Bryan, from my last ship. He's a sweet older guy with silver hair in the places he still has it. He's given up asking me to sing with the band now, but for a while when I first got here, he couldn't accept that I'd packed it all up.

Tonight's game is a slower form of bingo where, instead of calling out numbers, the jazz band plays each song through and people cross it off if they've got it on their card, and then they sit back and enjoy the music. I keep stealing glances at Eliza. I can't help myself. She isn't someone who ever has to make a lot of effort – she always looks beautiful – but I secretly love formal nights. You can see the pride she takes in dressing up a little more glamorously, just like she did on our date.

After fifteen minutes or so, the first "bingo!" is called for a line of five. I check the ticket against the band's set list with Eliza and then let her award them their prize.

"I love this kind of music," she admits when the next song starts.

"Me too."

We hum along to it until we can't help but sing the chorus quietly. I make the mistake of peeking up at Tom, who purposely looks at his watch and back down at me. When the band plays "My Shadow and Me", I know exactly what I want to do.

"Care to dance?" I whisper to Eliza, who looks up at me in confusion.

"Really?"

"Why not? We've got time."

The next bingo for two lines won't be called for a while.

She smiles, and I take her hand, guide her around in front of our table, and pull her into me. She follows my lead, her body moulding to mine so naturally. It doesn't take long for some other couples to get up and join us in dancing by their tables. Displays of affection between crew members in public areas definitely aren't tolerated. Okay, so I don't have my tongue down her throat – unfortunately – but it's affection. And it's public. *Hmm.* If only.

"Oscar?"

"Yes, Chapman?" I look down at her bright blue eyes staring up at me.

"Maddison said something today…about requesting a ship for her next contract. She doesn't want to come back here again." She swallows, looking nervous all of a sudden, and it makes my heart ache. "What, um—?"

"I haven't been asked yet." Which I guess is a good sign I'm still being considered for the activities manager position, but a very bad sign I could be about to lose her.

"Do you want to come back here?"

I lock eyes with her. "More than anything." I want to tell her the truth about everything, but with the smile she gives me before she settles her head back against my chest, and with the way her fingers tighten on my hand, I know it would only hurt her. And there's no need to upset her over something that might never happen. This isn't the first time in the past few days I've hoped it actually doesn't.

Eliza and I sing quietly together again, and when the song picks up, I can't help but spin and dip her while she giggles and squeals with delight, neither of us holding back anymore, and it feels so right. The band is smiling away at us, and when I peer around the room, so is everyone else.

I check in with Tom, but he's no longer alone. Valentina and Maddison are by his side, clearly having been briefed on my forfeit and wanting in on the entertainment. Tom cocks an eyebrow at me as if to say, "Is that it?" What more does he want? It's not like I can run on stage and…

"Oh, fuck," I sigh under my breath.

"What's wrong?"

"I'm about to do something potentially very stupid."

"Okay." Eliza looks up at me, confused. "Want me to stop you?"

"Nope."

I catch Bryan's eye and nod, and his face lights up with understanding. As the band plays the final few bars of the song, I dart up the steps at the side of the stage, not forgetting to grab one of our microphones from our table on the way. I bend down next to him, confirming the next song.

"Sure this is okay?" I check.

"I thought you'd never ask," he says with a triumphant smile, then he leans into his mic, and I step back out of his way. "Ladies and gentlemen, we have a very special guest joining us for this next one. Please welcome to the stage a good friend of mine, Mr Oscar Harvey!"

It's hard to block out the applause as I take a spot at the side of the band.

The piano and trumpet play the intro to "Beyond the Sea", and anxiety almost bowls me over. *Deep breaths.* Three minutes and it'll all be over. The song for sure, but quite possibly my career too.

Singing up on a stage again shouldn't feel as good as this. I don't deserve for it to. But I will cherish this performance

277

more than anything I've ever done before because Eliza's here, watching me with such pride. The spotlights are bright, but I can just about make out faces. Dumbfounded but not horrified. Good. My voice isn't as shaky as my insides feel then.

When the song ends, Bryan looks more than pleased. I read his lips: "One more?"

I've completed my mission. Tom isn't pushing me anymore, but seeing as how this hasn't blown up in my face, I can't bring myself to get off the stage. Not yet.

"One more," I agree.

He gestures with an open palm for me to pick a song. I step closer to him and glance at the setlist over his shoulder, the perfect song instantly jumping out at me. He eyes me with curious excitement, granting me permission before I can even ask the question.

Please forgive me for this, Eliza.

"I'd like to extend this very generous welcome to an incredibly gifted performer. An undiscovered talent, you could say." It's then, as I look over at her, that I spot the fear in Eliza's eyes. "Miss Chapman, would you care to join me up here?"

The guests cheer in support. It's possibly because I've earned their trust, but most likely it's because she's captured their hearts in just a matter of days. There's no way she can refuse now.

Eliza panics, nervously picking up her microphone before joining me onstage. The band watch her as she passes them, avidly waiting to hear her sing. She has a professional smile fixed on her face, but her eyes aren't committed to it. I whisper the name of the song at her to make sure she knows it. When she nods, still unsure, I give Bryan the go-ahead.

I used to be fearless. And fun. I used to back myself to do anything and everything. Though I think his intention was to see me sweat, Tom's actually done something far kinder. He's liberated a part of me I've been hiding for fear that was the thing that made me a bad person. Turns out being spontaneous and a little bold doesn't make me an arsehole. Being an arsehole made me an arsehole.

He's done me a favour, and it would be selfish of me not to pay it forward.

TOM

"I didn't know she sang. *Can* she sing?" I look to the others for confirmation.

"Guess so. They get together with the actors on Wednesdays," Valentina reveals like it's no big deal.

"What?" Maddison's jaw drops wide open. "How do you know?"

How did I *not* know?

An acoustic guitar starts playing, and Valentina shuts Maddison up. I break out in goose bumps the second Eliza opens her mouth. I'm speechless. Why have I never heard her sing before? And what else don't I know about her?

Her smile tells me she's relaxing into the song, and the guilt I felt when he pulled her up there loosens its grip on my stomach. Their voices sound good together. Annoyingly good together. And, of course, it's a romantic song. I'm not sure what it's called, but they keep saying "something stupid" and telling each other how much they love each other. Of all the songs he could have picked…

Their eyes barely leave one another. Eliza looks over at him like he's the night sky she belongs in, and the way he looks back at her summons the green monster that's typically only reserved for my brother. He's not acted on his crush though. Not properly. He wouldn't have moved me into her cabin if he were planning to. Or has he and that's just another thing I don't know?

"Good work, Tom." Valentina pats me once on the shoulder.

"Oh, shit. Henry. Five o'clock." Maddison freaks out.

I look down and spot Henry watching them, but they haven't seen him yet.

"We're going to leave you to enjoy Neptune's incredible Big Band once again. Thank you for letting us share your stage."

Harvey and Eliza initiate a round of applause for the band and head offstage. The smiley old guy takes charge again, and the game continues.

Henry meets them back at their table. Their faces are calm, but I know their minds won't be. This is my fault. I sidestep past the girls. I need to go and take at least some of the hit on this.

"Oh, thank God," Maddison sighs, and I look back down to see Henry shaking their hands with a huge grin on his face.

Relief visibly washes over them. *Crisis averted.*

Once Henry leaves, Eliza and Harvey glow with excitement. Everything about her sparkles like glitter. He points up to us on the balcony, I guess having explained why all that just happened because her eyes narrow and she points an accusing finger my way with the cutest little smile. It's like her glitter is on me now too.

She isn't mine, I know that, but I don't want her to be his. Who am I kidding? She'd never pick me over him. I can't give her what he can. I'm stupid to have ever believed I could, and selfish to have ever stopped him from trying.

That's the difference between us. When he's selfish, he gives her a night she'll never forget. When I'm selfish, I deny her the chance to get close to the people I never want her to remember.

EIGHTEEN

ELIZA

I've been on cloud nine for the past few days. Passengers keep coming up to me to tell me what a lovely voice I have, and each time they do I get this wave of emotion like I'm going to cry. After so much external *in*validation, I started to believe my voice was in fact atrocious and I'd just been delusional this whole time, thinking I was talented enough to even *apply* to drama school, let alone get in. Yet the past few Wednesdays I've sung with Oscar and his friends – our friends – have been so healing that I'm finally starting to love my voice again.

I successfully pitched a pirate ship–themed, story-led haunted house to Henry and Jerry yesterday. It'll start off with a lighthearted Long John Silver sending the audience on a quest to retrieve their stolen treasure from The Flying Dutchman as they believe that will lift the curse on their own vessel. They'll hand over a key and warn them of the dangers, telling them of the countless sailors they've lost to the mission and the nightmares the rare few who have returned unsuccessfully have been plagued with ever since. The guests will go from room to room in search of the treasure, encountering mutated fish pirates along the way. In the final room there'll be a huge treasure chest, and when the key is inserted into it the guests will be plunged into near darkness and will face the wrath of the formidable captain of The Flying Dutchman, forced to run for their lives or have their souls claimed.

All of this will be part of the fifteen-and-unders time in the early evening, but then for the sixteen-and-overs from 9 p.m., there'll be more actors, more gore, and more aggression.

Over the coming weeks I'll be collaborating with theatre production staff from every department, who will then design and build the set, create soundscapes and lighting sequences, and source, make, or order props and costumes and special effects makeup to really bring it all to life. Henry and Jerry even agreed to let me teach a scaring masterclass to the other staff because after seeing that YouTube video and how everyone repeatedly shouted "boo" or "rah" at people, they realised they clearly need some help. I almost can't believe they want my opinions, let alone my whole idea, but apparently, Henry has meticulously studied the guest comment cards from previous Halloween weeks, and none of them ever praised the haunted house. This year he wants to take full advantage of having an expert on board – not that I'd call myself that, but as the only person here who's dedicated nearly two years of their life to scaring people, in their eyes, I am.

Tom and I are allowed off the ship today, and we're determined to do it right this time. On the team's recommendation we go to the nice beach cafe for lunch. We order burgers and mocktails, and Tom buries my feet in the warm sand under the table while we wait despite my attempts to bury his first.

"I have a confession to make." He looks at me with a cheeky grin, and I buzz with curiosity. "I dropped my suitcase on purpose."

"No, you didn't," I say in a playful tone, thinking back to that morning waiting outside the hotel.

"I swear!"

"Why on earth would you do that?"

"I wanted an excuse to talk to you."

"So you're saying you saw a random girl from behind and instead of talking to her like a normal person, you *yeeted* all your belongings down a flight of steps. What does that say about you, Thomas?"

"Wow, so you didn't remember me as the hunk from breakfast. Elizabeth, I'm offended." He presses a hand to his chest.

"What?"

"I saw you in the restaurant sitting there all alone with your eggs. I actually did the whole 'hey, is this seat taken?' thing just to strike up a conversation."

I can't help the cackle that comes out. "Stop it. I would have remembered."

"Of course you would have. Look at me – I'm sensational, but you didn't even look up. You had your headphones on, talking to someone saying how much you were going to miss them, so I just sat quietly on the table next to you."

That call I do remember. I gasp and bite my lip. "I feel so bad."

"Don't. Hearing that *cute little accent* of yours was enough." Whenever he puts on a British accent he just ends up sounding like Moira Rose from "Schitt's Creek". "But when I saw you again outside, I knew I had to make sure my grand entrance was more memorable."

"You're such a wally."

"Hey, it worked, didn't it?"

"I guess it did."

Our mocktails arrive, and we both bob our heads and smile as we enjoy our first sips of the fruity concoction.

"So when you eventually noticed me, what did you think?"

"I thought you were a hot mess."

"You said hot. I'm takin' it!"

"But you were about to get on a ship for six months – why bother even talking to me?"

"I dunno. I guess I felt like a troop being deployed; I just wanted one last memory to keep me going. A girl to come back for. Maybe even a departing kiss…" He looks off into the distance wistfully.

"Oh, shut it, you. You were shagging Polly within a week."

We both giggle. It's nice that we can laugh about it now. I really love being his friend. Even if some days it feels like it's possible to be more.

Sharing a room with him, although an amazing change from Gwen, has been…difficult. We made a list of rules before we accepted Daniel's offer, and the first two were already in place: no nudity, and no communal showers. The third, which he was pretty insistent upon, was that the room was a sex-free zone. I can't work out if that was said as a final backstop to make sure neither of us gave in to the temptation that's never fully gone away, a warning to me that I'd better not even think about inviting Oscar back after catching us in the pool, or if he was politely letting me know he plans to hook up with people and he's going to be considerate about it. But either way, knowing that was where his head was at, I couldn't see why we'd say no. And with that, our mutual friend-zoning pact was set.

Followed almost instantly by another. I completely tanked my date with Oscar. But am I really shocked after I turned up late, bitched about my ex, and whined about what a failure I am? It's no wonder he didn't want to kiss me. In fact, he couldn't have made it any clearer that he wasn't interested if he'd tried. Sitting us down with the others like that instead of at a quiet table in the corner or walking me to my door. Though of course, it took me until the morning to see it without the rose-tinted glasses.

Ugh. So awkward. At least I can play it off as just a dare, even if for a second I thought it might have been real.

Tom and I ban any and all ship-talk and enjoy our delicious lunch in the sun. He tells me all about his psychology degree he didn't quite finish, which makes me feel a bit better about not having any higher education experience to my name. I ask a million questions about frat and sorority houses, which still baffle me. From what I've seen online and in movies, they're basically just cults for sexy people. He wasn't in one, but he couldn't tell me a single thing to sway my opinion.

We slag off our older brothers and hypothesise about how different we'd be if we grew up in the other's country. He thinks he'd be a full-fledged alcoholic if he were legally allowed to start drinking at eighteen, even though it's not like he waited until he was twenty-one. My instinct is to defend that theory, and then I think of everyone I know who's my age or older and still out binge-drinking, pushing through each day with a hangover, so I admit he's probably got a point. I decide I'd be the size of a house because I love American sweets and have terrible impulse control.

When he gets his wallet out to pay his share, I can't resist making a demand.

"Show me your ID."

"I'll show you mine if you show me yours," he flirts.

I roll my eyes and make the trade.

So worth it.

"You're so tiny and squishy!" I coo.

"Shut up. We can't all be pretty like you. Some of us are late bloomers!"

I study it a bit more. His date of birth doesn't look right. There aren't twenty-eight months. *Oh, right, Americans are weird.*

"Wait… Is it your birthday tomorrow?"

He snatches the card back and looks around desperately for the waiter to return, which only confirms it.

"Why the hell haven't you said anything?"

"Because…I don't really care about my birthday."

"'Don't really.' Not 'really don't'. Ha! Psychology! You do care! Everyone cares about their birthday, and those who say they don't are actually the ones who want the biggest fuss made."

"Please don't make a fuss."

"You can't stop me."

"Elizabeth," he pleads in the same tone you'd reason with a dog to drop its favourite toy. "Promise me you won't make a fuss." He holds out his pinkie and waits for me to lock mine with it.

"Fine," I succumb, crossing two fingers on my other hand behind my back.

Tom

Elizabeth stays true to her word. No one, not a soul, seems to know it's my birthday today. I spend all lunch with her and she doesn't even mention it once. Maybe she forgot. The only acknowledgment was from Mom and Bobby this morning, but apart from that, nothing.

It's our first birthday without Dad, and I didn't expect it to hit me quite so hard. Eliza was right: maybe I do want a little fuss. Or just something to take my mind off everything. If only I could track her down to tell her. If only I could track *anyone* down. It's 9 p.m. on a Sunday and the bar is completely empty of familiar faces. People can't be too tired to have at least one drink before bed, can they?

I finish my lap of the room and head back out. I guess I'll go knock on more doors again in case I just missed people a minute ago. Or didn't knock loud enough.

I bump into a scatty blonde thing when I step out the door. She drops a pile of clothes on the floor in the collision, so I help her pick them up.

"Eliza, there you are! Want to grab a drink?" *What is all this?*

It's a lot of spandex, that's what it is, and then I spot the famous Superman logo.

"Sorry, I haven't got time."

"Not even for a quick birthday drink?" I cringe hearing how desperate I sound.

Her whole face freezes, her eyes slowly giving away her panic.

"Fuck. Tom, I'm so sorry."

She forgot. She actually forgot. She looks devastated.

"Today's just been—"

"Don't sweat it. Are you okay? Do you need a hand with something?

"Yeah. Actually, are you free now?"

I spread my arms wide. "As a bird."

"Thank God. I can't find anyone. You haven't had a drink, have you?"

"Not yet."

"Good."

"What's going on?"

"No time. Come with me." She hightails it to our room, and I chase after her. When we get inside, she throws a Superman costume at me and immediately strips down to her underwear. Without thinking, I do the same. "There was a fuck-up. Some VIP guest booked a superhero party for their son."

"What, now? Bit late, isn't it?" I force my leg into the tight costume.

"Tell me about it. The guys managing the bookings thought it was a mistake and corrected it to 9 a.m. tomorrow."

"Why would they assume the mix-up was with the a.m./p.m. and not the date? Like, why wouldn't they have moved it to 9 a.m. today?"

"That would have made a lot more sense..."

"How did that even happen? We use twenty-four-hour time here."

"Who knows, but someone's getting fired. Anyway, the passenger turned up about twenty minutes ago and went mental. The kids' team are already several drinks deep, and guess who was right next to them, sober as a judge, with no choice but to say yes? I have no idea where the hell everyone else is. Thank you."

"Yeah, no problem."

"I'm so sorry I forgot your birthday. I'll steal some of this little shit's cake and we can eat it after?"

"You're gonna be such a good aunt, I can tell."

She glares at me. *Got it. Less jokes, more changing.* "Come on – we have, like, two minutes."

"All right, all right, two seconds." There's a weird cup built into the crotch of the costume that I'm having a hard time getting comfortable in.

She yanks the door open and runs down the corridor. Her cape flows behind her and her white sneakers carry her as fast as they can. Superwoman's a good look on her. Way too good to be going to some kid's party.

"How do you even host a kid's party?" I ask.

"I don't know. Shit. We'll just play musical statues, musical bumps, musical…lions? I'm not sure. We'll figure something out, but whatever happens, I think music will be a winner."

We fly up several flights of stairs and through the back routes so we don't crash into any guests until we get to a part of the ship I didn't even know existed.

"Slow down, Elizabeth. I'm Superman, not The Flash!"

"I'm sure that would be funny if I knew who that was."

Oh, this girl needs educating.

"Where are we?"

"Fuck should I know? Some boardroom they've thank-fully kitted out in advance." She knocks on the door and waits.

I finally catch up with her, so out of breath my lungs sting.

"Hang on…can we just…*aghh*," I huff.

"No." She fixes my hair quickly and pushes me forwards to open the door. She owes me. *Big time.*

"SURPRISE!"

She didn't…

No wonder I couldn't find anyone – they're all here. The whole room is full of our friends dressed in superhero costumes of their own. The space is covered from head to toe in balloons, banners, and photos from the past month, the latest Spiderman film is playing silently on a projector screen at the back of the room, and the table is full of candy and snacks from the crew shop and alcohol snuck up from the bar. Maddison's filming us like a proud mom, and only now do I notice Eliza and I are in matching costumes. I used to hate being put in the same things as Bobby, made to look like clones of one another, when all I wanted was to be seen as an individual. But tonight I feel so lucky to be her clone.

I have no words.

I turn to look behind me. Surely this isn't all for me. It must be someone else's birthday too. It has to be. Everyone laughs at me like I'm doing a bit, but I'm in total disbelief. I've never had my own birthday party before. I fight back the burning tears in my eyes.

My own birthday party.

"Tom, you okay?" Eliza's sweet voice asks me.

"Yeah." I clear my throat. "I'm just so relieved I don't have to host a kids' party!" I let out a big sigh, no longer sure if I'm out of breath from running or the shock.

Everyone laughs except Eliza, who's looking at me nervously. She went against my wishes, but I love her even more for it. Sometimes I think she knows me better than I know myself.

"I'm so getting you back for this, Elizabeth." I squeeze her in a tight hug. "Someone get this girl an Oscar because *boy,* did she have me fooled!" I pull myself away to take a look at her scheming face, phones flashing all around us as photos are taken.

"He's right here." Daniel pats Harvey on the back, earning him the same kind of groan he always gets for his dad jokes.

The party is exactly what I needed. Exactly what I've always wanted. It's silly and fun and it reminds me of all the good times, the carefree part of my life before Dad got sick, before Bobby and I became rivals. I can't believe what Eliza's managed to pull off in such a short space of time. She roped the girls into helping plan party games, sort all the decorations, and spread the news, and the guys she assigned to food and finding costumes for everyone. There's even a cake with my name, and my name *only*, frosted on top. We aren't allowed candles, but I couldn't care less. I feel like the luckiest guy in the whole world. I can't believe she'd go to all this effort for a guy she hated just a few weeks ago.

It's late by the time we've packed up the room and gone back down to our rooms.

"Eliza, thank you. That was beyond amazing," I say when it's just us walking down the hall.

"Really? You're not mad?"

"Why would I be mad?"

"Because you specifically said 'don't make a fuss', and I specifically and deliberately made a fuss."

"I was wrong."

She gasps loudly and stops dead, falling into me as if she's passing out.

"Oh, can it, you." I laugh and drag her the last few steps.

We brush our teeth together, and I leave her to take her makeup off. I stick the fairy lights on and peel this horrendously tight Lycra skin off me before slipping into my bed. I avert my eyes while she changes into her pyjamas but don't miss the tiny scraps of paper that fall out of her costume onto the floor.

"So, Valentina and Sophie, huh? Gonna explain what you were up to there?"

We had bits of paper just like that with dares written on them to give to other people during some twisted form of beer pong. Eliza's clearly didn't say "kiss the closest person of the same sex for twenty seconds" when I peered over her shoulder, but that's what she said to Valentina.

"I was up to nunya."

I crinkle my face at her nonsense.

"Nunya business!"

"Elizabeth, it's dangerous to meddle in affairs of the heart."

"You can talk. 'Hold hands with the birthday boy for the rest of the night.' What was that about? My hand has never been so clammy!"

"Hey, that was only after I realised we could just make up anything we wanted, and trust me, you should be thanking me because what was really written down was pure filth!" *"Give a lap dance to the tallest person in the room."* Whoever wrote it wanted to watch Harvey squirm, and no way in hell was I about to endure watching her do that to him. *Especially* not on my birthday.

"What was it really?"

I beckon her closer to me, then closer still, getting her to come right up to me so I can whisper in her ear, "Nunya. Business."

With fake annoyance she throws herself on me, causing us to fall back on my bed. I wriggle while she tries to tickle the answer out of me, saying, "Tell me, tell me!" over and over again. Finally, I summon the strength to overpower and restrain her, both of us giggling and squealing as I bear down on top of her.

For a second it's just our breaths panting, and every

scenario plays out in my head, my dick coming to life in my boxers at all the possible ways I could thank her for tonight.

Nope.

I release my hold on her and roll onto my back, making sure the sheets cover my lap as we lie side by side for a while.

"Tonight was really special." I finally break the silence.

"I'm glad you had a good time."

"Do you do this for all your friends?"

Friends. We're just friends.

"I used to." She smiles, but there's something missing. "Damn, if I had more time I could have done party bags," she sighs. "Ooh! Or a lucky dip!"

I laugh at her adorable ideas. "It was perfect. *More* than perfect. It was literally the best birthday party I've ever had."

"Now you're just being nice."

"Seriously." I turn my head to look at her, needing her to know I mean it. The warmth in her smile returns, and even with her lips *right there*, I'm not going to give in to the temptation. After tonight, I know for sure this isn't a friendship worth putting on the line again.

NINETEEN

ELIZA

By the time next Sunday rolls around, I'm exhausted but exhilarated as if I've just climbed Mount Everest. If Everest were fun or in any way of interest to me. And despite the long days and late nights, it hasn't felt like work at all.

Two or three months ago, I never could have imagined life being like this, and now I can't imagine working anywhere else.

Having watched and met some of the solo performers on the ship, I start wondering if I could ever make that gig work for me in the unlikely event this particular role gets boring. They get a pretty sweet deal on here – whole days off to explore, and then performing in one of the ship's bars, smaller venues, or even the main theatre in the evenings. But then they aren't here for nearly as long as the entertainment staff. Some of them seem quite lonely as they don't have a regular bunch of people to hang out with, and also, I really like the variety I get from hosting. Besides, it's not like I'd ever actually get booked. It's fun to dream though.

I finally got to see Tom do stand-up at an open mic night in the crew bar this week. I was weirdly nervous to see him perform because I'm not typically a fan of amateur male stand-ups. After one or two half-decent jokes, their material usually peters out into minute after painful minute of crude jokes – if you can even call them that – about their penises. Either they can't get it up or they can't stop touching it or no one else wants to touch it. Like, we get it, you have a penis, big whoop. Imagine if I went on stage and just talked about my flaps for ten minutes. The same misogynists who find those penis jokes hilarious would be saying "women aren't funny" and wouldn't see the hypocrisy.

But Tom's jokes, to my relief, were more sophisticated than that, and side-splittingly funny. His set was seamless and his timing spot-on. He was so confident up there I was able to actually relax and just enjoy being entertained by him.

With all the attention he was getting after his performance, I wasn't surprised when he didn't come back to the room with me, although I was surprised when he got in at 3 a.m. immediately needing a shower.

When I get to the bar after Laser Tag, I find everyone sitting around a table raising their glasses. FOMO instantly kicks in as they knock them together, and I rush over without first getting myself a drink.

"Hey, what are we celebrating?" I take an empty seat next to Oscar, but he doesn't look at me.

"Harvey's just been promoted to activities manager!" Maddison speaks for him.

"Wow! A promotion? That's great! Congrats!" I respond, excited for him but confused by his body language. It's amazing news – why isn't he happy about it? And why won't he look at me?

"Gonna miss you, Harvs," Obi says, wrapping an arm around Oscar's shoulders.

Miss him?

"Why've none a y'all said you're gonna miss me yet? He's not the only one leavin'," Maddison huffs playfully.

Leaving?

"Hey, you *chose* to leave us – that privilege has been revoked."

My heart beats faster at their bickering. I need someone to explain exactly what's going on before I explode.

"Oscar...?" My eyes don't leave the side of his face until he finally lifts his head to look at me.

Defeated, he says, "I'm moving over to Atlantis."

My heart shatters into a million pieces.

"I'm really happy for you." I don't know why I say it; both of us know it's a lie.

As the only one without a drink, I excuse myself from the table with no intention of getting one or even returning. Instead, I sneak out of the bar and walk as fast as my legs will carry me. I don't know where to yet, but if I'd sat there for a second longer I would have burst. I'm not strong enough to spend the rest of the night pretending to be happy when the person I...care about...*a lot* is leaving for good. Letting him celebrate without me is the kindest thing I can do. Not that he looked like he was in the mood to celebrate.

Before I know it, I'm up in our spot wiping tears off my cheeks and listening to the crashing waves. It's safe up here, and it's the only way to feel close to him even when I'm not.

Christ, pull yourself together, woman. He's leaving, not dying.

How long has he known he might be going? I assume there was an interview process and it's not something that's just been sprung on him. Was that a lie the other night when he said he'd come back? It didn't feel like one. But then I'm not exactly the world's greatest lie detector.

I'm overwhelmed with grief for something that never

was, but my breathing has settled and my tears have dried by the time I'm found. Without saying a word, Oscar joins me on the bench, and we watch the world go by together.

"I heard Norovirus runs rife on Atlantis," I fib. "And no one sings, ever. Like they've banned it or something. And all the guests are like Mrs Pigeon."

His amusement is a tuneful hum. "Is that what we're calling her now?"

"Doves are birds of peace. She's a bird of chaos and disease." My eyes narrow like a cartoon villain plotting revenge.

"Makes sense. Where'd you hear all that about Atlantis?"

I look over at him but can't maintain eye contact for more than a split second. "Meticulous research."

"Seems legit."

"It is."

"Well, I'd better stay here then."

"Yeah. You probably should." I find the strength to latch onto those impossibly blue eyes of his but struggle to keep my composure. "I'd say congratulations, but I don't mean it." The words sound childish, but I'm hoping my tone is soft enough that he sees it's coming from a place of honesty.

"That's probably the most genuine thing anyone's said all night."

There's another long silence. I study him out the corner of my eye.

"Why aren't you happy?"

He doesn't reply. Instead he slips his hand in mine, and we stay like that for a while. I scowl to prevent any more tears from forming and twist my tongue in my mouth, doing anything to settle my wobbling chin and the ache in my throat from holding back my sobs.

"When you said you wanted to come back, I thought maybe…" I can't bring myself to finish my sentence.

"I thought maybe too."

I turn my head towards him. His eyes are as dark and pained as mine feel. He lets go of my hand and wraps his arm around me. I rest my head on his shoulder and hold onto his other hand with both of mine. He plants a long kiss on the top of my head.

"This is so stupid. Like, we're not even…" I flap my hands between us, unable to find the words because there aren't any. "And yet I feel so…"

"Ship life's a bit of a headfuck."

"Tell me about it."

"Do you think you'll do another contract after this?" he asks.

"Yeah. I really like it here. Or I thought I did." I feel his cheeks rise in a smile against me. "Why?"

"I was just thinking, you could—" He cuts himself off.

"What could I do?" I ask, but he shakes his head.

I sit up to look at him.

He hesitates before speaking again. "You could always request Atlantis for your next contract. If you wanted to."

Maddison said she requested another ship after her first contract, but they brought her back to this one because it needed the staff. This time they've done as she requested, maybe because she's earned some kind of loyalty points. Or what more likely has happened is they need her somewhere else. Plus, her request wasn't as specific as one particular ship like before; it was to just *not* be on this one.

"I'd wait for you, Chapman."

The air in my lungs suddenly thins. Hearing that and seeing the care in his eyes should fill me with all the courage I need to say yes. But it feels more like I'm being waterboarded. Right here, I've been gifted with the kindest, most thoughtful and patient man I've ever met in my life, and I can't have him.

"And if I don't get placed on your ship…?"

"I might have a say." His voice is full of hope.

"And what if you don't?"

I think back to the research I did on the company before I left. They have a fleet of twenty ships that operate worldwide. So I have a five percent chance of getting that ship without saying anything. Maybe…what, ten percent if my request has any bearing on the decision? Fifty percent if Oscar's does? I'm pulling numbers out of my arse now – I have no idea. And what if we wait seven months to be reunited and I'm sent to one of the nineteen other ships he's not on?

But what if I'm not?

But what if I wait that long and get lucky, only to turn up on day one and find out he's met someone else and has been sleeping with them behind my back? I'd then have to endure six months of torture pretending to be happy for him. Twat-face moved on the second I left the building. We were just a few tube stops away and he forgot all about me. I know Oscar isn't him, but this is the other side of the world we're talking about.

"That was a lot to ask. Sorry," he backtracks, the arm around my shoulders loosening.

"No, please don't apologise." I want to reassure him, but I have no assurance to give. "I wasn't expecting… I'm not… I can't ask you to wait for me."

"You don't need to ask. But I know that's a lot of me to ask of you."

"I'm not sure I'd cope if I weren't able to join you." I had so much hope when I thought he could come back, but that's vanished, and I feel naïve for even having hope in the first place now. I'm upset I didn't know about the job. Not upset with him – I get that he probably didn't want to jinx anything. But I'm upset I didn't see it coming. "So I didn't tank our date then?"

He studies my face, shaking his head in confusion.

"I just thought…because you didn't— Because we didn't—"

My stuttering is interrupted by his soft lips on mine, and for a second, the whole world stills. For someone so strong, he's so gentle with the way his hand cups my cheek, as if I'm made of glass and he thinks I might break if he kisses me any harder. The shock prevents me from acting fast enough to kiss him back.

He pulls away, looking deep into my eyes. "I'm sorry if I made you think that." He kisses me on the forehead again, and we sit there for a while longer before heading down for the night.

I want nothing more than to kiss him again and climb into bed with him to spend as much of our limited time together as possible, but I need a second to gather my thoughts.

By the morning, I know I can't start anything now. It'll only make this more painful when it's time for him to leave. And no matter how much I might want to, I don't trust anyone to go that long and not stray.

Another week passes and we act like things are normal. Each time I enjoy his company, I'm hit with another wave of sadness that I can't have him. The only time I truly stop pining over him is when I'm working on the haunted house. It opens the weekend before Maddison leaves, with Oscar leaving the week after her, and I'm working extra hard to make it as fun as I can for everyone who'll be involved so the two of them get the send-off they deserve.

The following Tuesday I'm assigned to another excursion. I'm close to storming into the office and demanding to be taken off the programme after what happened last time, but snorkelling sounds just too good to pass up. And it's not like I'm going to be put on another minibus again, right?

Wrong. The minibus taunts me from where it's parked just by the ship. Before we start signing people onto the bus, I throw open the passenger door up front and immediately check to see if the air-con works.

Okay. We're safe. For now.

My leg jiggles with post-traumatic stress symptoms, and I successfully manifest a peaceful journey there. The beach is stunning. I want to stay put, but we board a small fishing boat and sail out ten minutes or so to a prime spot for snorkelling. We divvy up the fins, masks, and life jackets to those who want them and let the guests swim away before we get in ourselves.

The water is so still and clear I can see right to the bottom, and the sun is so warm it's heated the sea to the point it feels like jumping into a bath – or a bath compared to the English Channel anyway. After a nice paddle marvelling over fish of every colour and laughing at phallic-looking sea cucumbers, I lift my head up to take stock of where I am. And even though I almost drown myself in the process by forgetting I still have a snorkel attached to me, I allow myself to relax into the outing. This is already a million times better than that bloody sightseeing trip.

I dutifully splash my way over to a huge cave that a few

guests are exploring. *Excellent escorting, Eliza.* It's nice to have a chance to hang out with guests off the ship in a way that doesn't include my lap being treated like a toilet. Because of the sick, not because…

Never mind.

A sudden wave from a nearby boat leaving the spot presses me against the large rocks just outside the cave, but thankfully not with too much force. One of my fins gets caught on the rocks, though, and slips off my foot, so it's now floating beside me. I grab hold of it, check my watch, and decide to head back to the boat. I want to get back earlier than the guests were told to be back anyway so I can get dry and dressed, ready to be helpful. I don't bother putting my lost fin on just yet and prioritise getting away from the rocks so I can't be pummelled into them again.

I press my bare foot against the rock to push myself off. *Ow! What the fuck was that?*

I'm signed off work for the rest of the day by the onboard medics. The girls come by my room to check on me after I don't show up for the Sail Away Party – *again*. Once they establish I'm fine, they do nothing but make fun of me. I don't mind though. It's a nice distraction from the pain.

It doesn't take long for Oscar to find me, the worry on his face fading when he sees me laughing.

"What have you done?" His eyes sweep down to my swollen foot, which is resting on the chair so I can elevate it from where I'm perched on the end of Tom's bed.

"She stepped on a sea urchin," Maddison titters.

"What did you do that for?"

"The attention, obviously," I snip. "And I didn't step on one; I was *attacked.* By *several.*"

"Oh, Chapman. How long you out for?"

"At least tonight. I'm seeing the doctor again in the morning."

Maddison's watch beeps. "All right, I need to scoot along to karaoke. Rest up, Buttercup!"

Valentina follows her, but not before casting her gaze between Oscar and me.

"I'm cursed," I whinge when we're alone.

"You're not cursed, Cricket."

Parking *that* for a minute…

"I am. Bad things happen when I get off this ship, I tell you."

"What are you gonna do now?"

"Not sure. I've been waiting for an opportunity to sit and stare at the wall feeling sorry for myself for a while, so it looks like I'm in for a big night."

He smiles at my melodramatics. "Well, unlucky for you then, I'm finished for the evening, and I have been waiting for the perfect opportunity to play doctor."

"Kinky."

"Never said I wasn't."

That comment takes us both by surprise. We blink back and forth for too long while he thinks of something to change the subject with.

"Have you eaten yet?"

"No, and I'm *starving.*"

I've been dying to eat again so I can actually take the ibuprofen my foot desperately needs to help with the swelling, but I couldn't cope with the potential embarrassment of hopping to the mess alone and then having to ask for help when I got there. I had visions of doing it myself, flinging the contents of my tray everywhere as I kept hopping towards a table. No, thanks. I'd rather bodyslam another sea urchin.

"Come on then."

I slide one flip-flop on easily, and the second somewhat tentatively, before hobbling over to the door Oscar's now holding open for me. Barely a metre down the hall, he decides to give me a piggyback the rest of the way. My arms wrap tightly around his broad chest, and his hands hook under my thighs to fasten me to him.

In the mess he sits me down on an empty table, makes sure I can rest my foot on a chair opposite me, and heads off to fetch us both dinner. He's too good to me.

We stop by his room on the way back to mine to pick up his hard drive, having decided to spend the rest of the evening working our way through the musicals he has stored on there. He puts me down on his desk to save me from standing uncomfortably while he digs around in his drawers.

"I'm gonna change real quick."

"Outdoor clothes," we both say at the same time, making us laugh.

He remembers my distress at people napping in their beds in their uniforms. Maybe it's a germaphobe quirk I picked up in London. The things I've seen people do on tube and bus seats... Ugh. I wouldn't even sit on my sofa in my jeans when I got home, let alone get into my *bed* in them.

He strips off his polo shirt, and when he catches me staring, an amused smile tugs at his lips.

The door opens with gusto. "Oh, *helloooo*, didn't know I was walking into a private showing of the Chippendales. I can't bear to look." Obi covers his face with his hands – everything except his eyes, which couldn't be more open if he tried.

"Shut up, it's your favourite part of the day," Oscar retorts with a sass I've not seen from him before. He finds a clean T-shirt and unfortunately puts it on.

"Aren't they chipmunks?" I ask.

"You're thinking of Chip 'n' Dale. Very different things. The Chippendales are the US equivalent of Dreamboys," Oscar clarifies.

"Ah, don't wanna mix those two up."

"No, you do *not*. What are you two up to?"

"Movie night at mine," I say.

"Ahh, the old Hard Drive and Chill technique. Nice."

Oscar ignores him and changes his shorts for tracksuit bottoms.

"Careful not to accidentally show her your porn stash," Obi warns him before turning to me. "Honestly, the shit that guy has on there. The most obscene videos of people asking each other how their days were and caring about the answer, pizza delivery guys *just* delivering pizza, plumbers *actually* fixing lonely housewives' drains, and he even has pictures of people…holding hands." He gasps in mock horror.

Oscar walks into the bathroom rolling his eyes with quirked lips, leaving the door open while he freshens up.

"And worst of all…" Obi continues, leaning in closer to stage-whisper. "Some of them are straight!"

I can't help but laugh. "Oscar, I didn't realise you were such a pervert."

"That's me." He gives me a certain look and I know he's thinking about my own porn stash again.

Obi reaches under his bed to retrieve something. "In case those smutty videos get you all hot and bothered." He offers forwards a box of condoms so casually they could be a box of chocolates.

"Obi!" Oscar scolds him, his face stern in the mirror.

"No, thanks. I've been impaled enough today as it is." I reject his offering, and Oscar returns to the room chuckling.

"Well, I hope you were careful."

"I wasn't."

"Suit yourselves." Obi puts the box back where he found it.

"Besides, someone's got to fulfil the role of Ship Virgin when he's gone," I joke.

"Harvey, you've created a monster."

Oscar smiles, but he seems lost in thought. Probably still thinking about porn.

"Ready to go, Chapman?" He swings the door open.

I slide off the desk and shuffle out of the room. He crouches down and I climb back onto my noble steed.

"Have fun, kids!" Obi calls out after us. "Don't stay up too late!"

We pass by Valentina in the hall in a dress. *A dress!* I ask her who she's so dolled up for, but as always, she just responds with a frosty glare. I take great pleasure in watching her break into a smile. I glance back over my shoulder to find she's giving me the same "I'm happy for you" kind of look I'm giving her.

When we get back, I grab a quick shower, keen to finally wash the seawater and sun cream off my skin. I contemplate leaving the door unlocked in case I lose my balance and knock myself out, but then I think better of it. The last thing I want is to be discovered nude and wet in a heap on the floor – by Oscar, no less. I'd never recover from that. Like women who have a heart attack at work and can never return – not because the revival was unsuccessful, but because for a good length of time, they were surrounded by an entire circle of peers, superiors, and subordinates all watching on as her lifeless boobs convulsed while the miracle of resurrection took place.

It's a very niche fear, but a fear nonetheless.

I manage. That's the best way to sum up my shower. Keeping myself steady by resting on the tips of my toes on my swollen stump of a foot, I change into my PJs (the skimpier ones I own, fine, you got me) and come out to see Oscar's hooked the hard drive up to the small TV on the wall and is perched on the desk scrolling on his phone with grave concern written all over his face.

"Whatcha looking at?"

"Paralysis, respiratory failure, tissue necrosis, and death are all possible complications of sea urchin stings," he reads out.

"Yeah, not sure I'm into this whole doctor role-play thing, actually."

TWENTY

OSCAR

It's not fair. None of this is fair. She shouldn't be hurt. I should be the one making her laugh, not the other way round. And she should be mine.

Fresh face. Rosy cheeks. Wet hair splayed on the towel wrapped around her shoulders. The pebble of her nipples visible through her tight vest top. And those tiny silk shorts… They are something else entirely.

Since her last excursion, I haven't been able to get the image of her wet, soapy body out of my head. And as much as seeing her like that was some kind of sex dream, seeing her like this is just as breathtaking.

Tom gets to see this every night. *Lucky bastard.*

Her words play over in my head. *Ship Virgin.* Did she really mean that? I thought she and Tom had… It doesn't change how I feel about her – I don't have some twisted Madonna-whore complex – but knowing that maybe she hasn't been with him stirs something in me.

She treads with caution, throwing her hairbrush up onto her bunk.

"Need a hand?"

"No, I'm good." She reaches the ladder, and I sit back to watch her consider which foot she should step with first.

"Sure?"

"Yep."

Stubborn little madam.

She takes a nervous step onto the first rung of the ladder with her good foot, emitting a pained squeak for the brief second her bad foot is supporting her. She gives me a coy look over her shoulder.

"Come on, Cricket." I take a firm hold of her hips.

She pulls herself up on the rails, and I lift her easily up to the next step, and then the next. I see the bottom of her foot properly for the first time. There's black and purple bruising around each dot of the urchin's assault.

"Your poor foot."

"You've been awfully obsessed with my feet tonight."

"Don't even start with me, Chapman."

She looks back down at me. "You can see why I have trouble believing you don't have—"

"I *don't* have a foot fetish."

"Mmm, no smoke without fire."

"Doesn't count when you're the one starting the fire."

"If it's not feet, then tell me what your kink is."

"Not happening. Now get into bed."

She emits a cute grunt and hops up the last step, spoiling me with the most spectacular view of her arse. If she wasn't injured I wouldn't be able to resist bending her over the top bunk and burying my face between her legs. But she is injured. Just another thing I'll save for the shower.

She crawls along to the head of the bed where I've propped her pillows against the wall, and I climb up to join her.

"What have you picked?" she asks.

"My all-time favourite. Something I'd never be cast as the lead in."

"'Annie'? 'Legally Blonde'? 'Mean Girls'?"

"'Little Shop of Horrors'."

"Agh, so close. You could so be Seymour though."

"Mmm, I'm not sure."

"Why not?"

"Because I'm—"

"A big hunk of flesh?"

I attempt to act unfazed by her description, but it's difficult. All I was going to say was I don't look the part. I lean back and let her wriggle until she gets comfy next to me.

"Exactly. Took the words right out of my mouth."

"That could be half the joke though. All the words and songs depict him as this scrawny, lovable weakling, and then *you* show up." Her eyes widen to emphasise her point, and heat rises in my cheeks. "People would eat that up, no question."

"Thanks, Chapman."

"I'd cast you. Though you'd also make a great Dentist too."

"Now, *that* I think I could do."

Making sure Eliza's foot is comfortable, I hit play, and we settle in for the next few hours. I want to hold her close to me, but I'm aware Tom could burst through the door any minute now.

We sing along, quote our favourite lines, and take turns to do our ridiculous impressions of the plant. She doesn't mind me geeking out over behind-the-scenes facts – she actually has a bunch herself. Turns out she played Audrey in her school production, but Seymour didn't want to kiss her, so they just hugged. I tell her I'd have kissed her, at which point she closes her eyes tight and pouts her lips, opening one eye to peek at me when I don't.

"You couldn't handle one of my stage kisses," I say.

"There's only one way to find out."

I lean in close, my lips brushing her ear. "But it's so much more fun watching you crave it." That and one second of her mouth on mine is all it would take for me to lose my composure.

She doesn't say anything more, but the two peaks pressing against her top tell me it isn't because she didn't like it.

This could be forever, I think while settling into the next film, *if we quit cruising*. Or we could be reunited in something like six months' time and have another few months of this pure joy I've felt ever since I met her. I will do everything in my power to make that happen if that's what she wants.

We haven't addressed it since. I know it was a lot to put on her, but I don't regret saying it. She hasn't been distant, and that's all the confirmation I need to know she wants to say yes. Though the lack of an answer is also all the confirmation I need to know she's considering saying no.

Maybe one day we'll reconnect on land. We live close enough that we could give this a real go. I'll get a do-over, take her on a real date and be sure to kiss her at every opportunity. That'll be the start of forever then. Or maybe she'll always be my "one that got away" even though she's never been my one to begin with.

Right person, wrong time.

My heart's full after carrying a sleepy Eliza off the bed for a bathroom break and returning her again, tucking her up under the covers. I love looking after her. She's been on her own in the world for so long – we both have – and even if it's just for one night, I want to take the weight off her shoulders.

There's still no sign of Tom by the time we stick the third musical on, even though it's getting late. She said he probably won't be back until two or three if he's not back by now. She's confident, but it isn't enough to let me relax entirely.

Noticing how I tense every time a door slams shut out in the corridor, Eliza tugs the curtain across her bunk to conceal us both from being discovered in preparation for his unpredictable but inevitable return.

It's stupid to be scared of him catching us like this, but I am. It's no secret he's moved on from his infatuation with Eliza, but in his eyes, I'd be betraying him and contradicting the advice I gave. I would assume the same thing if I didn't know Eliza was so much more than a friend now.

I won't forget the things he said about me. I forgave him after he apologised, but there's always going to be a part of me that knows he thinks the worst of me. What did I do to earn that assessment from him? *You'll hurt her just like I did.* Sure, I had a number of meaningless liaisons on the last ship, but I was always upfront about my intentions. I never led anyone on, never treated anyone without respect, never hurt anybody.

"I should go after this."

She looks up at me, disappointment written all over her face. "Paralysis, respiratory failure, tissue neck-something, and death, did you say? A good doctor wouldn't abandon a patient in such a critical condition."

"I suppose not."

So that's settled then. I'm staying the night. And I'll face the consequences in the morning.

We lie down, and she curls up against me, resting her bad foot on top of me. I plant a long kiss in her hair, squeeze her tight, and before long, she's falling asleep on my chest.

Her small, warm body lengthens alongside me when she wakes up. We smile at each other with bleary eyes, careful not to make a sound.

Eliza double-taps my stomach before pushing on it to sit up when I tense for her. Adorable. She peeks around the curtain and cranes her neck down to inspect Tom's bed. Her face is confused when she retreats. "Did you hear him come back?" she asks, and I shake my head. "Hmm. Must have had a good night."

I scan her eyes for signs of jealousy, but she seems indifferent about it. She lies back down in my arms. *Hmm.*

"Still breathing?" I check, my voice coming out low like it always does first thing.

She takes a deep breath in and out. "Still breathing."

I smile back at her. "Guess you weren't a fan of 'Into the Woods'?"

Her face says "oops" for her. "Let me guess, they sing some more songs and all live happily ever after?"

"Not quite."

"Oh. We'll have to watch it again then before—" She catches herself and decides not to finish her sentence.

The swelling on Eliza's foot has gone down significantly, so she's able to walk herself down to the medical centre. That doesn't stop me from accompanying her though. Both in case she needs me to carry her again and because I know as soon as I leave her side, the day will go back to normal and I'll have to return to acting like I'm not obsessed with her.

The doctor deems Eliza fit to return to work with a warning to take it easy (like that means anything on here), and we head to breakfast, where I sit her down with Obi and get us both something to eat.

I'm not even halfway through my omelette when Obi whispers the rules of improv to us with urgency. "Yes and, kids. Yes and."

What does he need us to go along with?

"Oh my God, Eliza, are you okay?" Tom stands beside us.

"Yes," she says quickly then staggers through the "and". "And…the Doctor's given me the all-clear." Her eyes keep darting over to Obi for a clue as to what she's supposed to be doing.

Tom heaves a sigh of relief. "Great! So I can come back now?"

"Yes and…I…would…like you to."

"Cool. I'm gonna have a nap after this. Daniel and Gwen are so much worse now that it's *their* room."

"Yes *and* I can imagine how bad that must have been."

Tom narrows his eyes on her. "Sure you're okay?"

Eliza nods with an absent smile, done with whatever game Obi's made her play, and when Tom nips off to get breakfast, both of us swing our heads over to Obi.

"That was odd, wasn't it, Oscar?" she says in a deliberately stiff manner.

"Yes, it was. *And* I think Obi owes us an explanation."

"Yes and I will right after I get my thank-you card." He holds out his hand like he's waiting for it.

"Obi. What did you do?"

"I may have told him Eliza came into contact with a toxic

sea urchin and risked spreading a very dangerous and contagious disease to anyone she came close to."

I could kill him. Or kiss him.

"I trust you both had a good night's sleep. Or didn't…?"
He tilts his head forwards and widens his eyes, eagerly
searching both our faces for the answer neither of us give. He
crumples in disappointment. "Ugh, can you two just fuck and
get it over with already? All this 'will they, won't they?' crap
is driving me insane."

I've been on edge for the past two weeks. Silence has broken
out both times I've entered the rehearsal studio, and today
I've finally found out why.

As it's the penultimate Friday before I leave, and we'll be
too busy with Halloween festivities next weekend, the gang
have planned a surprise outing on a catamaran as a send-off.
It's extravagant, and everyone's chipped in a bit extra to
cover my share, which doesn't sit right with me – but with a
crew discount and enough people to split the cost between,
I've been assured no one's broken the bank for this. They all
consider it a treat for themselves too, so that reduces the guilt
a little.

It should feel redundant, going from one boat straight
onto another, but it doesn't. On Neptune, I'm always on.
Always alert. And though we've struck no disasters, I'm
aware one could come at any moment and I'd need to be
ready to help. But today, just for a few hours, I can switch off
from "Ship-Dad Mode", as the others call it, and just enjoy
the trip.

As we sail across the coast, I sit back with the guys while
the ladies sunbathe on the netting up on the bow of the ship. I

can't stop myself from smiling every time Eliza squeals with the others when the spray from the ocean splashes them all from underneath. I'm so grateful to everyone for welcoming her in like they did. It's comforting to know she'll still have them when I go.

Fuck, I don't want to go.

I take full advantage of the sunglasses I'm wearing to finally study her body like I've been trying not to on the rare occasions I've had the opportunity to see her like this. Trying and often failing. My eyes secretly admire every delicious curve, freckle, and the elegant tattoo on her ribcage. Her skin's darker and her hair's even lighter for spending time in the sun over the past two months. It's gone from shades of gold to almost white, as if she has an angelic glow all around her. I've often found myself wondering what those perfect locks would feel like brushing against my chest as she rides me.

She squeaks with delight again as the boat rises and falls hard over another wave, and I wonder if I'll ever be the one to cause her to make that noise. Or be the one to make her breasts bounce like that. I shift my position to hide the place where my trunks have gotten tighter and force my eyes away.

It's serene in the bay we've anchored up in – perfect sky, perfect sea, perfect breeze – despite the various creative jumping competitions that have been going on since we got here. Each time I offer up the soft drinks or snacks I bought last-minute as some kind of feeble contribution to the trip, or whenever I attempt to be the one taking photos for once, I'm told off and forced overboard to play in the sea.

"Come on, Eliza, your turn!" Sophie shouts over to where Eliza's sunbathing.

"No, thanks. I'm good. Not taking any chances today!"

"There aren't any urchins out here, I promise," Sophie tries to reassure her.

It's been over a week since urchin-gate and she's thankfully made a full recovery. Is that why she's not been joining in? When she said no to me before, I assumed it was a time of the month thing and didn't push her any further to save her from having to spell it out for me.

"Anyone feeling seasick?" Valentina asks around. "No? Good. Looks like you're safe from a puke shower today then too," she adds in a way only she could.

Even though it's only the Wednesday meet-up crowd, Valentina managed to get the sign-off to come too, and I'm glad. She's been different these past few weeks. Happier. It looks like she's finally found someone worth letting in too.

Eliza reluctantly gets up but looks over at me. "I'm gonna get got."

"You're not gonna get got, Cricket. I'll protect you."

"You've got to go first then."

"Deal."

Someone comes up with a game they coin "Death Drop" that raises the eyebrows of the captain and skipper in concern for our safety. Not that they try to stop us though. The idea is that one person steps over the railings at the side of the boat, and instead of holding onto those before jumping into the water, someone else holds tightly onto their wrists and asks them various questions until they're wrong and they let them go. It's stupid, but it's good fun.

I step over the railings and go to take Eliza's hands. "Someone hold her down, else Mr Muscle over here is going to take her with him," one of the older guys who plays Harry in "Mamma Mia" says, which prompts a whole line of people to form behind Eliza, anchoring her down like she's Winnie the Pooh and I'm a rabbit hole she's stuck in.

"All right, I'm not that heavy!"

"We've all seen you at the gym, mate. You don't know your own strength!" Max shouts from the back of the line.

"Take my wrists instead," she says, and I do, squinting at her curiously as I lean back over the side. The way her arms are being pulled by me pushes her tits together, and the stakes could not be any higher for me to be good at this game. "I want *you* to let go as soon as I guess your kink."

With the chorus of excited noises, I don't get a chance to argue before she's off.

"Choking, spanking, tickling, BDSM, group sex, butt…stuff…?"

"My sexuality is not a kink."

"I know, but you might just be a freak for it."

I shrug indifferently – as much as one can when their arms are being hauled by a chain of people.

"Feet." She pauses like she's waiting for me to cave then sighs with frustration when I don't. "Role play. Dom/sub. Public sex—"

With a smile I let go, falling backwards. I won't ever forget the way her whole face lights up as the penny drops. I resurface to the sound of jubilant cheers for Eliza for finally getting some dirt out of me. She's my weak spot, and I'm glad they've not discovered that until now.

Over the uproar, I can just about make out that she's losing her nerve.

"That was the deal," Max reasons with her.

She looks down at me with terror in her eyes.

"It's not a long way down. I'll fend off any urchins."

"Promise?"

"Promise. They'll have to fight me first."

Eliza tentatively climbs over the railing, giving me the

most magnificent view of her behind. Max steps forwards to take her hands.

"Eliza Chapman, your challenge is…to sing the opening lines of these musicals. Hesitate too long and you're in."

"Okay." She leans back with a tiny nervous shriek.

Max starts listing them off, and without missing a beat, Eliza is able to keep up. She's like some kind of human juke-box. It gets to the point where Max has to stop for a second to think of more.

"So, do I win now, or…?" Eliza looks around smugly, hoping to be spared.

"Go on, give her a hard one!" Valentina shouts.

"Or you can give up because I'm never going in."

"'Urinetown'."

"'What is Urinetown'?"

Max lets her go.

"No, the song! It's a song!" she pleads, her arms wind-milling to keep her upright until she lands feet first with a splash.

Max looks over the railings down at her when she resurfaces. "You're right. It *is* a song, just not the first one, unfortunately."

"Dammit." She slaps her hands against the surface of the water. She earned herself a round of applause from everyone though.

Despite Eliza's earlier reluctance to be in the water, we stay in the sea, bobbing about and watching the others mess about above and around us for a long while after our death drops. She presses me for all kinds of details about past public exploits, which I don't divulge. Instead I tease her for her sudden interest.

"Need someone to show you the ropes, Chapman?"

"You've taught me how to do everything else here." Her eyes lock on mine. "Why stop now?"

For just a second, my hand purposely skims her waist, the gentle waves lifting her up so the voluptuous curve of her bum slides into my palm. To keep it there any longer so I can squeeze it would risk us both drowning, so for her – and the chance to do it in the future – I stop.

Once we've had enough, we head to the back of the boat. I let Eliza get out first without thinking of the tremendous torment I'll have to endure watching her rinse the saltwater off her body with the small shower head. I lose myself in a million different fantasies, all involving my tongue and various parts of her skin. She holds out the hose for me, but I make a point of refusing to board the boat. The dirtiest grin appears on her face, and without breaking eye contact, she bends down deliberately slowly and returns the hose to the hook before strutting away.

When I finally get back on board, I have every intention of throwing Eliza over my shoulder and sequestering her somewhere for the rest of the trip. But as soon as I get round to the front of the boat, the attention's back on me, as is the expectation to take part in whatever mischief the gang's getting up to now.

I didn't see her sneak off, but her absence is noticeable. It always is. Eventually, I tear myself away from everyone and go in search of her. I head inside, down some steps, and into the cabin we abandoned our belongings in earlier. In the small walkway at the bottom of the raised bed, I'm greeted with her tanned body, slick with freshly applied sun cream. The smell of coconuts and summer floods my senses and my heart starts pounding.

"There you are."

"Here I am," she sings, flashing me a smile before applying her candy-floss lip balm.

Much like a shark smelling blood, I'm hit with a dangerous hunger that needs satiating. I swallow. "I thought you might have got got. Or perhaps a gull had swooped down and flown you away."

"Wouldn't rule it out." She returns the lid to the stick and puts it back in her bag. "You okay? Having a nice day?"

"The nicest."

We smile together, her words from that night in the pool hanging in the air. I feel incredibly lucky to have been given a day like today, and even more so that I got to have one afternoon with Eliza away from everything. It will never be enough, but it's something.

"I wish I could say I helped plan it, but turns out I'm not the only one who's sad you're leaving."

"Mmm, sure this isn't to celebrate my departure?"

"I'm sure." She takes a step forwards just as a strong wave hits, and I reach out to catch her. She blushes, straightens up, and tucks a strand of hair behind her ear. That's when I notice a tiny streak of sun cream still on her cheekbone.

"Missed a bit." I place my hand on the side of her face and gently sweep my thumb across her cheek. Her chest rises and falls a little faster, her eyes wide and full as if she has the whole universe in them. Neither of us move. It's only then that I become very aware we're alone.

Lips ravenous. Hands desperate. I lift her onto the bed, my hips lining up with hers. Pulling, pawing, tasting. Skin against skin. Small sighs against my mouth. Our worlds have finally collided, and nothing will ever be the same again.

Everything. She is everything.

Delicate hands on my neck pull me with meaning. Not leaving her lips, I step on a ledge and then I'm over her. Scrambling back further. Our hungry kisses have me starving for more. Like a sailor returning home to their favourite meal, realising all they've tasted up until now has been bland, empty, stale, and that the things they thought they could live without are in fact the very reason they want to live, nothing will fill me. Even when I've devoured every last piece of her, I will still want more.

Her legs wrap around me, demanding me closer. My lips fervently explore her neck, ignoring giggled warnings of sun cream and lingering salt from the sea on her skin. I don't care; I need to kiss everything. Worship everything. She pulls me back to her lips. Just a few seconds without them and I missed them.

Bodies move together; soft moans grow louder. Braver. More urgent. Breasts unable to be ignored any longer. Fabric pulled aside. Pretty, pink, firm nipples beg to be sampled. Her body writhes, toes curl, and legs tighten, silently screaming, "Give me more!" And more I give. But my giving is also my taking.

Curious hands through tight fabric wrap around the hardest part of me. Kisses pause so we can breathe. When did I last breathe? Who cares – she's my oxygen now. A dangerous smile gets kissed away, but it's contagious. Waistband pulled at, her fingers take hold of my—

A door slams. *Cover her.* Hearts in our throats. Lungs panting as we stare at the door. No one. But there was someone. Panicking. Relaxing. Kissing away fear from her forehead between a promise: "One day…I am going to take you away…somewhere secluded…and make you come…for every time…we've been interrupted…"

We shuffle down to the end of the bed. I climb off, but she doesn't follow. Her eyes look back at me, no longer happy.

"I'll find them, stop them telling—"

Her head shakes.

What is it? Anything – I'll do *anything* to make her happy again.

"When we step out of here I'll lose you again." The urgency to return to the deck above disappears in a split second. "I've only just found you." Her voice is weak.

My throat aches and my eyes sting. I hold her and kiss her with every overwhelming feeling racing through me. "You could never lose me."

A single tear staining her perfect face protests against my comfort.

"I know, Cricket. But this isn't forever. Let's have today. We owe ourselves one day."

Her arms wrap around me tightly, her face burying into my neck. "Today."

I step out first to check for whisperings of a salacious discovery, but everyone is too occupied in their own fun to have even noticed our disappearance. Eliza follows shortly after, taking a shy seat near but not next to me on the large cushioned sun lounger, hiding herself within a few other bodies, making it clear she wants to be discreet.

We might be giving ourselves today, but we still have to consider tomorrow.

People are vultures for gossip in this place, sticking their noses in anything they can just to distract them from the noth-ingness that comes from being at sea for so long. And because of the elusive snoozefest of a man I've become here, this will be gossip that gets everyone's attention. I don't care because of me – I'll be gone, and if people want to waste their time speculating then so be it. But I care because of Eliza. She's the one who'll suffer the incessant barrage of questions. The sideways glances. The leering from creeps who think they know what she's like in bed because they heard from a friend of a friend of a friend that I have some sick appetite for something specific only she could give me. I don't want her to face it at all, but especially not alone, so careful we have to be.

I catch a glimpse of the redness the roughness around my lips left behind on her neck. Before I can get her attention, Valentina, never one for being tactile, reaches over to Eliza and pulls her hair forwards to cover it. A bashful but grateful half-smile shared between the two of them and a stern look back at me warning me to be more careful is all I need to know that our secret is safe. Valentina settles herself back against Sophie and gives Eliza a nod – something that's hard-earned from her. The cogs start to turn. Warning looks were fired her way a lot the night of Tom's party and I couldn't work out why. Maybe her first kiss with Sophie wasn't a coincidence at all.

My little ally.

My openness to connection has always been what closed others off from me. Irony at its finest. The gay community called me a fraud. The straight community didn't trust me not to stray. I was good enough for a night or two, but nothing more. I haven't had to explain myself to Eliza. She hasn't swept my sexuality under the rug. She's welcomed it. She *likes* it.

Laughter and singing fills the air on the sail back. Every-one's glowing from spending a day out in the sun and desperate to bask in every last bit of joy the trip has left to offer. But I can't bring myself to join in. Instead I sit back on the lounger with Valentina, who, shock horror, is content with not singing either.

I am both the happiest and the saddest I've been since I got here. Eliza looks back at me and smiles, and my heart can't decide whether to shine or shatter.

"You gonna be all right?" Valentina breaks our silence.

I work to find the answer before realising there isn't one. "I don't know."

This afternoon has been perfect. More than anything I could have possibly asked for. Everything that's kept Eliza and me apart until today and all the upset that came with it has been worth it. Because today, we got just a sliver of what we wanted. Today is a good day.

But this isn't forever.

TWENTY-ONE
ELIZA

I never thought Austin Powers could be sexy, but *somehow*, Oscar finds a way to prove me wrong.

It's sixties night, and I've managed to nab a cute flower-power go-go dress from the costume store. It's the same colours as a Fruit Salad sweet and flares out at the wrists and waist. It's been non-stop since we got back on the ship, with a Sail Away Party, game show, disco, and barely any time between all that to grab something for dinner and get showered and dressed up. Oscar sneaks up behind me in the dark but lively room where I stand back and watch Valentina run a groove-off. God, I've missed him so much, and it's barely been a few hours since I last saw him.

"You nearly finished?" His impatient words land on the bare skin of my neck, which the high ponytail has granted him access to.

Suddenly breathless, all I can manage is a nod.

"You know where to find me."

The heat behind me disappears, and I wish away the final fifteen minutes of my shift.

Valentina and I leave the venue, and as soon as we're out

of sight, she corners me against the wall. Without saying a word, her finger slips inside the low neckline of my dress and she slides something sharp and crinkly into the top of my bra. I sputter her name with all kinds of questions, but I'm unable to form any of them quickly enough. Her intrusive hand retreats and returns to her pocket, and I pat the item through my dress, the circular ring unmistakable.

"Valentina, I don't—"

"Maybe not now, but it's not like I've got a use for them anymore." She gives me a satisfied smile.

I won't need it, will I? Though if she hadn't caught us earlier, would we have stopped? Neither of us were prepared. We would have had to stop, but I wouldn't have wanted to. When I stepped into that cabin earlier, I had no idea Oscar would find me or what would happen once he did. But now it would be ignorant of me to assume being unprepared is an option.

She places a mint in my hand and frees me from the wall before nudging my frozen body onwards when it doesn't move of its own accord. "Have fun," she calls out after me.

I think I will.

I climb up and up and up and consider pausing so as not to reach him a puffing mess, but every second I'm not with him makes my body ache. He's there, still in the Austin suit, but with fewer frills now, leaning against the railings and watching me with hungry eyes as I arrive.

"Any cameras up here?" I ask, striding towards him, my white patent knee-high boots click-clacking along the decking.

"Nope."

"Good."

In an instant I'm up in his arms, my legs are wrapped around him, and my lips are drowning in his. I pull away to gasp for the breath I never caught, and he moves his attention to my neck, humming against my skin.

"Do you have any idea how good you look in this outfit?" His hands rub down my thighs and back up to my bum, this time sliding under my dress. There's a strained breath when he finally feels the soft, almost silk-like fabric barely covering any skin from this angle.

"I have a feeling you're about to let me know."

He lets out a low rumble as he squeezes me and steals my lips again. He carries me over to the bench and sits with me straddled on his lap. It's impossible not to feel the strength between his thighs, and I can't help but rock against it.

His gentle hand cradles my face, fingers entwining with my hair, and the kisses slow as we savour every sensation. Peppermint tingles along my spearmint-infused taste buds, and each time the tip of his tongue touches mine it's as if stars are shooting inside me. I love the idea that he's been preparing to see me, that he wanted to make sure he tasted good for me. How else did he busy himself while he waited around for me to finish my shift? Was he nervous? No, surely I can't shake the king of composure.

I pull back, suddenly anxious to see him and check he's real, that this isn't just some bizarre fever dream brought on by sunstroke. I make sure to take in every beautiful detail of him, terrified I'll wake up tomorrow having fabricated the whole thing.

Tomorrow.

We only gave ourselves today, but I can't imagine spending another day without him being mine. And he's not mine. Because of me, *my* trust issues, *my* doubts, *my* fears, *my* concerns.

No. I can't allow Twatface to take anything else away from me. I won't.

"I'll wait for you," I promise him, desperately hoping his offer wasn't revoked the second I didn't take it.

His face softens, disbelief piercing his ocean eyes as they search mine for any trace of doubt, but he won't find any. He makes me confident. He makes me trust again. He makes me feel wanted. And I want every part of him. Any fear that he might not want every part of me too is gone, kissed away with a fervour I've never known.

I'm overcome with every emotion, every endorphin. My eyes sting, but I can't stop smiling. Happiness bursts out of me in any way it can, and I find myself laughing against his lips. When I open my eyes he has the same sting in his too. I spatter his face with kisses, paying extra attention to the lines on his cheeks as he laughs with me.

"There aren't enough words for how happy you've just made me."

"Words are overrated."

"I'm not sure you're ready for my actions."

"Try me." The quirk of my lips is all it takes to unleash whatever he was holding back. Without another word, he manoeuvres me until I'm sitting facing away from him.

My neck is decorated with kisses from behind, his hands heavy on my waist as I grind against him. He spreads his legs slowly, mine following. His fingers begin to trace the inside of my thigh, creeping higher and higher. I rest my hands back on his thighs and squeeze him with want, not expecting to hear the unmistakable crinkle of a foil wrapper in his pocket.

"Just in case," he reassures me with a voice as rough as gravel.

I reach into my bra and pull out the gift Valentina bestowed upon me, placing it on the bench next to us. An unbridled tremble is the last thing I feel before his fingers are against the fabric covering the most intimate part of me. Light strokes enthral me. So light they're barely there, which only makes me need more.

"Please," I beg with whimpered need.

His fingers press firmer, forming circles now instead of lines, and I gasp. My legs close as I tense with pleasure.

"Keep them open for me, Chapman."

If I didn't know it already, I certainly do now: I'd do anything for him. I open my legs, and as some kind of reward, his other hand comes up and pinches my nipple through my dress. Quiet sighs drift from me relentlessly, and I know my knickers are already wet for him. His fingers stroke down and he confirms it for himself. An unbidden groan escapes him.

Hooking a finger in the material, he pulls it aside, displaying me to the night. His strong but tender finger explores the soft places that crave him. He purposely stops over my entrance, circling in the slickness. "Is this what you want?" he asks, pressing just a little, and I nod. "Is it?" His voice is firmer.

"Yes. *Please*."

He as good as growls, and slowly, his large finger enters me. The rise and fall of his chest against my back slows as he stops breathing too. When he's all the way inside me we both release the trapped breath and heave for air. The very tip of his finger expertly strokes my favourite spot, and I fight against every instinct to pinch my legs together and come apart there and then. Not yet. Not yet. Not yet.

"Can you see all those people down there?" he rasps against my ear.

I open my eyes, not realising I had them blissfully shut, and clock the ant-like people pottering about under a whirl of coloured lights by the pool. I can't make out faces, but I can see them. I nod.

"Can you?"

"Yes."

"Do you like seeing them?"

Something about it sends a delicious shiver down my spine. "Yes."

"Do you like knowing that they could look up and see you?"

We're too high up and tucked away for that to happen, but I play along because I *do* like it. "Yes."

"I wonder what they'd think. Would they think, 'I wish I could have her too'? Or—"

"Look at that slut," I cut him off, reclaiming the word as my own and letting it stir something menacingly good in me. I want this, him and I misbehaving outside. I want the risk.

"Is that what you'd like them to think?"

"Yes."

His fingers are getting stronger and faster, and I can barely hold myself up.

"Is that what you are? My little slut?"

"Yes." I'm gone. Completely gone. I chase the rush all the way to the edge, and when his hand grips lightly around my neck, I fall. Headfirst. I can see nothing but stars and colours rushing all around me. Tighter. Harder. Faster. More. Everything. This is everything. *He* is everything. When I land, he catches me with his tender kisses and adoring words, covering me up but holding his hand against the wet fabric, nursing me as the aftershock continues to pulse through me.

"I was right. You do look pretty when you come."

I throw my head back on his shoulder and catch my breath. He is some kind of God. Never, *ever*, has someone been able to satisfy me like that – not without me having to ask or direct or settle for less. But I was just served every-

332

thing I needed, even the things I didn't know I wanted until now, on a silver platter.

"Where did you come from?" I pant.

Oscar purrs and twists my pleasure-drunk body to the side so he can hold and look at me. "And here I was thinking this was *my* kink."

I dip my eyes to hide from him, suddenly too embarrassed to be seen.

He lifts my chin and forces me to look into his kind eyes. "Never stop surprising me, Chapman." He kisses me deeply, and that's all I need to spring to life again.

Without leaving his lips, I stand, spin around, and straddle him again. He's so hard under me I swear I feel him throb. He shrugs out of his jacket while I rush to undo the buttons on his shirt. When I free all of them, I pull myself away so I can finally admire how perfect he is.

I attempt to push his shirt off completely, but he resists.

"In case we need to make a swift exit," he whispers.

Smart. Can't say I mind either – he looks like some kind of suit model right now. My fingers trace the hard lines of pure muscle, and I push him away each time he leans in to kiss me.

"I just need another second."

He chuckles, and I can't resist him any longer. My lips and hands are busy again, finding and unfastening his suit trousers. I reach inside and slowly rub his manhood through his boxers. My exploration was caught short earlier and I've been doubting myself ever since. There's no way it's as big as it felt. Or as big as it looked that night everyone came back to mine. No, I'm sure it's a very normal-sized—

Holy shit.

I pull back the tight waistband and uncover him, stroking him softly up and down before breaking away to study where my comparatively tiny hand grasps his length. He's not just long; he's thick. *Solid.* It's bordering on ginormous. That won't fit. It can't fit. I was joking when I referred to hypothetical sex with him as being impaled before, but now I think I was correct in my assumption. *Very* correct.

I swallow hard and look up at him to see he's already watching me. I always forget how he watches me.

"I'll make sure you're ready when the time comes."

Endlessly patient. Endlessly thoughtful. Endlessly big dick. That's what it'll say on his gravestone. And maybe that last part on my death certificate.

It's my turn to watch him now. His eyelids flutter closed as I play with him. When I wet my hand and replace it, he expels a groan, and I know exactly what I want to give him to earn more of them. I look around to check we really are still alone, and once I'm certain of it, I get up despite his feeble attempt to keep me on him, and kneel down in front of him. His eyes lock onto mine.

"Is this what you want?" I repeat his words back to him.

Nervous eyes do the same scan I just did. He nods, unable to find a voice to his answer. But two can play at his game. I patiently wait for a verbal "yes", and then my lips are on him. My tongue swirls, my mouth sucks, and my hands tug.

"Jesus, Eliza," he sighs under his breath, unable to look away.

I stop, sit back on my heels, and wait for him to correct himself.

"Chapman…" he grumbles.

That's better.

I return my lips and my hands to where he deserves them, treating myself to the sight of his abs tensing each time I hit a certain spot. He's every bit as relaxed as he is ecstatic. There's contradiction in his blissful eyes as they roll back, and in the way the moonlight bounces off his clenching jaw. He's fascinating to watch. I could genuinely do this all night, and I think I just might until he strokes my cheek. I release him with a *pop* and he leans down, pressing his forehead against mine.

"I'm not done with you yet." He helps me to my feet.

I look back down at the ready cock protruding from his lap with anticipation. Both his hands hold me in front of him, roaming up my dress, clutching the sides of my knickers, and after a querying glance up at me, he pulls them down and slides them over my boots. Oscar swaps places with me, pulling me right to the edge of the bench, and the sight of him kneeling in front of me makes the thump in my chest beat in double time.

"You're on lookout," he says with a sly smile. His lips glide along the inside of my leg, and when his warmth hovers over my core I tremble with anticipation. He presses a long, slow kiss on my centre before lapping his tongue over my pulsing bud. With every wet caress I become more unsure that I'm awake. But it's when his tongue enters me, greedily tasting my excitement, that I'm certain I have to be dreaming. He's like a castaway devouring his first and possibly last meal, and *fuck me*, do I want to be the last. He steals from me in the same way he gives. Which is to say that this is as much for me as it is for him.

"I need you," I finally cry out in an urgent whisper as he looks up at me. I flick my eyes to the condom on the bench beside me and then back to him.

There's no rushing or fumbling; he takes his time, holding me, kissing me, connecting with me. I'm straddling him again, his irrefutable lust between us, but he's in no hurry to act on it.

"You sure you don't want to take this inside?" he asks.

And what, get interrupted by every man and his dog? "I'm sure. Do you want to?"

His eyes do that thing I imagine a wild animal's do when they get a whiff of prey, and he shakes his head with a smile. "But if you change your mind, you tell me straight away." He plants kisses in my hair, fetches the Chekov's gun beside us, and tears it open.

"You too."

He stretches me slowly, but my body is so ready for him that each inch I'm given feels like a blessing. We both sigh a soft curse when he's as deep as he can be. He guides my hips as I roll back and forth, both of us fighting to contain our whimpers of euphoria. When I wrap my hands around the back of his neck and start bouncing, the fight only becomes more arduous.

I can't get enough of the way he looks up at me, watching every crease of my brow, every bite of my lip, and every time my eyes glaze over when he continues to hit my sweet spot. It's not my pleasure and his pleasure; it's ours.

"Fuck, I can't wait to see you naked," he mumbles.

"Imagine if I were now," I whisper in his ear, picking up my pace. "Completely exposed for you."

He groans.

"There'd be no hiding if someone came up here." I study him as arousal pools in his eyes. "Would you like that? If someone caught me now, fucking you naked?"

"Yes," he pants.

"Would you want me to keep going? Let them watch as your slut struggles to take your huge cock?"

He emits a heavy sigh. "Fuck yes."

"Would you let them touch me?"

"Mine," he growls, wrapping an arm tightly around my

waist and glaring up at me territorially as the answer I hoped for makes my heart beat faster.

"Your what?" I toy with him, grinding my hips slowly.

"My…little…slut."

I weaken against him. "Fuck me. Please, *please* fuck me," I beg.

He swoons. "You going to stay nice and quiet for me?" He snatches my lips in his, grazing my bottom lip with his teeth.

"Yes."

"Promise?" he teases.

"Yes, I promise."

"Good girl." He smirks as he leans back and then starts thrusting up into me at lightning speed.

My fingers dig into his neck harder and harder until I unravel. It's good. *So* good. *Too good.*

"Look at me, Chapman."

The priority for him isn't about his satisfaction, but our connection – though the satisfaction is an incredibly pleasant byproduct. I fight the reflex to keep my eyes clenched shut and look right into his. Seeing him on the edge too, desperate to share my orgasm, launches me into the stratosphere. I'm in oblivion. Nothing else exists, just us here…in this…*fuck!*

His relentless pounding into my tightened desire brings him crashing down. He holds me steadfastly as his body releases his tension in short shudders. He stifles his grunts in my neck and embellishes me with more kisses.

If I was the earthquake, he's the tsunami.

I twirl my fingers in the soft hair at the base of his skull as we hold and kiss each other on our comedown.

"Perfect." He sighs. "You are perfect. And this was…" His chest rumbles. "Perfect."

I giggle into his neck. "How long have you been wanting to do this?" I ask when my heart rate steadies.

"Probably since the first time I brought you up here."

"Only that long?" I tut, which makes him smile. "Kind of disappointed though."

His brow creases, and I ignore the guilt that sets in.

"Thought you'd at least say 'groovy, baby' or something when you came."

He laughs and squeezes me tight, probably in relief. "I'll be sure to take your Austin Powers fetish into consideration next time. Want to know why I'm disappointed?"

I frown.

"You promised me this wouldn't become another hookup spot."

Oops, so I did.

He kisses the smile off of my lips.

We stay in our newly claimed hookup spot talking and joking for a long time. It's only when it gets to two in the morning that we drag ourselves up and make a move, agreeing we can't share a bed tonight, as much as we might want to. Firstly, because I have a big day tomorrow and I'm already going to be somewhat sleep-deprived as it is – and sleep is the last thing I'll get if we share a bed – but mostly because we aren't ready for people to know yet. Having something for yourself on here is sacred, and we want to keep this secret for as long as possible. Plus, I'm not ready to host the inevitable summit that'll happen as soon as the news gets out – especially not on my own.

There's one person in particular we both don't want to know yet, which only solidifies our decision. Oscar finally tells me what happened with Tom that night after Scavenger, the advice he gave. He's nervous that now things have changed it'll seem like he said that to get him out of the way, but I don't see it like that for a second. He encouraged me and Tom to forgive each other and then facilitated Tom moving into my room, for Christ's sake – he couldn't have put Tom more *in* the way if he'd tried. I see it as the advice that saved my closest friendship on here.

We both know it'll hurt him when he finds out though. It doesn't matter that Tom and I are just friends now, or that he's busy sleeping his way around the ship. He's always been wary of Oscar, and the last thing Oscar wants is for our new relationship to put a crack in mine and Tom's friendship.

I appreciate how much Oscar cares about keeping us close. It would be so easy to hold a jealous grudge over the briefest fling Tom and I had and jump at the opportunity to drive a wedge between us, and a worse man probably would. I really don't deserve him.

On our way below deck, we pass the venue that's been converted into the haunted house. They started the build on it earlier in the week, but I haven't had a chance to see it yet. As if reading my thoughts, Oscar stops in his tracks and encourages me to go in.

Nothing could have prepared me for this. I did rough sketches for the theatre crew to do what they wanted with, not expecting anything as remarkable as this. My idea has well and truly been brought to life.

Long John Silver's briefing room feels like being on a dock, looking ahead at the gangway of the mysteriously green Flying Dutchman. Stepping through the archway of ripped fabric, I'm transported onto the ship. A maze of wooden panelling guides us through different rooms, all set-dressed to perfection to look like a real pirate ship. The sleeping quarters have bed sheets draped from the ceiling, the bar is full of those funny metal beer mugs I reckon we can make some amazing clattering noises with, the dungeon/jail room has a skeleton chained up and more bones and skulls scattered all over the floor, and finally, in the captain's office, an enormous treasure chest sits pride of place on top of the large wooden desk.

There's another archway to the side of the room that leads out into the foyer we came in from. It's incredible. And what's more, there are a million different hiding spots and secret walkways behind it all for the performers to appear and escape through. It looks like the creative team had as much fun making it as I did dreaming it up.

"It's just like my drawings," I mutter under my breath.

"You designed all this?" Oscar asks – not in a way that makes me think he doubts I could have, but more in quiet astonishment. He looks around the room with a new appreciation for it.

"Not intentionally. I kind of just gave them some doodles as a guide, like, 'this is what I'm thinking'. I didn't think they'd actually use them."

"Is there anything you can't do?"

My heart warms and I wrap my arms around him, resting my head on his chest. He always sees the best in me, always believes in me, always pushes me to do the things I want to do but never would without encouragement. I wouldn't have had the opportunity to do this had he not tried to include me in the conversation with Jerry in the first place. I'm buzzing all over, and I swear my heart is so full it might burst.

"Bake. I'm terrible at baking." My head bounces a little with the vibration of his laughter.

"Nah, I reckon you're better than you think. You always are."

I step onto my tiptoes and kiss him because if I don't, I'm scared I might say something stupid. His soft lips welcome mine and hold me there with slow and long pulls. I still can't get over the fact I can kiss him now. We wasted so much time not doing this before, though I'm more than happy to start making up for it. My hand dares to press against his pocket where I heard the foil crinkle earlier.

His mouth curls into a smile. "Now there are definitely cameras in here, Chapman."

I sink back down to my normal height with a little "hmph".

"I'll work out where the blackspots are tomorrow." He kisses my head. "Promise."

Aye aye, Captain.

TWENTY-TWO

ELIZA

"Don't touch the guests and the guests won't touch you. There are three main reasons for this rule. First reason – Maddison, can you do your best zombie impression and come touch me on the shoulder?"

I turn away from everyone to face the back of the room and listen to her slow footsteps pit-pat towards me across the rehearsal room floor. When I hear that she's close enough, I spin around quickly, her stiff outstretched hand landing straight on my boob, causing laughter to break out in the room.

"Do I need to explain why that's not good?" I joke. "Second reason…"

I retrieve a blindfold I got from guest services from my pocket, which earns me a few whistles that I lean into. I hand it to Maddison to put on and run over to whisper instructions to the excited cluster of entertainment and acting staff. When I return to Maddison, everyone quietly forms a line in front of her as requested. Electric butterflies flutter around my stomach when I catch Oscar's eye, remembering everything from the night before.

"Right, Mads, just walk straight ahead until I tell you to stop."

She only takes two steps forwards before the first person in the line suddenly grabs her shoulder. She shrieks and steps away before tittering nervously.

I line her up, helping her face the right way. "Keep going."

The next person down the line grabs her shoulder, then the next, and the next, and the next. By the end of the line, Maddison's stopped reacting at all. I relieve her of the blindfold and people reward her bravery with applause.

"Why did you stop screaming?"

"It wasn't scary anymore."

I address everyone. "So if every single person reaches out and grabs you, it gets old pretty quick. The same can be said for all the other scare tactics too, which is why we need to make sure we're all constantly varying our scares."

While the majority of the passengers are off exploring the port, I've been given two hours to run a scaring masterclass and rehearse with everyone ahead of next week. The haunted house doesn't open until Thursday night, which will be more of a test run ahead of Halloween on Friday, and then it'll run over the weekend evenings while people are still in the spooky spirit. I was half-joking when I first said I could teach everyone how to scare properly, but Jerry was insistent on it. He's been nodding along, taking mental notes the whole time. It's not like anything I'm saying is particularly mind-blowing – but then I think back to when I did my training all those years ago and how excited I was to learn how to really terrify people.

I've been liaising with the crew manager to get shifts worked out around everyone's other commitments. I'm going to be there all the time to oversee it and attend to any issues we – hopefully won't – come up against. Then we need a *minimum* of three other people working on it at any one time, which was a bit of a gamble before we saw how it was going to be built, but it's actually worked out perfectly. One person will play Long John Silver, at least two people will run around scaring – but it will feel like a heck of a lot more because of all the secret routes helping them to reappear in front of the guests mere seconds after they last encountered them – and then the Captain will be watching from the shadows in the final room, operating the lights before chasing people out of the haunted house. Long John Silver's briefing can last anywhere from one to five minutes depending on the queue times, so it should make for a steady flow of traffic through the house. And because everyone's learning how to do every part, shifts can change seamlessly to allow for breaks and people's other responsibilities without having to disrupt the show.

We work through the short script I wrote for Long John Silver, giving Tom full credit for all the jokes he helped me iron out before I learnt it ahead of presenting it today. I have something written out in full for those who don't enjoy improvising but the key story points are highlighted in bold for those who do. I encourage everyone to make the character their own as I want the focus to be on engaging with the guests and calming their nerves right down before they go in. The lower their heart rates, the bigger the impact the scares will have.

It feels amazing being able to empower everyone to make their own choices, just as Jerry and Henry empowered me. Back home, Lawrence would always micromanage me, to the point he basically did everything himself. After however many months of letting it bother me, I just gave in to it, accepting that that was how he wanted to do things, and I stopped caring, stopped trying to impress him, because what was the point when nothing I did was ever good enough? I was scared my nerves would push me to control everything like he did, but my instincts have only been telling me to let go.

I've worked really hard on this project, and I feel there's a lot riding on its success because for the first time in my professional career I've been entrusted with responsibility. If something like this had happened before I joined the ship it would have terrified me, but now I see it more as an opportunity to show them – and maybe more significantly, *myself* – what I'm capable of.

The guests' enjoyment will be determined by the team's enjoyment, and so theirs, over everything, is my priority.

Once I've taught the basics of scaring – different techniques, physicality, and noises they can make, stressing the importance of vocal warm-ups and not straining their voices because we all rely on them so much for our main jobs – we head over to the haunted house to play in the space. I thought it was unbelievable last night, but when the lights are on and the spooky nautical soundscape is playing, it's like a dream come true.

I split people into groups and let them take turns scaring each other, giving tips where I can, but mostly I'm just having fun watching my brainchild come to life. Each person seems to have come up with a signature scare or claimed their hiding spot as the best. Not that they needed to, but there's always a competitive edge to everything we do as a group.

When there are twenty minutes left, I call everyone together again. "Here's your challenge: scare me."

They all know by now I don't scare easily, but I can already see Obi rubbing his palms together like he's plotting something good.

"And if anyone shouts 'boo', I'm walking."

I go through the maze a number of times to give each group a chance to get me. I flinch once or twice, but mostly I give encouragement when I'm impressed by something they're doing. I spot Oscar stalking closer to me between the sheets in the sleeping quarters, his height suddenly intimidating when I'm being preyed on like this. Eventually, when he's towering over me as I walk slowly along the path, his deep voice whispers, "Outdoor clothes in bed."

"Harvey…" I scold – not very convincingly through my laughter. I can't miss the grunt I get in response to my use of his surname.

Daniel makes an excellent Long John Silver, as I knew he would, and Valentina is possibly the best Captain of the day. I mean, she can intimidate people even when she doesn't mean to, so her meaning to is quite something. Maddison masters sneaking around and appearing out of nowhere. Her signature scare is to whisper people's names as they come through. It's a great way to freak people out because it's unexpected. Usually, you have to hope someone in a group will shout a friend's name when you scare them, and even then it's quite tough to catch while everyone else is also shrieking at the scare, but here, where it's part of our job to learn people's names as quickly as possible, it's a piece of cake.

At the end of the session, I stay back with Jerry to iron out a few final details, refusing to accept his praise for how well it's all come together. I'm just the ideas girl; there was a whole team of people who made it actually happen.

The others all dart out as soon as they can to spend some time around the port while there are barely any passengers on board to entertain. Because I shifted some things around to get on the boat trip yesterday, I'm on port manning duty today, so unfortunately, I'm bound by maritime law to stay on the ship in case there's an emergency. The good news though? So is Oscar.

I catch Tom heading out of our room as I get there. He was in when I eventually went to bed last night. I used the excuse of working on the haunted house and losing track of time for why I wasn't involved in the usual Friday shenanigans, which he seemed to believe. It didn't feel good lying to him, but for now, until I'm ready to tell him, it's the right thing to do. Oscar reassured me what he doesn't know won't hurt him, and I really don't want to hurt him.

"Have fun out there!" I say, taking the weight of the door from him.

"Thanks. Well done for this morning, by the way – or just all of it. It's awesome."

"Thanks again for all of your help. Did you enjoy it?"

"Yeah, felt really good to scream."

I laugh. "I know, right? It's super therapeutic." I push into the room expecting him to walk away, but I feel his presence still behind me. I expect to see more humour on his face when I turn back, but his eyes are lost in thought.

"Yeah," he says quietly.

"Tom! Hurry up – we're all waitin' for ya!" Maddison shouts down the hall, and he hurries off before I can ask if he's okay.

I lose count of how many orgasms Oscar gives me. Every time I think I can't possibly have another, they just keep coming and coming. Or rather, I do. Our appetites for one another are insatiable. It's got to the point that as each one crests, I think I'm going to collapse in on myself like a dying star, and when I don't, it only spurs him on to try harder. And his stamina… *Uhh.* When he comes undone he pushes me over the edge as many times as it takes for him to recover before he can return to me again. And when he's in me, it feels like the perfect puzzle-piece fit, like we were designed for one another.

If bunk-bed sex were an Olympic sport, we'd need a wheelchair to cart us from our podium as we'd be too weighed down by all the gold medals to walk away with any shred of normality. Actually, I'd need a wheelchair to get there in the first place because I'm pretty sure my legs won't be of any use to me for a while.

I've never felt more beautiful than when he finally takes off my clothes. He's so brutally torn between committing every part of me to memory and making the most of the alone time we've been granted that I have to decide for him. And I choose the latter.

My tongue traces every hard line on his skin, and he lets me. I mean, of course he does – hardly a chore, is it, to have a woman worship you like that? There isn't a part of my body that doesn't meet his gentle touch or a freckle that his adoring lips don't find. He even sucks my toes in an attempt to clear his name as a foot fetishiser, but he only proves himself wrong. Apparently, watching me squirm at the ticklish sensation does it for him.

Every now and then we suggest locations around the ship we can take full advantage of now it's basically empty, but neither one of us is prepared for the other to put clothes on or face the professional distance we'll have to keep in order to get there.

Eventually, we're a heap of come-drunk limbs with panting lungs, and I don't think I've ever been this satisfied. In fact, I know I haven't. I never want to leave his bed.

"Important question," Oscar says once he's caught his breath.

"Mmm?"

"Can I have your number?" His kisses glide over my cheek, my neck, my collarbone.

"Bit keen," I tease.

"Damn, I knew it was too soon. I've blown it, haven't I?" He splits his attention between both of my nipples. "Let me make you forget I ever asked." He trails kisses down my body.

"Ooh, ooh, no, she's done. She's done."

He laughs against my stomach and looks up at me. "I guess I'll just have to take you on a date then. A real one."

"With kissing?"

"So much kissing."

"I'll check my diary, see if I can fit you in. Can't make any promises though."

"Mmm, but you've been doing such a good job of it so far." His lips make their way up my giggling chest, back to mine, and the warmth of his body returns over me.

The next few days race by in a blur of guest activities, stolen kisses, and careful distance-keeping. Every night it gets harder to separate ourselves, but we must. It was meant to be for Tom's benefit, but he's not slept here for the past few nights. He seemed indifferent when I tried to tease him about it, which isn't unusual, but typically I get at least a laugh out of him. Except this week, nothing. Has he cottoned on to Oscar and me? Or is he getting serious with someone else and is in fact keeping it secret from us?

Under the guise of wanting to show the security team

some hilarious reaction footage from the training session, Oscar makes good on his promise of locating the blackspots in the haunted house's surveillance, which later finds me bent over a cannon for a delightful portion of the evening.

On Thursday afternoon, after my last activity of the day, I head to the kit store to return the props and find Oscar already there waiting for me. This has become a pattern of ours. I have a copy of his schedule, and he mine, and whenever we can line up our spare time, we do. Sometimes we only have a few minutes to make out before having to dash off again, but this isn't one of those times.

I'm up in his arms in one fell swoop, my legs wrapping around him, and I devour his lips while he walks further into the room, past several rows of shelves packed with plastic storage boxes, until he presses me up against a metal locker in a hidden corner. His stubble grazes my neck as his lips wander.

"Careful!" I squeal.

He eases off my sensitive skin and returns to my mouth, his tongue wrestling with mine. The pulse between my legs is unreal. I tap for him to let me go. I need his fingers there. I need relief from the constant throb I get whenever I'm with him, and quite honestly, even when I'm not.

"What is it, Cricket?" he asks, his deep voice mischievous.

I reach for his hand where it palms my breasts under my top, but as I try to pull it down, he resists me.

"Such an impatient little thing, aren't you?"

This is both the best and worst thing about having more than five minutes together. He could easily satiate me in mere seconds, but instead, he chooses to tease me relentlessly.

I scowl at him, but it only adds to his amusement. He pushes his thick thigh between my legs and snatches up my downturned lips again. He pins both my hands above my head with just one of his when I keep reaching for his desperation even though I can feel it pressing against me.

He succeeds in distracting me, but as good as it is, the sensation of rubbing against him isn't enough. I grumble my frustration against his lips.

"Use your words, Chapman."

"Touch me."

"I am." Being deliberately facetious, he pinches my nipple hard to emphasise his point.

I grind myself over his leg, so wound up I could throw a tantrum. "Touch me *properly*."

"Show me what you mean." He loosens his grip on my hands, and I waste no time slipping one inside my shorts. "Well, I can't see if you do it like that." He tuts.

I peel my shorts down just a little – he has a real thing for seeing me with my clothes not quite off my body, as if I'm in too much of a rush for him to take them off completely – and get back to swirling circles against the wet cotton of my knickers. His Adam's apple bobs and his eyes struggle to decide whether to focus on my fingers or my face.

"Please," I whisper, but he shakes his head, mesmerised.

With a vexed grunt, I use my free hand to make a play for his pocket and snatch the condom I know he always has on him since that first night together. If I can just get it and rip it open, he won't be able to tease me for much longer.

He lets me rifle through his pocket, but it's empty. I check the other one too. Nothing. His smile is so devious I could dissolve into a puddle.

He knows full well that we've already depleted my supply. I bought the remainder of Valentina's stash off her as soon as I could. She didn't ask questions, and I had no intention of answering them if she did. He went out and got his own too, and I know we definitely haven't made our way through those yet. He did this on purpose.

I glower at him. "Why?"

"You're so cute when you're angry."

"Harvey," I snarl, provoking him to take hold of my neck. I purr with pleasure as he glares at me in warning. "You're so cute when you're angry." I goad him with his own words.

The next thing I know, his strong finger is entering me, silky with my need.

"This what you want?"

I nod desperately, unable to form words with the building satisfaction that races through me from the wavering pressure of his finger.

"Then what do you say?"

"Thank you," I whimper as my muscles tense.

The clash of the door bursting open cuts my orgasm off like a song being skipped just as the chorus is about to start. The scuttle of shoes and laughter falls into the room, followed by the squeaks of lip-locking.

I should be furious at the ache tearing apart my insides. We should be panicking about being caught. But both of those emotions get overshadowed by something else. Something new.

We're tucked away enough that we'll only be discovered if they come all the way back here – which, from the sound of things, isn't going to happen. Oscar's eased pressure becomes powerful again at the dwindling threat of discovery. He cocks his eyebrow: is this what I want?

Yes.

His eyes close blissfully for just a second as his arousal peaks, and then his devilish eyes lock onto mine and he works quickly to pick up where we left off. Shit, shit, *shit*. Being quiet has never been more important, and it only sends me spinning even faster. Oscar secures his hand over my mouth as I falter through the shudders of my ecstasy.

Before my breathing evens out, I'm tugging at his waistband, wanting to slip my hand inside it, but I stop when the other couple start talking.

"I've missed you," a woman sighs.

"Have you? Doesn't seem like you've had a problem replacing me," a man replies.

"He doesn't mean anything."

"Prove it."

When I hear frantic buckles and zips, I simply can't resist looking any longer; I need to know who it is. I pull up my shorts, and Oscar grins at my nosiness. I'm not going to watch – I just want a peek. If they wanted privacy they could've gone to one of their cabins. And it's not like we can still get away with the "we were putting away the kit" excuse if we announce ourselves now, so seeing as we're stuck here, I want to find out who with.

I step onto my tiptoes and peer through the shelf beside us, Oscar rubbing against me from behind. I look for a gap that lines up with the other gaps in the shelves past that...

And suddenly my blood runs cold.

OSCAR

She stills. Her curious face turns to stone and the rise and fall of her chest stops dead. I contemplate going out there myself or putting on my Danny Zuko accent to ask them to leave so I'll keep our identities hidden. I just want to put an end to whatever it is that's caused her such upset.

But she beats me to it.

"Does he really mean nothing to you?" she asks loud enough to get their attention.

The tryst ceases. I hear the sound of clothes being straightened out, alongside whispered words I can't quite hear. One set of footsteps retreats. The heavy door clicks open and slams shut. Eliza stays firmly planted exactly where she is. A single tear falls from her eye, but she isn't crying. Her features are hardened by anger.

I step forwards to hold her, but no matter how tightly I do, she's already slipping through my fingers.

"Gwen." *No.* "Answer me."

"And who are *you*, exactly?" Gwen responds with contempt.

Eliza wipes her cheek and shoots past me without giving it a second thought. I know better than to stop her, but the distance is already making me dizzy. I manage to catch her wrist, but my thoughts don't form into words.

Let me handle this. Let me help. Let me fight for you.

She shakes her head and slips out of my grip.

No, no, no.

"It's not what it looks like." Gwen's voice is small now, no longer defiant like before.

I position myself where Eliza was, crouching down to watch on through cluttered shelves because I'm not sure what else I can do without compromising us both.

Eliza holds strong, waiting for Gwen to explain.

"I was so lonely without—"

Eliza interrupts her. "Does Daniel know?"

Gwen stutters nothing conclusive, which is as good as a "no".

"Tell him soon. Or I will."

Eliza walks out of the room, leaving Gwen alone. She stands there for a while before snapping out a few choice words. She takes her time to collect herself before leaving, at which point I have no chance of catching up with Eliza, but I'm determined to find her before my next activity starts.

In spite of my fearful heart and my sadness for Daniel, I'm once again blown away by Eliza. Her moral compass. Her ability to speak up when so many people would have stayed quiet or revelled in the scandal. She just had a front-row seat to her worst nightmare, forced to relive it vicariously, and yet she fought through her own hurt to stand up for a friend.

I eventually track her down in the rehearsal room we've commandeered as a dressing room and warm-up space for the haunted house. The lights are off, but the low sun warms the space. She's now changed into a long maroon skirt with a pirate shirt tucked into it and she's struggling to tighten the ribbons at the back of a corset. She looks up at me when I step through the door, and in that one look, I know I'm at risk of losing her.

"Please don't let this change anything," I plead, crossing over to her.

"I just need a minute."

I stop in my tracks, but I refuse to leave. Our time is limited as it is. I don't have a minute I'm prepared to give up, especially not now.

I watch her in silence as her frustration with the corset builds. "Let me help you." I walk the rest of the way over to her, and she relinquishes control of the ribbons.

With all the mucking about in period costumes at drama school, I have a rough idea of how to tie her into it – though I might act a little more clueless if it'll buy me more time. Sweeping the soft blonde locks over her shoulder, I begin to tidy the tangle she's gotten herself into.

We stay in silence for a while. I want to reassure her we'll work, that that would never be us, just as much as I want the reassurance from her that she believes in us.

"I always saw them as proof long-distance can work," she finally says. "I saw how patient Daniel was while they were apart, how happy they were – or seemed to be – when she arrived. Lucky. I thought they were lucky to have found the person who made the pain of spending all those months without each other worth it."

I rest my head against hers. "Please don't give up on us."

She doesn't answer, but her head pushes lightly back.

I steel my spine and finish tying her in with unsteady hands. The black ribbon blurs the longer I look at it.

"I've only just found you," I whisper, my throat tightening as I place a kiss on her bare neck. Her hand finds mine on her waist and squeezes me. "Do you trust me?"

"I want to. But trusting you will only make it hurt more wh—"

I spin her around before she can finish that sentence. "I'm not him, Eliza. I will never be him." My forehead is on hers, her troubled eyes looking up into mine. "Please give me a chance to prove it."

I place my lips on hers, and she welcomes them again and again. Which only confirms she wants us to work but she's terrified of trying. I hold her as if it's the last chance I'll get. Because it might be.

The door opens, and Eliza pulls away from me. We can't catch a fucking break in this place. Both of us turn our heads to see Jerry, who's already twisted away in an awkward apology for disturbing us, combing through the side of his hair with his fingers. He's holding a box that looks like it contains an outrageous amount of fake blood among other makeup pots.

I look down at Eliza, shutting him out. "Give us until I go," I bargain.

Her attention flashes back to me. Eyes wide. Lips rouged. She nods quickly, blinking away the emotion clouding her vision.

"Break a leg. I'll come through when I finish."

I take one step to go, but my skin prickles the instant I leave her side. I turn back and kiss her once more. Her mouth is like heavenly clouds against mine. Jerry's already caught us – one more kiss can't cause any more damage. Besides, people knowing about us is the least of my concerns right now.

"You're everything to me, Chapman," I say under my breath before giving her one last kiss on her forehead and walking away.

Jerry and I share a small nod as I pass him.

The whole entertainment team and actors, bar those currently scaring, make a plan to go through the haunted house at the end of the night, but the queue is so long by the time we get there that we have to beg security to let us join the back of it. Turns out they had to start turning away guests about an hour ago or else they wouldn't be able to finish on time.

Daniel's still his playful self, and guilt tears through me. But it's not my place to get involved. Not yet. I need to allow Gwen the chance to tell him herself, and I respect Eliza enormously for encouraging her to do so. Daniel deserves that at the very least.

There's a huge buzz outside as everyone watches guests tumble out of the exit screeching and laughing. And from what I've heard from Henry, who's been patrolling the line and keeping passengers entertained between his other commitments, the family sessions earlier went well too. Kids freaked out but didn't cry, and that's a tick in everyone's boxes.

When we finally get to go in, we drag Henry in with us, pushing him to the front of our group. He claims he's been too busy to go through yet, but we all know he's actually just been too scared.

Eliza frightens us right from the off even though we all knew her sudden appearance in the briefing dock was coming. Henry lets out a little yelp and tries to hide behind everyone else, but the gang stay strong and keep him at the front.

I hate the way Eliza started tonight. This was her big night, and she had to go into it with a brave face on. But I see it, that thing she talked about, forgetting everything when she's performing. Or if she hasn't, she does well to cover it.

It's amazing to see everyone in full costume and makeup. When Max gets up in my face in the jail room I can't help the instinct to cower away. I collect myself and notice he has what looks like gills on the sides of his neck. His eyes are whitened out with contact lenses, scales have been painted on his face in a shimmering mix of blue, green, and purple, and there's frighteningly realistic fake blood drenching him. Did Eliza do all that too?

We bolt out of the exit clutching our sides with laughter as Henry pants and tries to regain some composure. Jerry and an excited Eliza are outside waiting for us like parents at the bottom of a waterslide.

"Good, right?" Jerry says with a smug grin.

"Good to see what all the fuss is about," Henry replies, shivering the tension away and approaching Eliza with his hand outstretched.

She shakes it, and I can feel her vibrating with pride from here.

"I'll never forgive you for that, I hope you know," he jokes with her.

"I wouldn't be satisfied with myself if you did." She smiles.

Everyone bundles back in through the exit to see the others now the show's over. I want to spin Eliza around in my arms and tell her how incredible she is. How proud I am of her. But even though we slipped up in front of Jerry earlier, I'm not about to compromise us any further. A shared smile between us as she's whisked away will have to do for now.

A hand on my shoulder holds me back from following the group inside.

TWENTY-THREE

ELIZA

"Hold still!" I move Maddison's head back to where I need it to be and hold a cut-up piece of fishnet stocking against her cheek so I can brush on more scales with eyeshadow. Despite the step-by-step instructions I made and stuck up on the mirrored wall yesterday, she claimed she was no good at these things and demanded my help.

"All I'm sayin', Daniel's never taken a sick day and Gwen's eyes were red as hell this mornin'."

I thought I'd feel good when I found out Gwen had come clean. Well, not *good*, but better than this. I helped. I saved him from wasting any more of his time in a one-sided relationship, or from finding out the hard way. I did the right thing. But he's hurting, and I'm hurting for him.

"Tell you what gossip I actually care about…" I change the subject. "Where's Tom been lately? I feel like I barely see him anymore."

"But y'all are roommates."

"I know, but he's almost never in. Obviously, I see him when we work together, but I dunno, he just hasn't been himself."

"He's probably just exhausted from chasin' all that tail."

"But do you think he's, like, secretly dating anyone?"

"Like you are? No."

I still the makeup brush on her face.

"Come on, Eliza. The only time people think others are keepin' secrets is when they're keepin' some of their own."

Shit.

"Also, when did you and Harvey *ever* sit on opposite ends of the table? To an untrained eye you might be pullin' it off, but to the icon that is Gossip Girl" – she means herself – "it couldn't be more obvious."

"Please don't tell—"

She holds up a hand to stop me. "I have *some* restraint."

I breathe a quiet sigh of relief.

"I know the two of y'all appreciate your privacy. Take my silence as a partin' gift to you both."

"Thank you." I paint the sides of her neck with a final layer of liquid latex, which I'll get her to blend in with her foundation once it dries, ready to then cut gills into and cover in *just enough* fake blood. The dousing starts at nine. "So, Tom…should I be worried?"

"Nah, every guy goes through a ship-mattress phase. He'll take it easy soon."

This comforts me a little, though not completely.

Maddison preps her gills, and I start on my own. I'm one of the mutant pirates today, and I'll play the Captain tomorrow. Though I'll miss playing Long John Silver, I'm so excited to be part of the real action tonight.

Once everyone else arrives for the first shift, I'm on standby to help get them ready, but most already know how to do their makeup from yesterday. I lead them all in a physical and vocal warm-up, and then we head to the haunted house in character as a fun way to drum up some excitement

– which seemed to work well yesterday, though it doesn't look like we need it today. When we get to the venue there's already a huge queue of families lined up waiting to go through. *People really like Halloween, huh?*

Whenever I'm not in the haunted house itself, I'm either hoofing down dinner, running warm-ups for the people arriving to take over, fixing costumes, or teaching people how to apply the special effects makeup. I don't mind how much people lean on me for help; it feels good to be needed, and seeing how much everyone wants to make sure they're "living up to my vision" – yes, someone actually said that – warms my heart.

My last shift of the night finishes with Oscar, Valentina, and a handful of the actors. As we get to the rehearsal room, I go to praise them all for another great night, but nothing comes out. I've been growling, gasping, and screaming for the past five and a half hours and my voice is completely shot.

Oscar chuckles his way through an "aww" and wraps his strong arm around my shoulder in a side hug.

"Thank you, everyone," I force out in a husky, broken whisper.

It's 11.30 p.m. and the crew's Halloween party is well underway, so after grabbing their things, the others rush off to get clean and into their chosen costumes for the evening. Everyone, that is, except Oscar, who's attempting to remove some of the fake blood with face wipes even though I told everyone the only way to get it off properly is to take a shower.

I thought we might talk things through last night, but he disappeared. When he didn't come back into the Captain's office I assumed he'd be at the bar when we all piled down there, but he wasn't. I slipped away to knock on his door, but there was no answer. I even schlepped my way up to our spot expecting him to be waiting for me there, but he was nowhere to be seen.

Today we've been acting like nothing's changed, but we've not been alone since Jerry caught us yesterday. And now we're very much alone. Though doing this – whatever this is – until he goes doesn't feel right. Although if we both know this is temporary, if we've both agreed to make the most of a shitty situation, then that's okay, right? It took Oscar so long to finally allow himself the things he wants, and if this is what he wants – me for just one more week – I can't deny him that.

All right, and maybe I can't deny *myself* that either.

Oscar slowly walks towards the door and twists the lock. "Cruel. That's what you are." A daring smile pulls at his lips as he turns around, striding over to me.

He's still in his ripped striped T-shirt, which on everyone else looks like they've been caught up in a rough storm or attacked by another creature, as it should. But on him it looks like his bulging muscles have done that to the shirt, and it's hot as fuck.

"How so?" I attempt to ask with sexy curiosity, but it comes out like a squeak.

"Oh, you know what you did, Chapman."

I turn my head to the side and pretend to be confused. "What could you possibly mean?" is what I'd say if I could.

"Squeezing past me in all those tight corridors. Hiding with me in those insufferably tiny corners. Pressing yourself up against me any chance you could."

I smirk proudly. I knew exactly what I was doing.

He takes my chin possessively between his thumb and forefinger. His one whitened-out eye is frighteningly sexy.

"Don't think for a second that I'm going to let you get away with it."

Yeah, we're going to be late for that party.

I eventually turn up to the crew bar in my makeshift "Powerpuff Girls" costume, clean of any fake blood and scales. What with it being Maddison's last crew party, we three girls made sure to coordinate. Valentina as Buttercup, the feisty green one, obviously. Maddison, our outgoing leader, in pink as Blossom. And little old me as Bubbles in blue. If only Oscar could have waited. I look way better in this than I did half an hour ago.

It takes a second to adjust to the loud music and dark, smoke-filled room. The club lights flash from orange to purple, and there are cobwebs hanging from just about everything. I walk further in and look around for the gang. Oscar catches my eye from the table he's sitting at with the girls, smiling sweetly as if he didn't just fuck the living daylights out of me. I watched horror porn once, and despite my passion for both of those things it did nothing for me. However, watching him in the mirror as he made me pay for teasing him has me reconsidering the category.

He's dressed as Fred from "Scooby Doo". An exceptionally jacked Fred. Good *grief*. He raises a drink at me, which I picked up early on as the international sign for "I've got you one", but for some unknown reason, it's a cup of tea. Of course he brought a cup of tea to a fancy dress party.

"You took your time," Valentina mumbles when I get to them, knowing full well why I did. I give her the side-eye while purposely sitting in the empty chair beside Oscar and not as far away from him as I can, which Maddison seems to approve of.

"Aww, if only you dressed up as Daphne," Maddison says, and I glare at her, reminding her of her promise to keep her mouth shut. Though I guess by her logic it would be more obvious not to be setting me up with Oscar every waking minute of the day.

Obi totters over with drinks in full drag as Velma.

"Why are you still keeping it quiet? Everyone knows," Valentina questions.

As if on cue, Tom, who's dressed as Shaggy, turns up with more drinks. Maddison fills in the gaps instantly, and Valentina soon after.

Turns out Oscar didn't bring me tea. He made me hot honey and lemon for my sore throat, and it takes all my strength not to cry at the thought of losing him next week.

I shift my attention to Tom opposite me. "Didn't expect to see you here," I toy with him, my warm drink already soothing me.

"Missed me, Elizabeth?"

"I won't miss the 3 a.m. door slam," I tease. He knows it winds me up. No matter how quietly he tries to come in, the door is still the clunkiest thing ever.

"Night's still young." He grins, and I roll my eyes.

Despite his taunt, for the first time in a long time he stays with the group all night – or for however much of it is left. He heads to bed when I do, and in the morning he's still in the room when I wake up.

I have the whole morning off and I'm in desperate need of more sleep, but I don't want to pass up an opportunity to spend time with Tom. Maybe I feel guilty for having spent so much time sneaking around with Oscar, but I know for sure that I really, really miss my friend.

It's more than just being horny, this phase of his. I went through the same thing while I was rediscovering myself after everything happened. I spent my days surrounded by people at Lawrence's company who looked right through me, and all I wanted was to be seen. I didn't have any friends anymore, so after work I'd go on dates as often as I could, but it was just a quick fix. No matter how many dates I went on or how much I tried to connect with someone, it never made me feel any better, and it took me forever to work out that I was just lonely. So now I need to remind Tom that I see him. Friends make time for each other, and I haven't made time for him lately. I mean, neither has he for me, but it goes both ways. Otherwise we risk becoming mere colleagues, and he's always felt like more than that.

I lean over the side of my bunk. "Breakfast?"

Tom

Our plates are piled high, mine with a full English and hers with American pancakes – something I could spend all morning analysing if I had the energy to. She's in her cute oversized pink sweater, and though she can barely talk, she's dancing from side to side with each mouthful as if it's the best thing she ever tasted.

A stack of mail lands on the table and spills over to us.

"Don't y'all ever check your mailboxes?" Maddison stares at us both in disbelief.

"I have post?" Eliza's eyes glisten with happiness. "I didn't think…" Her thought drifts off. "I have post," she says, almost to herself.

"It's been sittin' there for weeks. Thought you knew."

There's a brief pause before Maddison goes to get food, and she nods at me. It shouldn't have taken her getting mad at me last night to see I've been a jerk lately. But it did.

Eliza's already tearing into the first letter before Maddison even has her back turned. The second she looks at the card she bares her teeth. "Oops, I think I'm in trouble." She flips it open and begins to read.

I look at the front. It's one of those personalised cards with a picture of Eliza in black-and-white. Above it is the word "MISSING", and underneath that, "HAVE YOU SEEN MY SISTER?" I laugh.

"I'm guessing that's not the first card she's sent you."

"Apparently not." Eliza reaches for another card in the messy stack. "Are you not going to open yours?"

"I'll take a look later," I lie. There's a reason I haven't checked it since the first time I got mail.

Photos fall outta her next one, and her mouth drops open. "Bump! Look! It's Bump!" Her voice breaks as she announces it, waving the baby scan at me.

"Wow, it really looks like something now, huh?"

She keeps opening letters, glowing brighter every time. I wish my letters from home had the same effect on me.

"Anythin' good?" Maddison asks, taking a seat next to Eliza.

They fuss over the scans for a while and laugh at family photos where her sister's written things like "in case you forgot what we look like" on the backs of them. Eliza opens the next letter, and after skimming it for just a second, she flinches and folds it again.

"Shit, sorry. That's one of yours." She hands it over, looking guilty.

"Committing mail fraud, are we, Elizabeth? Pretty sure they'll have your head for something like that," I tease and take it from her. It'd be weird if I didn't read it now. Maybe it's a nice letter this time. I convince myself it will be, but the first sentence is enough to prove me wrong.

You forgot Dad's birthday.

No, Bobby, I didn't "forget Dad's birthday". How could I? Despite every effort to, I've been unable to *stop* thinking about it. And what, I'm supposed to wish his happy birthdays to you now? Well, unhappy fucking birthday to your dead dad, asshole.

I'm so sick of his golden child shit. Painting me out like I'm some heartless monster. And now Eliza's looking at me like I'm the dick who forgot his own dad's birthday. Great.

Breathe.

I'm projecting. Maybe she didn't see it. Either way, I've lost my appetite now.

"Guess I'm spending my morning replying to all these then," she says.

Guess I'm spending my morning wishing I could burn all of mine.

It's later that night the reality check comes. We've all gathered in the haunted house to celebrate the end of it. Even Henry and Jerry are here giving Eliza the praise she deserves. She's pulled off this amazing event, made a name for herself here, and what have I been doing? Drinking and fucking anyone who even looks my way.

I thought I was done grieving. I should be. It's been

almost a year. But instead of getting easier, it's just getting worse. I should be ashamed of myself for using his name as an excuse for the way I've been acting. It's pathetic. But it's easier to lose myself in the distractions than to be alone with my thoughts.

This punching bag doesn't work. I keep thinking anytime now something will click and I'll be able to walk outta here with a clear head, but the red mist is only getting thicker.

"I wouldn't like to be that bag." A voice echoes around the empty gym.

Oh, great, *he's* here. The tip of my chin is all I can be bothered to give in response. I focus back on my target, chasing the relief I crave.

Why. Doesn't. This. Fucking. Thing. *Work?*

"Hey, hey, slow down – you're going to put your shoulder out."

Work. Dammit. WORK.

"Tom!"

Please work. Just work!

"Shit!" I snatch back my wrist. Shooting pain burns all the way up my arm. Harvey, already waiting on the sidelines, dives in to steady the bag before it does me any more damage. I cuss my way through the pain.

"Let's get you to medical."

"I'm fine."

"Sit down. Let me take a look at least."

"I said I'm fine!" I rage, waiting for the shouting match.

But he doesn't fight back. Doesn't walk away. He just stares at me with those stupid condescending eyes of his.

After a few more "motherfucker"s, my body moves

against my will, giving up and straddling a nearby bench. He does the same and then takes my hand to assess the damage.

"Wanna talk about it?"

"Not really."

I hiss when he tries to rotate my wrist outwards. "It's not healthy, keeping it all in."

"I don't have anger management issues if that's what you're getting at."

"I'm not saying you do. But you need to find a better outlet for it because these random outbursts you have aren't good for you. Wiggle your fingers."

I grimace as I do as I'm told, and silence passes between us.

"Who do you want to be?"

"What's that supposed to mean?"

"Just a question." He applies pressure lightly in different spots round my wrist, watching my face as I wince. *Sadist.* "Took me a long time to work out the answer isn't the same as *what* I want to be."

Guess I've never given it much thought. *What*, sure, but *who*... I don't even know where to start.

He lets go of my arm. "Yeah, I think you've sprained that pretty bad. You'll need to head down to the medical centre." He gets up and walks over to the weight rack.

I begin making my way to the door but turn back before I can think better of it. "Do I really seem that lost?"

He thinks for a second before he speaks. "My dad was never really around, and I didn't have any older siblings to look up to, so I wasted a lot of time figuring shit out for myself that I wouldn't have had to if someone had given me a nudge in the right direction. I don't know what home's like for you, but—"

"Everything's great at home."

He raises one eyebrow at me. "No one joins a ship because everything's great at home."

Why does he have to be right all the time?

"So you aren't angry anymore?" I ask.

"I was never angry, but I was a real bellend."

The joke's too good not to miss. "Was?" I look around as if I'm searching for the new and improved version of him.

He cocks his head to one side, a smile spreading from the corner of his mouth, and the tension in my chest eases a little. "All I'm saying is things got better when I stopped lying to myself."

"Tom! What have you done?" Eliza hurries over to me when she sees me on the main deck a few hours later, her wide eyes taking in my bandaged wrist in a sling.

A sling. Fucking humiliating.

"You should see the other guy."

She rolls her eyes, trying not to smile.

"It looks worse than it is, I promise. The sling's just a precaution – I should be out of it in a few days."

Her face quickly changes from concerned to stern, like she's been possessed by Valentina all of a sudden. "I swear to God, if you use this as bait for a pity shag with someone tonight, I won't speak to you again."

"Is that how little you think of me?" I spread my bad hand on my chest. "Elizabeth, I'm— Actually, that's a pretty good idea," I kid, and she swats my good arm. "Ow, ow, careful! I'm fragile."

She starts to lead me over to our activity spot and I get right up to her ear.

"Wanna shag?" I ask in my creepiest voice.

She giggles and whacks me again. As much as it hurts to admit, Harvey might have a point. I'm never going to get anywhere if I keep lying to myself.

There are lies I've been telling myself out of self-preservation: that I don't miss home; that I've fully processed losing Dad; and that college wasn't a complete waste of money. But there's one lie I refuse to tell myself any longer because everything seemed to get worse the minute I tried to believe it. So, it's time to be honest.

I'm in love with Eliza.

Shit, just by admitting it I feel a million pounds lighter. I'm not sure if I'm ready to admit it to her just yet, but I'm optimistic I'll get it right this time.

"What are you smiling at?"

"Nunya."

In the evening, the girls and I help Maddison pack. Or rather, Eliza and Valentina help while I sit up on Maddison's bunk heckling them like one of the old men from "The Muppets".

We all get up early for an emotional goodbye on Monday. I didn't expect it to hit me so hard, but Maddison's been like a big sister to me on here. I'll miss her a lot for sure.

"You next, man." I pat Harvey on the back, keeping the mood light as we watch her walk away.

Lying awake last night with an aching wrist – not as dirty as it sounds – I corrected one more lie: Harvey isn't out to get me. I thought I hated him because he was always getting in the way of Eliza and me. And because I thought he thought he was better than everyone. But knowing he used to be an asshole – like, an actual one – has given me hope. Even if I'm an asshole now at twenty-two, I can still turn it around and get my shit together by the time I'm almost twenty-five.

"I'll remember to bring tissues next time," I say, looking at all the tear-stained cheeks around me.

"I wouldn't bother. Don't think there'll be much upset," Harvey replies with a shrug before we all disperse.

Eliza's bottom lip trembles again, but she tries to hide it by walking ahead of me.

Yeah, I'm gonna bring tissues. And while I think of it, I'll stock up on Skittles too.

TWENTY-FOUR

ELIZA

Maddison's replacement, Sunshine from Barbados, seems lovely from what I know of her so far. I've never met someone so suited to their name. She's got the brightest smile and warmest presence. She's quite a bit older than the rest of us and a lot more experienced with cruising too. Even after just one day with her, I can already tell there's a real "Ship-Mum" vibe about her.

I'm sitting with her and Valentina in the theatre on Tuesday afternoon. They're polar opposites, like summer and winter, but I think they'll get on just fine as roommates. We've assembled for the monthly staff meeting while the guests are off exploring the port. The captain's giving various people around the room all kinds of praise – I think. She's smiling and people keep clapping, so I think it's praise.

I know I should be paying more attention, but it's more interesting to look around at the changing faces. Most people were here last month, but there's still a significant number of people I don't recognise who must have arrived in the past week or so. Some with more distinguishable features I'm certain I scared last week. Even though the haunted house was for the guests, the crew were still allowed to come through in their downtime so long as they didn't all come at once and overwhelm the queue.

The captain invites Henry onto the stage to speak, and I scan the room for the boys again. Obi, Daniel, and Tom are sitting a few rows down, but Oscar's nowhere to be seen. It's unlike him to miss something like this. I have to start getting used to not seeing him in a crowded room, though, I guess.

"Eliza Chapman!"

Huh?

The girls are nudging me with excited grins. Well, as close to a grin as Valentina can stomach. *What's going on?*

"You just won Employee of the Month!" Sunshine tells me, clapping.

I'm sure to the outside it looks like I'm doing that fake modest thing actors do at award shows, but I genuinely have no idea what's happening.

"Go!" Valentina nods towards the stage, rushing me up from my seat. I hurry down the aisle to people applauding and smiling at me, but I barely hear anything over the sound of my heartbeat.

Me? Employee of the Month? Come off it.

I ascend the stairs at the side of the stage with legs of jelly. I can't wait to write home about this – Mum and Dad will be so impressed. I wish I could see Lawrence's face when they tell him. "Queen of the circus? Wow, well done, Lizzie, what an achievement," he'll say sarcastically, but I won't care.

I shake Henry's hand, my face hurting from the smile threatening to rupture my cheeks, and he gives me a certificate.

"Well-deserved," he says with a nod and a proud smile.

I only just hear him over the boys' signature dog-bark

cheer. I look out to see them standing up with one hand around the side of their mouths as they shout, their other fists punching the air. My heart is so full. I wish Oscar were here to see this.

It's only when I get down from the stage that I discover he is. He's sitting in the front row, clapping with everyone else. Smile wide, eyes sparkling, and looking right at me.

I return his smile and float back to my seat, sticking my tongue out at Valentina when I see she's filming me on her phone.

"Well done, sweetie," Sunshine congratulates me.

The girls check out my certificate while people I know, and even some I don't, look back at me to give me a big thumbs-up or to mouth "well done".

Today's a good day.

Henry invites Jerry up to speak next, and I decide to pay attention, having learnt my lesson.

"As some of you know, I've been on this ship for a very long time. Too long, some might say."

There are a few titters from the head of departments sitting on the stage behind him and near the front of the auditorium, which prompts him to clap back with a sassy remark.

"And until recently, I thought I would be for a lot longer. But it's time for a new challenge. So, in a few months, I'll be heading to Atlantis to take over as activities manager there."

That's Oscar's ship. I look at Valentina, who looks back at me with the same confused expression. Did Oscar turn down the job? He'd better not have. I swear to God, I'll—

"And I couldn't think of anyone better to replace me here than our very own Oscar Harvey. Oscar, come on up."

What?

My heart stops beating. Every single muscle of mine grows so heavy. "Did he just say…?"

Valentina nods and starts clapping with everyone else. People whistle and cheer, but I can't believe my eyes. My six-foot-something Greek God of a man strides onto the stage, lights bouncing off his perfectly styled blond hair. He shakes Jerry's hand, and Jerry encourages him to say a few words.

Caught a little off-guard, Oscar takes a second to step forwards to the microphone. I'm at the back of the auditorium, but somehow he finds me, his eyes locking onto mine and his cheeks dimpling with a smile. "Thanks, everyone. I'm sure I'm not the only one who'll be sad to see Jerry go, and I know I've got some big shoes to fill, but I look forward to learning how to walk in them."

I restrain myself from showing too much emotion on the outside, but on the inside I want to burst with excitement. I want to cry with happiness. I want to run and hug him like we're two lovers reunited in an airport.

And here I was thinking today couldn't get any better.

He's staying. *He's really staying!*

OSCAR
DEVIL'S NIGHT

"Harvey, can I have a word?"

I turn towards the hand on my shoulder. Jerry looks serious, not jovial like he was just a minute earlier.

"Sure, what's up?" I hide my sudden nerves. *Is this about the kiss?*

"Walk with me."

We step away from the haunted house and head down the quiet boardwalk.

"You want to know why I selected you for the job?" he

asks me as though deep in thought, and I nod. "Because come rain or shine, you're there. The guests love you. Every crew member loves working with you. You never think twice before helping somebody else, and, hell, you've saved my ass more times than I dare to count. There was never any doubt that you were the right man for the job."

"Thanks, Jerry. That's very kind of you to say."

He falls silent again, but we keep walking. "I think I need a change of scene. I've felt it for a while, but... I was thinking of speaking to Henry tomorrow about moving to a different ship. Maybe even Atlantis."

Is he saying what I think he's saying?

"Jerry, I can't ask you to do that."

"You don't have to. Unless you would prefer I didn't." His eyes narrow on me like he's making sure he hasn't misread something.

I struggle to find the words. "No, I...I would love to stay here."

"That's settled then."

"You think they'll let us switch?"

"I won't take no for an answer."

I wait for her up in our spot. It's been horrible keeping this from her, but until things were one hundred percent confirmed, I couldn't get her hopes up.

When she arrives, not a word passes between our lips before they're on each other's. All candy floss and smiles. She's breathless from the stairs, and I'm breathless from her.

"How?"

"Pulled a few strings." I shrug, faking nonchalance. "I'm so proud of you."

She kisses me again. Tiny tears fall from her eyes, and she wipes them away, laughing at herself. I laugh with her and brush the next one that falls down her cheek.

"I still have to leave on Monday."

Her eyes fill with panic again.

"Just for six weeks. It's a timing thing with mine and Jerry's contracts, as well as the activities manager's on Atlantis. Sorry, Cricket, I really tried."

She shakes her head, dismissing my apology with a smile despite the tears streaming down her face. "But you're coming back?"

"I'm coming back."

She pulls me down to kiss her, and even though we're both here fighting back a tidal wave of emotions, I can say with confidence I've never been happier. "Thank you."

I hold her beautiful face away from mine. I need to make the most of seeing her in person before we have to spend the next six weeks apart. All the work I did on myself hasn't been for me at all; it's been for her. It was to make me the man she deserved to be with. Someone worthy of being loved by her.

"I love you, Chapman."

There's the slightest hitch in her breath as my words take her by surprise, and for just a second I worry I've overwhelmed her or she doesn't feel it too. But then her entire face softens and warmth spreads all over me.

"I love you too."

As part of Eliza's Employee of the Month award, not only does she get a significant bonus on this month's payslip, but she can also pick something from a number of perks to enjoy: a meal for two at Coral's, which she already won with Tom in their first week here but they haven't found the time to use yet; a big chunk of internet access; a day off; or an excursion – which, of course, she sees as a punishment. But what she ultimately picks is a guest cabin experience. An entire evening in a suite which she arranges for tonight. My last night on board.

I tell everyone I'll be locked away in my room packing all night, though almost no one buys it. Instead I'm here with her, saying a proper goodbye. I did remind her she'd be passing up a guaranteed day swimming with pigs, but she still chose this, and I'm honoured she did.

She opens the door to me looking utterly angelic, her golden hair and summer dress the perfect contradiction to the devil I'm confident just started dancing in her head.

Sex with Eliza is unlike any I've ever had before. My encounters up until now, while adventurous, were frivolous. There was passion but no chemistry. Fire but no spark. Falling for Eliza has unlocked a whole world of emotions and sensations I never thought possible. With her, I get to play. It's not about testing limits, pushing boundaries, or inflicting pain; it's about bringing our dirtiest fantasies to life, and *my God*, does she have the filthiest appetite. Every time we're together I get to delve deeper into that depraved part of her, as well as myself, and I revel in knowing I've barely even scratched the surface.

As much as I'm looking forward to making love to her in that real *full-size* bed and seeing what she looks like with her hair splayed over the pillows and her fists bunching up the sheets – though I love it when they're tugging and clawing at my shirt – the look in her eyes and the urgent pull of her welcoming kiss tells me she wants to play. Dropping my overnight bag on the floor, I restrain her wandering hands.

"Wait here," I instruct.

I stride out to the balcony, temporarily captivated by the view. The sun's low in the sky and the flat sea stretches on for eternity. Perfect though it seems, there's one thing that could improve it insurmountably.

I lean over the railings a little, checking for signs of life from the neighbouring cabins. Nothing for now. I turn back to see Eliza still standing in the exact spot I left her in. She's in the mood to behave herself this evening. Noted. Just before I call her over, I spot a pair of heels by her bag. Oh, she knew exactly what she was doing bringing those.

"Put those on then come outside."

A little taller now, she approaches me with an excited kind of anticipation.

"Hands on the railings."

She obeys. I stand a step or two behind her, place my hands on her hips, and tug her towards me, stretching her out so her back's beautifully arched and her incredible arse is pressing against me, perfectly aligned. I will myself not to get distracted by the sensation of it and take a step back, lifting the skirt of her dress to reveal the most incredible pair of satin knickers. Baby-blue. My favourite colour.

"Are these new?"

She nods.

"For me?"

She nods again.

Fuck. The thought of her scrolling online, deliberating which lingerie she wanted to wear for me, makes my pulse beat with thunderous intensity. It takes everything not to demand to see what I assume is a matching bra immediately.

Good things come to those who wait.

I run a light hand along her sensitive slit. The satin is soft against my fingers, and her tender warmth begs me to keep stroking. When her dampness soaks the fabric and her knees begin to buckle, I stop, step away, and take a seat just behind her on the cushioned metal chair.

She looks back at me, on the edge of desperation.

"Head forwards," I demand. "Spread your legs."

She slightly widens her stance.

I just want to look at her. That's not true. I want to do a lot of things, but I'm not going to let myself rush this.

"Pull them down for me."

Her painted fingers slide them down so they hug her thighs before she returns her hands to the railings without me even needing to ask. A rumble rolls through my chest. Obedient. Keen. *And all mine.*

The impulse to unbuckle my trousers and satiate the both of us is agonising to control, but there's something I want more. Getting to my knees behind her, I bury my face deep between her legs, tonguing her sweetness. She covers her mouth, but it doesn't stifle her squeaks of satisfaction. She's soaking, squirming on her tiptoes as pleasure wracks through her body.

"Oscar, I'm gonna—"

I pull myself away again, causing her breath to catch. *Not yet.* Once she stills, I indulge in one more stroke with my tongue before dragging myself up. Her thighs clench and she lets out a whine.

"Did you want something, Chapman?"

She grumbles, her body tensing and releasing with frustration.

"Use your words."

"More," she whispers.

"Can't hear you."

She looks back at me. "I want more," she states boldly.

"Greedy little thing, aren't you? Was that not enough?"

She shakes her head.

"Take it from me then." I once again tug her hips back against the front of my tightened trousers. "Take what you want."

She hesitates just a little, so I guide her hips with the motion I know feels as good for her as it does for me because she sighs softly with relief. I keep guiding her but still feel her holding back. Gathering her hair into a ponytail, I pull her up so my lips meet her ear.

"If I can't feel how wet you are through these soon, there'll be trouble."

She sighs, grinding against my straining muscle with more confidence.

Keeping my voice low, I check in with her. "Is this what you want?"

"Yes."

Hmm. "Good girl."

With one hand still tight on her hair, I lower her back down. Bent over so her clit gets the pressure it needs, she works herself up on my body. Using me. All the while, I throb with the need to be inside her. To fill her with my length.

"Six weeks without me is going to be hard for you, isn't it?"

"Yes."

"Are you going to fuck yourself with your fingers every night and pretend it's me?"

"Yes. I promise."

I reach forwards and work my way inside the top of her dress, fingering the lace trim there before pulling the cups away and exposing her breasts. I hover my hand close to feel them as they sway. "Mmm. I'm going to think about you all the time. Think about you watching those filthy videos with your hand inside your knickers like the depraved little animal you are."

She weakens with a sigh, and I pinch her hard nipple. Her muscles tense as she gets closer and closer to her finale, bringing me so close to my own, but I fight to keep my composure.

"My dirty. Fucking. Slut."

She whimpers. Her body tightens and loosens as she rides the wave of her orgasm, staining my clothes with her gratification.

Once her breath steadies itself and I can be sure I won't crumble with my next move, I relieve her from her position and snatch her lips in a deep kiss. "You're fucking incredible."

Taking one look at her, content and come-drunk, my obsession with her spirals. I have to get this dress off her. *Now.*

We take it inside. If this is the first time she doesn't have to hold back her noises, I want to make the most of it. And *my fuck*, is it worth moving. Who needs a sea view when I've got her to look at?

She's lying flat on her stomach, her legs together, as I kneel on either side of her, holding her tight where her hands are bound together with the cord of a bathrobe, and drill into her from behind. I'm so deep we're both seeing stars. Our reflection stares back at us in the mirror, but her eyes are unable to focus on anything with the way they roll into the back of her head. I don't want her to miss this though.

I slow my rhythm just a little. "Look up, Chapman."

She does as she's told, catching my eye with a wry smile.

"Tell me what I'm doing."

She bites her lip and her cheeks glow with shy pride. "You're fucking your favourite pussy." She's only just starting to believe it now. Even though I've told her almost every day since the boat trip.

"Why is it my favourite?"

"Because it's mine." Her words are spoken in fragments as I pick up the pace, her mouth forming a delicious circle.

"And who do you belong to?"

"You." She shudders as another orgasm ripples through her, tightening blissfully around me. "I belong to you," she pants, and my climax crescendos with hers.

This is the part I've been looking forward to the most. Taking care of her. Soothing her. Kissing her. With no rush to be anywhere else or hide how much I love her. Well, no rush if I ignore the ultimate countdown hanging over us, which I am.

After a warm shower, we sit outside in our complimentary robes and slippers, our hands intertwined as we watch the sun go down and wait for our room-service dinner. Speaking of which, I hope the Prosecco I ordered arrives soon. I have a very important question to ask.

Eliza looks over at me, a glint of mischief in her eye. "So are you, like, my boyfriend now, or…?"

Damn, she beat me to it.

"Bit keen." I pull her smiling lips in to kiss mine.

It's funny. When all this started between us, I thought today would be the end of our journey. But as it turns out, it's just the beginning.

TWENTY-FIVE

ELIZA

The second goodbye is tougher than the first. Oscar has to be off the ship first thing, so we wake up super early, pull the curtains back, and watch the sunrise from our bed with tear-filled eyes. Oscar spoons me while I fight off the immense pressure in my lungs willing me to sob, instead wanting to cry just a few cute tears. But we don't always get what we want. It's that heartbreaking fear there'll be a last kiss and a last hug any second and I can't do anything about it.

He leaves the guest cabin at 6 a.m. so he can sneak back to his room and pack up the last few things before we all escort him to the crew gangway. No more sobbing, no more lingering hugs, and definitely no more kissing.

He'll be back the Monday before Christmas, which is in exactly six weeks, when his obligatory contract break is up, and it can't come soon enough.

I journal my days in undelivered WhatsApp messages to Oscar, waiting until I can finally send them at an internet cafe in one of the ports. The second I'm connected, a whole storm of texts flood in from him, which gives me a weird E-gasm. I open our chat, scroll all the way up, and begin reading about his chaotic plane journey, getting tackled by his dog when he finally arrived home, and how good it is to see his family again. At the start of each new day he's put a countdown to when he's back.

It's lunchtime here, which means it's about dinnertime there. And before I have time to wonder if I'll be lucky enough to catch him, one little word appears under his name.

Online.

The grey ticks of my messages turn blue, and suddenly he's typing.

> How's my Cricket today? xx

My heart swells and the smile on my face grows even wider at my pet name. I can still hear him laughing at my subconscious "cricket legs" on Sunday night.

> Cricket's good. Alone in an internet cafe with time to kill… xx

In an instant, my phone starts to buzz with a FaceTime request. I connect my headphones and shut the rest of the world out while I chat to my *boyfriend*.

That night, I reread all his messages and snuggle into my pillow, which I sprayed with his aftershave. I spritzed the curtain with it too so when I open and close it every day I get a little waft of him.

I miss him so much already, but I'm not scared of the time

apart like I thought I'd be. I love him and I trust him, and I'm genuinely excited for him to be at home enjoying the comforts that come with it.

On Sunday, Tom and I finally go out for our dinner at Coral's. It's crazy we haven't gone before now, but everything's been so busy since we got here that only now do I feel some form of calm. Tom seems to feel it too. I'm not sure what's changed, but he's had a spring in his step this past week or so despite his sling limiting him quite substantially. You don't appreciate how physical this job is until you're one limb down. I should know.

He's been hooked up to a wireless headset mic like a pop star for all his activities because he quickly discovered that as soon as he held an actual microphone he couldn't do anything else. Does it make him look like a Justin Bieber tribute act? Absolutely. Will I ever let him live it down? Absolutely not.

But the sling's off tonight. It clashes with the tux, apparently. He still has to keep his wrist support on, but it's much less limiting. Tom insisted on the dress code, so I'm in my favourite pink off-the-shoulder dress, which I wore on my first formal night.

The food is *so good.* Which is to be expected considering Coral's has a Michelin star. We purposely order different things so we can sample as much as possible despite wanting the same dish as each other every course. It's not like we can keep coming back here given the prices.

It's so nice to hang out properly again. A sweet couple of older ladies on the table next to us keep giving us nostalgically loving smiles every time we laugh too loud. Maybe to them we look like we're on a very successful date. Actually, there have been a few times tonight where it's *felt* like a date too.

Shit. Am I flirting? No, this is how we've always talked. But I have a boyfriend now – should I be toning it down? Oscar knows this isn't anything, *I* know this isn't anything, but does Tom know? He does have a cheeky look in his eyes tonight, but he always has a cheeky look in his eyes – that's just him. And it's not like we're feeding each other with our own forks or playing footsie under the table.

For a second, I consider telling him about Oscar to defuse whatever romantic vibes might be floating around, and then I remember how he hurt his wrist and why we decided it best not to tell him yet. We wanted to give him time to work through whatever he's got going on while Oscar's away and then hope Tom's fist isn't aimed at Oscar's face when he gets back and we come out as an official couple. They're not sworn enemies or anything, but they certainly aren't friends.

"See, if you took girls here instead of eating out at theirs all the time, you might have more success locking one down," I comment, taking a nonchalant bite of crème brûlée. *Yep, remind him of all the other girls he's been with. Perfect date deterrent.*

His spoonful of tiramisu pauses just an inch away from his mouth as he registers my crude joke. Then we chortle like children who just typed "eight zero zero eight five" on a calculator and swap the last halves of our desserts over.

I haven't let on that I know what really happened in the gym last week, nor that I saw what was in that letter I didn't mean to open. I've avoided asking him anything about home despite my concern. He almost never talks about his family, but I didn't think things were so strained. I only told Oscar because I was worried. I knew he wouldn't share it around, and I thought it would be helpful if someone else kept their eye on him. No one else seemed to think there was anything the matter, but *I knew* something wasn't right.

Tom smiles even brighter at me after sucking the last traces of desert off his spoon. "This has been nice."

"It really has."

Silence spills between us, but it isn't uncomfortable; it's warm and cosy. That feeling doesn't last long though.

"I'm sorry I avoided you," he says.

My stomach tightens. *Avoided me?* Preoccupied, sure, but *avoiding*? I ask why, but the word barely brushes my lips.

"I've been telling myself it was because I've had a lot going on, but if I'm honest with myself, which I'm trying to be, a huge reason" – he swallows – "was because I couldn't be alone with you."

My heart thumps impossibly hard in my chest.

"And I can't be honest with myself without being honest with you too."

Warm isn't cosy; it's clammy and claustrophobic. The room could be spinning or squashing and I'd stay still in among it all, unmoving.

"I'm crazy about you, Elizabeth." His kind and beautiful brown eyes burn into mine. "And I would do anything for a second chance."

I'm lost for words. I don't— I can't— I shake my head, blinking away the sting in my eyes. "Tom, I…" I *what*? How do I—? What do I—? "Your friendship means everything to me."

The light in his eyes dwindles.

Please don't give up on our friendship.

"I need to be honest with you too." *Fuck*. "I'm seeing someone."

Confusion or hurt or a mix of both flickers across his face. His eyes glaze over as if he's trying to figure out how he missed it. I consider putting him out of his misery, but I know I'll only cause him more. His eyes snap back to mine, pleading with me through those long eyelashes of his.

"Harvey?"

I nod, shame clutching my insides.

He clears his throat like his has tightened too. "How long's that been going on for?"

I take a second to consider my answer. "I guess since the boat trip." I settle for this because numbering how many days or weeks I've been deceiving him for feels worse, though now I've probably given him all kinds of imagery he didn't need.

His eyebrows raise. "Wow. I was really that blind to it, huh?"

"I should have told you, I'm sorry. I—"

He shakes his head. "Are you happy?"

My heart starts to crack while watching his shatter. I nod again apologetically. "Tom—"

Our waiter comes by to clear our plates and offers us coffee, but we decline. With no bill to pay, we slip out of the restaurant in silence. I make for the crew stairway, but Tom hangs back.

"I'm gonna take a walk."

"Tom," I plead.

He gives me a sad smile. "Just need to clear my head. Sorry I said anything." He walks away before I can beg him not to.

I don't even get one flight down before tears start rolling over my cheeks. I hold back my sobs, hoping to make it to our room without drawing any attention to myself, but I'm unsuccessful. Valentina and Obi, seemingly on their way to the crew bar, stop me as I attempt to walk past them.

"Whoa, what happened, baby girl?" Obi asks, his gentle hand on my arm keeping me from running off.

I sniffle. "Tom found out."

"About what?" His confusion is fleeting as realisation quickly dawns. "Oh, honey, come here." He wraps me in a hug, and I hope my mascara doesn't stain his T-shirt.

Valentina watches me sympathetically.

"It should be illegal for someone as cute as you to cry. Especially when you're all dressed up like this."

I laugh a little.

"You wanna come hang out with us?" Obi asks. "We can go back to mine if you don't wanna go to the bar."

"Thanks, but I'm gonna see if I can call Oscar, I think."

"Okay. Come find us if you need anything."

They wait for me to walk off before they do.

With trembling hands, I buy half an hour of internet and FaceTime Oscar. I keep apologising for calling so late, but he keeps apologising for not being here to make things better – not that there's much he can do. The damage has been done. Tom and I can come back from this though. I know we can. We've done it before.

I'm hidden away on my bunk when the door clatters open. I take an earphone out and pull back the curtain a little, hiding the fact I'm on the phone. I want to ask him if he's okay, but I know he's not. He gives me a stifled smile and opens his drawers, pulling out a clean uniform.

"I'm gonna crash with Daniel," he says before getting his toothbrush from the bathroom.

"Okay." I hide my disappointment, but not very well.

"Night, Eliza." He looks up at me with sorry eyes.

"Night," I reply, but it sounds fractured, and he leaves.

Oscar's voice in my ear snaps me out of spiralling thoughts. "Just give him some time."

I pick the phone back up and nod, my teeth sinking into my lip. Neither of us speak for a while, both feeling equally helpless.

"I miss you," I say feebly.

"I miss you more."

I never meant for it to play out this way. I shouldn't have kept it from him. I knew it would hurt him, but I didn't factor in how much more damage the secrecy would do. I should have. Should have, should have, *should have*.

He's civil when we work together, but as soon as the activity ends he shuts me out again. It's not through anger or spite; I can see the upset when he dips his head and walks away, keeping his eyes down.

Come Friday, I learn he's officially moved out. I shouldn't be so shocked given his old bunk in Daniel's room is free again, but I am, mainly because I didn't hear it from him. I got back late to discover a half-empty room. I thought he'd at least tell me, give me an opportunity to apologise properly or convince him not to go. I contemplate going to the crew social and confronting him but think better of it.

I'm not much in the mood to socialise on Saturday night either.

I feel bad I haven't got to know the newbies very well, so I make an effort to join everyone for a drink on Sunday night. It's been a week and moping hasn't got me anywhere, so time to buck up and move on.

Oscar's replacement, Louise, is a funny girl from Essex who has to put up with Tom bombarding her with questions about the cast of TOWIE all night as if they're close personal friends of hers. I don't let myself linger on the feeling I've already been replaced. She's incredibly animated when she speaks; it's more like she's performing than talking. The table's in fits of laughter while she recounts a story from her first contract about how a bunch of them had a few too many to drink and tried to go skinny dipping.

"It's a miracle we weren't all fired, honestly. It was all thanks to this one guy who could charm his way out of anything, strutting out there starkers as the day he was born and chatting up the security guy."

"Shut. Up!" Obi squeals on the edge of his seat. "That really worked?"

"I still have a job, don't I?" She cocks her eyebrow. "Next thing you know, they're making out on the bar, we sneak out while he's distracted, and, well, we didn't see Oscar again for the rest of the night, so safe to say it was a win-win."

It's fine. Lots of people are called Oscar.

"Wait, what ship was this?" Obi asks.

"Deity."

Kill me.

"Are you talking about Oscar Harvey?" Obi clarifies.

"Yes! Oh my God, do you know him?"

Please kill me.

"He's due back in a few weeks to take over from Jerry."

"No way! He's *wild*!"

"I don't think we're talking about the same person," Tom says.

She picks up her phone and roots through her photo albums, finding what she was looking for all too quickly. "This guy, right?" She shows us all a picture of the guy. *Of Oscar.* He's shirtless with neon paint splattered all over his body. There are girls draped on either side of him also posing for the camera. He's got black hair too, which I wish I could say is the most unrecognisable thing about this photo.

"Jesus Christ!" Daniel gasps.

She makes an aside to Valentina and me while the boys all gawk at the picture. "In-*credible* in bed."

How do I shut my ears? Or better yet: *Hand over your phone, love. I'm sure there's a helpful tutorial on YouTube for how to perform some kind of eardrum-ectomy.* I think back to my first excursion on the hot, vomit-infused bus, and even then I didn't feel as nauseous as I do now. Tom's looking at me across the table with nothing short of pity in his eyes. My throat is dry, my cheeks are hot, and my legs have gone numb.

"Hate to disappoint, but he's got a girlfriend now," Valentina informs her so I don't have to.

"No way! Someone managed to pin him down? What a shame. Someone on here?"

Valentina nods once.

Louise looks around the bar as if she'll be able to tell just by looking. "Who?"

"You just told her what a good lay her boyfriend is." Valentina tips her head my way. I swear she's immune from feeling awkward. I hiss her name to scold her. Why can't I just keel over and die of embarrassment already?

Louise's hazel-coloured eyes widen with fresh mortification and she starts to spew her apology. I shake my head like it's nothing and smile as best I can to make her feel better. On land I could run and I'd never have to see her again, but here I have to keep the peace.

Over on the other side of the table, the boys and Sunshine have changed the subject and are talking among themselves, but I can still feel Tom's eyes on me.

I give the performance of a lifetime for the rest of the night, acting like the most unbothered, secure, emotionally stable woman who ever walked the face of the earth. Louise apologises again before bed, but I wave it off as if I haven't a care in the world, when in reality I have so many cares I might collapse under the weight of them all.

I'm not bothered that they slept together. Well, I am a bit, but only in that it's a little uncomfortable, like a needle prick or a paper cut. It'll sting for a while, but it won't break me. Everyone's got their past, me included, but is it too much to expect it to stay there?

He's *wild.*

It's unsettling that there are people from before who know him as someone else. I don't have the excuse of complete ignorance though; he told me he used to be different. He's worked hard to be the version of himself he wants to be, and he's proud of who he is now, so I can't let one conversation change my perception of him. I can only go off what I've seen. Even though deep down I'm terrified of being with someone who isn't who I thought they were. I can't take the humiliation of that again.

But trust is as much of a gut feeling as it is a choice. And I'm choosing to trust him. Because my gut is telling me to.

If Thanos could snap his fingers right about now, that'd be great. I just need to Blip for a week, a month tops.

Mom's here, which is okay. She was pretty mad at me for taking off like I did, but I think she's mostly over it now. I've missed her smell and the way she squeezes me when we hug, and more than anything I've missed her smile. But it's been more than three months since I've seen that.

Mom's not the problem though; Bobby is. I can barely look in the mirror some days because all I see is him – though I'd never admit that to the people who say they can't tell us apart – and now I have to endure the sight of him for seven days straight.

Who am I kidding? This week was always going to be shitty even if they weren't here for it.

I gave them a copy of my schedule in case they wanted to see me, and, credit to them, they've turned up to everything I've run so far. I spy Mom yawning as she turns up to my last activity on Wednesday night.

"Go get some rest. I'll see you tomorrow."

"I don't know when you get time to sleep or eat or do

anything besides work," she says, wrestling with her heavy eyelids. "When's your day off?"

"Tomorrow will be the first day off I've had in…" I do the math quickly in my head. "Almost ninety days."

Bobby's face contorts like he thinks I'm exaggerating.

"And only because I asked nicely. Don't even have time to check my mailbox half the time. Good thing I've never been sent anything important." I stare at him pointedly and wait for him to retaliate, but he doesn't – not in front of Mom. Go figure.

"I'm so proud of you, sweetie." She raises her arms to hug me, but I stop her.

"I can't hug you here. I'll get in trouble."

"Oops, sorry. I forgot you were too important to be seen with your mom," she teases and pinches my cheek anyway in an act of defiance. She's not the first older lady to pinch my cheek on here, and she probably won't be the last.

"Night, Mom."

My tense muscles relax when Bobby follows her out.

"Is it just me or does that guy look *exactly* like you?" Daniel contemplates when I get back to him by the stage.

"Just you."

Admitting to the team that my family is here means I have to explain I'm a twin. *The younger twin*, I'll have to clarify instantly because that question is always first. And then I'll have to explain where my dad is, and I don't have the strength to do that.

Not this week.

This time last year I was thankful for Dad's health. We were told not to expect him to make it to Thanksgiving, but Dad loved proving people wrong and did exactly that, passing away peacefully in his sleep in the early hours of the morning after. If only the doctors could have set the finish line as Christmas or New Year or sometime ten years from now.

I meet Mom and Bobby for breakfast and then take them on a tour of the port. Dad wouldn't have wanted us to stay hung up on the past; he'd want us to be out here joshing around, goofing off, making nice memories, but we've said almost nothing to each other all morning. I think Bobby and I are too scared we'll upset Mom, who's in a surprisingly good mood today considering.

We head to a nice place on the beach I've been to a few times for lunch. Bobby and Mom haven't adjusted to the heat yet, so we choose to sit inside where there's AC. I ask for a table for three, but we're seated at a table set up for four. It doesn't go unnoticed. Eventually, someone comes to clear it away, but Mom simply puts her hand on the placemat. The waiter backs away, and I give a small nod as a thank-you.

When our food arrives, I expect to be relieved it isn't turkey, but I'm not. I feel guilty. Because by refusing to eat something that reminds me of Dad, I'm ignoring him. And I know Mom and Bobby feel the same.

Enough is enough. Today isn't about forgetting him or moving on; it's about remembering him and celebrating his life.

I raise my glass of club soda. "To Dad." My eyes flick between them.

Bobby raises his glass too. "To Dad." His voice breaks a little as he says it.

Both of us are holding back tears, but they spill out of Mom's eyes as she raises her glass of white wine. "To Dad." The words barely come out, but she's doing her best to keep her smile in place.

Bobby and I fumble for napkins to give her while wiping our wet eyes with our hands.

Emotions a little more under control, I take Mom's hand, and Bobby rests his on her shoulder. She titters a little while she dabs at her eyes.

"He'll be looking down telling us to stop being such train wrecks."

Bobby and I both snicker too. Relief washes over me instantly as the heavy fog blows away. She's right: he would totally say that. For a minute we can't stop, each of us setting the other off for no reason until I can't tell if I'm crying because I'm laughing or laughing because I'm crying. The waiters probably think we're lunatics, but we don't care.

"It's so nice to hear you boys laugh together again."

I cast my eyes over to Bobby and the shame sets in. All week I've been poking and pushing him to fight with me, and for what? He hasn't risen to it even when Mom hasn't been around. I swear I don't even recognise myself. It's as if all this one-sided anger has mutated me into some kind of monster. Here I was thinking I was the hero in my story – keeping Dad smiling, leading the way by moving on with my life – but in reality I'm the villain. I'm the one who ran away when my family needed me most, and I'm the one who chose to ignore them. Right then I make a pact with myself to patch things up with him before he goes.

Our food's gone cold by the time we eat it, but we don't complain. I don't know the last time the three of us had a meal all together like this, but whatever broken thing inside of me I've been patching up with a Band-Aid of alcohol and sex until now is finally starting to heal. We reminisce about Dad, telling funny stories we've all told and heard a million times that still don't feel old. When we get back to the ship, I drop them to their room so they can get ready for formal night. I managed to sell them both on coming with me to see my magician/comedian friend performing in the theatre tonight because I thought we could do with a light evening, but when I go to leave, Mom seems anxious again.

"What is it, Mom?" I step back into her room, letting the door close behind me. Bobby and I sit her down on the small armchair by the window and perch on the edge of the bed.

Her eyes are already watery. "I can't help but think…if I'd made him a separate meal or didn't let him pile so much onto his plate, his body would have had the energy to fight just a little bit longer."

"Mom," we both interrupt her.

"I know, I know. But I just can't shake the guilt. I was so stressed with getting everything on the table in time that I didn't pay him the attention I should have."

"Mom, please don't for a second blame yourself," Bobby pleads. "Despite it being a busy day, you spent the whole day taking care of him. By hosting, cooking for, and entertaining all the family. And don't forget you guys teamed up and anni-hilated us all at Monopoly."

She smiles a little as if she's correcting the memory she twisted in her mind, and I hold her hand.

"Do you not think that instead of being too full, maybe he saw all his family one last time, saw us all happy, and he knew we'd be okay without him? It must have felt safe to finally let go."

"You gave him the best last day he could have possibly wanted," Bobby adds.

She considers this new perspective for a moment. "Thank you, boys," she tries to say.

We don't make it to the show. Instead we spend a cathartic evening crying and watching crappy films together, heckling the way Dad would have done whenever the actors speak too quietly or the plot is too predictable.

I never thought I'd have anything to be thankful for again, but I've been proven wrong. I am thankful. I'm thankful that instead of spending today alone and away from home, home came to me.

"I wish I were more like you," Bobby admits, looking down at his bare feet as they tread on the cool sand.

It's not a nice day to be outside – grey clouds pollute the sky, and the wind is so strong we have to lean forwards as we walk – but I thought we could use some one-on-one time while Mom's taking a dance class.

"Me? *Why?*"

"You're…carefree. Doing something you love, and doing it well, clearly."

A *compliment*? Jeez, what did I do to deserve that?

"Are you not happy?"

He sighs. "Not really. I've been summoning the courage to quit for…too long."

"So why haven't you?"

"Mom. I dunno. When Dad…when you dropped out, she put me on this pedestal like, 'Well, *this* son is going to be a lawyer. He's going to do something meaningful.'" He flashes me an apologetic look. "No offence. Her words, not mine."

I shrug. "None taken."

"I was already struggling before, but I kept going. I didn't want to disappoint her any further."

"Gee, thanks."

"I'm not— You know what I'm trying to say. If I was the

one constant thing that could keep her going, I wasn't going to quit. I couldn't. But I was so jealous of you, man."

"I'm sorry. I should have told you before I did it. My heart just wasn't in it. In my defence, Dad was the one who suggested this."

He takes a deep breath but smiles. "Good ol' Dad."

"Do you know what you would rather do?"

"No idea. Maybe travel? I dunno, but I'm kinda excited to figure it out. Just seeing it all work out so well for you, I have hope it could for me too."

All that time I thought I was the only one busting a gut to keep the peace at home, I never realised how much responsibility Bobby took on too, nor how much my sudden exit would affect him.

"How about I take on the role of the golden child for now so you go off the rails?"

"I would like that. *A lot*." He laughs with relief, and then we're almost knocked off-balance as the wind dies down without warning. I have to squint to see Bobby's smile as the sun breaks through the clouds.

Huh, so Dad thinks that's a good idea too?

"I'm sorry I left."

"I'm sorry I was an asshole about it."

We wrap each other in a tight bear hug, patting each other's backs before continuing to walk side by side.

"Who's the cute British girl?"

"You'll have to be more specific." I play dumb even though I already know exactly who he's talking about.

"Short, blonde, talked a bit like, *'Tom, what are you doing in your civvies?'* Know the one?"

I can't help but smile at his impression. "Yeah."

"She really misses me, apparently, so…maybe you wanna do something about that."

Yeah, maybe I do. If this week's taught me anything, it's that my reactions aren't always rational. I was pissed off at myself for not seeing it, and I was pissed off at Harvey for manipulating me – or doing what I thought was manipulation anyway. But now I've had some time to think about it, he lasted – what, two months? Two entire months before they hooked up – or whatever happened on that boat trip – which must have been hell given I know he's liked her since week one. I didn't wanna see it before, but that's proof he at least *tried* to follow his own advice.

What I've also learnt since that night at Coral's is that everyone knew. Everyone else had worked it out for themselves, and yet I'd completely missed it. I pushed her away because I couldn't handle my feelings for her and freaked out when she didn't come running back to me the second I wanted her to. It wasn't fair of me to expect that then, and it isn't fair of me to expect her to forgive me easily now.

I think I finally know the answer to Harvey's question: I want to be a good friend.

So after keeping Bobby in the dark for so long, I let him in. I tell him what happened between me and Eliza, everything from the start, and he helps me come up with a plan to fix it. I messed up big-time, so my apology has to be even bigger.

And it might just involve a magician.

My good buddy, Paul, is running a magic masterclass the next morning, which Eliza just so happens to be helping out with. Bobby and I slip backstage towards the end of the session and, following the briefing Paul gave us yesterday, get into the tall wooden box on wheels, me in the front section, Bobby in the back.

Paul finishes up by performing a short routine to show the guests how to put all the tricks they've just learnt together. Before he goes, he announces a new act he's been working on, asking the guests if they wouldn't mind being a tester audience for it, and he earns a chorus of cheers in response.

"All right then, Eliza, my love, I need you to give me a hand with this one. Just wait there for me."

I'm assuming he's brought her up on stage. Footsteps draw near, and Paul knocks on the box. As planned, Bobby and I knock back. The brakes snap off and we almost fall when we start moving.

"Eliza, can you close your eyes really tight for me? Perfect. Now, can you think of a person – any person, but someone on this ship – someone who…maybe you're tired of seeing by now. Got one?"

"Got one."

"Okay, open your eyes."

She lets out a tiny "oh".

"Please could you open the box and tell me if they're in there."

Footsteps pad closer, and light suddenly pours into the box. The guests start to laugh as I smile sweetly at her.

"Are you tired of seeing this guy by now?"

"I couldn't possibly comment." She grins a purposely fake smile, prompting more titters around the room.

"Shall I make him go away?"

"Could you?" she asks hopefully.

"Anything for you, Eliza. I'll fix it. I'll fix it." He slams the wardrobe-like doors comically on my face, and Bobby slips through the trap wall to join me. Paul gets the crowd to say some magic words before asking Eliza to open the box again to check I'm definitely gone. She reveals us both standing there – and yes, I did make Bobby put on my uniform so we'd look even more identical – and jumps back with a little squeak.

After everything I did to try to scare her in the haunted house, two of me in a box is all it takes to finally get her.

There are gasps from the audience before they twig a second later we're obviously twins, not clones. Eliza giggles nervously, her eyes wide as she looks back and forth between the two of us.

"Now, here's the real question," Paul says. "Which one's Tom?"

"Elizabeth…" Bobby says in the way I taught him to, and I echo him.

The audience laugh while she struggles to decide, which in turn makes me laugh, giving me away. She reaches for my arm and holds it up in the air with hers like a winning fighter. People cheer, but Paul plays up to it, looking back at us, stage-whispering, "Is she right? How am I meant to know?"

I nod, and he makes sure the audience celebrates her correct guess. Bobby and I slip off to the side of the room, leaving Eliza to wrap up Paul's session while we eagerly wait for her to come see us.

"So *this* is Bobby. How did you not tell me you're a twin?" she quietly snips.

Bobby speaks before I can, putting his hand on his puffed-out chest. "It's not his fault – he's spent a lifetime in my shadow," he jokes as if it isn't the *exact* reason I didn't tell anyone. Not that he knows that, of course. "Pleasure to meet you." He holds out his hand, which she shakes.

Eliza looks at me with a sarcastic smile. "And here I was thinking you'd be the humble one."

Bobby pretends to be wounded. "Ooh, okay, I deserve that."

They laugh, and it's good to see her relax, even just a little.

"Go get changed before someone thinks you're me." I usher him away.

"I'm not going anywhere looking like this."

"Ugh, fine, go wait over there. I'll come with you in a sec." I dismiss him and turn back to Eliza. "Hey," I say with a grin, but her smile has vanished. "So I'm a twin."

"Yeah, I got that."

Ah, shit. The magic only charmed her for so long.

"Can we talk?" I look over at my brother waiting by the doors. People are already confusing him for me. "Later? I owe you an apology."

Her brow furrows with either anger or confusion – I'm not sure. She looks around to check no one can hear us. There are guests taking photos with Paul not far from us, so she drops down to a whisper, "You've ignored me for the best part of two weeks and you think a magic act will fix every-thing. Have you *actually* gone insane?"

"No, I don't think that at all. I thought it might help ease the tension."

"Well, it hasn't."

Fuck. "Can I come find you later?"

"I'd rather you didn't. Or is there a secret triplet you'd like to introduce to me through the medium of mime? Or maybe he'll pop out of my drawers tonight like a fucking jack-in-the-box." She tries to walk away.

"Eliza."

She turns back to me. "Sorry, I thought the appropriate reaction to discovering a secret part of your best friend's life was to skulk off and ignore them for two weeks. Spoiler alert:

in two weeks' time I'll sit my secret boyfriend on my knee, shove my hand up his arse like a ventriloquist doll, and put on a little show for you because, *apparently*, the only way you think we'll have an adult conversation is if I give you the ol' razzle-dazzle first." And with that, she storms off.

Well, that told me.

"So, did it work?" Bobby asks when I pull myself together enough to move.

"I think it did the opposite."

TWENTY-SEVEN

ELIZA

Who the *fuck* does he think he is, Derren *shitting* Brown?

I poured my heart out to him, or so I thought, but now I'm guessing that was actually his brother. It does explain an awful lot about the past few days, and I have to say I'm a little relieved. I thought I was going mad, seeing him in the faces of guests, even an older lady…which now makes me think maybe his parents are on board too. I did want to talk to him and sort this all out, but that little display he just put on has made it blindingly obvious he doesn't know, even slightly, just how much he hurt me.

He *ignored* me. Moved out *without saying a word.* Acted as if *I'd* betrayed *him* in some way, and I've spent the past two weeks believing I did. Well, no more. He's not a real friend if he thinks I deserved that.

I huff my way down the hall. I would have loved to stay and berate him some more, but I have *actual* friends to hang out with before they all disappear tomorrow. Oh God, I'm not ready for them to go. Our Wednesday nights together have been everything to me, and now they're over. We didn't even get one last session this week because they were with the new cast. I haven't spent much time with them yet – they're all too busy getting to grips with ship life, bum-licking the leaving cast, and tech rehearsing "We Will Rock You", which opens next week, so there hasn't been much interest from them in socialising outside their bubble. And I'm not in their bubble, so…

Whatever. I'm not giving them a choice today. I have half a day left to spend time with my friends, and these newbies will just have to get over it.

There's a whole horde of people in the gangway saying their goodbyes the next morning, including some of the now resident actors getting all emotional as if their connection could be so strong inside just a week. *Oh, piss off.*

Deep breath, Chapman.

I'm jealous. That's what's really going on. I hate them because I want to be them. Half of them are making their professional debuts tonight – something I could be doing if only I were as talented as them.

Valentina's here with me, parting ways with Sophie. They were planning to tough it out and make the long-distance thing work, but all that changed last week. Sophie's been self-taping her auditions for a few different upcoming shows the company were casting for and just found out she got the part of Penny in "Hairspray". She's pretty much going straight into rehearsals when she gets home, and then she's joining Poseidon, which just so happens to need a new entertainment host in eight weeks too. A vacancy that already has Valentina's name on it.

Seeing it all fall into place for them has definitely given me hope for mine and Oscar's long-term future, which I'd previously tried not to think too much about.

Max gives me a tight squeeze. "Never stop singing," he whispers and pulls away to look me in the eye. "Promise?"

I give a shell-shocked kind of nod. I owe him so much for helping me build my confidence, and I really hope our paths cross again soon.

Valentina and I take a walk around the ship before breakfast because she wants to be forced to "snap out of her hysterics". (She shed one tear. I'd say half if that were even possible.) Being in public will help her, apparently. Not that there are many guests about to smile for – they're all either packing or disembarking.

The ship's had a festive transformation overnight. There are fairy lights, tinsel, giant baubles, wreaths, and snowflakes everywhere. They haven't quite stuck on a Bublé album yet, but I know it's coming.

Strolling along the boardwalk, we pass a bunch of workmen erecting a gigantic Christmas tree that was apparently carted on the second we docked in PortMiami in the early hours this morning. And that means one thing: Oscar's nearly back.

Now I'm not saying a whopping great erection in the middle of the ship reminded me of Oscar, but I'm not *not* saying that either.

"How's Oscar's present coming along?" I ask to get Valentina's mind on something else. It's his birthday this weekend, and I'm very excited to FaceTime him and show him what I commissioned.

It was no easy task working out what to get him. For a long while I had no idea – or, correction: I had too many ideas, none of which were possible given we live at sea. I much prefer giving people experiences than presents. If he were here, I'd throw him a "Night at the Oscars"-themed party. If we were both back home, I'd want to wake him up with omelettes and Earl Grey tea, take too long to get ready because we can't keep our hands off each other, head into London to see a matinee of a West End show, go for dinner somewhere romantic, and hope we don't get caught misbehaving in the train toilet on the way home. That would be the perfect day. If we weren't currently four and a half thousand miles apart.

Presents are hard to get right here too. If it's too big or awkward it won't be able to fit in his suitcase, let alone his new room. And given that minimalism is the only way to not overwhelm your surroundings with clutter, it has to be something either practical or small and decorative. That's where Valentina comes in. I asked her to paint Oscar as Seymour from "Little Shop of Horrors" on top of a page of sheet music I printed out in the library. It's one of the songs in the stage version but not the film, which he was very excited to tell me all about, and even more excited when he found out I also knew those songs. I've ordered a magnetic photo frame so it can go straight up on the wall in his new *single occupancy* cabin (sweet Jesus, I can't *wait* for that!), and as a side present, which is also kind of for me too, I ordered a buttload of condoms.

"Almost done. We've got 'til Saturday, right?"

I nod in response.

"Yeah, it'll be finished way before then."

"Amazing, thank you!" I take a stab at injecting some energy into her, but Valentina just keeps walking along in silence. "What do you make of the new actors?" I move us onto a new topic. I didn't realise how much I relied on Maddison for intel before she left, and now I feel like I owe her an apology for taking her gossip for granted.

"Obnoxious and annoying. But I thought the same thing about the others until I got to know them. Or one of them at least. You gonna catch the show tonight?"

"Yeah, hopefully, if I can finish in time." I put more effort into sounding convincing than I know I'll put into getting to the theatre later.

I'm as petty this week with Tom as he was with me. All smiles when we have to work together, and then I shut him out the second it's over.

How's that medicine taste?

Ugh, listen to me. He's always brought out this childish side of me. Before, it was a good thing; I was playful whenever I was around him, but now I'm being petulant. I can't stop though. I'm mad. *Really* fucking mad. I keep playing that stupid trick back in my mind. It's like he was proud to show me how much I don't know about him, how many secrets he's kept from me. Who does that? It's just another thing to convince me we were never actually friends. When we leave here, he'll go back to his secret life, and I'll go back to mine.

"Chapman, that's incredible!"

"You like it?" I flip the camera around to face me again and hold up the framed painting beside me.

"I love it! It's so thoughtful, thank you. I'll message Valentina too – she must have put so much time into this."

"She did, though I think she enjoyed the distraction."

His face softens with sympathy.

"Love you." I smile at his perfect face on my screen.

"Love you."

"Got anything planned for tonight?"

"Just a quiet one. Going for dinner with Mum, Nan, and Gemma. Wish you could be here."

"Me too. That'll be nice though, have a good time." I hide the upset creeping up on me. It's been so hard here without him. With my biggest friendship group leaving and everything that's going on with Tom, I've been so lonely. But I'm not going to cry at him again. I won't drag him down like some anchor of misery.

"When do I next get to see you?"

"I can go to the internet cafe on Tuesday."

His face drops with disappointment.

"*Or*...I could log back in again later after Valentina's leaving do, before I go to bed…"

Mischief twists his smile. "I'd like that a lot."

There's a pregnant pause as we both wrestle with our lewd thoughts until he's able to distract us.

"What's the new cast like?"

"Loud…"

He chuckles, and my whole body tingles as if I'm being wrapped in a blanket. "They'll calm down soon. They're just in survival mode."

"Mmm, feels more like spring break mode."

"That might be what it looks like on the outside, but trust me, coming on in a big group like that is more daunting than it seems. Plus, it's opening week – they're all running on a crazy amount of stress, nerves, and adrenaline right now. Give them time."

After we end the call, I use my last five minutes of Wi-Fi to share something on my Instagram story. Valentina airdropped me a bunch of photos the other day, and I want to tag Oscar in something for his birthday. Okay, fine, and I want to show off that I have a fit new boyfriend so when people look at my story they'll see how great I'm doing without them.

I find a photo of Oscar and me on the catamaran. We're sitting next to one another on the long, sofa-like lounger, his arm around my shoulder. I'm smiling at the camera, and he's looking at me with the biggest smile on his face. This was pre-fumble when we could still be next to each other and honestly say nothing was going on. But holy shit, when he tucked me up against him, I swear I nearly died.

Story uploaded, I switch my phone off for the day, looking forward to turning it on again later to talk to him. And to see who'll decide to crawl out of the woodwork to look at my story.

After my final activity, I get to the bar to find Obi, true to form, dancing on a table while some of the others dance on the floor around him. It takes a while to match their energy, but with the help of a few shots, eventually I'm there.

We carry a very tipsy Valentina back to her room when the bar closes, and the party continues there for a while. Thankfully, it stays pretty PG-13 despite the new actors' best efforts to spice things up. Tom's here, but he keeps out of my way. Well, as best as one can in a shoebox-sized cabin.

Around three in the morning I call it a night because I'm

exhausted, but also because through various not-drinking games it's become quite clear a fair few of the new arrivals know Oscar the same way Louise does. Thankfully, Valentina doesn't speak up this time and the rest of the entertainment staff keep hurrying to change the subject before too much is revealed, but that doesn't stop them all from sending not-so-subtle "you okay, hun?" glances my way every five seconds.

I FaceTime Oscar, but he doesn't pick up. It's almost 9 a.m. in the UK now, so he should be up. He might have gone to make a cup of tea or something, so I ping him a message to let him know I'm free, turning the ringer on so I don't miss his reply while I'm getting ready for bed.

I'm not going to bring up my latest discoveries with him, the same way I didn't bring up the Louise thing. It's none of my business who he slept with before me – unless he has a secret child he's one day expecting me to step-mother or, you know, some life-threatening STD. Those things would be my business, but I'm confident he would have disclosed something like that to me by now.

Fifteen minutes later and he's still not called. My message hasn't even delivered. Something twists in my stomach, and I wrestle to ignore it. There were times my messages didn't deliver to Twatface for hours, which I later found out was because he turned his phone on airplane mode whenever he was with her.

Oscar isn't him.

I climb into bed and call him again, but there's no answer, so I distract myself on Instagram. Oh, look – over a hundred people have seen my story. I scroll down the list of viewers and revel in the fact all these people who forgot about me the second I got a normal job have now borne witness to my perfect new life.

Still nothing from Oscar, and still no answer.

Back on Instagram, I spot that he's uploaded something to his story. He reposted my picture with a heart and cricket emoji. A few other people have also wished him happy birthday, which he's shared too. There are some adorable pictures of him when he was little, shared by I'm guessing family members or old school friends. Tiny Oscar is *so cute.* My goodness, we'd make beautiful babies.

Out of nosiness and an attempt to kill some time before he eventually calls, I stalk the friends whose stories he shared.

My stomach twists again.

One of them has uploaded a video to their story. It's of a bunch of people around a table in a noisy pub, and from the collection of empty glasses in front of them all it's quite clear the drinks are flowing. The camera focuses on Oscar at the head of the table. He isn't looking at the camera though; he's engrossed in lively conversation with some blonde girl next to him. She throws her arms around him in a tight hug. And he hugs her back.

I tap left for it to play again just to be sure it's not his sister.

It's not her. I'm certain of it.

With my heart pounding in my ears, I tap for the next post on their story. There's a picture of everyone posing for the camera. *What is this?* I dart my eyes between all the faces, particularly the ones perched closest to him. Why is everyone there attractive? Who are they all? Why is his fucking arm around that girl, and why isn't he answering his phone?

I feel so forgotten.

Everyone's been tagged, and so, with nothing better to do, I stalk them all one by one. From the looks of it, they're all professional actors with proudly public accounts, most of them mentioning the same drama school Oscar went to in their bios. Except for that blonde girl. She's just some model he knows, apparently.

A shitting model.

Gemma's out with him, but there's no sign of his mum or his nan. Did he lie this morning so I wouldn't ask too many questions? Or this could have been a surprise party. Yes. That's a possibility. But then why wouldn't he have texted me to say that? I get maybe not wanting to be on his phone when he's catching up with friends, but they've all clearly been on their phones throughout the evening posting on socials.

Nothing feels good about this.

I go back to WhatsApp. My message *still* hasn't bloody delivered. I fight off the rising frustration. He knew I was going to call this morning, so why isn't he up checking his phone to see if I'm logged in yet, realising he's got no signal or his phone has died, and doing everything to rectify it so he can talk to me ASAP?

I go back to story-stalking. Someone else from the group uploaded a video of them at Revenge, a popular gay nightclub in Brighton. Everyone from the pub is dancing around Oscar and shout-singing along to the song that's playing.

This is anything other than a quiet one.

You can tell from the floppiness of his body that he's had a lot to drink. I've never seen him drunk before. This is so out of character I almost don't believe it's even him.

What if he never went home? What if he's at that blonde model's house? I know how many bad choices I've made because of alcohol. Is he a horny drunk too? I hate that I don't know the answer to that. I hate that I don't know my own boyfriend. Why would he be loyal to someone who doesn't even know him? What if he's cheated on me because he can, because he thinks I'll never find out? All these hot friends of his have history with him –

years of history. I have three months. Or three weeks, depending on how you look at it. How could I ever compete with that?

I'm going out with a stranger. And I've just told the whole world he's mine.

I dig around for one more story – I can't help myself – clinging to the hope that any second now I'll see a glimpse of *my* Oscar and everything will be okay.

I click on the story of some guy who was tagged in the last video and instantly wish I hadn't. Oscar's carrying the model wedding-style along Brighton Promenade. She's laughing hysterically, her arms wrapped around his neck. Gemma's walking barefoot beside them carrying her heels, and upon realising she's being filmed, she covers her face like a celeb being papped and whines, "Dylan, stop filming!"

He turns it around to selfie mode. "Sorry, Miss Influencer!" He spins to get Oscar back in the frame and starts walking backwards to keep up with them.

I don't catch what Oscar says next, but the model's response sends me over the edge.

"Shut up and take me home."

Paranoia and pure panic control my fingers. Back on the model's profile, there's a pink ring around her picture where there wasn't before. Her story loads, and the evidence I was looking for but never hoped to find stares me in the face.

The walls close in around me.

He cheated.

He fucking cheated.

All the time I was fixated on the model, I failed to notice this guy, *Dylan*, at Oscar's side in every single shot I saw. At the pub, Oscar's arm was around the model, but it was also around Dylan. Dancing in the club, I focused on the girls draped over him, but not on Dylan singing with him. Walking along the seafront, I focused on the girl he was carrying, not on Dylan following him home.

Posted five minutes ago. Oscar's in bed with him, undressed and under the covers, fast asleep, *spooning* him. "Just like the old days," the caption reads.

I choke on my tears.

Valentina was right all along: he is too good. Too good to be true.

TWENTY-EIGHT

ELIZA

I wasn't surprised when Valentina snuck off the ship without a sendoff – she's not one for big displays of emotions after all – but I had hoped to see her one last time considering she specifically said she'd see me in the morning when I left her room late on Sunday.

I walk back to my room from the gangway feeling utterly alone. I briefly consider going to find Tom but think better of it.

I just want to go home.

How could I be so stupid as to trust someone again? I will always be enough for someone until I'm not. Until someone better, prettier, or actually talented comes along.

I didn't bother messaging Oscar again before the internet cut out. My phone's back in the safe where it always should have stayed, and if he thinks I'm going to waste any more of my time in an internet cafe listening to his lies, he's got another thing coming.

I keep it together for the sake of the team, but Sunshine pulls me to one side at lunch to check on me. I brush it off as tiredness and then feel guilty for lying and immediately want to tell her everything, but I stop myself. I hate Oscar. I hate him with every fibre of my being, but when he gets back he becomes our superior, and as much as I couldn't give a shit about him, I give a shit about my job.

I consider confiding in Obi, but he's busy training the new guy. Plus, he's Oscar's best friend on here, so it's not like he's going to be Team Eliza. Instead I keep it all in and work harder on making my "everything is fine" front more convincing.

The Sail Away Party cheers me up a bit. Kind of hard not to feel good on the inside when on the outside I'm pretending to have the time of my life. Unpopular opinion, but the first Sail Away of the week is always my favourite because even though the new passengers are shy and more wary about joining in, I like the challenge. I like winning them over, focusing on a small group of people, teaching them just a few steps, building up their confidence, and then watching them eagerly learn the routine for the next song and the next, until everyone around them has joined in too. Being the reason people smile is one of the best parts of this job.

"Why do I recognise that girl?" Tom asks the gang when the party's over. "Is she famous or something?"

"Nope, never seen her before." Daniel dismisses it.

I have no intention of breaking my cone of silence for Tom, but my curious eyes follow his to where everyone's still staring.

"Guys, stop, she's looking!" Louise panics.

All the air gets trapped in my lungs.

Tara and Kate stand on the other side of the deck. Tara waves with all the warmth of a golden retriever while Kate tucks herself behind Tara, acting like a nervous Staffy at a shelter.

Great. This is exactly what I needed…

"Kind of looks like they know you, Lize," Obi observes.

"Wait – she's from that photo in your room!" Tom twigs, and I nod.

Tara and Kate going on holiday together makes sense, but I never thought I'd see the day Kate would come within a hundred yards of me again. I don't for a second let myself believe they came all this way to see me, especially after what happened between me and Kate, but it's also too unlikely to be a coincidence.

After whittling down my options for escape, I'm left with no choice but to suck in a deep breath, slap on an even faker smile than the one I'm already wearing, and go to greet them. I'm overcome with self-consciousness, wondering what they're thinking of me. Did I do anything weird before I noticed them? Were they laughing at me? Comparing me to a sports mascot? I'm now painfully aware these basic dance moves to cheesy songs make me look like one of The Wiggles.

"Well, this is unexpected!" I greet them.

Tara bundles me in a tight hug, and a hefty chunk of my unease subsides. I didn't know how much I needed to see a familiar face.

"You have no idea how excited I've been to see you," she chirps.

They planned this?

After just too long to be comfortable as we both decide how to play this, Kate and I exchange "hi"s awkwardly like we're rallying a tennis ball. Tara's eyes bounce back and forth between us like the world's most adoring umpire.

"You're a social-climbing narcissist!"

"Yeah? Well at least I have something going for me. All you'll ever be is a third wheel. A little fucking tagalong. Here, at home, even in your own bloody relationship. No

423

wonder he found something better – it wasn't hard. You're a nobody."

"I thought you were on tour," I say to Tara.

"I've got a two-week break before we're back on the road again. There's no way I wasn't going to come see you out here. How is it all going?"

"Love it," I say through somewhat gritted teeth. "Finally found my thing, you know."

"And excuse me, have you got a boyfriend now?" She tries to include Kate in the conversation, but she's as stiff as a dead hamster.

A pang of stress makes my heart thump so hard I could keel over. Oscar must have seen the message and missed calls by now – did he come up with some shit excuse as to why he missed me or not even bother to reply? What else has he been doing that I just don't know about?

Shut up, shut up, shut up!

"Oh, uh, no. He's just…"

"Say no more. I know how these things work on cruise ships." She gasps suddenly. "Have you been to an orgy yet?"

I flinch, shooting my eyes around to all the guests bustling past us.

"Sorry. But…" She raises her brow in question, and I shake my head, much to her disappointment. "What are you working on tonight?"

She's already got out her itinerary and highlighter. It's so hard not to love this girl. I take it from her and highlight "Blind Date", waffling on about having some other duties to rush off to before then. I'm not busy now, but I need a second to process the fact they're here. No, that *Kate's* here. *All week.* The audacity.

"Oh my God, *please* pull Kate up onstage. She needs a holiday romance so bad."

I pretend to laugh. "I'll see what I can do. How are you, Kate?" I manage to say without letting on that I'm absolutely *seething* on the inside.

"Good, thanks." Though her response is short, it isn't as cold as I expected, but I'm glad when she doesn't elaborate.

An old lady chooses that exact moment to approach me asking where the toilet is, and I want to dissolve. "It's easier if I show you." I take the excuse to leave the girls and lead the guest away.

People ask Tara for selfies and autographs when she finishes a shift while I just get asked where people can relieve themselves. If anyone needed a metaphor for how our careers are going, that's the perfect one.

I drop the passenger off and make a pitstop of my own in the crew bathroom so I can fuss over myself in the mirror. Do I look okay? Do I have anything in my teeth? Do I smell nice? Do I have any weird marks on my white shorts? I'm past embarrassment at this stage; I just need to know how bad it was. Luckily, I seem to be in good nick.

I work to unscramble my brain from their unanticipated reappearance, but I can't ignore that intrusive thought I put to bed so long ago. I never should have moved with them to London. I was always clawing for some shred of what they had and never got anywhere close.

I think back to the last time I saw Kate in person. It was my twentieth birthday and my parents had bought us tickets to "& Juliet". I'd been so excited to see it. Tara was on holiday with her family and couldn't come, but she at least sent a card, FaceTimed me, and got me this cute star neck-lace. Kate spent the whole pre-show dinner talking about herself, never once asking me a question. Whenever I could get a word in edgeways, she'd get her phone out and text people while doing that fake "active listening" crap. *Mmm, yeah, oh wow, really?*

I don't know when it happened, but she became so image-obsessed that nothing could happen without it being posted online. Despite the fact we got a stranger to take our photo, she only posted the picture I took of just her. If Tara were in the photo, Kate would have posted it.

Kate spent the first half of the show checking the time. She left at the interval, claiming something she ate at dinner was making her feel unwell. She's gluten intolerant – it was a feasible excuse. If it wasn't so obviously just that. She didn't think I remembered that she'd – no, *we'd* – been invited to another party that night and only registered she couldn't go when Tara pointed out it was my birthday. And it would *look* bad if she turned me down for it.

After watching the second act alone and soaking the sleeve of my cardigan while trying to hide the fact I was crying, I decided I wasn't going to let her get away with it anymore. I'd been quiet for too long.

"It's cute you're giving it a go," she'd said after seeing the show my Cellar friends and I put on. I wasn't "giving it a go"; I'd worked hard at that. I got paid to do that. We sold out most nights and got great reviews. And don't even get me started on the "cute" thing.

"I always thought he was a prick," she'd said when I came home from Twatface's house crying into a carrier bag full of my things. It wasn't in solidarity; she'd always spoken highly of him before. She just wanted to pretend she was right about something, that she had something else over me, the ability to spot an arsehole from a mile off.

Takes one to know one, I guess.

"It's a drama school thing – you wouldn't get it," she'd said on multiple occasions, such as when I came back to the table from the bar to find everyone laughing at a joke I missed, or literally anytime she and Tara talked about their days.

I lost count of the amount of times she turned down my suggestions to hang out or accepted them and then bailed on me as soon as she had another offer. And how often she'd cut me out of plans her own friends included me in on. She'd hog Tara, invite her and only her to things, share secrets with her. We were always a three until Kate wanted to be a two.

I had my own friends, my own life – until I quit – and I was always happy to share it with her, but she stopped wanting to share hers with me.

That night of my birthday I so badly wanted to believe she was ill, but I knew deep down exactly where she'd gone. I skipped my usual trip to the merchandise booth, plucked up the courage to go to the party, and sure enough, she was there. I caught her in the middle of making a toast to her new flat-mates. Turns out she'd given our landlord our two months' notice and committed to a new flat without telling me. I knew Tara was moving in with her boyfriend, but the plan was for someone else to move in. Or that was *my* plan at least.

Then the screaming match began.

When I come out of the bathroom, Kate's right there across the busy corridor waiting for me. I don't think; I just act. I stride over to her.

"What are you doing here?" I whisper, not bothering to hide my anger.

"I want to apologise."

"Do you? Or does Tara want you to? Go for it, apologise – I'm sure she'll be so proud of you. Oh, and don't forget to film it for your followers!"

"I've changed."

"No. You've had over a year. You didn't even bother

texting me a simple 'sorry'. You had to come all the way out here to *look* like you're sorry. You haven't changed at all. This is still the same shit you were always up to."

"Can we just sit down and talk this through?"

"Sure, when did you have in mind?"

She perks up at my change of attitude. "Tomorrow morning?"

"Damn, I'm walking my goldfish. Evening's all booked up too – chocolate teapot demonstration."

"Lize."

"Fuck. Off." I spin on my heel and walk away.

Excellent, I finally see my nemesis and can't escape her. Why couldn't I have bumped into her while I silently snivelled my way down Southbank heading back to a tiny flat I shared with strangers after yet another soul-destroying day in the office, or while eating lunch alone for the millionth time? Either of those would have been preferable to being forced to work while she watches on. She's getting exclusive access to witness my failure to make it, and it's humiliating. All of this is *utterly humiliating*.

Over the next few days, it feels like I'm watching everything from the outside while my body runs on autopilot. Every pleasant interaction with a guest, every activity, every time Tara talks about something she and Kate did together, all expertly faked. And then I get back to my empty room and cry into my pillow until I tire myself out, and when I wake up, it all starts again. I might as well be a severely throttled battery at this point. No amount of charging will get me back to my old self; I just need to be thrown out and replaced by someone shiny and new.

It's late on Wednesday night when I snap out of it. There's a knock at my door and I hurry to dry my wet cheeks, climb down from my bunk, and discard the mountain of used tissues littered about the room. I look in the mirror. *Jesus, I can't answer the door like this.* My nose is pink, my eyes are red, and my lavender top has damp splotches of violet all down the front. It won't be anyone looking for my roommate – she might as well have never moved in. She spends all her time in her boyfriend's room.

I call out to ask who's there, but they reply with another knock. *Fine. Who fucking cares anymore?* I tug the door open to find a worried-looking Tom. We just stare at each other for what feels like an eternity until suddenly he's holding me so tight it's like he's scared I might crumble if he lets go.

The door closes behind him.

I sob into his shoulder, my breathing jagged, my head thumping, my ears ringing.

"It's okay. It's okay. You're okay," he whispers, stroking the back of my head.

"I can't—" is all I manage to get out between uncontrollable cries.

Tom soothes me, not letting go until my lungs are matching the same rhythm as his. He finds my water bottle on the table and makes me drink while he gets more tissues from the bathroom.

"I'm so sor—"

I shake my head. I'm not going to let him apologise when I've been just as shitty to him recently. I take the loo roll from him and sit on the bed. He perches on the desk.

"What's going on?"

"I can't be here anymore."

His brows crease. "You're not thinking of leaving, are you?" he asks as if it's the craziest thing he can suggest.

I don't answer. That's exactly what I'm thinking.

"Eliza, you can't!"

I'm fully aware of the consequences of leaving mid-contract. I'll owe the company a bunch of money, I'll have to pay for my flights home, and I'll get blacklisted from working here again. But that's the least of my problems right now.

I shrug in response.

"What about Harvey?"

I shrug again.

"What happened?"

"I was wrong about him."

Tom looks at me as if I'm speaking another language. "What are you going to do instead?" His tone is more than a little panicked.

"I'm going to apply to drama school." The words stun me as much as they do him, but only from the sense of clarity that washes over me when I finally say them out loud. "I've missed this year's application deadline by a long shot, but I can work for my brother again and spend the year preparing. I got so close this year. Next year *has* to be my year."

"But you hate working for your brother."

"It's a job. I can use it to save up for the course fees."

"Slow down a second. Where's all this coming from?"

"I'll never be happy until I get into drama school. And when I do, I can finally stop feeling like some massive failure."

"Why do you think you're a *failure*?"

"Because I'm not good enough! I've never been good enough to do the things I want, to *have* the things I want, or… to keep them."

Tom shakes his head. "You're perfect. Do you have any idea how hard I work just to *try* to keep up with you? You're instantly loved by guests, you're a natural at hosting, and you have a whole bunch of friends. You're Employee of the Month, for crying out loud!"

Had a whole bunch of friends. *Was* employee of the month. What have I achieved since? Nothing. How many friends do I have now? None.

"Elizabeth, this isn't you."

We sit in silence. I don't have the energy to explain myself any further. He'll get over it. He'll forget me like everyone else has.

He looks up at my bunk, frowns at something, then trains his eyes back on me. "It's them, isn't it? Your friends who showed up this week. Did they say something?"

"No, I've barely spoken to them."

"Why?"

"Because they're both living the life I want and I would literally rather hug a hornet's nest than waste another second entertaining Kate's fucking ego."

"You're not making sense right now." He paces. "Why don't you grab a shower? We can stick on a movie. Talk about it some more, sleep on it—"

"I'm good. I'm gonna give my mum a call."

"And tell her you're leaving?"

I nod.

"I really think you need to sleep on it."

"Why? I'll still want to leave tomorrow."

"You have to sit with any big decision for twenty-four hours before you make it. It's a psychology thing."

I'm almost certain he's bullshitting me, but I pretend to believe him because I know that's the only way he'll drop it. "Okay, twenty-four hours."

He looks at his watch. "So if you still wanna leave at midnight tomorrow, you can act on it then."

We make an agreement I only half-intend to keep.

"Let me go grab my things and I'll stay here."

"Why?"

"I don't think you should be alone right now."

"I'm fine."

He's not buying it, but I need him to.

"Promise."

He concedes but starts rifling through my drawers.

"What are you doing?"

"I won't sleep over, but I'm not leaving yet. Where's your iPad?"

"Tom."

"Elizabeth." We stare each other down, but he throws a packet of Skittles on the desk and soon goes back to looting.

I reluctantly give in, and we end up watching a few episodes of "The Office" until he decides it's safe enough to leave.

"Eliza, I'm so sorry about—"

"I'm sorry too."

"Friends?"

"Friends."

As soon as the door closes behind him, I open my cupboard and key in the code to the safe. I'm not acting on my decision; I'm just telling someone about it. My phone pings like crazy when I connect to the Wi-Fi, mostly with messages from Oscar that I have no desire to read.

Mum picks up after just a few rings. "Eliza! How lovely to hear from you!" It's times like this I'm glad she's an early riser. "Peter, it's Eliza," she calls out to Dad, swinging the camera around to him in the kitchen.

"Hi, darling!" His slippers shuffle along the floor as he comes to sit by Mum in the lounge.

Damn, I was hoping to get Mum on her own.

"What time is it there?" Dad pauses to do some quick time-math. "What are you doing calling us at this hour?"

My bottom lip trembles. "I want to come home." I thought I'd be out of tears by now, but that's not the case.

"Oh, sweetheart, you're just homesick. I worried that would happen when Tara asked what ship you were on."

"Why would you tell them to come? You know how I feel about Kate."

"She took Kate? Sorry, Lize, I had no idea. But they'll be gone in a couple of days. It's a big ship – you can ignore them, can't you?"

"Not really And it's not just that. It isn't…" I sniff. "It's not working out. I really, really want to come home."

Dad takes control of the phone. "Eliza, you're being silly. Come on – take a deep breath. It can't be that bad. You loved it last month. The Employee of the Month can't just quit!"

"It's just not what I want to be doing."

They sigh and stare at me with more than a hint of exasperation.

"We were expecting this call to come at some point," Mum admits.

What does that mean?

"And what do you want to do instead?" Dad asks.

"I want to give drama school another shot. I know I can do it. I'll work with Lawrence again until then. I've been dancing and singing with the actors here – they've really helped me work on my techniques and—" I stop when I see them looking at each other, having their own silent conversation. "What?"

"We'll talk about what you do next when you get back in March," Mum says softly.

"But—"

"It isn't up for discussion," Dad says firmly, both of them

softening the blow with "we love you"s before the call cuts out.

I call my sister, but she doesn't answer. I throw my phone on the mattress and yank the suitcase out from under the bed, unzipping it to find a lone pair of jeans. I whip open some drawers and start throwing my belongings in with them.

My phone starts to ring. For a second I think it might be my parents calling to be more reasonable, but dread hits me when I see it's Lawrence. That didn't take long. And because I can't hate myself any more than I do already, I answer it.

"Lizzie," he snips before I can even say a word, "what's this I hear about you quitting?"

"I—"

"I don't know why you think I'd hire you back. Your CV's fucking terrible."

"Fuck off, Lawrence."

"You've had three jobs, I see…" He puts on a snobby interviewer voice. "All before the age of twenty-two. Hmm, and which of these *didn't* you quit?"

I don't give him the satisfaction of a reaction.

"No amount of running will ever make you happy, Lizzie. Contrary to what you believe, the grass is not always greener. Sometimes it's muddy and covered in piles of cow shit, but you have to keep walking to get to the top of the hill."

"Is that Dr Seuss?"

"You aren't quitting. I will never let you live it down if you do."

"But there's nothing here for me anymore."

"Tough. *Make* something there for you."

"It's not as simple as that."

"Isn't it? Or are you just making it harder than it needs to be?"

I hurry to think of a comeback, but nothing comes fast

enough.

"Tell me honestly, if you came home on Monday and people ask you, 'How was that cruise ship you went on? Your mum told me you've been entertaining people all over the Caribbean!' and you have to look them in the eye and tell them you quit, would you feel good about yourself?"

"She's not told anyone." I sidestep his interrogation.

"Of course she has! She tells anyone who'll listen – Dad too. They won't shut up about it."

"Why would they do that?"

"Because they're proud of you! We all are! The only one who isn't is you, and I'm sick of this 'woe is me' bollocks you pull every time something doesn't go your way. You're not a child anymore. I'm not going to save you this time."

Silence falls on the line. There's a lot of truth in what he's saying, but I don't want to hear it. All the justification I want to give makes me sound like a whiny little bitch with a victim complex: *"You don't know what it's like living in your shadow"*; *"It's all right for you – you've never faced any kind of adversity"*.

"This is me *not* giving up on drama school," I mutter finally.

"And what if you go to one of these schools and you hit a rough patch there? You're just going to quit, are you?"

"No, it'll be different. I'll love it there."

"You said the same about this job and now look where you are. You're not even three months in and you want to give up. I kept telling Mum and Dad this would happen if they were soft on you. They've made you weak."

"I'm not *weak*!" I shout.

"Yes, you are! And it's time to toughen up. The world isn't perfect, and neither are you."

"I hate you."

He laughs – actually laughs. "Oh, I know. You know why you don't like me?"

"Because you're an arsehole."

"Because I'm the only one in this family who treats you like an actual adult, and you see anything other than coddling as spite. What I don't get is how just a few weeks ago you were telling us all how much you loved it there, and yet now you call to say not only do you not like it anymore, but that you hate it so much you want to leave. I swear to God, if this has something to do with a boy again—"

"It doesn't have anything to do with a boy," I snap.

"Mm-hmm."

"It doesn't!"

"Prove it.

"I don't have to prove anything to you."

"No, you don't, but you should want to prove it to yourself."

He's wrong. He doesn't know anything about me. He's never known me.

"Stick. It. Out," he orders before hanging up the phone.

Fuck him. Fuck *everyone*.

I throw open my wardrobe, gather everything, and dump it in my suitcase, hangers and all. I don't fucking need him. I'll make it without him. He'll see. I move onto the shelves, grabbing armfuls of clothes and adding them to the growing pile.

I'll get a job in London. I'll find a cheap room to rent. I'll make it this time. I know I will. I have to, because if I don't…

I collapse on the floor in front of all my things, fresh upset pouring out of my eyes again. I'm so used to it now that the stinging doesn't even faze me.

If I don't make it again I'll have to finally accept that I'll never amount to anything.

TWENTY-NINE

TOM

"What the fuck did you do?" I fret into my phone, wiping the condensation off the plastic cup with my shake in.

"Excuse me?" Even when verbally assaulted he's still polite. *Brits.*

"Eliza's leaving." I pretended I didn't see her full suitcase when I came to get her for breakfast this morning, but my head's been spinning ever since.

Harvey falls over his words in his hurry to get them out. "Why would she leave? What have *I* done? Did she say something?"

"'*I was wrong about him*'," I say, doing my best impression of her.

"Everything was good. She was meant to call on Tuesday... I just thought she was busy."

"Well, if she's heard half the shit that I have about you since this new crowd got here then I'm not surprised."

"What does that mean?"

"Dude! Was there anyone you *didn't* fuck on your last ship?"

He sighs. "Can you get her to call me? Or just…get her to an internet cafe. Please." His voice is urgent.

"I can give it a shot."

He sighs, and I take a sip of my drink, going back to staring out the window. I decide to ease up on him a little.

"All right, it might not be entirely your fault."

"So then…" He pauses mid-thought. "What did *you* do?"

Oh shit, angry Harvey exists.

"Whoa, nothing, I'm a saint. She and I are good now. Kinda."

"If you and your bruised ego hadn't shut her out, she might not have gotten to this point."

"Hey, I had enough going on already, and I'm not about to explain all that to you."

"No, but you can blame me for everything, can't you?"

"This isn't about *us*, dammit! There are some girls on here – old friends of hers, I think. Something's not been right since they—"

I leap outta my seat, spotting her walking by. I race out the door, not straying too far so I won't disconnect from the Wi-Fi.

"Tom, are you there? What's going on?"

I call out to her, and reluctantly she leaves her friend where she is. I put the phone to her ear when she's close enough so she doesn't get a chance to see the caller ID.

"Tom, wha—?" She pulls the phone away and sees his name then gives me the dirtiest look.

I bare my teeth at her with an "I'm just trying to help" kinda smile.

After a heartbeat of hesitation, she ends the call, forcing the phone back into my hand. "Thanks for that." She storms off to rejoin her friend.

"Can't you just talk it out?" I beg, but she ignores me. I

answer my vibrating phone.

"Did you lose signal?"

"Not exactly."

"She hung up on me." It's a statement, not a question, so I don't respond. *"Fuck."*

For once we're on the same page.

Fuck.

ELIZA

"Autopilot Eliza" agreed to spend time with Tara off the ship today, which I could have handled had I not just been ambushed. I mean, I was already in a shit mood before that, but now, with the reminder that Oscar hasn't in fact been dragged into the fiery pits of hell – or, better yet, The Bog of Eternal Stench – I feel even worse. Not that I'm going to let that show, however. I've got to be all smiles for Tara; I can't let her see I'm falling apart here.

I take her for a stroll down the beach because going for a drink or lunch somewhere makes it more to endure, whereas a beach walk can be half an hour and it's over with. My anger was always aimed at Kate before, but I've been harbouring resentment towards Tara ever since seeing that picture of them together outside stage door. Either she never saw Kate's dark side or she did and still picked her over me.

"I'm sorry I brought Kate."

Guess we'd better get this over with. "She didn't know I was here, did she?"

She looks down regretfully. *I'll take that as a "no" then.*

"Actually, can we sit?"

I agree like it fills me with anything other than dread. We

find a shaded spot and park ourselves in the sand.

"The night we got here she told me what happened on your birthday. Why you *really* moved out. I knew you guys fell out, but I only ever heard her version of events." She glances off into the distance with a troubled expression. "I thought coming here would be a chance to make some new memories, put whatever happened behind both of you. I missed us. You were always such a good friend to me, and I took that for granted. Big-time. I got lost in the boyfriend bubble and didn't put in the effort I should have. This trip was me wanting to make up for that, and if I'd known—"

"It's okay," I say. She tried to do a kind thing, but it back-fired. I watch my feet as I bury them deep in the warm sand.

"I'm sorry I didn't ask you for your side of the story. I wish you'd told me."

"It wouldn't have changed anything."

"Of course it would have. You're my best friend."

"So's she," I argue.

Her reaction tells me she's not so sure about that anymore, but I don't encourage it. Our eyes meet briefly, our mouths forming sorry smiles.

"I'm really proud of you. Being out here, finally doing what you always wanted to do. You're crushing it." She changes the subject.

I pull my feet out of the sand, wiggling my toes until all the grains fall off my skin. I could pretend that's true and take the compliment, but not being open with her has kept us apart for long enough.

"No, I'm not. I'm a failure compared to you."

"Oh my God, you don't really think that, do you? Eliza, tell me you don't think that."

She stares me down but I don't correct myself.

"How are you a failure for doing something that makes

you happy?"

"Well, it doesn't make me happy, so there's that." I twiddle a loose thread on my sundress, sensing her sympathetic stare.

"What's up?"

I take a long breath in and out. *Here goes nothing.* "I wish I was good enough to do what you do."

"Are you kidding? I wish I was good enough to do what *you* do. Not only do you have to run all these events, but you have to interact with people, improvise, *entertain* them twenty-four-seven. I perform the exact same thing day in, day out. Sure, there's the odd crazy day, but I get to go home and never see the audience again. Also, you have a job pretty much guaranteed after this, whereas I have no idea what I'm going to do after 'Waitress'. I've been auditioning for weeks and I've got nowhere."

I cast my eyes over to the shore and watch the waves come and go. Tara's talented, trained, and has a professional gig *as a freaking understudy* on her CV, and yet people aren't throwing jobs at her. I'm not stupid enough to think an actor's life is plain sailing, but I thought it got easier once that first role was in the bag.

"You know why everyone always thinks actors are narcissists?"

I shake my head.

"It's because we have to be. Every audition, every meeting with a prospective agent, every single day, we're told we're not right for something. Imagine if I believed that every time I heard it – I wouldn't last a second in the industry. 'Good enough' only depends on who you're asking."

Have I really been so naïve as to believe it all this time? To take every rejection to heart. For all my "I don't care what people think about me" attitude, I've discovered another blackspot: audition panels. I really, *really* care what they think. But where has that got me? I'm miserable, jealous, and I hate myself.

"You've never been one to follow the crowd or change who you are to please people. It's one of the best things about you. Every audition I go to I'm meant to become this blank canvas the casting director can paint on – or that's one school of thought anyway – but you're anything other than a blank canvas. You were always going to carve your own path. I mean, just look at your family. Lawrence started his own business because he hated working for other people, I hear Simon's going to be a stay-at-home dad because Sarah's the main breadwinner in her soon-to-be family – congratulations, by the way. And then there's you, entertaining thousands of people a day in this unique job of a lifetime. You shine on here, Lize. I really mean it."

I'd never really thought about it like that. Any of it. "Thank you."

It's so good to clear the air with Tara after all this time, but naturally, just as one thing from my past resolves itself, my future is nothing but murky.

When I get back to my room it takes me a second to recognise it as mine. If I didn't know any better, I'd think I was raided. Thank God inspections aren't today. I dig out the dress I want to wear for formal night tonight from the middle of the pile and hang it up so it has time to unwrinkle. I need to sort through the rest of my shit too, but right now I only have enough time to get into uniform before a busy afternoon and evening of activities.

Tom's wary of me at the Sail Away Party, as he should be.

That stunt he pulled this morning was the last thing I needed.

He approaches me cautiously once the party's over. "How was your walk?"

"Good."

"Good."

There's a long silence as we head below deck.

"You thought much more about leaving, or…?"

"Yep."

"Oh." He sounds disheartened. "So you're really going?"

"Nope."

"You're staying?" His mood flips on a dime.

"Yep."

"Was it because of—?"

"Nope." He doesn't get any credit for this revelation, but that doesn't stop his face from breaking out in a relieved smile from ear to ear. He slips off to his room to change into his tux for the evening, and I keep walking on to mine thinking of the actual reason I've decided to stay. It's a piece of advice my grandad lives by: "if in doubt, do nowt". And right now I have a lot of doubts. Therefore, I will do nothing. For now.

At the end of the night, I steal myself away from the others as they all head to the crew bar, and I enter my room determined to put it right. I take a deep breath, change into my PJs, stick on some music, and get to work reorganising the chaos. *Just one thing at a time*, I keep telling myself whenever I feel overwhelmed – which is every five minutes at the start, but eventually I find a rhythm to it.

I originally unpacked with Maddison's input, most of which was extremely helpful, but there were some things that didn't work. So I make the space my own, and in doing so, I find a bunch of things I'd completely forgotten about hiding at the very back of various drawers and shelves.

It looks like an entirely different room by the time I'm finished. It's quite cathartic, actually, giving myself a fresh start like this.

The last item to put away is my jeans. I debate leaving them in the case like before, but because of the air-con, they actually wouldn't be too unthinkable to wear on here like I originally thought. I find a spot for them in a drawer, but I take them right back out again when I hear a crinkle. A tiny bit of excitement shivers through me. Who doesn't love finding money in their pockets? I slide my hand in to find it's not money at all; it's the note I wrote to myself on the plane. One of the reasons this job would be good for me. There in my own frantic handwriting is:

There's nothing left for me at home.

And where would I be without that charming reminder?

I consider scrunching it up and throwing it away, but I can't quite bring myself to. I continue to read the list of reasons…

I'm tired of being the family screw-up.

Drama schools don't want me, and I don't want to be where I'm not wanted.

I was never meant to have a normal job, and I can't work another second with Lawrence.

. . .

This is a chance to make some real friends.

The sunshine will do me some good, and I'm excited to see the world.

I need a new challenge.

~~I might meet the love of my life.~~ Don't even <u>think</u> about meeting the love of your life!

This is my dream job. Please don't fuck this up.

I was happy here. I loved every bit of my job…before I started thinking with my vagina.

This is exactly why I didn't want to get involved with anyone while I was out here: it's complicated so much. You know what? I refuse to let another bloody man make me want to quit my job. Fuck Twatface, fuck Lawrence, and fuck Oscar.

I sigh, knowing deep down that's not all it is. I can either keep letting this happen, blame everyone other than myself and be perpetually miserable, *or* I can take some damn ownership of the part I played in my own undoing, take back control, and break the cycle. And I choose the latter. *I* will be the one who ruins this job for me, not them! Yeah, that's the spirit. No. I'm responsible for my own job fulfilment, my own happiness, my own damn success. I can think about drama school when this contract is over. I can deal with Oscar when he's back, but right now I'm going to stick out this job to prove everyone, including myself, wrong. I can't keep quitting when things get tough. Sure, I might want to, but this time I won't.

I finally shove my suitcase away and get ready for bed, where I read the list once more with a new outlook. I'm still the family screw-up and drama schools still don't want me. But there are things for me at home now. Tara for one, Sarah's baby for another, so that's something. For a while, it felt like I had made real friends here, but it's tough to say when I don't check my phone enough to see if Maddison, Valentina, or any of the actors have messaged. I could message. Why do I have to wait for them to? *Take. Back. Control.* I also shouldn't dismiss the people currently on the ship too. Sure, I've made a terrible first impression, but it's not like I can make their opinion of me any worse by trying.

Better late than never.

Have I seen much of the world? Sure, the catamaran trip was a good day out, but any other time I've ventured further than the beach or the restaurants around the main port it's ended in disaster. Actually, the catamaran trip also ended in disaster – it just took longer for it to transpire. But in the spirit of taking back control, I'm going to go somewhere that won't end in disaster. I will manifest a positive experience, and it will be fine. I am more than willing to settle with it being just fine.

Right, that's it, I've decided I'm not going to let myself go home without doing at least three things on this list. That seems fair.

Make friends, see the world, don't fuck it up.

Yeah, I think I can manage that.

THIRTY

ELIZA

I might be on a path of enlightenment, but Kate's still dead to me. I made it clear to Tara that if she wants to be her friend I won't stop her. I didn't bother to go into detail about every one of Kate's toxic wrongdoings because she simply isn't worth my time. They have their own relationship, and I'd be no better than Kate if I tried to drag Tara away from her.

I don't believe Kate would be apologising if it weren't for being stuck here with me against her will, but that's not to say she's not having some kind of Christmas Carol/Grinch-esque epiphany now she's finally having to face up to the fact she's an awful person.

Unlike earlier in the week, I'm actually happy when Tara turns up to my activities. When I see her laughing, I don't let myself wonder if it's at me because I know it's with me.

It's Latin Night tonight, and instead of skipping the Friday social like I have been recently, I decide to turn up. I finish late, but I'm still the first one at the Salsa masterclass from our gang. I linger awkwardly on the sidelines hoping I don't look like I'm dying with self-consciousness. Maybe they're not coming. Maybe there's a cabin party I wasn't invited to. Maybe I should leave.

Just as I think I might, one of the dance teachers clocks me as someone without a partner and volunteers me to the room, dragging me into the centre of the crowd with them. The other teacher does the same with more loners, and to my relief, one of them is Louise. Has she been here all this time? I offer to be the one who leads, and she agrees to partner up, but I can feel her hesitation in the rigidity of her body. I've been distant from everyone lately, but I have a hunch she thinks it's personal. Starting now, I'm going to make sure she knows that isn't the case.

The professional couple walk us through the moves, and by the time we're running the dance through fully, we're cheering each other on and giggling away at any mistakes we make. We're not walking away from this as the best of friends, but it's a step in the right direction.

At the expense of my now slightly bruised toes, Tom spends the rest of the night playing class clown, focusing on making me and the others crack up rather than learning any moves he could use for the rest of the night. He's got so much confidence for someone with two left feet.

All the entertainment staff bundle together after the class and commandeer a few tables. Other than Valentina's leaving party, I've pretty much never spoken to the actors. I thought they didn't really want to know us, but the more I look around at how chummy they've become with the other hosts, it dawns on me *they* didn't shut *me* out; *I* shut *them* out. Discomfort gnaws at me when I first integrate with them, but after another drink and a small pep talk to myself in the bathroom it gets easier.

When the bar closes I get Tom to walk me back to mine.

"I wanted to apologise. It was petty of me to—" I begin, but he half-smiles and shakes his head.

"There's something I should tell you."

I've rarely seen him this serious, so I invite him in.

I perch on the desk and he settles on the edge of his old bunk, and it doesn't take long for all my tiny, feeble problems to be put into perspective. Tom opens up about home, how in the past few years he's had his entire life turned upside down, and how coming here was his chance to feel normal for a few months. We find ourselves sitting next to each other on the bed, holding each other by the hand, as he explains what was going on the week his family was here.

"I'm sorry I wasn't there for you."

"I'm sorry I didn't let you be."

We make a deal to never shut the other out again, but more than anything, we both want to be able to have fun like we used to.

So that's what we do.

All weekend we mess around, playing things like a day-long round of ship-tag with the rest of the team and making stupid bets he somehow always ends up doing the forfeit for.

On Monday I get up early to see Tara off, promising to catch up with her when I'm back and meaning it. Kate lingers on the sidelines, and I take a leaf out of Valentina's book, holding firm on any emotional displays and giving her a stoic nod instead of a rigid hug or half-hearted wave. I hope this trip has changed her, but if it hasn't, I trust that something else will. It's not my job to teach someone how to be a good person, especially not at the cost of my own mental health. Nor when I'm not perfect either.

My jealousy has kept me back from enjoying the things I love, the things that make me happy, so that evening, I put my pride to one side and go see "We Will Rock You". If I took a punch for each time I compare myself to them or wallow in my own shitty self-esteem, I'd be black-and-blue. I almost wish I *was* being punched, just so I'd be forced to see the damage I'm doing to myself. The show is phenomenal. I, however, am still a work-in-progress.

But I'm going to put in the work.

Later in the week, Tom treats us all to another hilarious stand-up routine at the crew's open mic night before forcing me to go up and sing something. I refuse and refuse and refuse, but before the end of the night he manages to track down Bryan, who's keen and willing to accompany me on the piano. It's him I can't say no to.

Inspired by the breakup playlist I compiled and have been listening to on a loop whenever I'm alone, I ask him to play "Burn" from Hamilton. It's from the part in the show where Hamilton's wife, Eliza, finds out he cheated on her and burns all their love letters. It's rather fitting to my current situation, and singing my heart out to a room full of people is freeing as hell. The actors and other professional solo performers are so supportive, and maybe it is just what I needed to feel like I'm on level ground with them all. I even muster up the courage to mention our old Wednesday meet-ups, which, to my delight, everyone seems up for restarting in the new year.

Come Sunday night I'm a nervous wreck. I'm not ready to see him. I'll never be ready. But it's happening whether I like it or not, and I'm not going to let him ruin the progress I've made.

THIRTY-ONE

OSCAR

When I left, I had visions of Eliza waiting for me at the gangway upon my return. She'd jump up into my arms like she always does, smother me with kisses without a care in the world for who saw us, and refuse to get down until I'd staggered to my new room and given her exactly what we'd both been starved of over the past six weeks. But the reality is the opposite. Not knowing where I'll see her or how I'll get her to talk to me is maddening.

I've forced myself to relive every escapade from my last ship – the ones I can remember anyway – and spent sleepless nights putting myself in her shoes, imagining being surrounded by half the people she's slept with, hearing them tell stories after hours and not knowing if they were about her – or worse, knowing for sure they were.

The last I heard from Tom was that she's decided to stay, but that was as much as I could get out of him and maybe as much as he knew at the time. Every few hours for two weeks I've been checking to see if those first grey two-tick messages have turned blue, or if the one-tick messages have turned into two at the very least, but her phone's clearly been locked away. Because I'm not worth getting it out for anymore. That's what kills me. She didn't even want to *try* to talk to me. I wouldn't have cared if she'd screamed and shouted, just as long as she was communicating with me.

I haven't quite decided how I'm going to play this, but I have faith I'll know what to do when I see her.

It's lunchtime when I finally spot her on the other side of the main deck before the Captain's Welcome. My pulse quickens and my limbs weaken briefly with nerves. She's every bit as beautiful as I remember – more so even. Her hair is blowing in the wind as she laughs and jokes with Sunshine and another girl who wasn't here when I left but whom I eventually recognise from my last ship. *Ah.* From what Tom said, I'm regretfully confident I've come up in conversation between them, and yet here Eliza is, clearly having made friends with her despite it.

I hope to get her attention but don't manage to before the captain introduces Henry, who subsequently introduces me and Jerry. I smile and wave at the guests, and for a split second I catch her gaze before she quickly looks away again. It physically pains me to hold myself back from running right over to her in front of all these people.

Henry launches the week's first Sail Away Party, and it comforts me to know this is Eliza's favourite part of a Monday. If seeing me is the nightmare she's been dreading, at least she has something she enjoys to distract her for at least the next half an hour. Jerry leads me away to his next duty of the day, and I hide my reluctance to follow him. My head isn't on right today. I haven't been able to think straight all morning, let alone now I've seen her. However, when Jerry hands me a master schedule of all the festive activities happening this week and who's running them, I instantly perk up.

At 2.55 p.m. I'm meant to be on my break, but instead I'm hovering outside the pub where Eliza's due to finish a quiz any minute now. I hide out of her line of sight and listen to her announcing the scores and awarding prizes. The room's full of merriment as it always is when she's around, and the second I hear her sign off and the chatter around the room starts up again, I seize the opportunity.

When I first met her, there was always a hint of panic in her eyes. Then slowly, day by day, I saw it fade, replaced by the sparkle that made me fall in love with her. Now, though, the panic returns. I've changed that look before, and I'll be damned if I can't do it again. I just need to talk to her.

Striding over, her startled blue eyes leave mine and focus on packing up, but her fingers are skittish and incapable of doing anything useful. When I get to her, she gives up and reluctantly lifts her head to look at me. Her face is as still as anything, but I see her swallow her discomfort.

"Hey," I say softly.

She doesn't reply. Her jaw tightens and she blinks a little more.

"Can we talk?"

"Sorry to disturb you, dears." An older couple approach us, and from the voucher they've got in their hand I ascertain they're the lucky winners of the quiz. "Just wanted to find out where we could go next. I've been a bit of a ditz and left the schedule in our room." The woman's voice is sweet and calm, and I instantly feel bad for wishing she hadn't bothered us.

Whipping out the master schedule from my pocket, I take a look. "Have either of you ever played bowls?"

They shake their heads.

"Well, there's a…" – I breathe a heavy sigh at the awful attempt at a pun – "jingle bowls for beginners class you could take in about fifteen minutes' time on deck nine. There's a tournament later on in the week you could win big at too, so it might be worth a go."

"Oh, that sounds fantastic. Where was that again?"

"Deck nine. I'll take you," Eliza offers without missing a beat.

"That's all right, I'm sure we'll find it." The lady smiles and heads out of the pub. Her husband thanks us with a nod and follows on behind her.

I don't miss the blush on Eliza's cheeks now she has to face me after attempting to run away. She looks around at the room still full of players enjoying their drinks, none of them in any rush to leave like she is. She doesn't meet my eye again.

"Now's not a good ti—"

"Later then? Please."

She looks at me briefly then down again, taking a few seconds to faff with her quiz sheets and pens before responding. "I think I finish around ten."

"I'll see you then."

I leave her in peace. It kills me to see her so unhappy to see me, but at least I got to talk to her. Christ, I'm like a bird desperately pecking at the breadcrumbs she's throwing, but I don't care.

I pace as I wait for her up in our spot. I'm aware we didn't set a meeting place, but I was confident we didn't need to. We should be clear of the wet season by now, but it's horrid outside. The heavy wind makes the spit of the rain feel like pinpricks on my face. Hardly the ideal weather to be outside in, but still, it's warm out – it always is. Maybe I should search for her inside instead.

"Nice of you to have brought the English weather back with you."

She takes me by surprise. I must not have heard her footsteps over the weather or the faint music from the pool deck below, or perhaps just the noise in my own head.

I hadn't grasped the extent to which I missed her voice or sarky comments until now.

She comes closer, just enough to go down the two steps onto the deck, and then she stops, not daring to come any closer, keeping herself tucked into the railings. We both stand still. For a while, it's as if time has frozen.

"Chapman, whatever you've heard about me, I'm so, *so* sorry. I can't imagine how awful it's been to be stuck here with people from my past. I promise that's not who I am now. I'm better than that, and I will do whatever it takes to show you."

"Is that why you think I'm mad?"

"Why wouldn't it—? I thought— What else—?"

"What I don't know won't hurt me, right?" Her glare makes my heart sink to my stomach.

"Please tell me what you think I did."

"You fucking *cheated* on me!"

Confusion strikes my body, almost knocking me over. I *what*? "Eliza, I would never—"

She shakes her head sternly. "Don't do that. I know. You got caught. Just admit it and we can get this over with."

"I have *no idea*—"

She scoffs and turns to leave.

"Could you give me a clue at least?"

She looks back, staring me dead in the eye. "Your birthday. When you bailed on me. To sleep with *some guy*."

Relief hits me like a tonne of bricks and I can't help but laugh.

She gets to the top of the steps and panic takes over. "Don't fucking laugh at me. Prick."

"No, Eliza, wait! He's my cousin. The guy I was in bed with was my *cousin*."

She freezes in her tracks. From her shoulders, I can tell her breathing is laboured with adrenaline.

"So unless you want to accuse me of something more sinister…"

"Prove it," she says, still with her back to me.

I don't want to know what lies she's been told before to make it so her immediate reaction isn't to believe me. She wants to. But she's been made a fool of before, and she won't let it happen again.

I can't get to my phone soon enough. I find the family album on iPhotos and hand it to her, letting her scan through years' worth of images. As many as she needs. Christmases. Birthdays. Summer holidays. I watch on nervously, waiting for her to be satisfied with the evidence.

Her eyes close and she takes a deep breath. One of her hands comes up to cover her face while her other drops down by her side, and I see the photo she's landed on – the same one I now know she saw on Instagram, but taken twenty years ago. Dylan and me as kids, fast asleep in bed, spooning. After we got my other cousin's twisted ankle iced, Gemma thought it would be funny to recreate childhood photos with them. This was before she started throwing up and couldn't stop for long enough for us to get home.

"Amazing how little context one picture can give you."

She hands my phone back, shame written all over her face. "My messages weren't delivering. You weren't answering my calls. And when that's happened before—" She chokes back a sob.

"My phone was dying, so I left it at home thinking I'd only be gone an hour or two. Then I got blindsided." I sent her a whole wave of messages when I finally got home the next day telling her everything, but it was too late. She'd already seen the picture.

"I'm so sorry."

It breaks my heart to know this whole time she's been getting over what she thought was another betrayal. I'm hurt – of course I am – but it's forgivable given what happened to her in the past. And though she's yet to admit it, I'm sure whatever she's heard from whoever else is here has only further smeared the picture she was painting of me. I *wish* I took my bloody phone out with me. I *wish* she'd read my messages. I'm sure she wishes she did too.

I take a few steps towards her. "It's okay."

She looks up at me, shaking her head again, and I stop just short of her.

"We'll be okay."

She presses her lips together hard, and then her eyes well up.

"Chapman."

"You deserve to be with someone who trusts you." She sounds resolute even as her voice breaks.

"I want *you*."

She lifts her eyes up to mine and teardrops start to fall. I take two more steps, sweep my arms around her, and hold on tight until it soothes her, but then she tenses again.

"This is…" – she pulls back, stepping away – "toxic. You shouldn't be comforting me. I'm in the wrong here. I swear I'm not turning this around and playing the victim. *I* hurt *you*. And I don't deserve to be with someone as good as you."

I wipe a tear from her rain-soaked cheek with my thumb before remembering I have a packet of tissues in my jacket pocket and retrieve them for her. I'm embarrassed to admit there's even a condom in that pocket too because I wanted to be prepared *just in case* make-up sex was on the cards.

"I'm clearly not over what happened before, and it's not fair of me to take it out on you."

"I want to work it out with you."

She shakes her head. "That's not your responsibility. You have enough going on. You've worked so hard for this job – I'll only be a distraction."

"Eliza—"

"Please. Can we...go back to being friends or whatever?"

Looking into her eyes, I know I'm not going to be able to change her mind tonight, but that doesn't mean I have any intention of not trying again tomorrow. "Okay," I agree.

The rain starts to pour down, but I remain unmoved.

She looks up, water falling on her face and cleaning away the evidence of her sadness. "We should go," she whispers and slips away. She heads down the steps until she thinks she's out of sight, takes a deep breath, and straightens up, plastering on a smile before continuing down. It's a routine she seems to have mastered. How many times has she had to hide how she felt from guests while I've not been around? It hurts to think about it.

I wait a short while so as not to follow her, and then I head inside too. Despite being soaking wet, I go to the bar to see if the guys are still around. I promised them a drink earlier and I'm more than a little late to turn up for it, but luckily they're here. Perhaps not waiting for me, but here nonetheless.

Daniel and Obi get up from the table and each bundle me into the tight hugs we couldn't give each other earlier out on the main deck. Tom's welcome is a little warier. Does he think I fucked my cousin too?

"Cor, stand in the rain much?" Daniel teases, wiping the excess rainwater off his top.

There's no sign of the newer crowd, which is a relief. I'd rather not have to put on a brave face for them right now. I grab myself a soda and lime from the bar and rejoin them.

"Good first day, big man?"

Let's see, less than twenty-four hours in and the love of my life broke up with me. I puff out my cheeks and slowly push all the air out of my lungs. "Could've been better," is all I choose to say.

"Surprised you joined us at all, to be honest. Thought you'd be breaking in your new bed," Obi ribs me.

Thankfully, I'm saved from having to come up with a response when the double doors to the bar burst wide open behind me, announcing the arrival of – I'm guessing – the actors riding their post-show high. I look around and it's like the Ghost of Hookups Past. I can't help but sigh. I was a real piece of work.

And then it dawns on me. Despite her meeting half the skeletons in my closet, Eliza still thinks *she* doesn't deserve *me*. Calling me a man-whore was the easiest way to get out of our relationship and she didn't use it. She didn't shame me like I expected her to, and now I realise that even though she claims she thought the worst of me, in expecting her to hate me because of who I was, I thought the worst of her. She's wrong. It's me who doesn't deserve her.

"Harvey?"

Someone coaxes me out of my trance. All the guys are looking at me with concern.

"I need your help with something."

THIRTY-TWO

ELIZA

It's Christmas Eve, and for the past two days Oscar has been kind enough to keep his distance. I pass him around the ship, and even though he smiles at me, he doesn't stop to talk. It's weird seeing him at breakfast at another table with Jerry and the other heads of departments. I may or may not have watched him from afar while he made himself tea this morning and secretly wished it were for me.

How did I get it *so* wrong? Serves me right for going full psycho on him.

I still love him. I think I'll always love him. I'm sure I'll move on one day in years to come and be happy, but I'll always love him.

Tom's been doing his best to keep up his end of the "fun pact". The others have all got in on our crazy games too, although Tom and I both vetoed Obi's suggestion of a round of sardines very quickly.

I call home during my lunch break to wish them all an early Merry Christmas as I'll be too busy to call them at a reasonable hour tomorrow. I'm a little tense calling Mum and Dad, but they don't bring up our last conversation. Lawrence doesn't bug me about it either. I wonder if they've already forgotten it, swept it under the rug with the many other times I've wanted to quit something. Although I barely give him a chance to say anything – I'm too busy demanding to see Sarah and her bump. Now six months into her pregnancy, she's really showing, and she periodically squeals for everyone to come and feel her stomach when there's a kick. I beg her to make sure the bump doesn't pop out until I'm home, because this is my first opportunity to touch a pregnant belly that wouldn't be obscenely inappropriate, and I don't want to miss it.

It's a bittersweet goodbye when I finally hang up. I didn't think I'd care too much about missing out on Christmas, but now I've seen everyone all together I'm a little bit gutted I'm not there. I'm happy I'm still here though. I'm surrounded by friends and it's almost thirty degrees outside. Plus, it's a port day tomorrow, and I've planned a beach trip for us all in the hopes I can tick off my "see the world" mission.

I can't not look at Oscar's messages before I turn off my phone. I don't know how long I sit and read them, but my heart, which is doing its best to be strong, is in utter pieces by the time I get to the last one.

I pushed him away because it was the right thing to do. I pushed him away because it was the right thing to do. I pushed him away because it was the right thing to do.

My thoughts are stuck on a loop, but no matter how many times I tell myself that, I don't seem to believe it.

That night we all flock to our pigeonholes and meet up at the bar with our Secret Santa gifts. Everyone's looking festive wearing Santa hats, snowman head boppers, and DIY

Christmas jumpers. I'm in a cute red skater dress that gives off just the right amount of Mrs Claus vibes.

I ordered Daniel this amazing handmade festive Dungeons and Dragons dice set from Etsy, which I rather modestly think was a stroke of genius. What I hate about Secret Santa is the secrecy; I want to take *full* credit for the joy on his face as he fusses over the mini snowman, Santa, reindeer, and gingerbread people trapped inside the weird resin dice.

We slowly go around the group and I struggle to keep up as each of the other hosts and actors have their own conflicting opinions on who their gift was from It finally gets around to me, and I'd be lying if I said curiosity hasn't been clawing at me while I've been waiting for my turn.

My gift is in a small square box with a blue bow on top. Like something you might get from a jewellers, maybe. There's no paper to tear through, just a lid to lift off. Inside the box is a tiny piece of white card with handwriting on it that reads:

Remember me? x

When I look under the note my heart almost jumps out of my chest.

"So? What is it?" someone asks from the other side of the table.

I have no clue how to explain the significance of it. I scan the circle to catch my Santa giving themselves away with a particularly guilty look, but everyone's curious eyes are on me and I can't pinpoint anyone.

I take the gift out of the box to show everyone. "It's my name badge."

People pretend to be excited for me because they can see I'm clearly moved by it, but they're more than eager to move on to Tom beside me for something more interesting to react to.

I go to put the badge back in the box but stop myself when I notice another piece of card at the bottom that says:

Santa's grotto. 11 p.m. Try not to hurt yourself this time. x

I'm delirious by the time I arrive at the grotto. It's an adorably made-up room with giant light-up candy canes all over the place. There's a perfectly decorated Christmas tree in the corner and a sleigh packed with presents being led by an army of plastic reindeer. At the end of the room is a huge red armchair grand enough to be described as a throne, and on the floor next to it is a large red sack bulging with more wrapped boxes.

Bulging sack? Really? That's the worst thing I've ever said, and yet I'm still turned on. That's the power badge boy has over me, I guess.

I had well and truly put my crush on him to bed. Albeit reluctantly. It was a game I read into way too much, and he obviously didn't feel what I did when we kissed. So why now? Wants a bit of action at Christmas, I guess. And you know what? Maybe it's what I need. I'm single now after all.

Colourful hues glow from the fairy lights draped over the snow-covered cabin-like roof above the throne. This is the most excited I've been on Christmas Eve since I was about twelve.

With no sign of him yet, I take a seat on the throne. Wow, this is *comf-ter-ble*.

Just as I relax, I'm plunged into darkness. That's when the door opens and closes, but I can't see who enters.

Oh my God. Oh my God. Oh my God!

Though his footsteps are muffled by the carpeted floor, the strides sound confident as he gets closer. Meanwhile, I'm shaking like a leaf. A very horny leaf. My chest pounds and my stomach flutters with nerves.

It's virtually pitch-black, but I can just about make out the dark figure as he stops in front of me. I eye the stranger's form intently as he kneels down, aligning himself to match my height. His hand touches mine where it rests on the arm of the chair. He takes it and guides it to the side of his face. Roughness grates my palm, but I revel in it. He lets go and finds his way to the side of my face, his other hand taking its time sliding up my thigh before settling on my waist.

He slowly pulls me closer, the smell of peppermint teasing me before he places his lips on mine, immediately setting off fireworks within me. I've never needed a kiss from anyone as much as I need one from him. I didn't make it up. It wasn't the alcohol or the side effects of a debaucherous afterparty. It's cosmic – it has to be. I mean, we literally collided the first time we met, and let's be honest, with the way he's kissing me, I'm anticipating a big bang of some kind in our near future.

He makes my dizzy world stop spinning and my fear turn into courage. He makes the pain go away.

This isn't just a steamy hookup; there's something so much bigger here. For months he's hidden in plain sight, I thought avoiding me, but now it feels more like he was watching over me. I wonder if he's ever spoken to me. He must have done. It's a small ship, and I'm sure I've seen everyone who was at my party since then. I wonder what we talked about. It should be creepy, but I've never felt safer or more connected to anyone.

We devour each other's lips, the tips of our tongues tangling in between our parted mouths, and the pulse between my legs beats harder with every passing second. I'm right on the edge of the seat with my chest pressed up against his, the sensation pebbling my nipples, which silently beg to be touched and squeezed and pulled. I'm unable to contain my sighs, and he releases a low groan that makes it impossible not to start taking off his clothes. But I'm stopped when I notice the lights are starting to glow around us again.

I pull away from him and look at my secret admirer. *Holy fucking shit.* How did I not work it out?

"It's you."

"It's me."

"But your accent…"

Of course he can fake an American accent. He had one for six months.

Oscar kneels nervously before me, his lips pink, eyes guilty, and hands gentle on my body like he's scared if he holds me too tight I'll notice he's there and push him away. "I told you I'd stay close by."

Questions flood my mind, leaving my thoughts to sink. There's one word that keeps swimming to the surface and gasping for air though.

"Why?"

Why didn't you tell me sooner? Why did you hide? Why didn't you want me then? Why do you want me now?

"Because I was a coward when you met me. I thought I had it all figured out, and then you turned up and I knew I'd

466

got it all wrong. I thought I wanted to be invisible, and you made me realise how much I wanted to be seen. But more than that, I wanted to be seen by the girl who appeared in my cabin, stripped down to her underwear, and tried to kick me out."

I titter at the embarrassing memory.

"You always looked at me as if I had the answers to the universe, but I knew nothing. I hid behind party games because I thought they were what made me brave, but they didn't; *you* did. And I'm done hiding." His blue eyes drop to his chest. He takes off his badge and places it in my hand.

I nibble my twisted lip as shame clouds my vision. "I wasn't good to you," I object.

He shakes his head in disagreement. "If we were in a show and your voice gave out one night because it was tired from weeks of being pushed to its limits, I wouldn't blame you for not wanting to turn up the next night. But 'the show must go on', as they say. *I* want the show to go on. And I will do whatever it takes to make that happen. I'll make you hot honey and lemons, I'll run extra warm-ups, I'll rehearse with you, I'll get them to change the key, I'll sing all of your songs with you night after night until you're confident again." He wipes the happy tears from my cheeks with his thumb. "You're the star of this show, Chapman and without you, there is no show. And before you say it, I refuse to work with an understudy."

"Diva," I whisper.

We break out into giggles, and my soul feels whole again.

"Will you please be my leading lady?"

I nod with enthusiasm because now my voice really has gone. His face lights up and he kisses me, our relief evident in the desperate grip we cling to each other with.

"I love you," I gasp.

"I love you too."

I pull him back into me, our lips meeting fervently. Then, out of nowhere, I hear cheering and clapping, and upon opening my eyes to investigate, I find it's snowing. Obi pokes his head out from behind the Christmas tree, Tom pops up from inside the sleigh, and Daniel appears from the small tech desk I hadn't spotted in another corner until now, and Oscar and I burst out laughing.

"Have you been here the whole time!" I shout in amusement and a little embarrassment.

"Sorry, I had a little help," Oscar confesses, kissing me once more before getting up to see them out. "Right, kids, scram."

Tom throws Oscar a set of keys and locks the door behind them. That doesn't stop them from making a bunch of playful jeering noises at us through it though.

"I have a very important question to ask you, Chapman," he says, stalking closer.

I bite down on my smiling lip. "What's that?"

"Have you been naughty or nice?"

Guilt clutches my stomach. "Well, we both know I haven't been nice."

Oscar frowns, taking my chin in his hand and lifting my head to meet his stare. "That's not true. Even when you thought I'd hurt you, you didn't shout, you didn't scream – you just let me go. You're a good person, Eliza."

I still don't feel like one.

He kneels beside me, patiently waiting for me to process my thoughts.

"I think I need to redeem myself," I mumble.

"Would that make you feel better?"

I nod, and he kisses me deeply before standing again.

"Up," he demands with an edge to him, My body fizzes

468

with excitement at the same time as my mind relaxes completely knowing he's in control.

He's going to make everything okay again.

He leans into my ear. "You're right: you haven't been good to me." He's so close but not touching me, and it's setting my skin on fire with a need to feel him. "You promised me you were mine, but you came up here to kiss a stranger. And you liked it, didn't you?"

I nod with faux-shame. Then, in the blink of an eye, his hand is up my skirt. There's fake anger in his eyes as he notices how wet I am already. Then there's a flash of something else, and he pulls away quickly.

"Lift up your dress."

I hesitate, looking around.

His features soften as he whispers, "The door's locked, the camera's blocked. It's safe here if you want to do this."

We look back to where the security camera should be, but it's covered up entirely by the star on top of the tree. And now that I really examine the tree's position, it looks a little off-centre. He's cautious – he has to be even more so now with his new role. I watched him lock the door with my own two eyes, and I trust him to know this is a good idea.

I do as he asks, revealing the nice knickers I got for him. And now I have to admit I was prepared for a little more than just a kiss. And he's not going to like that.

His jaw tightens as he mulls something over with a look of disapproval. "Care to explain those?"

"I wanted to look good for him."

He sighs a deep, frustrated growl. "If those lights hadn't turned on, you'd have fucked him, wouldn't you?" His eyes scan my chest.

"I wouldn't have."

The back of his finger traces my bra. I know what he's looking for. That's where I always kept the condoms before.

Even though he's playing up the jealousy, he seems genuinely relieved not to find one. "Good girl." He claims me with his mouth, one hand gripping me tightly around my waist, the other on my cheek.

God, I've missed him.

"Do you have any idea…how hard it was…all this time… knowing what you feel like…when you want me?"

Pressed against him now, I know exactly how hard it was.

"The things I've done thinking about you, Chapman." His tongue feels like a hit of sugar against mine. Sweet and sinful. "I was so well-behaved before you got here. You broke me. Are you proud of yourself?"

I smile against his lips and nod. "I really am."

His hands roam over me, gathering the bottom of my dress and lifting if all the way off. He takes in the sight of me in my lingerie before his fingers begin to unbutton his trousers.

"On your knees. Mouth open. Tongue out."

I submit to his orders, and seeing him loom powerfully over me wreaks havoc on my desire. He teases himself on my tongue, and my eagerness to please him pushes me to hold him and take him deeper. An unsolicited sigh of relief leaves him, but he pulls away.

"Did I tell you to do that?"

"No. Sorry."

"Do you want all of it?"

"Yes, please."

He arches an eyebrow at me. "You sure about that?"

"I'm sure." I smile.

His impressive length slides into my waiting mouth as

deep as it can go. I may have overestimated myself here. My eyes water, but I will do anything to please him.

He scrapes my hair away from my face, holding it in a ponytail, moving me slowly back and forth. "Eyes on me."

I look up and continue eagerly taking him in over and over again, hoping tonight will be enough to wipe the slate clean, but knowing I wouldn't be all that upset if it took a few more nights of this. Worshipping him in the way only I can.

"Please can I touch you?"

"Mmm, since you asked so nicely."

I wrap my hand around him and pull him in sync with my lips.

"Look at you, so desperate to earn my forgiveness." He curses and grunts as I work him harder and faster.

Squeezing my thumb inside my palm, I push myself to take him all the way down until I can't take it anymore, spluttering and panting as I pull back. He sighs with satisfaction, and I look up at him, waiting for his praise and approval.

"God, you look so good with me in your mouth, Chapman. You know that?" he mumbles, softly stroking my cheek. He offers out his hand to help me up then leans down to my ear. "My pretty little slut. Let me see you." He takes a step back, eyes trailing all over me as he puffs out a breath. "Jesus Christ, look at you. You really think I'd do anything to compromise this?"

I drop my head to hide how sick I still feel about my mix-up.

"Hey." He lifts my chin again, the moment shifting once more. "Stay with me, Cricket." He kisses a smile back onto my lips before returning to checking me out.

I feel unworthy being the subject of such adoration and reach across myself to hold my other arm.

"Don't go shy on me now. Just give me a minute." He

goes to sit on the throne and rests his head on his hand, mesmerised.

I blush as I giggle.

"Come here."

I walk towards him and straddle his lap. We both take a second to study the other's face and enjoy our closeness after being apart for so long. As I lose myself in the taste of him again, my hips begin to chase the relief I crave, and I slowly start undressing him down to his underwear. I've missed the warmth of his skin. The feel of it against mine. The smell of his cologne in the air.

His fingers snap the clasp of my bra and his lips glide down my neck before teasing my firm nipples, eliciting gasps from me. When he straightens, I notice his eyes are pooled.

"You okay?" I ask, and he nods, but he pulls his lips in tightly. "Tell me."

"I was just so scared I'd lost you."

"Me too." Both of us fail to keep it together. "Never again."

"Never."

Crying during sex doesn't sound like a good thing, but I'm on top of the world. We're both shedding tears of relief and happiness, laughing at how silly it is but how good it feels to share ourselves with each other like this. No secrets, no holding back. It's cleansing. Being naked with him – not just literally – is pure and perfect. Because we're finally letting ourselves express our love fully without worrying about him leaving tomorrow or having to hide what we are to each other anymore. He's mine, I'm his, and I'm never letting him go again.

We're met with all kinds of knowing grins from the others when we join them for breakfast the next morning, but I don't care. Not one bit. I'm too busy watching Oscar make us tea. After a month and a half of utter heartbreak and misery without him, waking up in his arms this morning was exactly what I needed.

Tom flicks the white pom-pom at the end of my Santa hat. "Your cheeks match the colour of your hat, Queenie."

I roll my eyes and smile, unable to come up with a witty retort. I blow on my tea before taking a sip and immediately pout at Oscar. "Why would you do this to me? It's Christmas," I whinge.

He laughs and swaps our mugs over, taking the Earl Grey from me and replacing it with the English Breakfast in front of him. I scrunch my face up dubiously. *Why's he got that?*

He smirks at having been caught. "Like I said, you broke me, Chapman."

If you'd told me a year ago I'd be spending this Christmas in a bikini, I would have cut off your eggnog supply.

We're playing some kind of lazy mix between American football and rugby, which amazingly, Sunshine, Louise, and I are winning. I think it has nothing to do with our skills and everything to do with our attire. Obi claims he's scared of boobs, and both Tom and Daniel have been too nervous to go for the tackle in case they touch something they shouldn't.

When Oscar arrives, our lead completely disappears even though I make nothing *but* illegal tackles whenever he has possession of the ball. We finally admit defeat and Oscar throws me over his shoulder, marching me into the sea while I squeal and shout, "Ref! Ref!"

"You're well past saving now, Cricket."

The others all run in around us, the splashes flicking up onto my skin.

"I need to get the smell of sun cream off you before I do something that could get us both arrested," Oscar warns under his breath before gently tossing me in.

The fact I'm making money today baffles me. The sun is shining, I'm surrounded by friends and the person I love, and when playtime is over, I get to go and do a job that doesn't even feel like work. And after *that*, I'll dance the night away to festive songs at the bar.

Life is good.

THIRTY-THREE

ELIZA

January flies by. Any thoughts I had about applying for drama school again have completely gone from my mind. I mean, I'd be crazy to quit this when I've found something that makes me so happy. Some*one* too, but even without him I can't imagine myself being so satisfied doing anything else. I swear that's only partly as dirty as it sounds…

Our musical theatre meet-ups are going well. Oscar's been a whole new level of busy but still finds time to pop in, even if just long enough to watch me sing and then leave again. He's uncomfortable there, both for himself and for me, but I've made it very clear I will never hold his past against him. He's made no secret of being mine, and of the people in this room who've had drunk hookups with him, whom I now consider friends, none of them have tried to cross any lines. They've either moved on themselves or respect that he has.

Being secure doesn't come naturally to me, but if our time apart taught me anything, it's that the reward for trusting him is so much greater than the punishment when I don't.

It was sad saying goodbye to Daniel, and losing Obi soon will be just as tough, but Daniel's replacement already feels like part of the gang, and I'm sure Obi's will too. Plus, it's not like we won't keep in touch. I set up a group chat for us all, and it's thriving. Mostly with Maddison's gossip about complete strangers, but no one's complaining.

That's a part of the job I've come to accept now: as hard as the goodbyes are, the people I get to say hello to always make it worth it. I guess I should have known everyone would be nice, seeing as one of the main requirements in the job description was "must be friendly and approachable". Though God only knows why Valentina saw that and still thought, "Yep that's the job for me!" She's friendly in her own way, and that's what I like about her.

My six months are up at the beginning of March. I thought about extending my contract by a few more months, but it would mean I'd miss the arrival of Sarah's baby, and I really want to be on hand if she needs me for anything while she's recovering and they're both acclimatising to parenthood. So I'll have six weeks off, which I've vowed not to make harder for us, and then my new contract will start in April for nine whole months instead of six.

The only thing is, I haven't been assigned my ship yet. We've registered with HR as a couple, I've put my request in, and Oscar's sent a polite but pleading email to staffing in a bid to up my chances of coming back. We're not letting ourselves worry about what will happen if our request isn't accepted yet.

"Nope. I'm not going. You can't make me." I dig in my heels like a stubborn child while Oscar laughs and drags me down the corridor.

I've completed my mission to get off the ship more. The

girls and I have been shopping around ports, the Christmas beach day was a success, and Oscar even took me to the ice cream place he wanted to and nothing adverse happened. But I've ticked it off now. I don't want to leave the ship again and risk my lucky streak wearing off. I've been absolved of my personal commitment to do any more, but unfortunately not my professional commitment. I'm still on the excursions programme. *Even though* I took myself off it. This is all one big mistake.

"You'll have a good time, trust me."

I don't believe him, especially since he looks like he knows exactly where I'm going. He would tell me if it was nice, and the fact he hasn't means it's something I'll hate.

He continues to pull me along, no amount of sexual bribery or threats of celibacy deterring him from doing so.

"I'm not getting on another fucking bus. I'd rather shit in my hands and clap."

He chuckles. "What happened to manifesting a positive experience?"

"Sorry, I'm *grateful* for the *opportunity* to get off the ship, and I'm *excited* to *embrace* a *magical new advent—* Nope. I'm not doing that. It's going to suck."

"Chapman…"

"Bite me."

There's a younger crowd on this minibus, which relaxes me a little, but not enough to let down my guard. At least I'll be working with iPhone cameras instead of navigating the bricks I've been handed before.

Anxiety whirls around in my stomach on the drive over, but as soon as we pull up it all goes away. There's a new hazard I hadn't considered being a problem before I left, but now that I'm here I don't care if it kills me because at least I'll die happy.

Today, I'm swimming with pigs.

Aside from one idiot getting nipped by a pig because he decides to ignore the rules and pick it up for a cuddle, the outing is perfect. I develop some form of kinship with a little pink pig with black spots who follows me around the whole time. The few hours we have together will never be enough, but I'm so happy I got *something*.

"You set this up, didn't you?" I burst into Oscar's soon-to-be office with a huge smile on my face when I get back.

He hums and wraps me in a hug. "You have a good time?"

"The *best*! Thank you. I'm so happy," I say into his chest.

"I haven't even told you the good news yet."

I crane my neck to see a grin brushing the corner of his lips. "What?"

He doesn't reply. His smile just keeps getting wider and wider until it clicks.

"I got my contract renewed?"

He nods, finally letting his excitement out, and leans in for a kiss.

Life honestly can't get any better than this.

I'm practically flinging myself over the moon when I call home the next day. My parents don't fling themselves with me though. Their mouths say they're happy for me, but their faces tell a different story.

"There was something we were going to tell you when you got home," Mum says sheepishly.

"Right…"

They look between one another, and I suddenly panic thinking of every possible disaster they could have kept from me while I've been away. I know what they're like, they wouldn't have wanted to upset me, especially given my penchant for misery.

"Has Sarah given birth already? Is the baby okay? Is *she* okay? Or is it Grandad? Is Grandad—"

"No, darling, nothing like that. It's a good thing, it's just…"

They do that look again.

"Just tell me already!"

Dad gives Mum a reassuring nod.

"You got into drama school, sweetheart."

What? My heart thumps so hard it could burst through my chest at any minute. "I… What? How? *When*?"

"The emails came in after you'd already set your heart on this job. Well, you were on the reserve list for one before that, and we didn't know if we'd hear any more, so we didn't want to get your hopes up. Then when the actual offers came in, you'd already committed to this and you were so excited."

"Offers? *Plural*?"

"Yes, Lize. You got into all three."

"You're lying."

"No, you did it. You really did it! We're so proud of you, darling," Dad praises me.

I've imagined my reaction to this news every day since my mum signed me up to Stagecoach when I was five. I thought I might cry with happiness or jump and scream or swoon onto a chaise longue like a Victorian housewife – if a chaise longue so happened to be available – but now it's happening, I can't process it at all. Everything's spinning and I can't breathe.

What. The actual. *Fuck?*

"So that's it? All that work and I never got to go."

"No, no, we deferred your places. You can pick which one you accept when you're back. Take some time to think about it," Mum says.

"I can't believe you didn't tell me."

"I know, we're really sorry, but look, you're so happy now! Would you even want to go?"

I...don't know.

After years of heartbreak and rejection, I've been handed a golden ticket to my dream life, and now I don't even know if I want to take it.

I end the call feeling completely lost. So, after taking a second to collect myself, I call the one person I can trust to give it to me straight.

"Hi, Frizz-head."

And I instantly regret it.

"Did you know about drama school?" I cut straight to the chase.

"Oh, I may have heard that somewhere, yes, but I assumed it was a disturbing hallucination or something."

"Why didn't you tell me?" I snap.

"Guess it wasn't my place to say..." he muses in an airy-fairy tone like he couldn't be more thrilled to have kept it from me. I can picture him right now leaning back in his office chair with his feet crossed on the desk, staring out the window or pretending to look at his nails. "Have you called me to brag about going behind my back after I offered you a lifeline, or to whine about not being able to choose which school? Make it quick either way – I haven't got all day."

"Lawrence, stop being a prick."

"Fine. What do you want?" His voice returns to his normal no-nonsense tone.

"I, uh...I really like it here now. But would it be totally

stupid not to do the whole drama school thing? It could open so many more doors for me."

"*Totally stupid.* God, you've got even worse. Pack your bags, get on the next flight home, and save yourself from further corruption."

"Lawrence! I'm serious," I whinge.

"It's so hard to keep up with you. One minute it's all about the boat, the next it's drama school, and now, what, you *don't* want to go to drama school? What's changed since we last spoke?" He pauses for a second, and I think about it. "Sarah told me about that boyfriend of yours. Is that it? Is he being nice to you again?"

"No!" I shut him up but know how that sounds. "He was never— Ugh! You're infuriating, you know that?"

"Mmm, well it seems to me you've gone and got all googly-eyed for someone and want to give up your dreams for him. *Again.* I'm sure that boy of yours is very nice right now, but don't throw this away over him. You did that once before and it didn't go your way, did it?"

My stomach twists into a knot as I remember just how perfect I thought everything was going with Twatface... before it wasn't.

Lawrence must work out he's hit the very flimsy nail on the head because his approach softens. "I'm honestly not sure what's right for you, Liz. Only you can decide that. But whatever you pick, you need to make sure it's the right decision for *you* and *your* future, not his."

I hate how well he knows me.

"You still there?" he checks when I don't respond.

"Yeah. Sorry, just too relieved to speak knowing I'll never have to work for you again."

"That was never an option."

I ignore him. "You're a horrendous boss."

"I know."

"You should do something about that."

"Nope. I did everything just right."

Of course he would think that.

"I was never going to let you get comfy there, Lizzie. You were always capable of so much more than being a PA to your shitty brother."

This is the first time my brother's made me smile in *years*.

"Yeah, you are shitty."

"Proud of you, freak."

"Bye, loser. Thank you."

"What was that? *A thank-you*? Lizzie, I—"

I hang up the call and hope he keeps harping on to himself for a while longer until he twigs I'm not listening.

So I guess there's one more thing I need to achieve on my list – with a small adjustment:

Don't even <u>think</u> about ~~meeting~~ the love of your life.

Lying in bed with Oscar that night, I feel like a fraud.

"What's wrong, Cricket?" His words warm my neck.

Despite every effort to act normal, I have a tell. My legs aren't wiggling. I can't work out whether to panic because I've been caught or celebrate because I'm with an emotionally intelligent and thoughtful guy (not to mention a freaking sex God who can *sing*!). In the end, I do neither, choosing instead to lie.

"Just homesick, I think."

I should tell him. It doesn't feel right to keep it in, but

he's pulled so many strings for this to work I can hardly just throw it back in his face. He'd be so hurt to know I was even considering the possibility of leaving him and this new life we've created for ourselves. *I'm* hurt and I'm the one with the power to stop it.

Just a month ago I swore I'd never let him go again, and I'm already beginning to break that promise.

He kisses my bare skin. "Anything I can do?"

I shake my head before kissing the arm that's wrapped around me and snuggling in closer to him. All I ever wanted was to be good enough, and now that it turns out I am, I wish I wasn't.

I still haven't signed my contract over a week later, and I'm hoping to God that Oscar doesn't have some inside knowledge about it. Though if he does, he hasn't let on.

Lawrence really got in my head this time. But it's not just him. From the things Tara was saying and the stories I've heard from the actors I've met here, life in the spotlight doesn't seem like it's all it's cracked up to be. And yet...I can't help but wonder if it'd be different for me. That maybe they all set their sights too high, and if I go into it with a different attitude I'll be okay with just being in the chorus. I'll consider myself lucky to take whatever I can get.

I introduce the guests to the Big Band and run through the rules of bingo like I've done so many times before. Bryan and I have our usual back-and-forth banter where he asks me if I plan on joining them for a song or two and I make some joke about breaking glassware or attracting a swarm of angry dolphins, and we begin the game.

When I get offstage, Henry's appeared, and he's bouncing

by my table. My eyes dart to his feet as they always do to check for springs on the bottom of his shoes.

"Do you know what you're going to sing yet?" He eyes the setlist in front of us.

"Oh, no, I couldn't—"

"I sincerely hope you do," he says, cutting off my jumbled refusal with a keen smile.

I'm not sure if this is him *telling* me to do it or if he's just being friendly, but I decide to play along either way. "Maybe I will."

"Maybe I'll be back in time to catch it," he says before he bounds away.

The night plays out the way it normally does. The only difference, however, is that I'm unbearably shaky and hot, and yet my skin is ice-cold. When the bingo is called for two lines and he's still not returned, I let myself breathe a little. Just a few more songs to go until someone will have a full house and I can relax.

But of course, *Zebedee* leaps into view. Okay, so he doesn't leap, but he's just got that energy about him. Henry's eyes take a quick sweep around the room at the guests and then lock directly on mine. His eyebrows quirk up as if to say, "Well, I'm here – aren't you going to sing?"

Fuck. I guess it's showtime.

I catch Bryan's attention and give him a knowing nod, and when the current song ends he waits for me to go up to him and request the song from the bottom of the setlist that I've kept my eye on just in case this happened. He seems pleased with my choice and welcomes me to the stage on the mic.

I take a deep breath to calm my nerves. *I've got this. I'm good enough to do this.*

For the band to add a song to their repertoire it either has to be a classic swing song, a song about the sea, or have some reference to "the good old days". So the song I've picked from those options is Adele's "When We Were Young". It's more of a ballad than swing, but I'm confident I know all the words to this at the very least, and it's definitely in a register I'm comfortable with.

I get tingles all over my skin as soon as I start to sing. Remembering the advice Max and the others gave me in our Wednesday night sessions, I make sure to connect with everyone in the room and not just myself. Although, that was easier to do in the rehearsal room. Here, with the lights shining in my eyes, I have to work harder to find people. But when I do, it's magical.

This. This right here is what makes my heart sparkle.

For the split second between the end of the song and the start of the generous applause, I finally get a sense of clarity. I have to pursue my dreams. I have to do whatever it takes to be worthy of doing this night after night.

I push down the mild discomfort of being in my own skin when I return to my table, because aside from this awkward need I have to apologise for taking up space – which I only think I have to do because I was born with a V between my legs and not a big ol' P – I feel fucking incredible right now. Henry smiles at me from the door, and it takes me a second to register who's next to him.

Oscar runs his hand through his ruffled hair, tones down his smile, and walks over to me. Henry gives me a small nod before slipping out of the venue. As Oscar gets closer, I spot that he's panting. I keep one eye on the room and work extra hard on maintaining my composure because the sight of him in a tux and out of breath makes me unbelievably horny.

He comes up beside me and looks out at the room too. He leans a smidge closer to say something quietly the way he always used to, except his words are what I *dreamed* of hearing back before anything happened between us.

"And there I was thinking I couldn't fancy you any more than I already do."

I bite back my immense smile. "Why are you out of breath?"

"I was listening to the band through the PA in my office. I don't think I've ever run so fast," he says, still a little puffed out.

"Guess you'd better work on your cardio."

He emits a low rumble, and I know exactly where his mind's gone. "Proud of you, Chapman. Come find me when you're done."

"Keep the tux on."

I catch his hungry eyes and my hormones go into overdrive. It's not until the door swings closed behind him that I remember what huge revelation I came to about my future – *our* future – mere seconds ago. Doing what I did tonight professionally would mean the world. But in exchange, I'd have to give up *my* world.

With a muddled mind, I head down to Oscar's office ready to tell him everything. Maybe the reason I can't come to a decision is because the dishonesty is clouding my judgement. It won't be an easy conversation, but it has to happen sooner or later. He could easily tell me all the bad things about his time at drama school to put me off, but knowing him, he'll only encourage me to go.

Just as I get down to the I-95, I catch Henry zooming about, stopping himself when he sees me.

"Eliza! Incredible performance. Thank you for humouring me."

"My pleasure."

He smiles and then falters. "I noticed you haven't signed your contract yet. Is there any particular reason for that?"

I instantly clam up, unsure of what to say at all. I tense even more as a bunch of staff walk between us.

"Why don't you come to my office? We can talk there," he invites me as if that will comfort me, but it does the opposite.

I never got in trouble at school. The threat of being sent to the headmaster's office was terrifying enough to work as a deterrent, and this feels just like those nightmares I used to have about being sent there. Except it's worse because I'm being escorted there by the "headmaster" himself.

He sits on the chair behind his desk but leans back, his body open and relaxed. I, however, sit on the edge of the inferior seat opposite him, making my body as small as possible.

"Are you happy here?" he asks.

I nod vehemently. "Very."

His face crinkles in confusion. "So what's stopping you from signing?" he asks kindly, more like he's curious than wishing to interrogate me.

I look back at the closed door, scared someone could be lurking around outside and might hear me.

"It's all right. Whatever you say stays between us."

Maybe it's because I trust him or look up to him, or maybe it's because I'm so exhausted from keeping everything in and his insistence is like a pin to my very full balloon, but whatever it is, I finally burst and tell him everything. About drama school, about how much I love this job, and about how until I sang tonight I thought I could stay, but now I know I have to leave. Even though that means breaking Oscar's heart, and my own along with it. And how if I don't take this opportunity I'll always wonder *what if?*

Henry takes his time, quietly mopping up my word vomit.

He nods slowly, his eyes looking elsewhere as if he's seeing it all for himself. "You seem to be suffering from a classic case of sliding doors syndrome."

"Exactly."

"So let's think this through. What happens after drama school? What's the dream?"

"I want to be on stage. Performing," I admit. "And be allowed to be there…because I earned it." I'm too embarrassed to add that auditioning for cruise ships would be the first thing I'd do once I graduate. I don't want him to think I've sung one Adele song and suddenly think I'm hot shit.

He nods again and takes his time before he responds. "I have to say, I'd be very sad to see you go, but I trust whatever decision you make will be the right one for you." He pauses, and I realise that he isn't the life coach I was hoping he might be. "Could I ask you for a favour?"

"Sure."

"Sleep on it for one more night. For my own conscience more than anything. I won't forgive myself if my suggestion earlier this evening rushes you into anything."

Has he been listening to Tom?

"Okay." I stand up and go to leave, but just before I can open the door, I turn back. "Could you not—?"

"My lips are sealed."

I give him a grateful nod and release myself from his den.

When I get to Oscar's office, which is only a few doors down, and see his warm smile, I can't bring myself to say anything. I want him to be happy. Even if it's just for one more night.

Henry comes to find me at lunch the next day. He stands still at the end of our table. *Too still.*

"Eliza, could you come and see me when you're done? Do you have time?"

"Of course." I smile politely.

He nods at Tom and Louise before walking away. When he's safely out of the room, they both make childish "ooooh" sounds at me, implying I'm in trouble. I shoot them both with a deadly glare and finish my lunch as quickly as possible.

Henry welcomes me into his office. I take a stab at adopting his laid-back body language but figure I probably look like a melting witch, so I stop.

"How are you doing today? Thinking any clearer?"

"I wish I could say the answer came to me in a dream, but…I'm still no closer to knowing what to do."

He presses his lips together sympathetically. "I've been thinking about our conversation a lot. And I couldn't help but wonder if there was some way we could help you." He retrieves a stapled document from beside him and places it in front of me. "Now, this isn't me persuading you to choose one thing over another, but I wanted you to know that you have options. Perhaps that isn't helpful right now, when you're already conflicted, but I hope you see just how valuable you are as part of our team."

I pick up the document. It's a contract. Instantly the pay jumps out at me. It's a staggering amount more than I was offered before, and sure, money's nice, but this decision is too big to be made for that alone. I struggle to work out why I'm suddenly worth so much to them – until I spot a change to the job role.

Entertainment Host and Lounge Singer.

. . .

What?

I keep reading to see that on top of my usual duties, I'll be contracted to a minimum of one performance a week with the ship's band. My mind is reeling. Why would he do this for me?

Oh.

"If this is about Oscar, that's unbelievably kind of you, really, but—"

"I'm flattered that you think I'd go to all this trouble to keep Oscar happy, but it's Bryan who gave me the idea. He told me yesterday how much he was hoping you'd sing with him, and I had a sneaking suspicion you might not go for it without a bit of encouragement."

I'm speechless. I keep reading the job title expecting to wake up any minute. "But I never auditioned. I—"

"That *was* your audition. Eliza, you earned this. Now take some time to think about it. There will be no hard feelings if you decide it isn't for you."

"Thank you. This is… *Thank you.*" I just about manage not to hug him.

"Oh, and these are for you too." He hands over a bunch more papers, questionnaires of some kind. "That's not all of them, but they're some of the best ones. Just in case they can help you decide. But again, no pressure."

I compose myself before leaving his office, and it physi-cally pains me not to skip or squeal with excitement as I head back to my room. My invisible roommate is in for a change, taking a nap, so I head up to mine and Oscar's secret spot, where I inspect the second bundle of papers he gave me. They're comment cards written by previous guests. I read page after page of praise saying how helpful I was, how funny I was, how I made people's holidays. Someone even mentioned the night Oscar and I sang together. The haunted house is mentioned a lot too, and I laugh at people's embarrassing admissions of wetting themselves in there.

My heart bursts with pride. I'm so touched that someone would even think to mention me. It wasn't just them I was making happy; it was me too. There must be, what, fifty of these? And these are just some he said. Gosh. I didn't know I could ever make this much of an impact.

I wanted to go to drama school because of where it could take me, but as luck would have it, I've found my own way there.

I look over the contract properly and know in my heart it's exactly what I want. I want the variety. I want this lifestyle. I want to keep making people smile. I want to sing.

And I want to be with Oscar.

THIRTY-FOUR

OSCAR

I've finally found out why Eliza's been acting so distant. I'm unbelievably glad she's staying, but nowhere near as glad as I am to hear she came to a decision she's happy with. I would have moved heaven and earth to make it work if she'd chosen to go, and I would've supported her choice no matter what, even though it's not one I would have made for myself knowing what I know now. But *God*, it would have broken my heart if she'd left.

For the past week she's been extra smiley too, and I'm not sure I buy that it's just because she's relieved to have told me about drama school. But who am I to question her for smiling too much?

I catch sight of a dress I don't recognise in the wardrobe while I get ready for the day.

"This is nice. Going to wear it tonight?"

She nods, hiding a grin so wide she gets dimples. Dimples so adorable they beckon me to join her back in bed.

"What's going on with you lately?"

"Nothing!" she sings innocently though she's anything but.

I kiss her neck, making her titter.

"I'm just excited to go to *prom* with my *boyfriend* tonight, that's all."

My hands wander all over her. "Mmm, I don't believe you, but with a bum as good as this…" I squeeze her. *Hmm.* "I'll let you off. But whatever you're scheming, Chapman, it better end tonight."

"It will, I promise."

I kiss her once more on the lips and drag myself away to get dressed.

I wrack my brain all day wondering what exactly it is she's up to. I have a few ideas, but nothing concrete.

Thankfully, I don't have too much longer to wait. One of my last things to do this evening is oversee the huge Valentine's Ball we're throwing in one of the larger venues and introduce the band. Everything seems to be going well so far as I pass by a whole crowd of couples looking more loved-up than usual, dancing to the romantic songs one of the DJs is currently playing.

A theatre technician hands me a mic in the wings as well as a piece of card.

"What's this?"

"They've asked to be introduced like this tonight."

Okay then?

The techie doesn't give me a second to read it before he's giving me my cue to go onstage. The music in the speakers fades down, and a spotlight finds me.

"Good evening, everyone, and happy Valentine's Day! I hope we're all having a *lovely* time so far." I roll my eyes. Ever since I got this job I haven't been able to stop using puns. "It's my pleasure to introduce you to your entertainment for the evening." I look down at the card. "Please give it up for Neptune's Big Band!"

I call out each of their names individually as I always do, then I refer back to the card. "Ladies and gents, it appears we have an incredibly exciting debut performance happening tonight too. Please could you give a warm welcome to the new lounge singer here on Neptune…"

P.T.O.

"Eliza Chapman!"

I stare at the card confused, *convinced* I've had one of those Freudian slips. She's always on my mind, and now everyone knows it.

But I look up to see her walking onto the stage with a microphone. Her dress looks even better on her than I imagined it would when I saw it this morning. Skintight, white with small iridescent sequins all over it, it fits her body perfectly. She's shining, and not just from the sequins. Her sparkling eyes look back at mine and render me speechless. Her smile lights up the entire room. I'm a weak man for her surprises.

I snap out of my daze and clap for her as I walk offstage, down into the auditorium with the rest of the guests. Henry's waiting for me among the crowd.

"She's not meant to start until she's back, but I couldn't resist giving her a warm-up gig."

I can't shake the smile off my face. "You organised all this?"

He shrugs, looking up at the stage. "Can't let a talent like that slip away."

"Thank you."

"I'll say the same thing to you as I said to her: I didn't do it to make you happy."

"Still happy about it though." I nudge him.

My heart swells when the music starts. Her grin widens like I've never seen before as she starts to sing Etta James's "At Last". Just like I chose my first song for her, she chose this one for me. She tries not to look at me for too long, whereas I've given up all hope of looking at anything else all night. She's spectacular. I have no idea how I got so lucky as to deserve someone as amazing as her.

"You stay – I've got you covered," Henry whispers, walking away before I can thank him.

I struggle to swallow the lump in my throat after she sings the final lines specifically to me.

That's right, I'm hers. At last.

THIRTY-FIVE

ELIZA

"All right, break it up, you two. You'll see each other in a few months." Tom prises us apart to get us off the ship before we miss the shuttle to the airport.

Tom's planning to take a long road trip around the coast with his brother like the one their dad took them on when they were kids, and they're going to spread his ashes at all their favourite spots along the way. His request to stay on this ship was approved too, so in six weeks we'll all be together again.

Sarah couldn't quite hang on long enough. My nephew, Samson, is already at home waiting to meet me, and even though I've only seen him through a screen, I already know he's perfect. My parents went along to some event my brother's company was throwing last week, and apparently, Lawrence couldn't stop boasting about how his little sister's some big cruise-ship star. He's since denied it, of course.

Guess I'm not the family screw-up after all.

I give Oscar one *final* kiss goodbye before grabbing my suitcase and heading off the gangway. Tom and I look back at the swarm of friends who've gathered to wave us off, and we blow them kisses.

I don't know what's on our horizon or how we'll weather it, but what I do know is I can't wait to come back.

BEWARE OF ARTISTIC LICENCE

Meticulous research went into creating More Than Shipmates, but please remember that this is a work of fiction, and various elements of ship life have been wildly romanticised. I take no responsibility if you uproot your life and don't fall madly in love.

COMING SOON...

Tom's about to find love with the one person he shouldn't. Oscar's sister.

For more info on future releases, sign up to my mailing list.

ACKNOWLEDGMENTS

* Plays "For the Dreamers" from "Back to the Future: The Musical" *

More Than Shipmates was a real passion project from start to finish. What originated as a sliding doors style daydream about a job that could have been and never was became my way to dissociate while 'that global event thingy' was going on. And it was in escaping to a made up world where people live far more adventurously than I do that this book was born.

There are some incredible people I need to thank because without them, I would never have got here.

First of all, Fae, thank you for introducing me to NaNoWriMo, being the first person to read a real life copy of More Than Shipmates and for all of your incredible thoughts and feedback. Sorry there wasn't a threesome.

Alicia, my cheerleader. Whenever I got stuck, I'd think, what would Alicia do? The answer: Work harder. Be kinder. And commit to my passions one hundred percent. Thank you for your endless enthusiasm in my hobbies.

Mazz, for making my first cruise so unforgettable that it inspired this whole obsession of mine and for checking in on me whenever I went quiet. Here's to our next trip!

Joe, for supporting my dreams and keeping my mug full of tea.

Ben, for answering my endless questions about life on board cruise ships and hyping me up every step of the way.

Kirsty and Zoe, you might have had the toughest job out of everyone: Telling me how shit my book was. Thank you for bravely accepting that responsibility, I needed every crumb of feedback you gave me, and I can't thank you enough for getting this bad boy ready for the edit.

And lastly, my incredible editor, Bryony. I couldn't have asked for a safer pair of hands for my book-baby. Thank you for reassuring me that this book isn't a dumpster fire and always letting me know where you laughed out loud.

IF YOU ENJOYED THIS BOOK, HERE'S HOW YOU CAN CONTINUE TO SUPPORT IT:

- Recommend it to friends
- Leave a review on Amazon & Goodreads
- Sign up to my mailing list to stay up to date with future releases.

Printed in Great Britain
by Amazon

33854346R00284